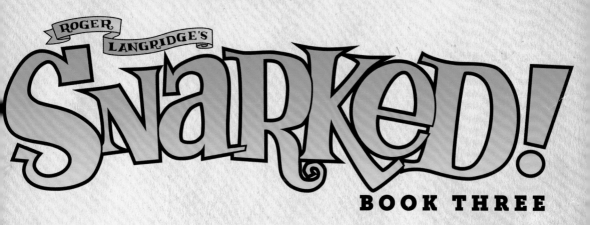

ROGER LANGRIDGE'S

SNARKED!

BOOK THREE

CABBAGES AND KINGS

ROSS RICHIE Chief Executive Officer • MATT GAGNON Editor-in-Chief • FILIP SABLIK VP-Publishing & Marketing • LANCE KREITER VP-Licensing & Merchandising • PHIL BARBARO Director of Finance
BRYCE CARLSON Managing Editor • DAFNA PLEBAN Editor • SHANNON WATTERS Editor • ERIC HARBURN Assistant Editor • ADAM STAFFARONI Assistant Editor
CHRIS ROSA Assistant Editor • STEPHANIE GONZAGA Graphic Designer • JASMINE AMIRI Operations Coordinator • DEVIN FUNCHES Marketing & Sales Assistant • BRIANNA HART Executive Assistant

kaboom!

SNARKED Volume Three — January 2013. Published by KaBOOM!, a division of Boom Entertainment, Inc. Snarked is Copyright © 2013 Boom Entertainment, Inc. and Roger Langridge. Originally published in single magazine form as SNARKED 9-12. Copyright © 2012 Boom Entertainment, Inc. and Roger Langridge. All rights reserved. KaBOOM!™ and the KaBOOM! logo are trademarks of Boom Entertainment, Inc., registered in various countries and categories. All characters, events, and institutions depicted herein are fictional. Any similarity between any of the names, characters, persons, events, and/or institutions in this publication to actual names, characters, and persons, whether living or dead, events, and/ or institutions is unintended and purely coincidental. KaBOOM! does not read or accept unsolicited submissions of ideas, stories, or artwork.

A catalog record of this book is available from OCLC and from the KaBOOM! website, www.kaboom-studios.com, on the Librarians Page.

BOOM! Studios, 5670 Wilshire Boulevard, Suite 450, Los Angeles, CA 90036-5679. Printed in China. First Printing. ISBN: 978-1-60886-295-5

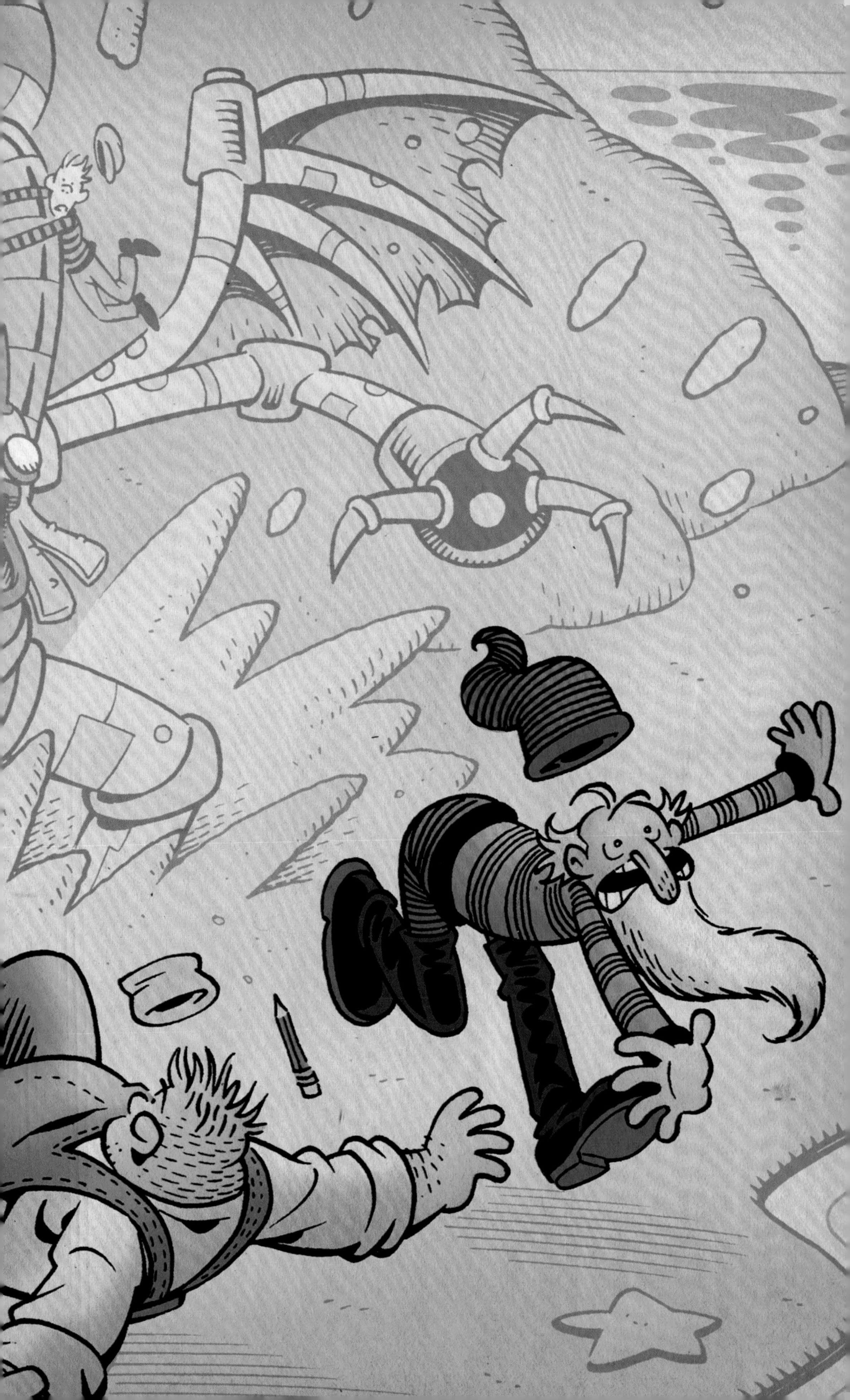

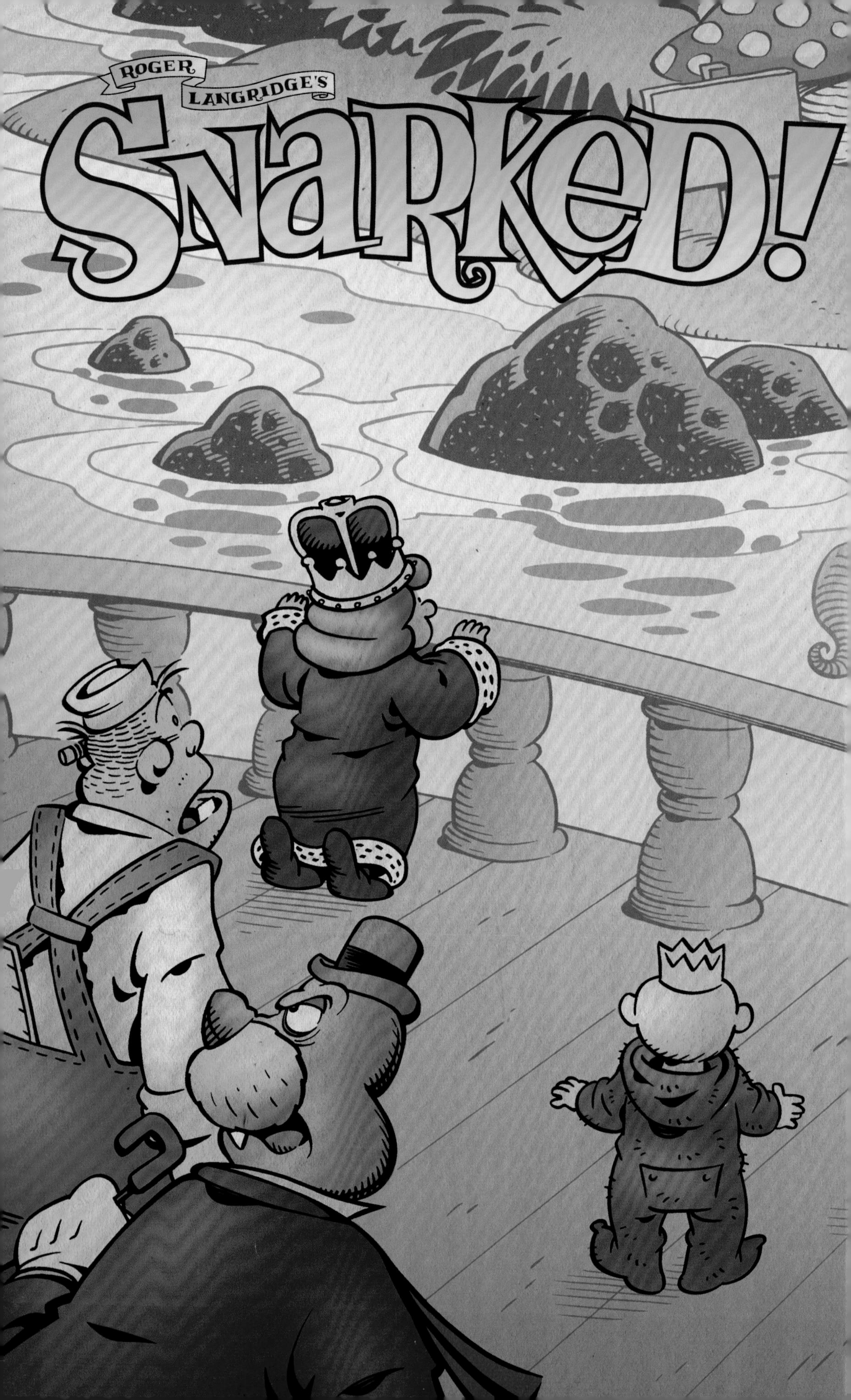
ROGER LANGRIDGE'S
SNARKED!

WRITTEN AND ILLUSTRATED BY
ROGER LANGRIDGE

WITH COLORS BY
LISA MOORE

COVER BY
ROGER LANGRIDGE

WITH COLORS BY
MATTHEW WILSON

ASSISTANT EDITOR
ERIC HARBURN

EDITOR
BRYCE CARLSON

GRAPHIC DESIGNER
STEPHANIE GONZAGA

INSPIRED BY THE WORKS OF
LEWIS CARROLL

SNARKED CREATED BY
ROGER LANGRIDGE

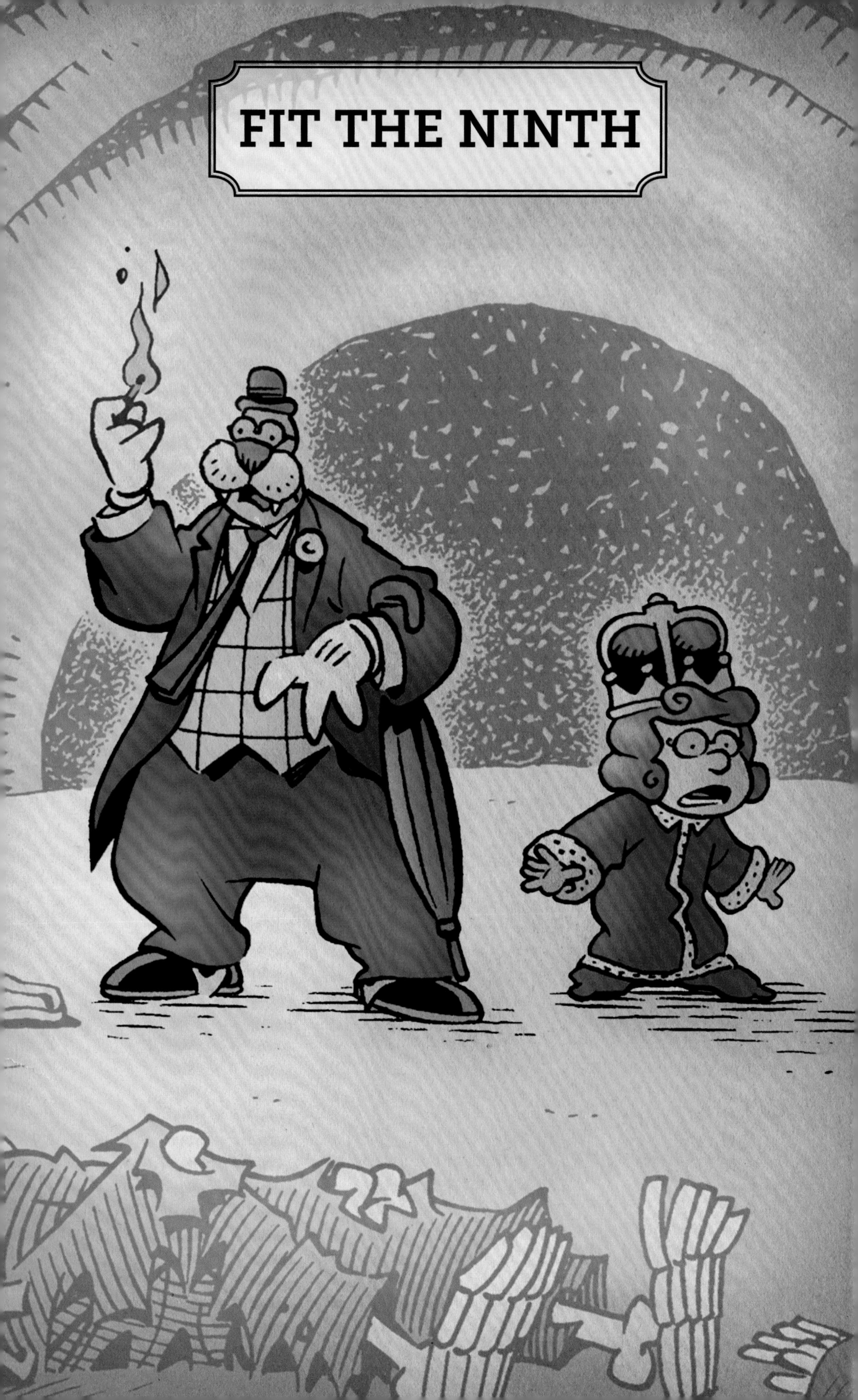
FIT THE NINTH

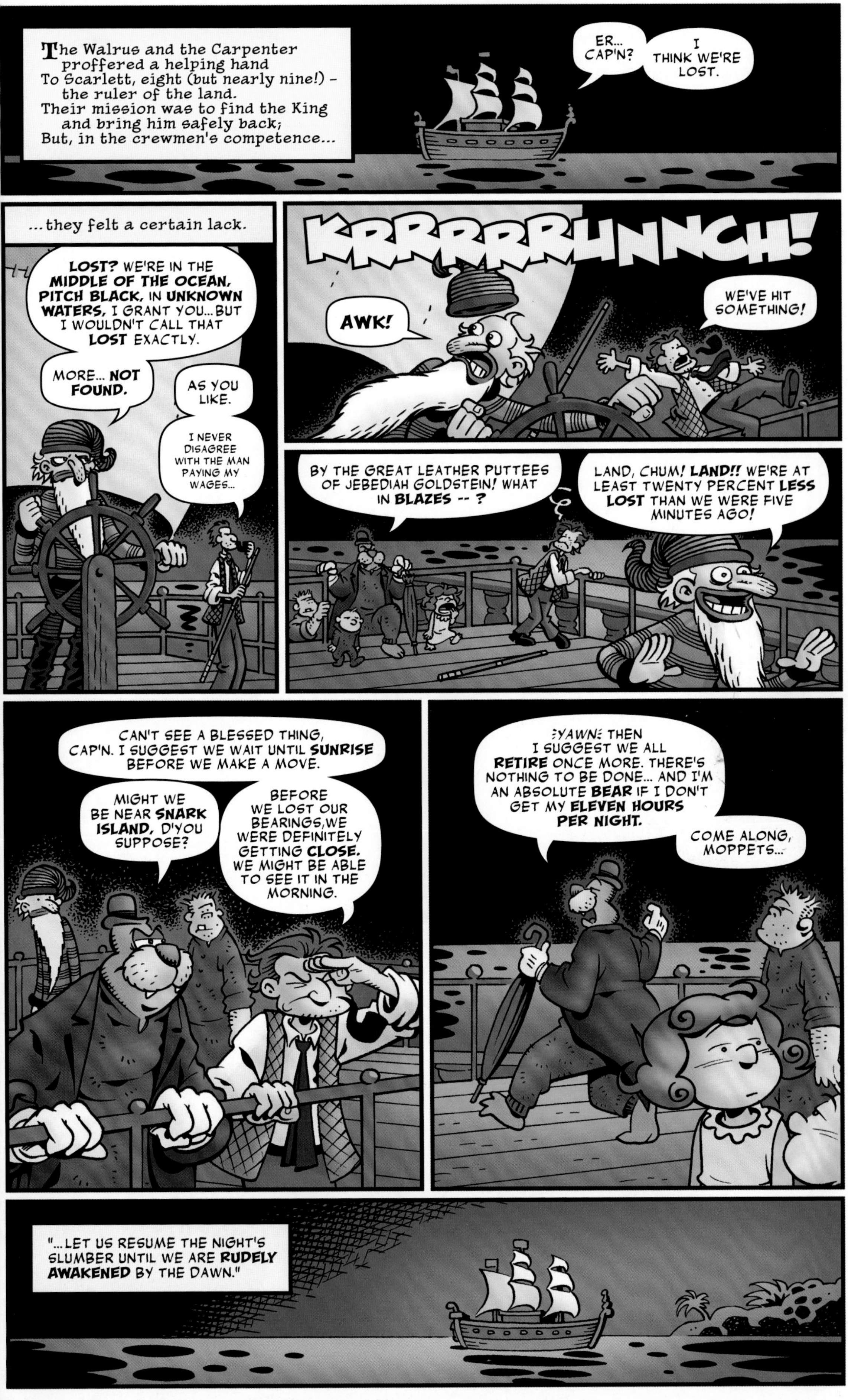

The Walrus and the Carpenter proffered a helping hand
To Scarlett, eight (but nearly nine!) – the ruler of the land.
Their mission was to find the King and bring him safely back;
But, in the crewmen's competence...
ER... CAP'N?
I THINK WE'RE LOST.
...they felt a certain lack.
LOST? WE'RE IN THE MIDDLE OF THE OCEAN, PITCH BLACK, IN UNKNOWN WATERS, I GRANT YOU... BUT I WOULDN'T CALL THAT LOST EXACTLY.
MORE... NOT FOUND.
AS YOU LIKE.
I NEVER DISAGREE WITH THE MAN PAYING MY WAGES...
KRRRRRRUNNCH!
AWK!
WE'VE HIT SOMETHING!
BY THE GREAT LEATHER PUTTEES OF JEBEDIAH GOLDSTEIN! WHAT IN BLAZES -- ?
LAND, CHUM! LAND!! WE'RE AT LEAST TWENTY PERCENT LESS LOST THAN WE WERE FIVE MINUTES AGO!
CAN'T SEE A BLESSED THING, CAP'N. I SUGGEST WE WAIT UNTIL SUNRISE BEFORE WE MAKE A MOVE.
MIGHT WE BE NEAR SNARK ISLAND, D'YOU SUPPOSE?
BEFORE WE LOST OUR BEARINGS,WE WERE DEFINITELY GETTING CLOSE. WE MIGHT BE ABLE TO SEE IT IN THE MORNING.
=YAWN= THEN I SUGGEST WE ALL RETIRE ONCE MORE. THERE'S NOTHING TO BE DONE... AND I'M AN ABSOLUTE BEAR IF I DON'T GET MY ELEVEN HOURS PER NIGHT.
COME ALONG, MOPPETS...
"...LET US RESUME THE NIGHT'S SLUMBER UNTIL WE ARE RUDELY AWAKENED BY THE DAWN."

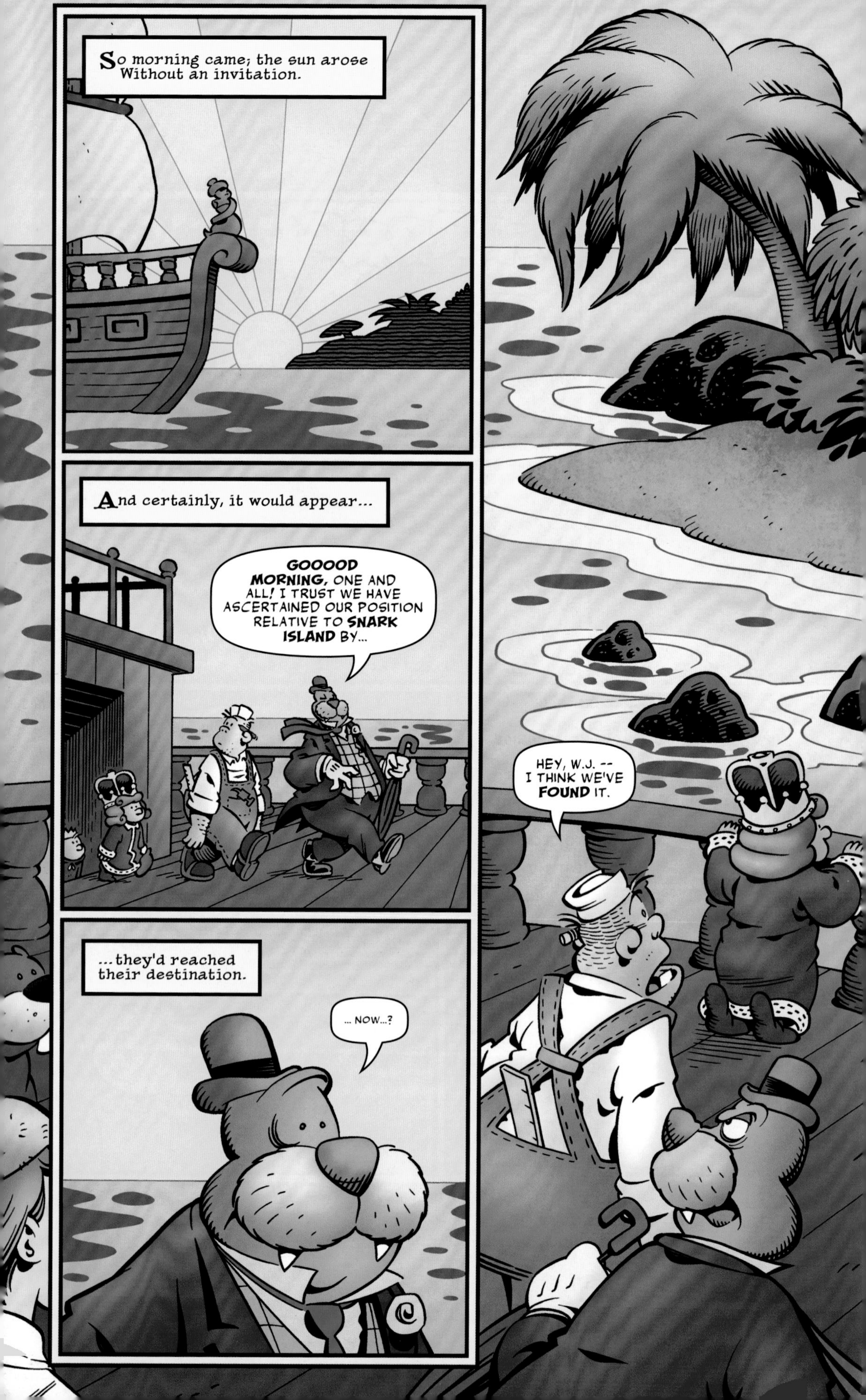
So morning came; the sun arose
Without an invitation.
And certainly, it would appear...
GOOOOD MORNING, ONE AND ALL! I TRUST WE HAVE ASCERTAINED OUR POSITION RELATIVE TO SNARK ISLAND BY...
...they'd reached their destination.
... NOW...?
HEY, W.J. -- I THINK WE'VE FOUND IT.

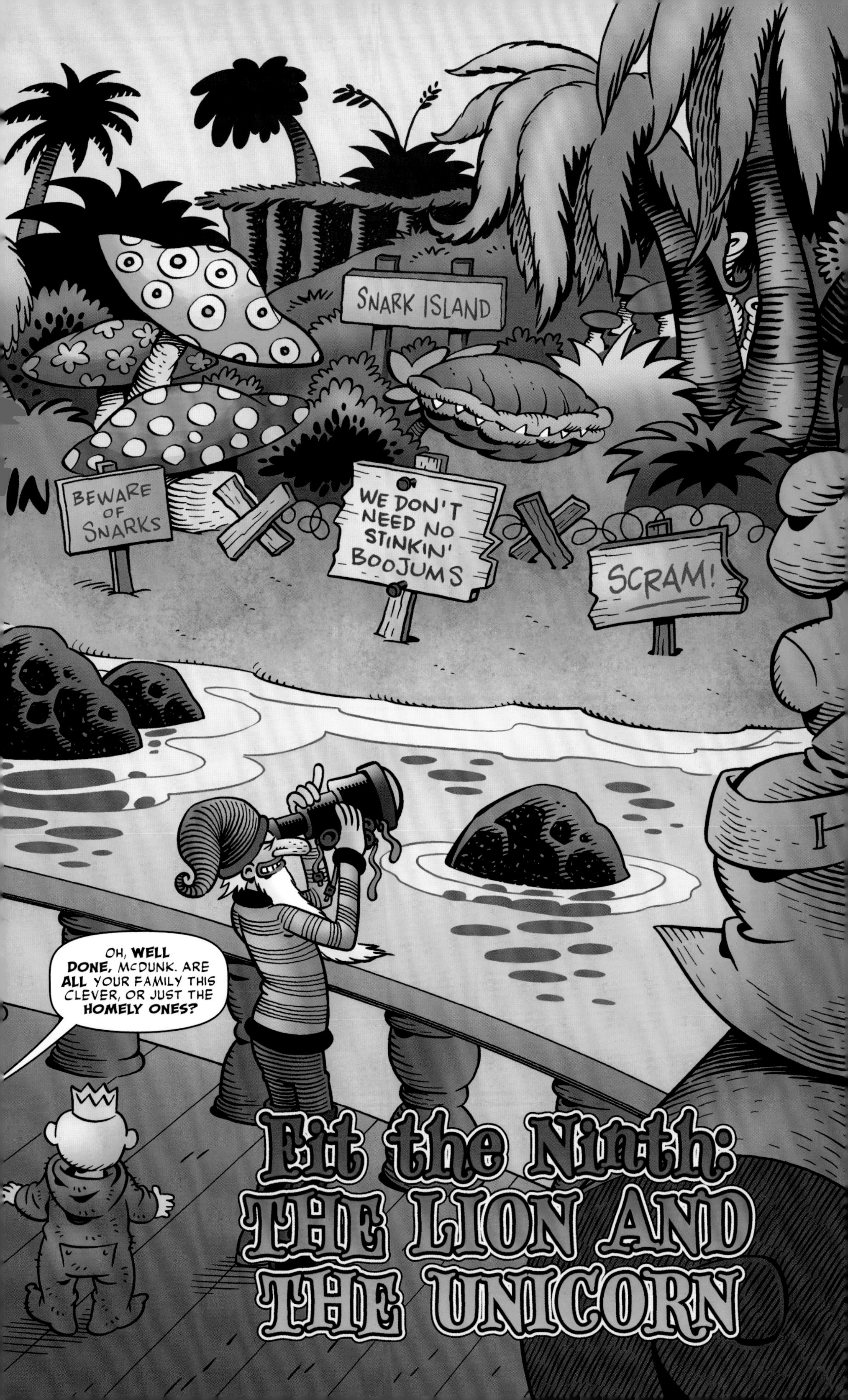
SNARK ISLAND
BEWARE OF SNARKS
WE DON'T NEED NO STINKIN' BOOJUMS
SCRAM!
OH, WELL DONE, McDUNK. ARE ALL YOUR FAMILY THIS CLEVER, OR JUST THE HOMELY ONES?
Fit the Ninth: THE LION AND THE UNICORN

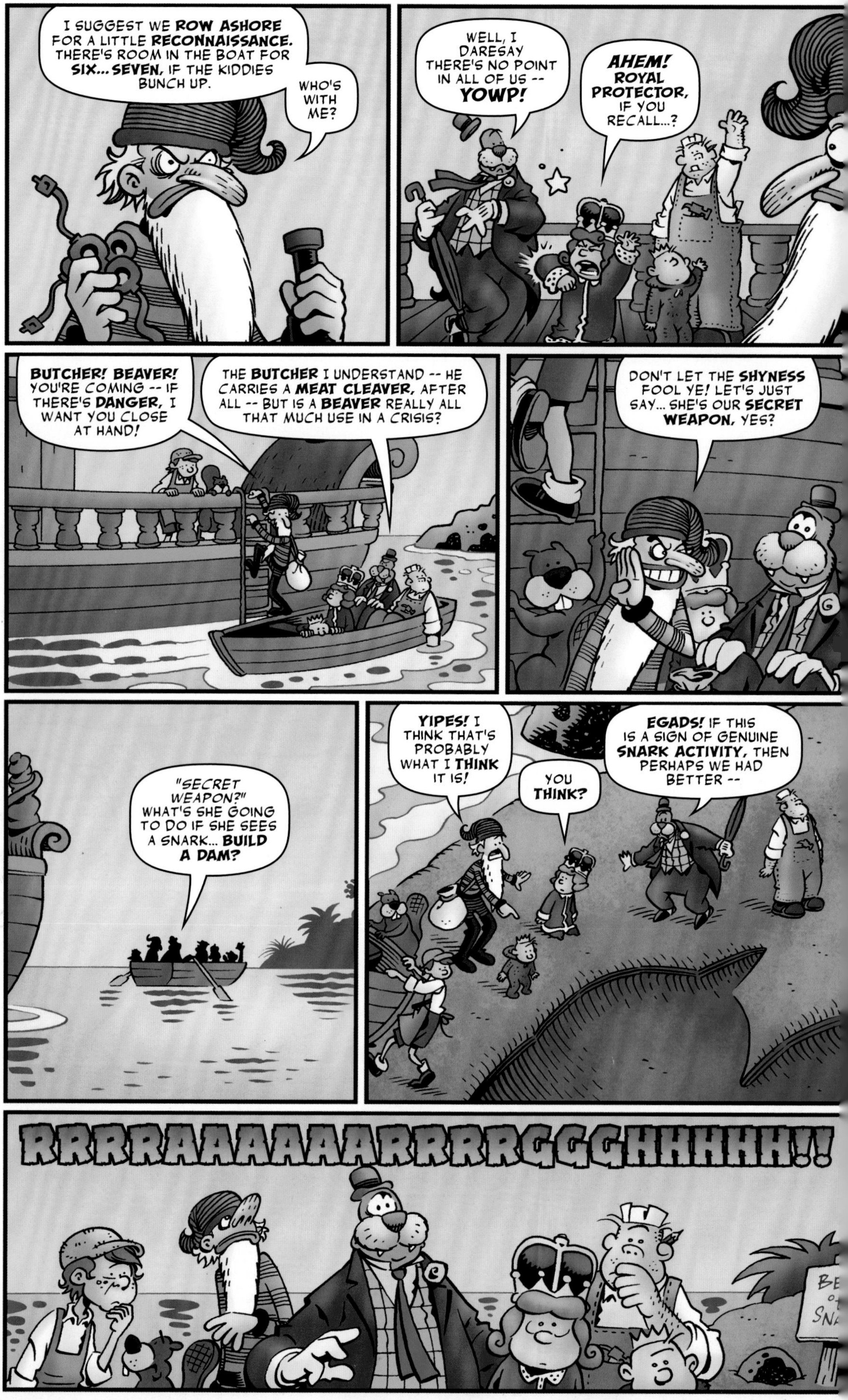
I SUGGEST WE ROW ASHORE FOR A LITTLE RECONNAISSANCE. THERE'S ROOM IN THE BOAT FOR SIX... SEVEN, IF THE KIDDIES BUNCH UP.
WHO'S WITH ME?
WELL, I DARESAY THERE'S NO POINT IN ALL OF US -- YOWP!
AHEM! ROYAL PROTECTOR, IF YOU RECALL...?
BUTCHER! BEAVER! YOU'RE COMING -- IF THERE'S DANGER, I WANT YOU CLOSE AT HAND!
THE BUTCHER I UNDERSTAND -- HE CARRIES A MEAT CLEAVER, AFTER ALL -- BUT IS A BEAVER REALLY ALL THAT MUCH USE IN A CRISIS?
DON'T LET THE SHYNESS FOOL YE! LET'S JUST SAY... SHE'S OUR SECRET WEAPON, YES?
"SECRET WEAPON?" WHAT'S SHE GOING TO DO IF SHE SEES A SNARK... BUILD A DAM?
YIPES! I THINK THAT'S PROBABLY WHAT I THINK IT IS!
YOU THINK?
EGADS! IF THIS IS A SIGN OF GENUINE SNARK ACTIVITY, THEN PERHAPS WE HAD BETTER --
RRRRAAAAAAAARRRRRGGGHHHHHH!!

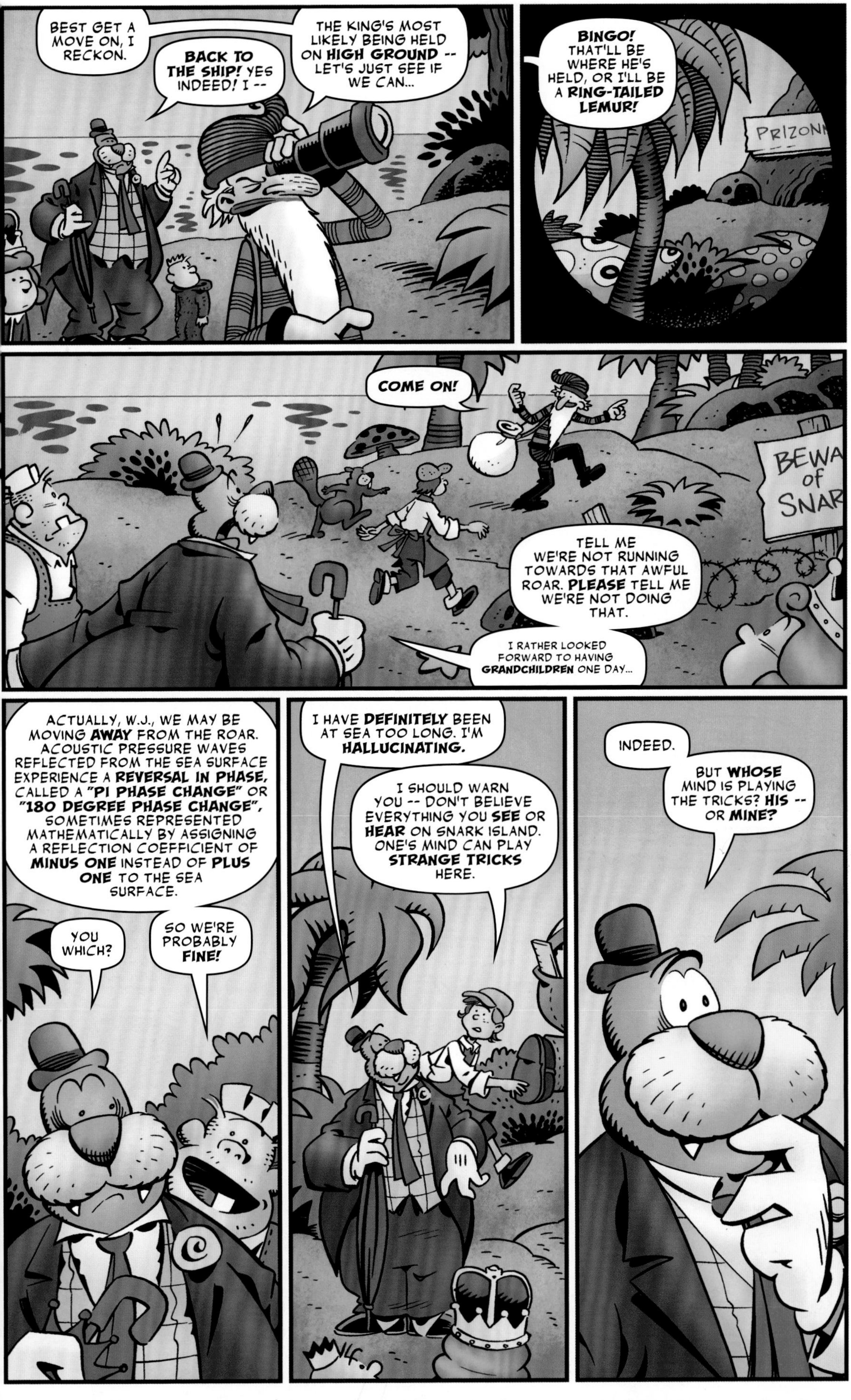
BEST GET A MOVE ON, I RECKON.
BACK TO THE SHIP! YES INDEED! I --
THE KING'S MOST LIKELY BEING HELD ON HIGH GROUND -- LET'S JUST SEE IF WE CAN...
BINGO! THAT'LL BE WHERE HE'S HELD, OR I'LL BE A RING-TAILED LEMUR!
PRIZONN
COME ON!
BEWA of SNAR
TELL ME WE'RE NOT RUNNING TOWARDS THAT AWFUL ROAR. PLEASE TELL ME WE'RE NOT DOING THAT.
I RATHER LOOKED FORWARD TO HAVING GRANDCHILDREN ONE DAY...
ACTUALLY, W.J., WE MAY BE MOVING AWAY FROM THE ROAR. ACOUSTIC PRESSURE WAVES REFLECTED FROM THE SEA SURFACE EXPERIENCE A REVERSAL IN PHASE, CALLED A "PI PHASE CHANGE" OR "180 DEGREE PHASE CHANGE", SOMETIMES REPRESENTED MATHEMATICALLY BY ASSIGNING A REFLECTION COEFFICIENT OF MINUS ONE INSTEAD OF PLUS ONE TO THE SEA SURFACE.
YOU WHICH?
SO WE'RE PROBABLY FINE!
I HAVE DEFINITELY BEEN AT SEA TOO LONG. I'M HALLUCINATING.
I SHOULD WARN YOU -- DON'T BELIEVE EVERYTHING YOU SEE OR HEAR ON SNARK ISLAND. ONE'S MIND CAN PLAY STRANGE TRICKS HERE.
INDEED.
BUT WHOSE MIND IS PLAYING THE TRICKS? HIS -- OR MINE?

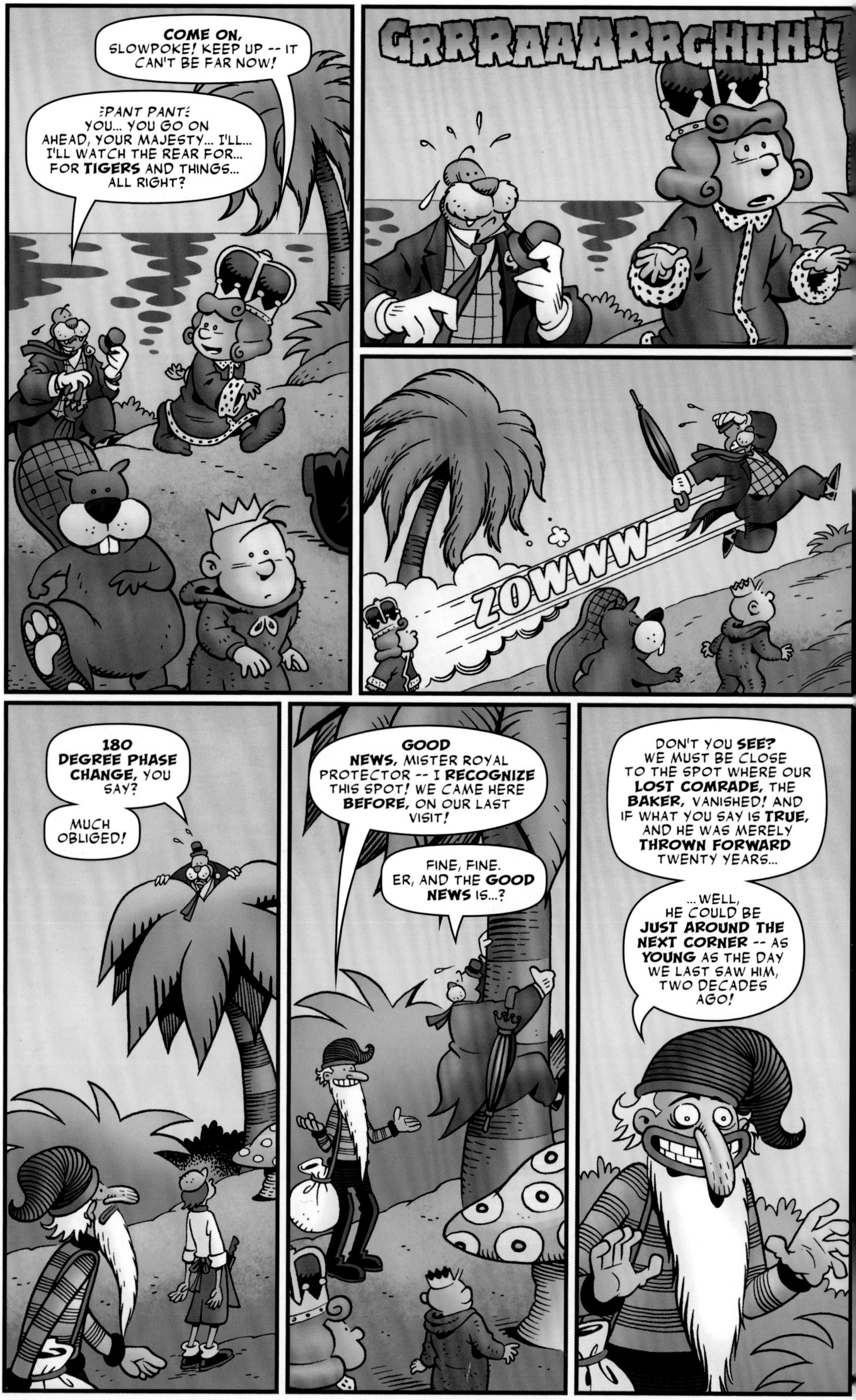
COME ON, SLOWPOKE! KEEP UP -- IT CAN'T BE FAR NOW!
=PANT PANT= YOU... YOU GO ON AHEAD, YOUR MAJESTY... I'LL... I'LL WATCH THE REAR FOR... FOR TIGERS AND THINGS... ALL RIGHT?
GRRRAAARRGHHH!!
ZOWWW
180 DEGREE PHASE CHANGE, YOU SAY?
MUCH OBLIGED!
GOOD NEWS, MISTER ROYAL PROTECTOR -- I RECOGNIZE THIS SPOT! WE CAME HERE BEFORE, ON OUR LAST VISIT!
FINE, FINE. ER, AND THE GOOD NEWS IS...?
DON'T YOU SEE? WE MUST BE CLOSE TO THE SPOT WHERE OUR LOST COMRADE, THE BAKER, VANISHED! AND IF WHAT YOU SAY IS TRUE, AND HE WAS MERELY THROWN FORWARD TWENTY YEARS...
...WELL, HE COULD BE JUST AROUND THE NEXT CORNER -- AS YOUNG AS THE DAY WE LAST SAW HIM, TWO DECADES AGO!

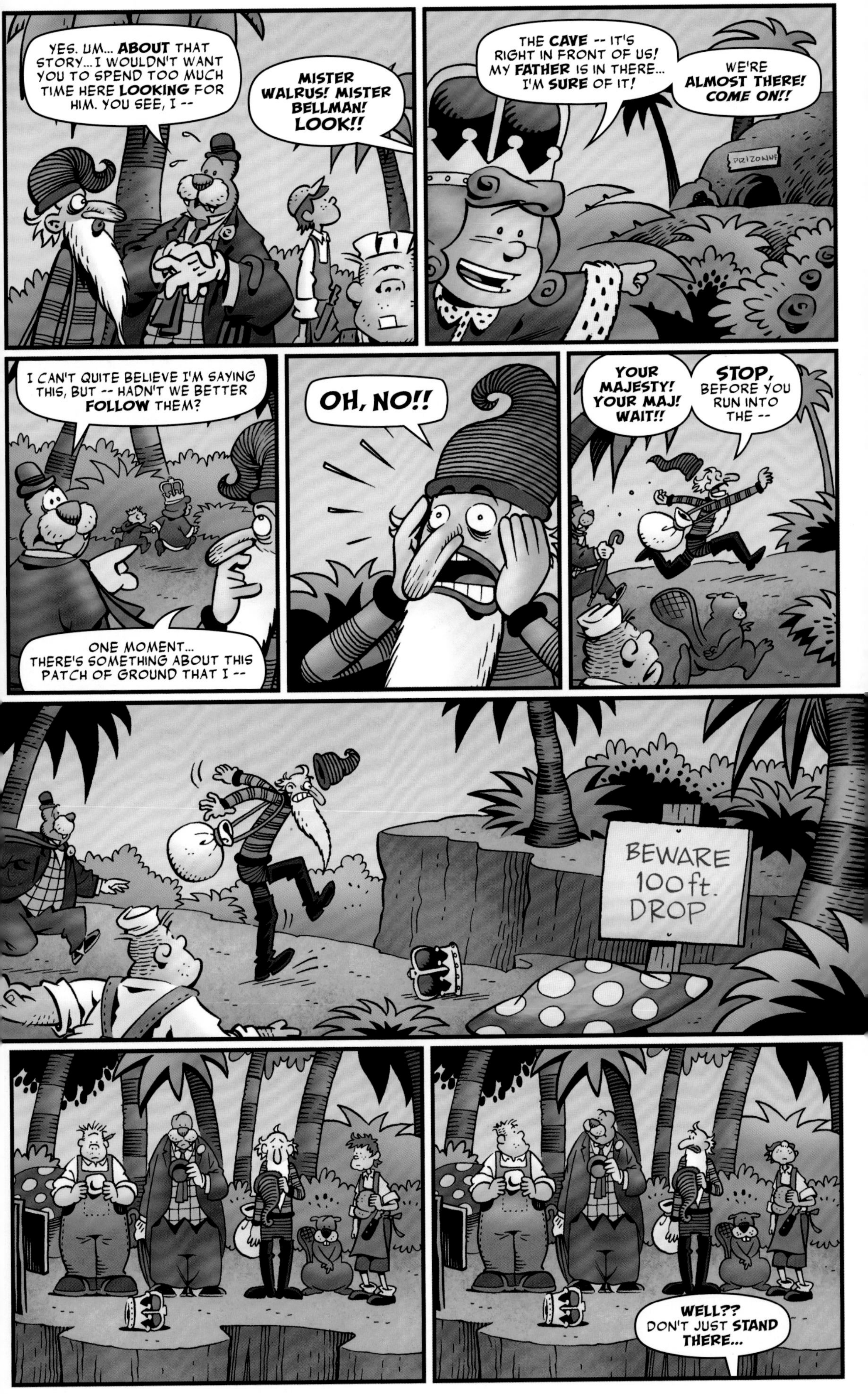
YES. UM... ABOUT THAT STORY... I WOULDN'T WANT YOU TO SPEND TOO MUCH TIME HERE LOOKING FOR HIM. YOU SEE, I --
MISTER WALRUS! MISTER BELLMAN! LOOK!!
THE CAVE -- IT'S RIGHT IN FRONT OF US! MY FATHER IS IN THERE... I'M SURE OF IT!
WE'RE ALMOST THERE! COME ON!!
PRIZONNE
I CAN'T QUITE BELIEVE I'M SAYING THIS, BUT -- HADN'T WE BETTER FOLLOW THEM?
ONE MOMENT... THERE'S SOMETHING ABOUT THIS PATCH OF GROUND THAT I --
OH, NO!!
YOUR MAJESTY! YOUR MAJ! WAIT!!
STOP, BEFORE YOU RUN INTO THE --
BEWARE 100 ft. DROP
WELL?? DON'T JUST STAND THERE...

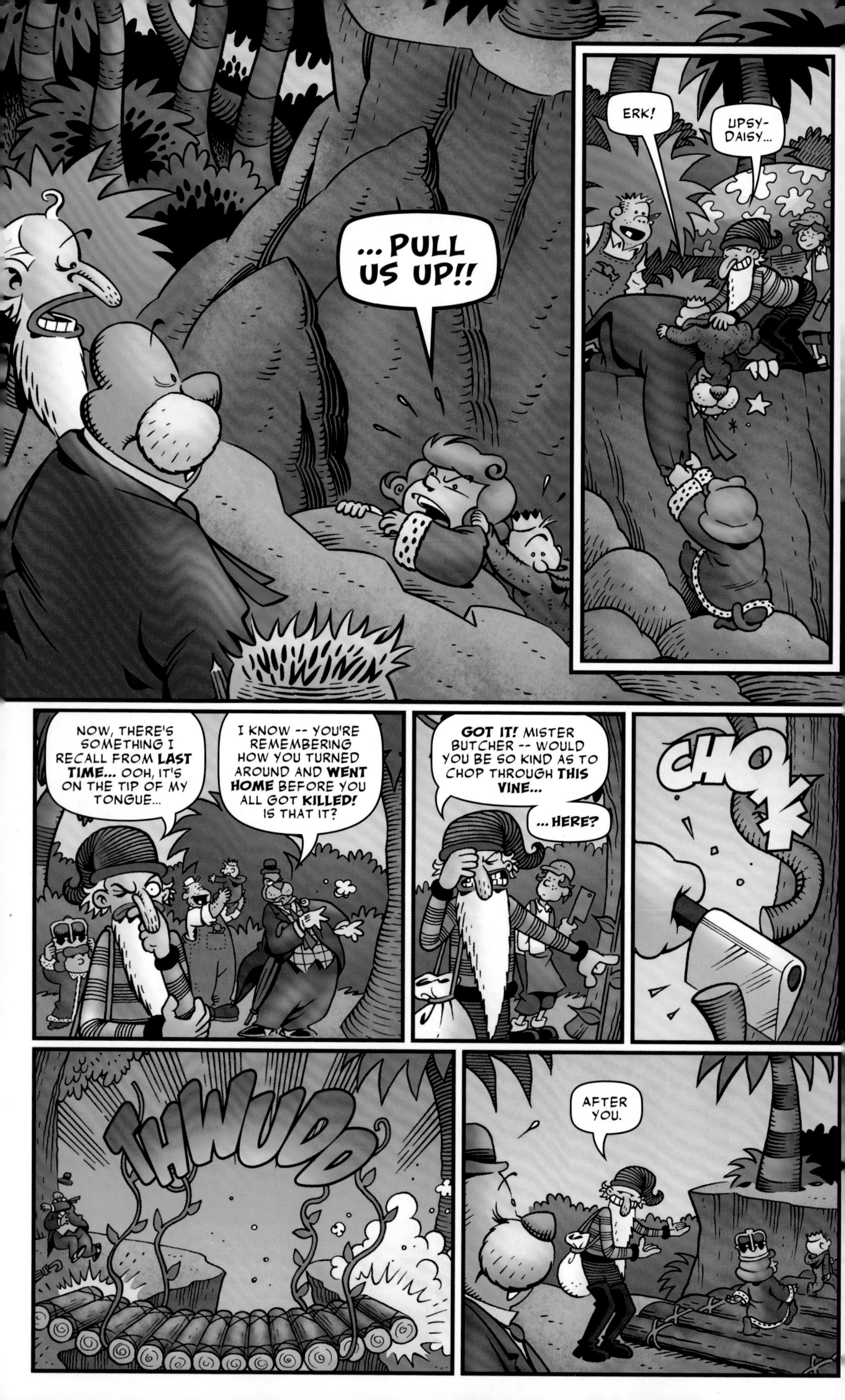
...PULL US UP!!
ERK!
UPSY-DAISY...
NOW, THERE'S SOMETHING I RECALL FROM LAST TIME... OOH, IT'S ON THE TIP OF MY TONGUE...
I KNOW -- YOU'RE REMEMBERING HOW YOU TURNED AROUND AND WENT HOME BEFORE YOU ALL GOT KILLED! IS THAT IT?
GOT IT! MISTER BUTCHER -- WOULD YOU BE SO KIND AS TO CHOP THROUGH THIS VINE...
...HERE?
CHOK
THWUDD
AFTER YOU.

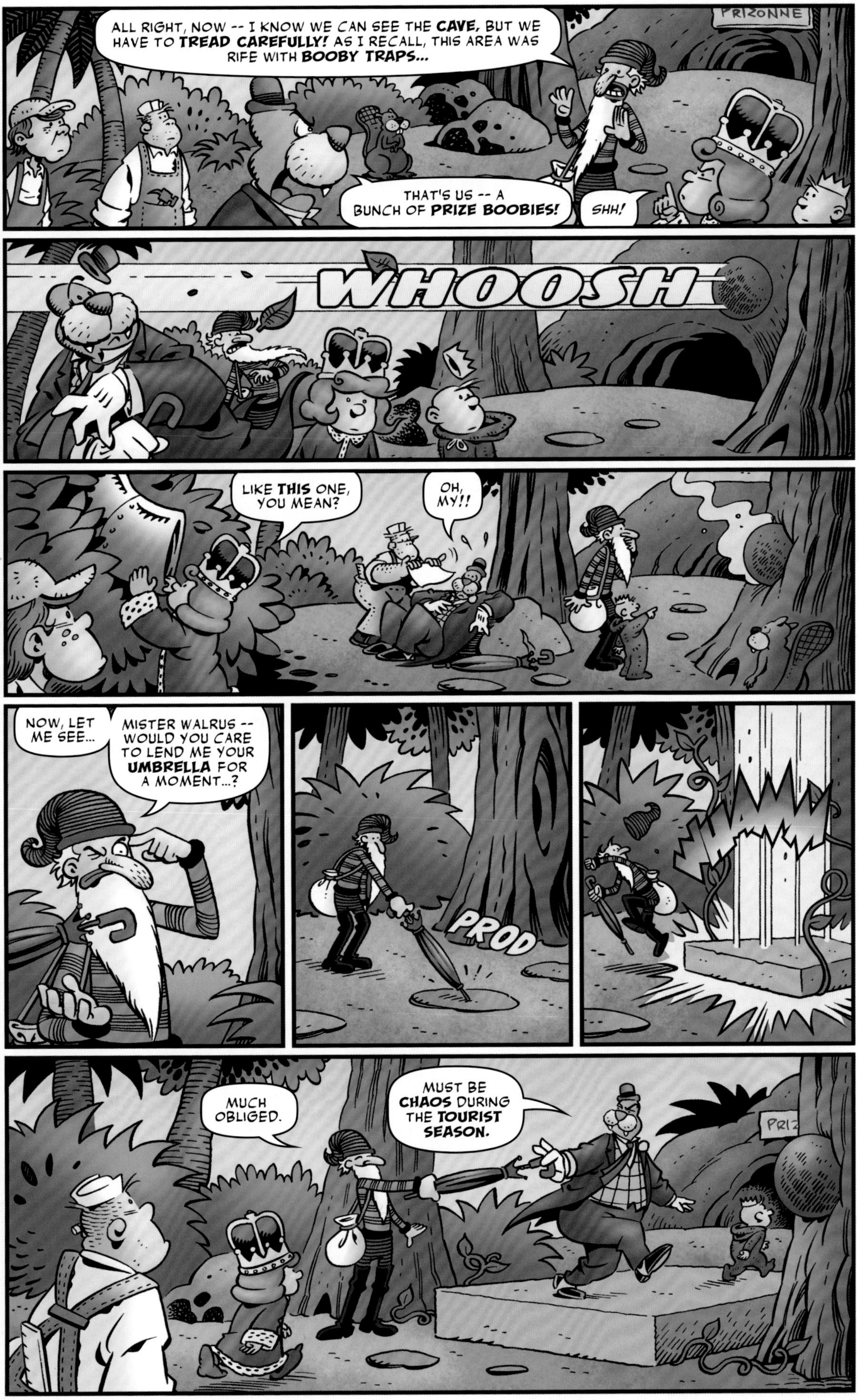
PRIZONNE
ALL RIGHT, NOW -- I KNOW WE CAN SEE THE CAVE, BUT WE HAVE TO TREAD CAREFULLY! AS I RECALL, THIS AREA WAS RIFE WITH BOOBY TRAPS...
THAT'S US -- A BUNCH OF PRIZE BOOBIES!
SHH!
WHOOSH
LIKE THIS ONE, YOU MEAN?
OH, MY!!
NOW, LET ME SEE...
MISTER WALRUS -- WOULD YOU CARE TO LEND ME YOUR UMBRELLA FOR A MOMENT...?
PROD
MUCH OBLIGED.
MUST BE CHAOS DURING THE TOURIST SEASON.
PRIZ

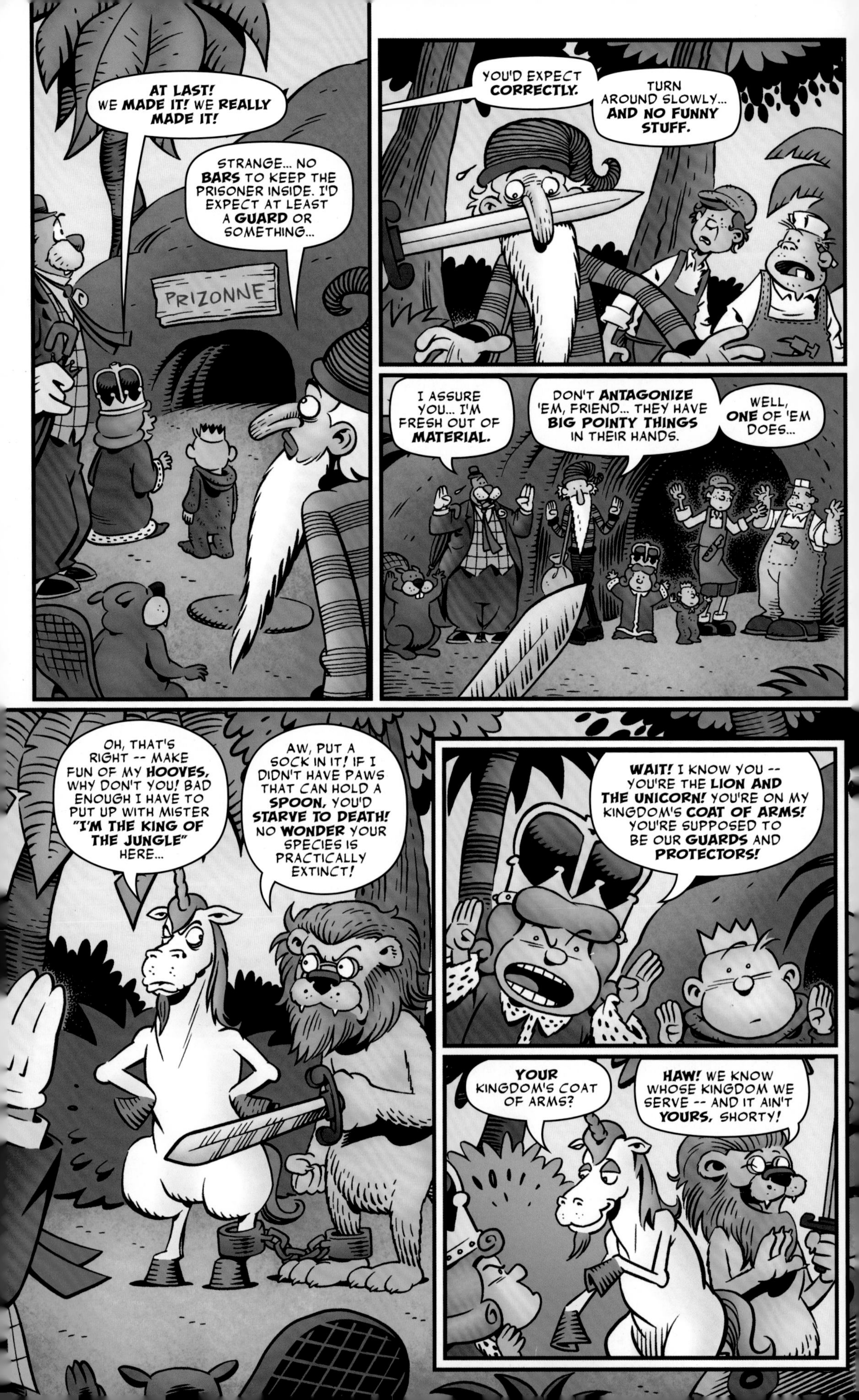

AT LAST! WE MADE IT! WE REALLY MADE IT!
STRANGE... NO BARS TO KEEP THE PRISONER INSIDE. I'D EXPECT AT LEAST A GUARD OR SOMETHING...
PRIZONNE
YOU'D EXPECT CORRECTLY.
TURN AROUND SLOWLY... AND NO FUNNY STUFF.
I ASSURE YOU... I'M FRESH OUT OF MATERIAL.
DON'T ANTAGONIZE 'EM, FRIEND... THEY HAVE BIG POINTY THINGS IN THEIR HANDS.
WELL, ONE OF 'EM DOES...
OH, THAT'S RIGHT -- MAKE FUN OF MY HOOVES, WHY DON'T YOU! BAD ENOUGH I HAVE TO PUT UP WITH MISTER "I'M THE KING OF THE JUNGLE" HERE...
AW, PUT A SOCK IN IT! IF I DIDN'T HAVE PAWS THAT CAN HOLD A SPOON, YOU'D STARVE TO DEATH! NO WONDER YOUR SPECIES IS PRACTICALLY EXTINCT!
WAIT! I KNOW YOU -- YOU'RE THE LION AND THE UNICORN! YOU'RE ON MY KINGDOM'S COAT OF ARMS! YOU'RE SUPPOSED TO BE OUR GUARDS AND PROTECTORS!
YOUR KINGDOM'S COAT OF ARMS?
HAW! WE KNOW WHOSE KINGDOM WE SERVE -- AND IT AIN'T YOURS, SHORTY!

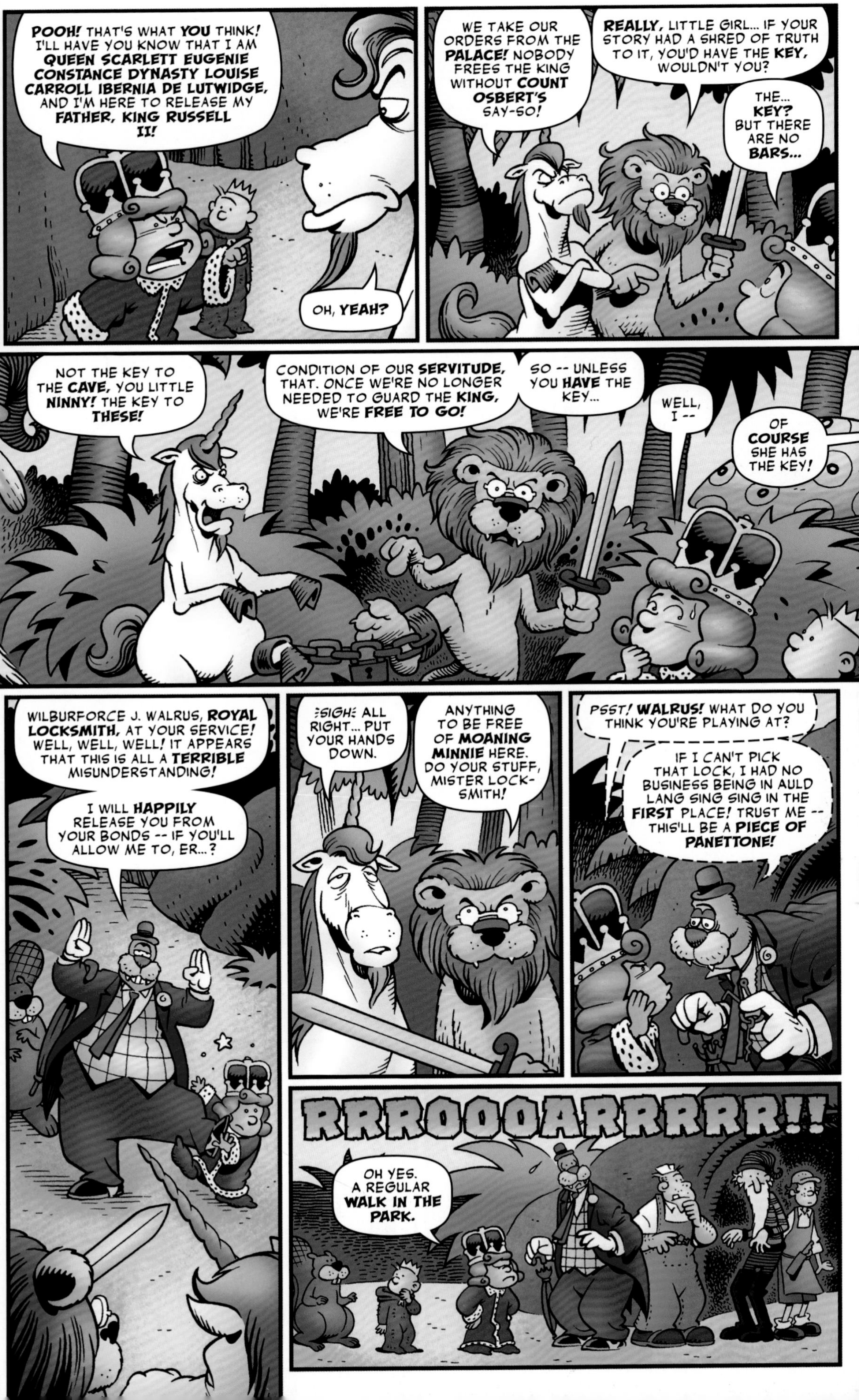
POOH! THAT'S WHAT YOU THINK! I'LL HAVE YOU KNOW THAT I AM QUEEN SCARLETT EUGENIE CONSTANCE DYNASTY LOUISE CARROLL IBERNIA DE LUTWIDGE, AND I'M HERE TO RELEASE MY FATHER, KING RUSSELL II!
OH, YEAH?
WE TAKE OUR ORDERS FROM THE PALACE! NOBODY FREES THE KING WITHOUT COUNT OSBERT'S SAY-SO!
REALLY, LITTLE GIRL... IF YOUR STORY HAD A SHRED OF TRUTH TO IT, YOU'D HAVE THE KEY, WOULDN'T YOU?
THE... KEY? BUT THERE ARE NO BARS...
NOT THE KEY TO THE CAVE, YOU LITTLE NINNY! THE KEY TO THESE!
CONDITION OF OUR SERVITUDE, THAT. ONCE WE'RE NO LONGER NEEDED TO GUARD THE KING, WE'RE FREE TO GO!
SO -- UNLESS YOU HAVE THE KEY...
WELL, I --
OF COURSE SHE HAS THE KEY!
WILBURFORCE J. WALRUS, ROYAL LOCKSMITH, AT YOUR SERVICE! WELL, WELL, WELL! IT APPEARS THAT THIS IS ALL A TERRIBLE MISUNDERSTANDING!
I WILL HAPPILY RELEASE YOU FROM YOUR BONDS -- IF YOU'LL ALLOW ME TO, ER...?
SIGH ALL RIGHT... PUT YOUR HANDS DOWN.
ANYTHING TO BE FREE OF MOANING MINNIE HERE. DO YOUR STUFF, MISTER LOCK-SMITH!
PSST! WALRUS! WHAT DO YOU THINK YOU'RE PLAYING AT?
IF I CAN'T PICK THAT LOCK, I HAD NO BUSINESS BEING IN AULD LANG SING SING IN THE FIRST PLACE! TRUST ME -- THIS'LL BE A PIECE OF PANETTONE!
RRROOOARRRRRR!!
OH YES. A REGULAR WALK IN THE PARK.

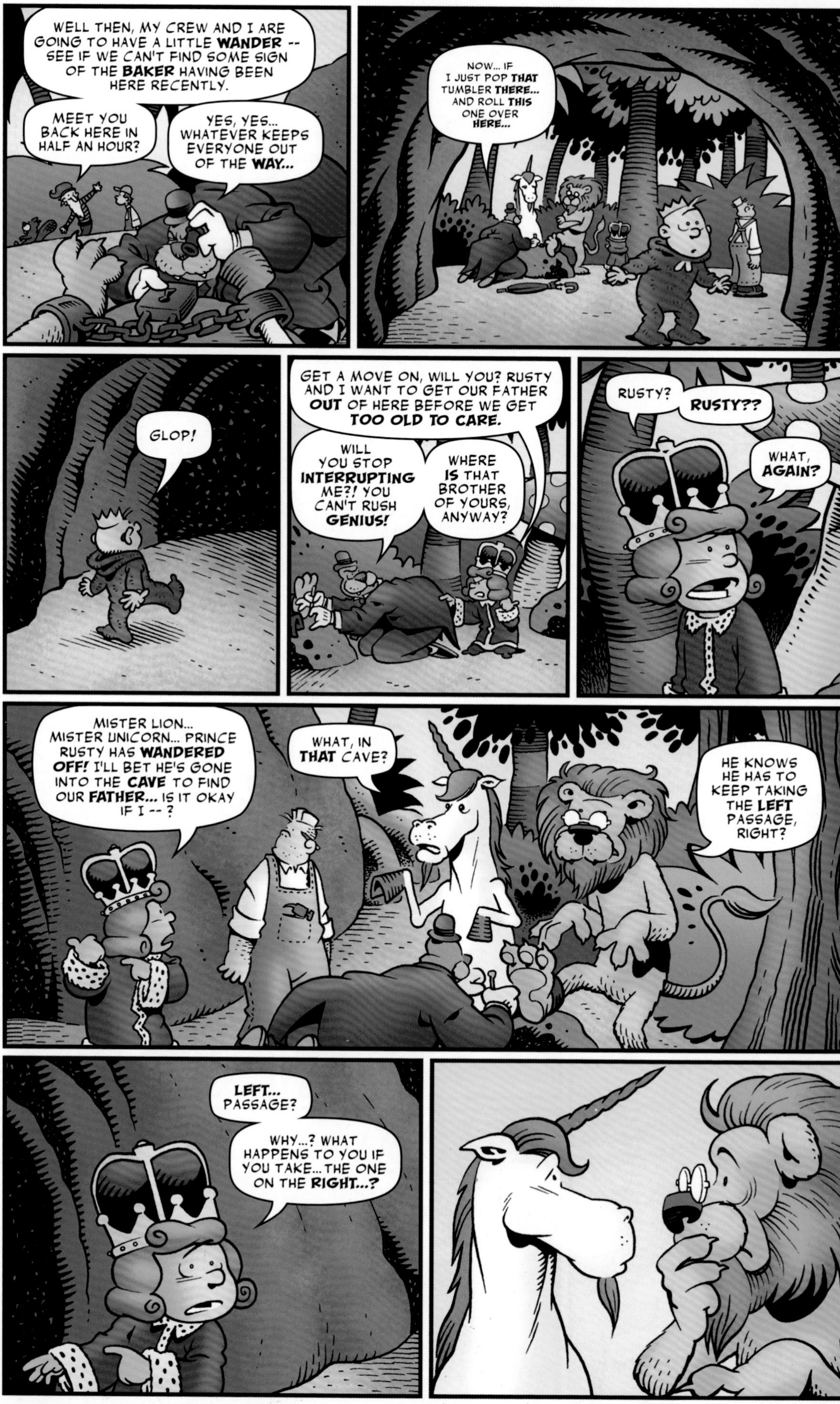
WELL THEN, MY CREW AND I ARE GOING TO HAVE A LITTLE WANDER -- SEE IF WE CAN'T FIND SOME SIGN OF THE BAKER HAVING BEEN HERE RECENTLY.
MEET YOU BACK HERE IN HALF AN HOUR?
YES, YES... WHATEVER KEEPS EVERYONE OUT OF THE WAY...
NOW... IF I JUST POP THAT TUMBLER THERE... AND ROLL THIS ONE OVER HERE...
GLOP!
GET A MOVE ON, WILL YOU? RUSTY AND I WANT TO GET OUR FATHER OUT OF HERE BEFORE WE GET TOO OLD TO CARE.
WILL YOU STOP INTERRUPTING ME?! YOU CAN'T RUSH GENIUS!
WHERE IS THAT BROTHER OF YOURS, ANYWAY?
RUSTY?
RUSTY??
WHAT, AGAIN?
MISTER LION... MISTER UNICORN... PRINCE RUSTY HAS WANDERED OFF! I'LL BET HE'S GONE INTO THE CAVE TO FIND OUR FATHER... IS IT OKAY IF I -- ?
WHAT, IN THAT CAVE?
HE KNOWS HE HAS TO KEEP TAKING THE LEFT PASSAGE, RIGHT?
LEFT... PASSAGE?
WHY...? WHAT HAPPENS TO YOU IF YOU TAKE... THE ONE ON THE RIGHT...?

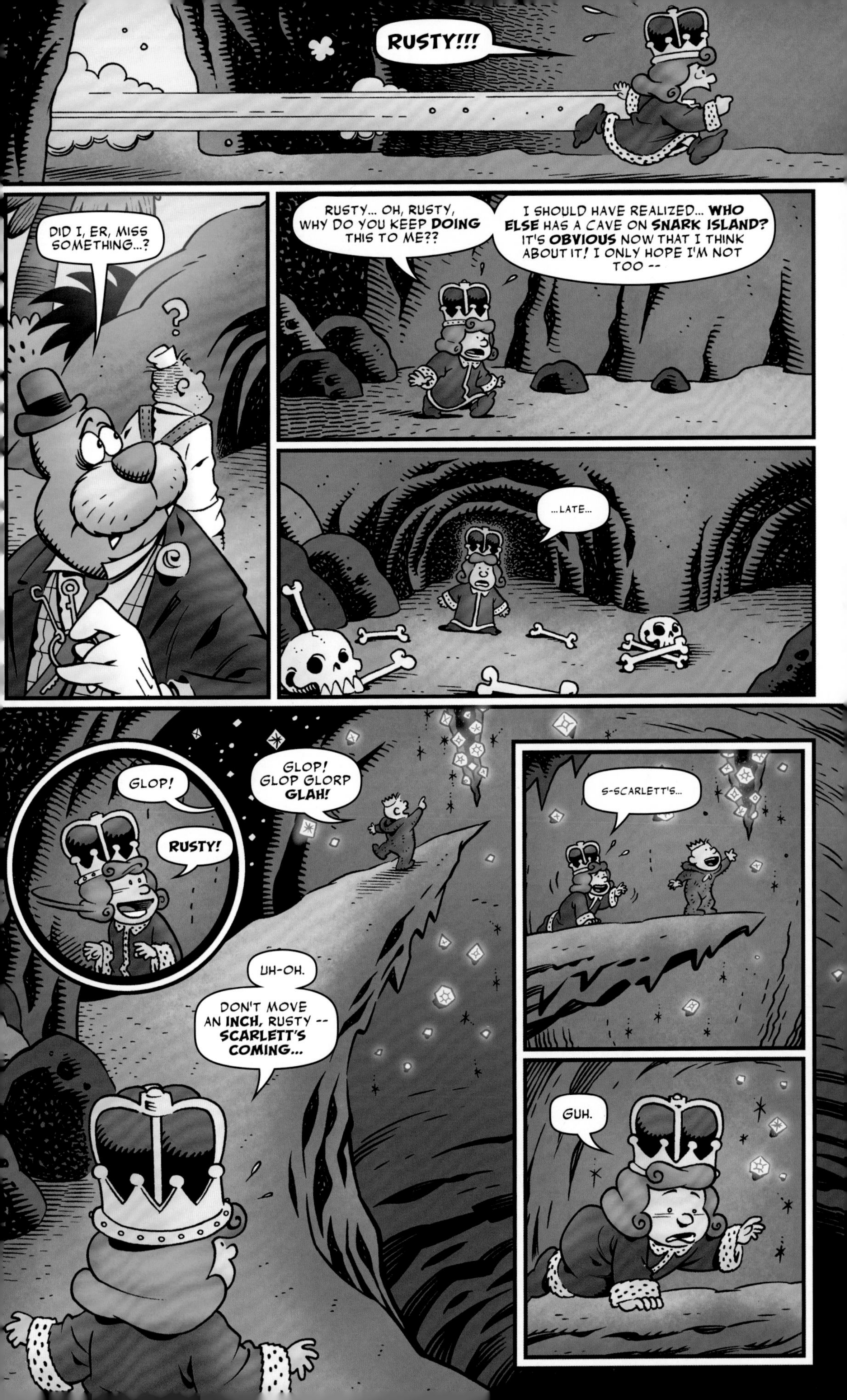
RUSTY!!!
DID I, ER, MISS SOMETHING...?
RUSTY... OH, RUSTY, WHY DO YOU KEEP DOING THIS TO ME??
I SHOULD HAVE REALIZED... WHO ELSE HAS A CAVE ON SNARK ISLAND? IT'S OBVIOUS NOW THAT I THINK ABOUT IT! I ONLY HOPE I'M NOT TOO --
...LATE...
GLOP!
RUSTY!
GLOP! GLOP GLORP GLAH!
UH-OH.
DON'T MOVE AN INCH, RUSTY -- SCARLETT'S COMING...
S-SCARLETT'S...
GUH.

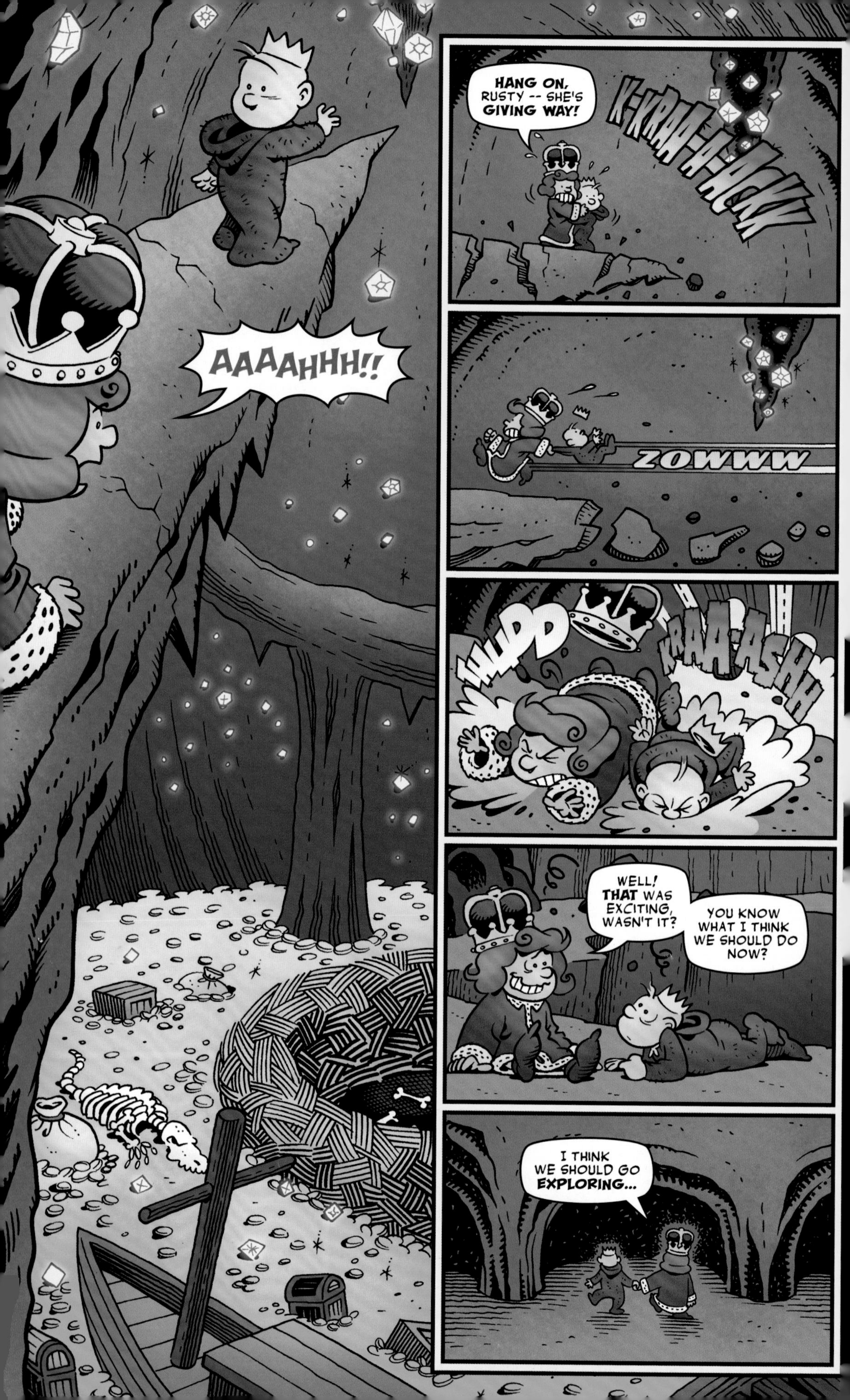
AAAAHHH!!
HANG ON, RUSTY -- SHE'S GIVING WAY!
K-KRAA-A-ACKK
ZOWWW
THUDD
KRAA-ASHH
WELL! THAT WAS EXCITING, WASN'T IT?
YOU KNOW WHAT I THINK WE SHOULD DO NOW?
I THINK WE SHOULD GO EXPLORING...

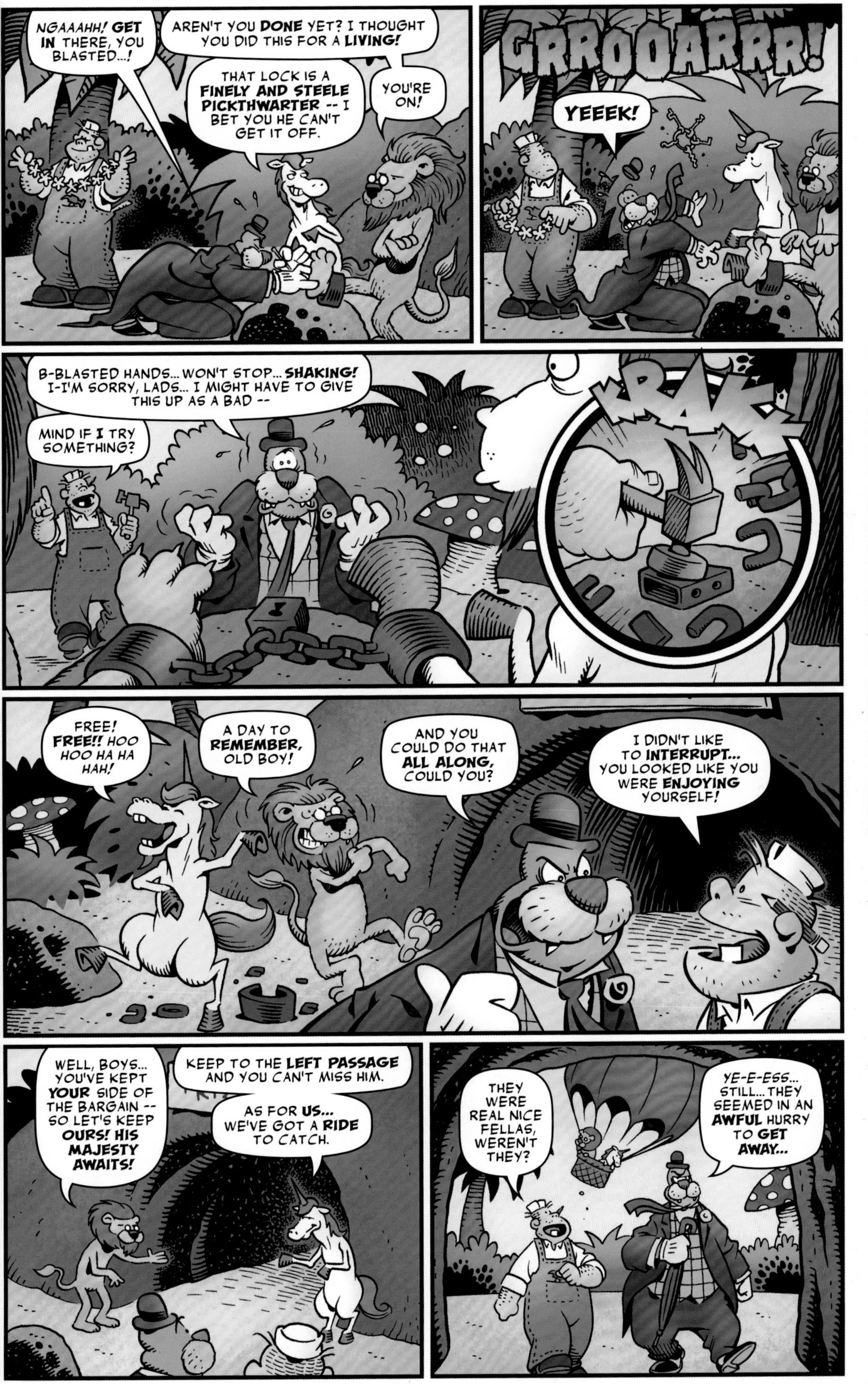
NGAAAHH! GET IN THERE, YOU BLASTED...!
AREN'T YOU DONE YET? I THOUGHT YOU DID THIS FOR A LIVING!
THAT LOCK IS A FINELY AND STEELE PICKTHWARTER -- I BET YOU HE CAN'T GET IT OFF.
YOU'RE ON!
GRROOARRR!
YEEEK!
B-BLASTED HANDS... WON'T STOP... SHAKING! I-I'M SORRY, LADS... I MIGHT HAVE TO GIVE THIS UP AS A BAD --
MIND IF I TRY SOMETHING?
FREE! FREE!! HOO HOO HA HA HAH!
A DAY TO REMEMBER, OLD BOY!
AND YOU COULD DO THAT ALL ALONG, COULD YOU?
I DIDN'T LIKE TO INTERRUPT... YOU LOOKED LIKE YOU WERE ENJOYING YOURSELF!
WELL, BOYS... YOU'VE KEPT YOUR SIDE OF THE BARGAIN -- SO LET'S KEEP OURS! HIS MAJESTY AWAITS!
KEEP TO THE LEFT PASSAGE AND YOU CAN'T MISS HIM.
AS FOR US... WE'VE GOT A RIDE TO CATCH.
THEY WERE REAL NICE FELLAS, WEREN'T THEY?
YE-E-ESS... STILL... THEY SEEMED IN AN AWFUL HURRY TO GET AWAY...

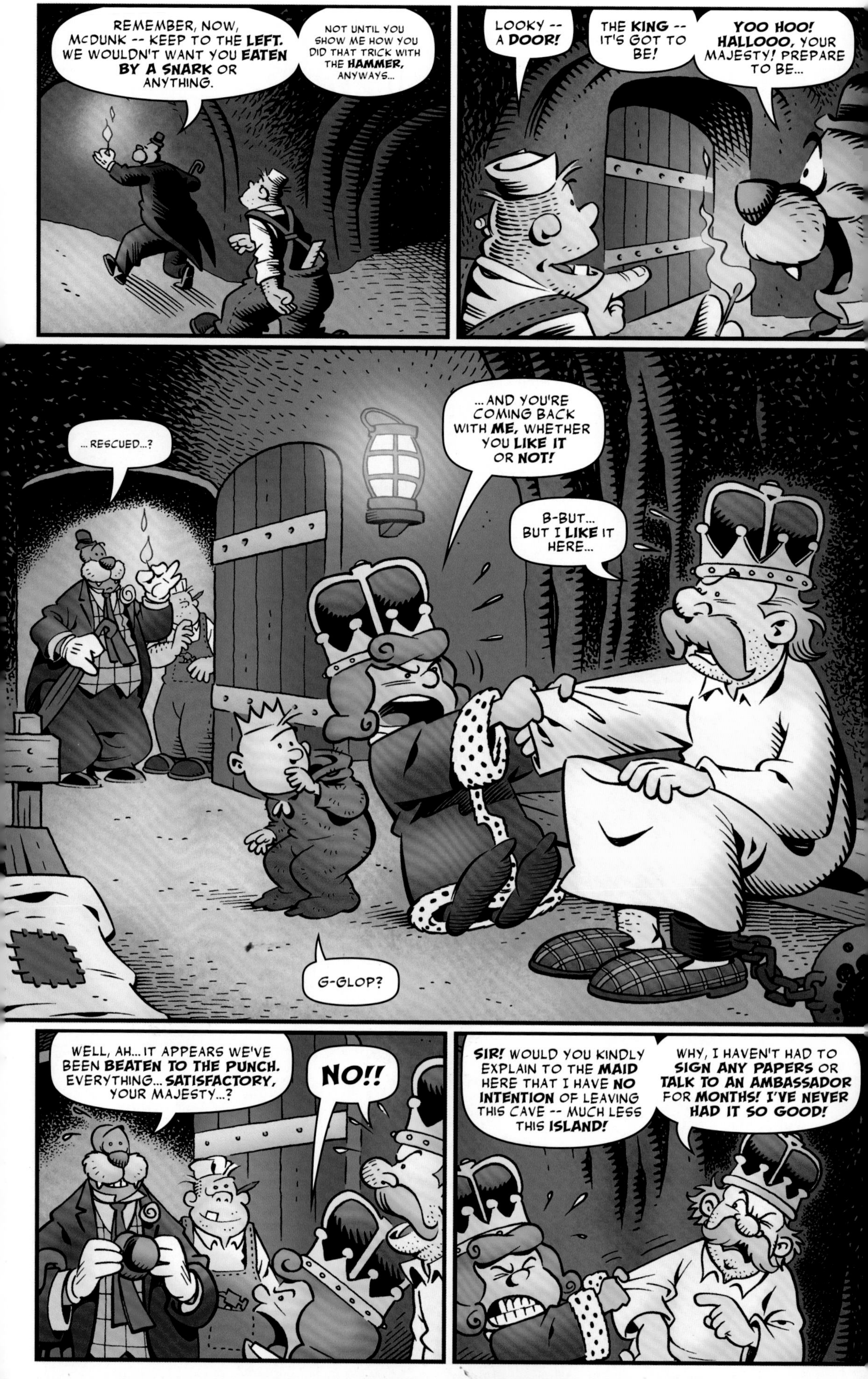
REMEMBER, NOW, McDUNK -- KEEP TO THE LEFT. WE WOULDN'T WANT YOU EATEN BY A SNARK OR ANYTHING.
NOT UNTIL YOU SHOW ME HOW YOU DID THAT TRICK WITH THE HAMMER, ANYWAYS...
LOOKY -- A DOOR!
THE KING -- IT'S GOT TO BE!
YOO HOO! HALLOOO, YOUR MAJESTY! PREPARE TO BE...
... RESCUED...?
... AND YOU'RE COMING BACK WITH ME, WHETHER YOU LIKE IT OR NOT!
B-BUT... BUT I LIKE IT HERE...
G-GLOP?
WELL, AH... IT APPEARS WE'VE BEEN BEATEN TO THE PUNCH. EVERYTHING... SATISFACTORY, YOUR MAJESTY...?
NO!!
SIR! WOULD YOU KINDLY EXPLAIN TO THE MAID HERE THAT I HAVE NO INTENTION OF LEAVING THIS CAVE -- MUCH LESS THIS ISLAND!
WHY, I HAVEN'T HAD TO SIGN ANY PAPERS OR TALK TO AN AMBASSADOR FOR MONTHS! I'VE NEVER HAD IT SO GOOD!

THE... **MAID.** RRRRRIGHT.

SCARLETT, MY DEAR... A QUICK **WORD,** IF I MAY...?

IT'S... IT'S NOT **FAIR,** MISTER WALRUS! AFTER ALL WE'VE BEEN THROUGH... HE WANTS TO **STAY HERE! HERE,** OF ALL PLACES!

YES, YES... **ABOUT** THAT...

I FEAR HE MAY HAVE BEEN **TORTURED** OR **TRAUMATIZED** IN SOME WAY. DID YOU NOTICE THAT HE CALLED YOU "THE MAID"? HE DOESN'T EVEN **RECOGNIZE** YOU!

I DON'T KNOW WHAT THOSE LION AND UNICORN BRUTES **DID** TO THE POOR CHAP, BUT...

IT... IT WASN'T THEM.

HMM?

HE DOESN'T RECOGNIZE ME... BECAUSE HE **NEVER HAS.**

THE TRUTH OF IT IS... I'VE BEEN RAISED BY **NANNIES** AND **GOVERNESSES** AND **TUTORS** ALL MY LIFE. I DOUBT I'VE EVEN **MET** MY FATHER MORE THAN HALF A DOZEN TIMES. HE'S ALWAYS BEEN... **TOO BUSY.**

THIS... THIS IS BUSINESS AS USUAL.

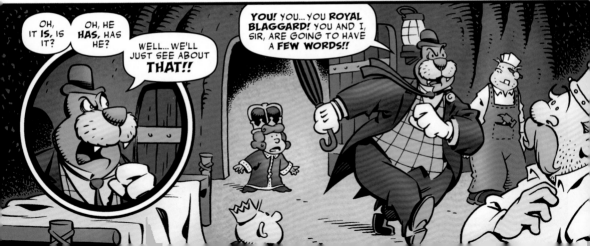

OH, IT **IS,** IS IT?

OH, HE **HAS,** HAS HE?

WELL... WE'LL JUST SEE ABOUT **THAT!!**

YOU! YOU... YOU **ROYAL BLAGGARD!** YOU AND I, SIR, ARE GOING TO HAVE A **FEW WORDS!!**

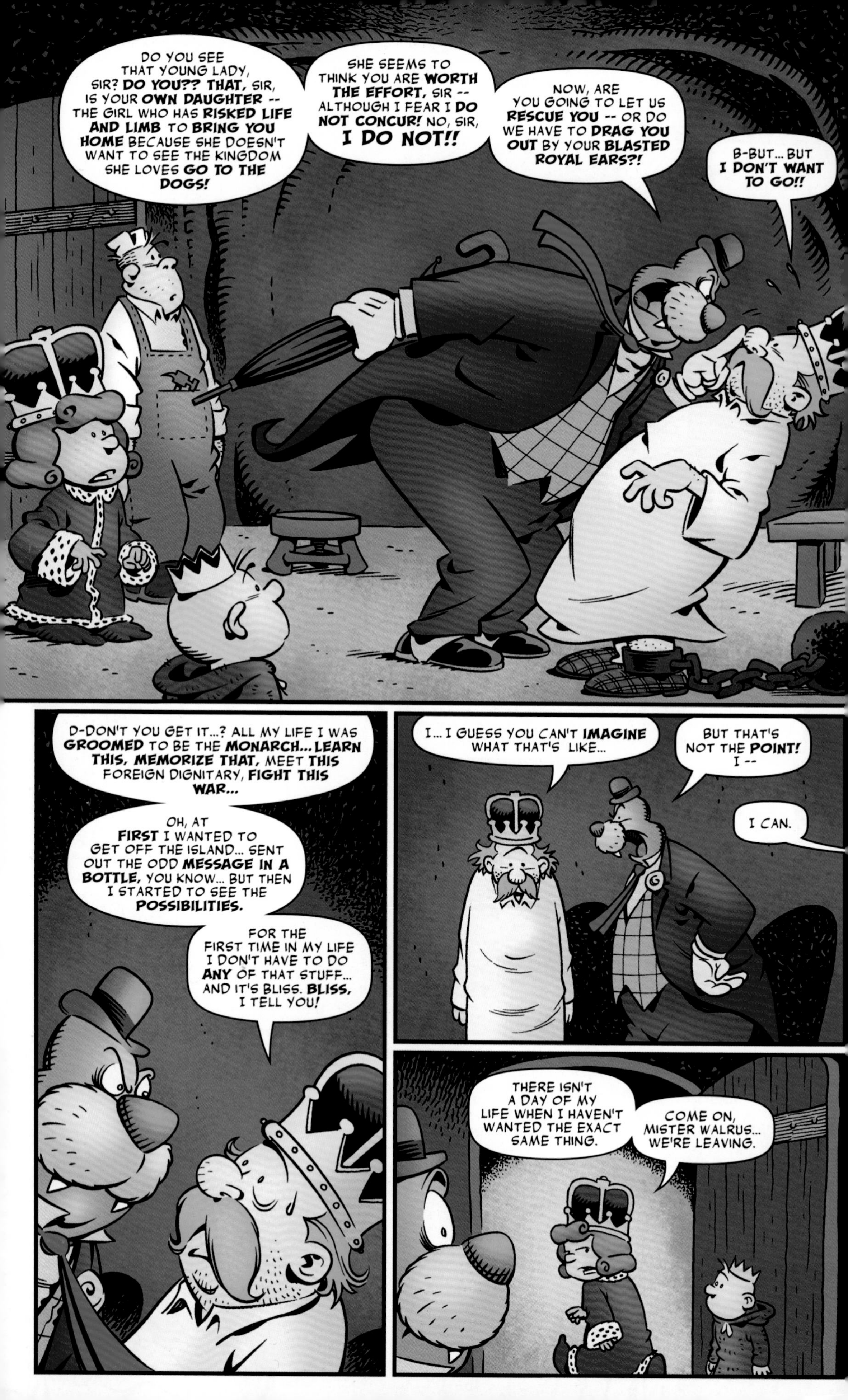
DO YOU SEE THAT YOUNG LADY, SIR? DO YOU?? THAT, SIR, IS YOUR OWN DAUGHTER -- THE GIRL WHO HAS RISKED LIFE AND LIMB TO BRING YOU HOME BECAUSE SHE DOESN'T WANT TO SEE THE KINGDOM SHE LOVES GO TO THE DOGS!
SHE SEEMS TO THINK YOU ARE WORTH THE EFFORT, SIR -- ALTHOUGH I FEAR I DO NOT CONCUR! NO, SIR, I DO NOT!!
NOW, ARE YOU GOING TO LET US RESCUE YOU -- OR DO WE HAVE TO DRAG YOU OUT BY YOUR BLASTED ROYAL EARS?!
B-BUT... BUT I DON'T WANT TO GO!!
D-DON'T YOU GET IT...? ALL MY LIFE I WAS GROOMED TO BE THE MONARCH... LEARN THIS, MEMORIZE THAT, MEET THIS FOREIGN DIGNITARY, FIGHT THIS WAR...
OH, AT FIRST I WANTED TO GET OFF THE ISLAND... SENT OUT THE ODD MESSAGE IN A BOTTLE, YOU KNOW... BUT THEN I STARTED TO SEE THE POSSIBILITIES.
FOR THE FIRST TIME IN MY LIFE I DON'T HAVE TO DO ANY OF THAT STUFF... AND IT'S BLISS. BLISS, I TELL YOU!
I... I GUESS YOU CAN'T IMAGINE WHAT THAT'S LIKE...
BUT THAT'S NOT THE POINT! I --
I CAN.
THERE ISN'T A DAY OF MY LIFE WHEN I HAVEN'T WANTED THE EXACT SAME THING.
COME ON, MISTER WALRUS... WE'RE LEAVING.

B-BUT... BUT THE **KINGDOM!** THE ECONOMY WILL **NEVER** RALLY UNLESS THE **KING** IS THERE TO **INSPIRE CONFIDENCE!** AND THOSE **ADVISORS** OF YOURS WILL **RUN ROUGHSHOD** OVER --

SO WE'LL BE JUST LIKE EVERY **OTHER** KINGDOM... **BROKE,** AND WITH A BUNCH OF **RATBAGS** AT THE TOP. BIG WHOOP.

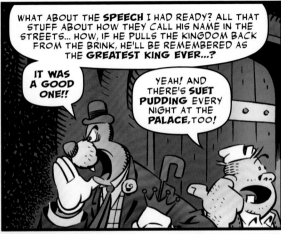

WHAT ABOUT THE **SPEECH** I HAD READY? ALL THAT STUFF ABOUT HOW THEY CALL HIS NAME IN THE STREETS... HOW, IF HE PULLS THE KINGDOM BACK FROM THE BRINK, HE'LL BE REMEMBERED AS THE **GREATEST KING EVER...?**

IT **WAS** A GOOD ONE!!

YEAH! AND THERE'S **SUET PUDDING** EVERY NIGHT AT THE **PALACE,** TOO!

RRAAHRR!!

GLEEP!

WUUHHHH!

AND THERE'S THE S-SMALL MATTER OF A **SNARK,** AS WELL!

GOOD AFTERNOON, YOUR MAJESTY... ANOTHER TIME, PERHAPS. MY PARTNER AND I MUST BE GETTING ON.

WAIT!

I'M COMING WITH YOU.

WH-WHAT...?

SUET PUDDING, YOU SAID! IF YOU KNEW HOW I'VE **CRAVED** SUET PUDDING THESE LONG MONTHS...!

WELL? ARE WE GOING OR WHAT?

ALL RIGHT, THEN... **COME,** IF YOU'RE COMING.

ROYALS... SHEESH.

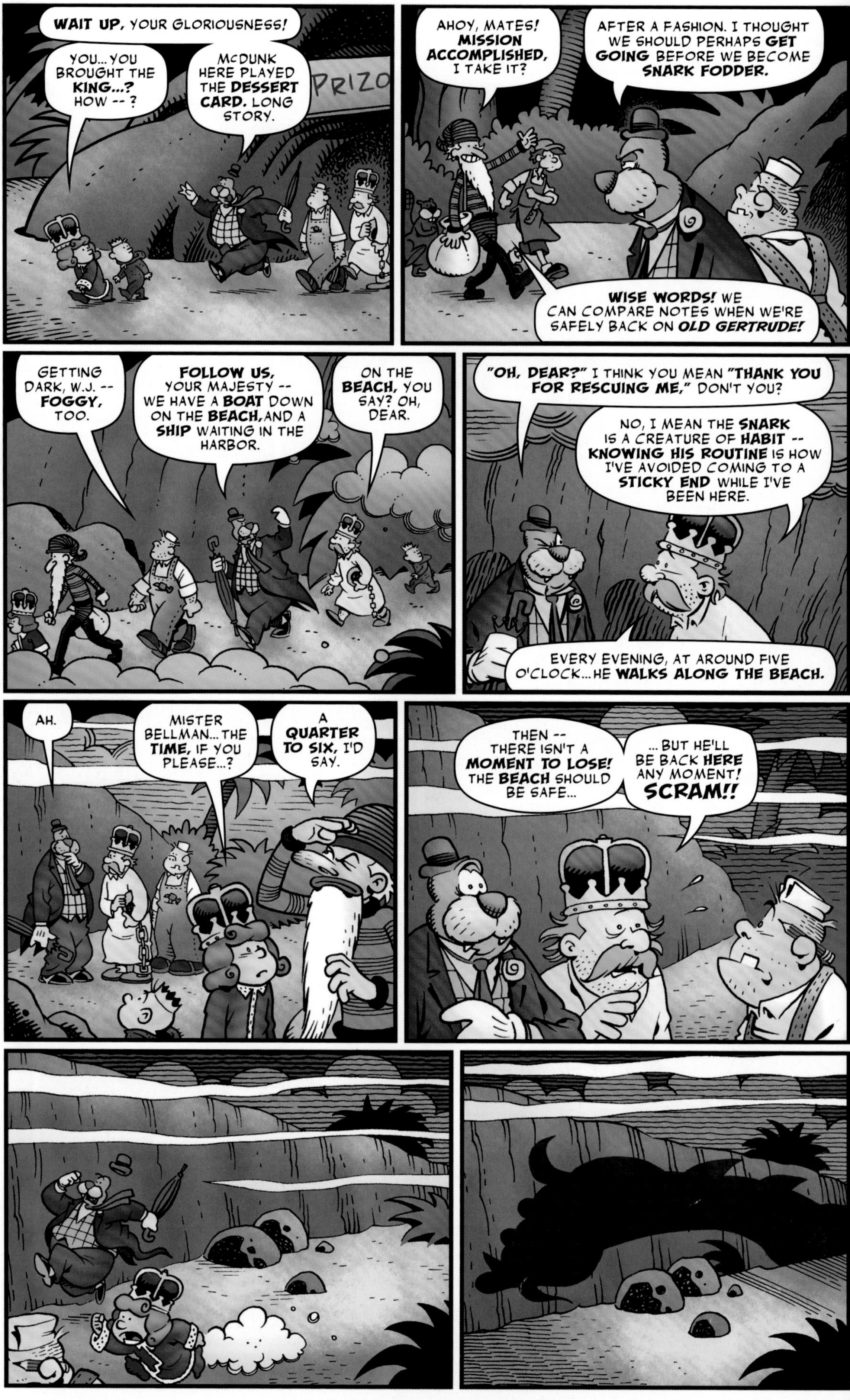
WAIT UP, YOUR GLORIOUSNESS!
YOU... YOU BROUGHT THE KING...? HOW -- ?
McDUNK HERE PLAYED THE DESSERT CARD. LONG STORY.
PRIZO
AHOY, MATES! MISSION ACCOMPLISHED, I TAKE IT?
AFTER A FASHION. I THOUGHT WE SHOULD PERHAPS GET GOING BEFORE WE BECOME SNARK FODDER.
WISE WORDS! WE CAN COMPARE NOTES WHEN WE'RE SAFELY BACK ON OLD GERTRUDE!
GETTING DARK, W.J. -- FOGGY, TOO.
FOLLOW US, YOUR MAJESTY -- WE HAVE A BOAT DOWN ON THE BEACH, AND A SHIP WAITING IN THE HARBOR.
ON THE BEACH, YOU SAY? OH, DEAR.
"OH, DEAR?" I THINK YOU MEAN "THANK YOU FOR RESCUING ME," DON'T YOU?
NO, I MEAN THE SNARK IS A CREATURE OF HABIT -- KNOWING HIS ROUTINE IS HOW I'VE AVOIDED COMING TO A STICKY END WHILE I'VE BEEN HERE.
EVERY EVENING, AT AROUND FIVE O'CLOCK... HE WALKS ALONG THE BEACH.
AH.
MISTER BELLMAN... THE TIME, IF YOU PLEASE...?
A QUARTER TO SIX, I'D SAY.
THEN -- THERE ISN'T A MOMENT TO LOSE! THE BEACH SHOULD BE SAFE...
... BUT HE'LL BE BACK HERE ANY MOMENT! SCRAM!!

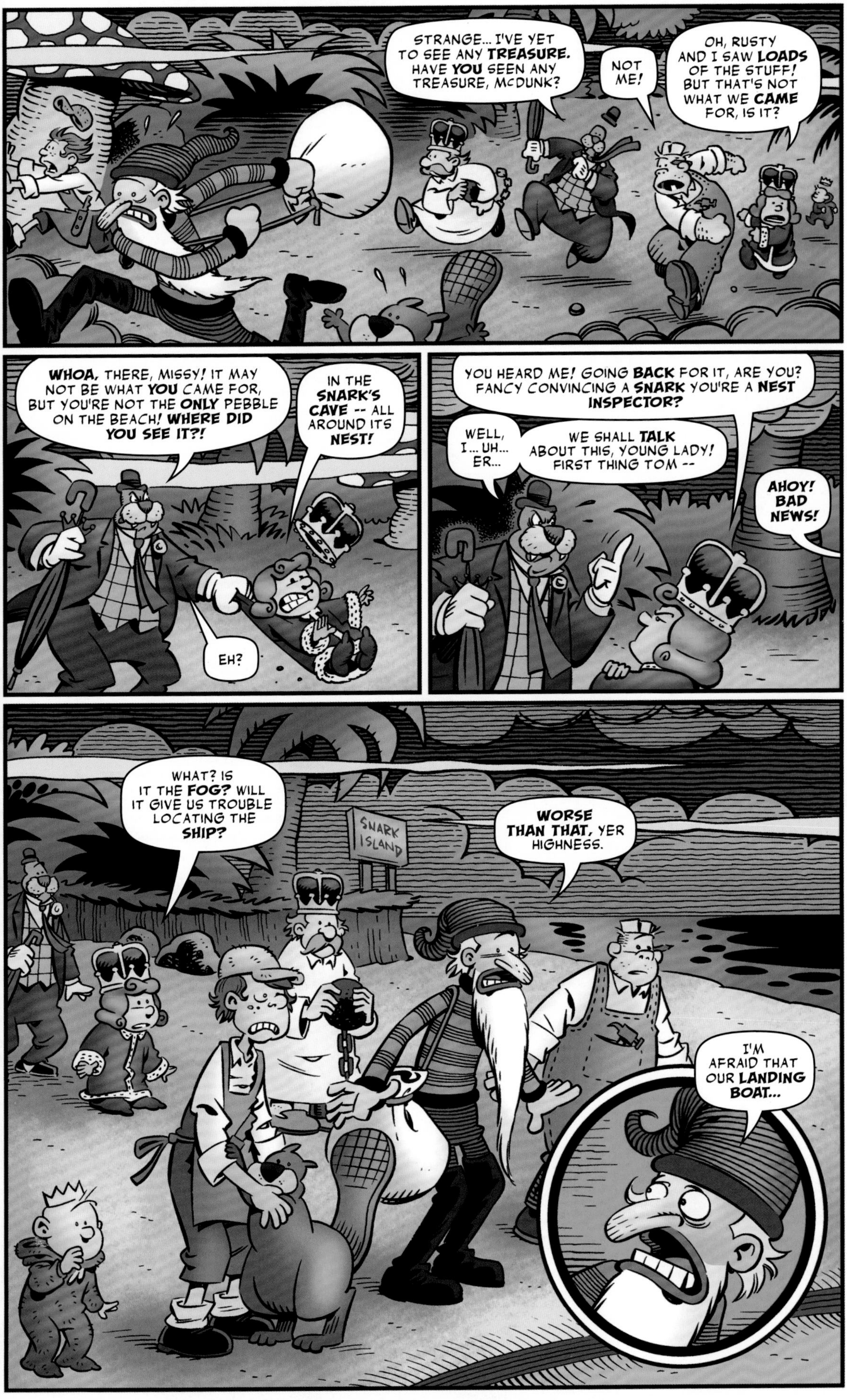
STRANGE... I'VE YET TO SEE ANY TREASURE. HAVE YOU SEEN ANY TREASURE, McDUNK?
NOT ME!
OH, RUSTY AND I SAW LOADS OF THE STUFF! BUT THAT'S NOT WHAT WE CAME FOR, IS IT?
WHOA, THERE, MISSY! IT MAY NOT BE WHAT YOU CAME FOR, BUT YOU'RE NOT THE ONLY PEBBLE ON THE BEACH! WHERE DID YOU SEE IT?!
IN THE SNARK'S CAVE -- ALL AROUND ITS NEST!
EH?
YOU HEARD ME! GOING BACK FOR IT, ARE YOU? FANCY CONVINCING A SNARK YOU'RE A NEST INSPECTOR?
WELL, I... UH... ER...
WE SHALL TALK ABOUT THIS, YOUNG LADY! FIRST THING TOM --
AHOY! BAD NEWS!
WHAT? IS IT THE FOG? WILL IT GIVE US TROUBLE LOCATING THE SHIP?
SNARK ISLAND
WORSE THAN THAT, YER HIGHNESS.
I'M AFRAID THAT OUR LANDING BOAT...

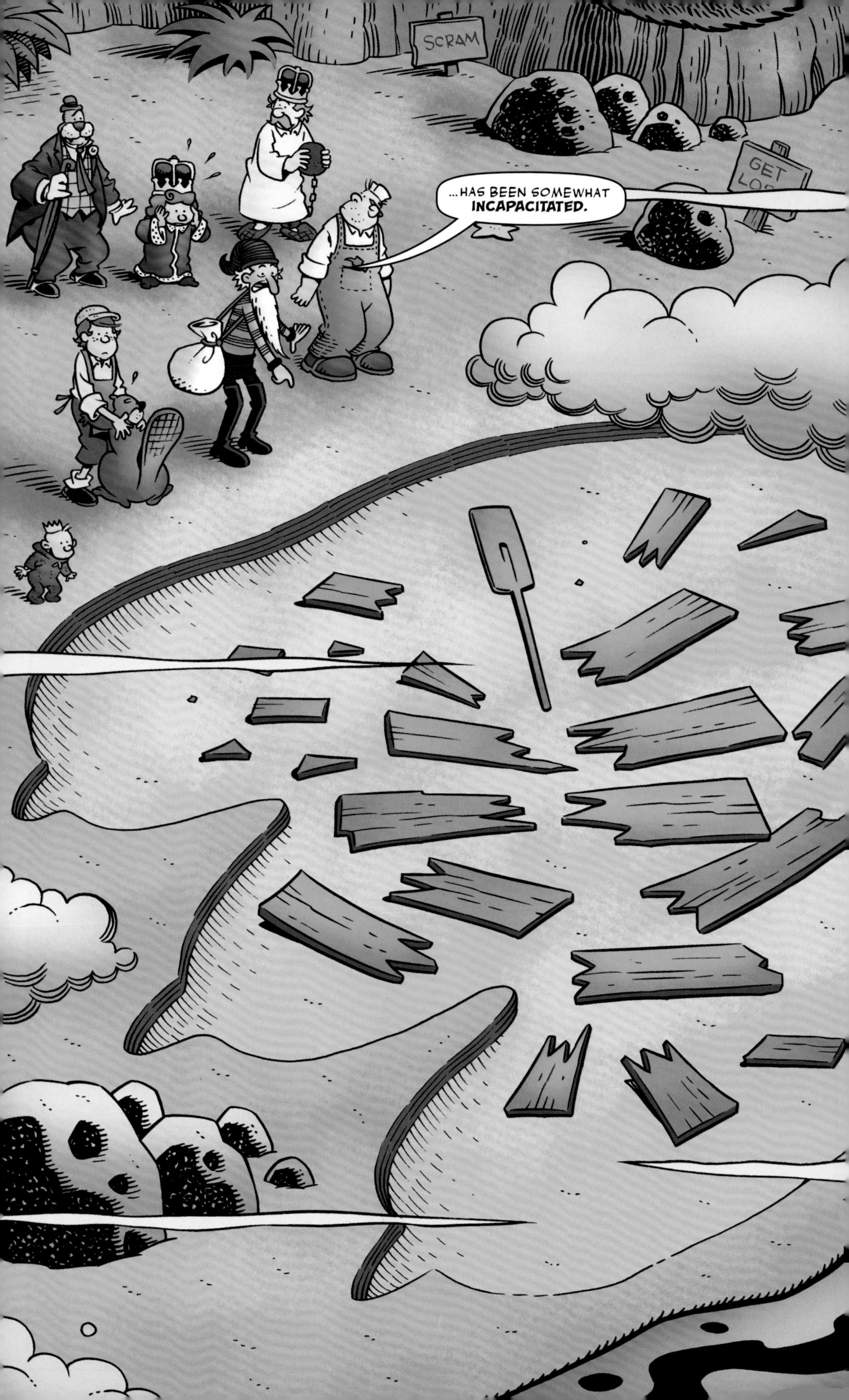
SCRAM
GET LOS
...HAS BEEN SOMEWHAT **INCAPACITATED.**

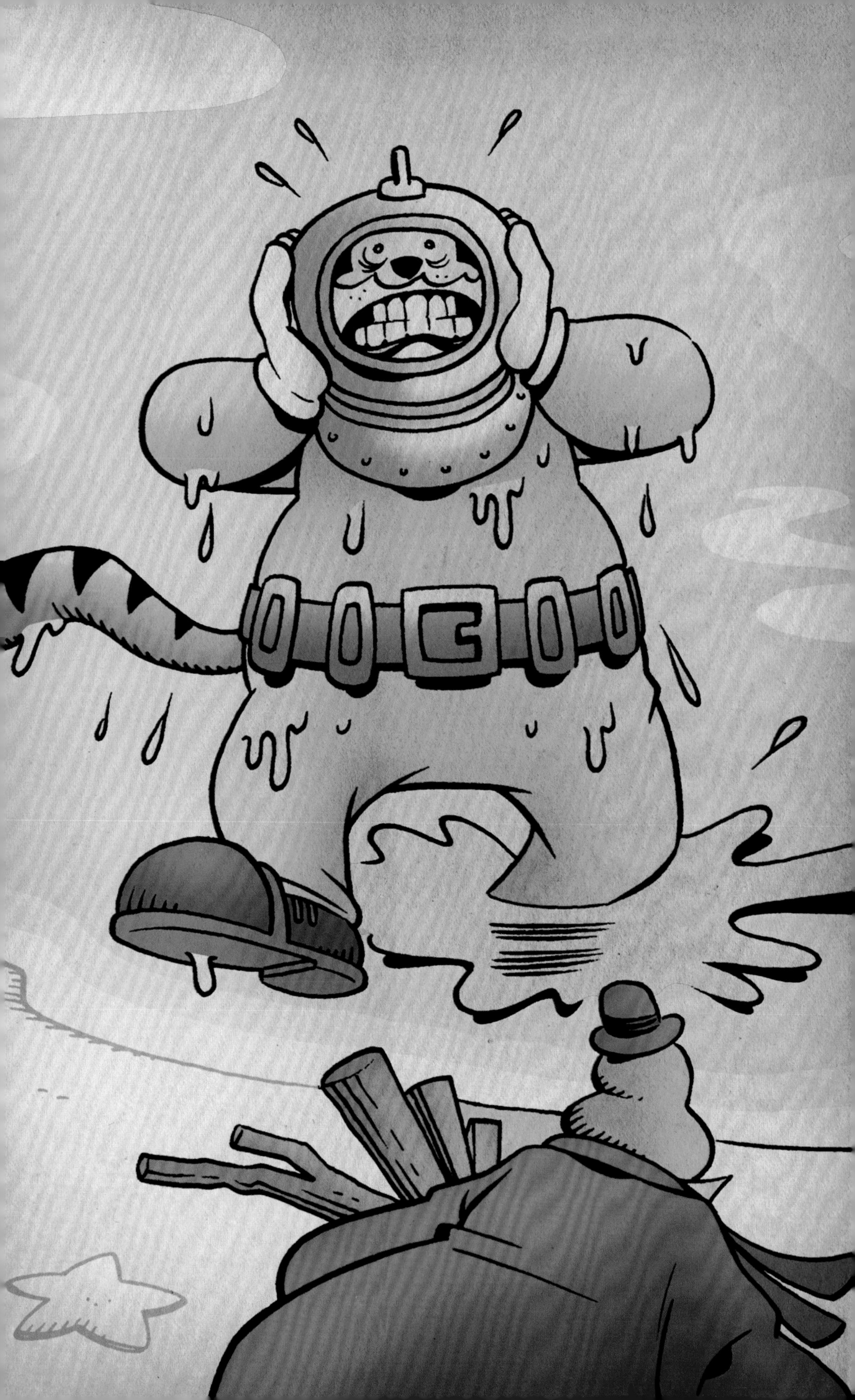

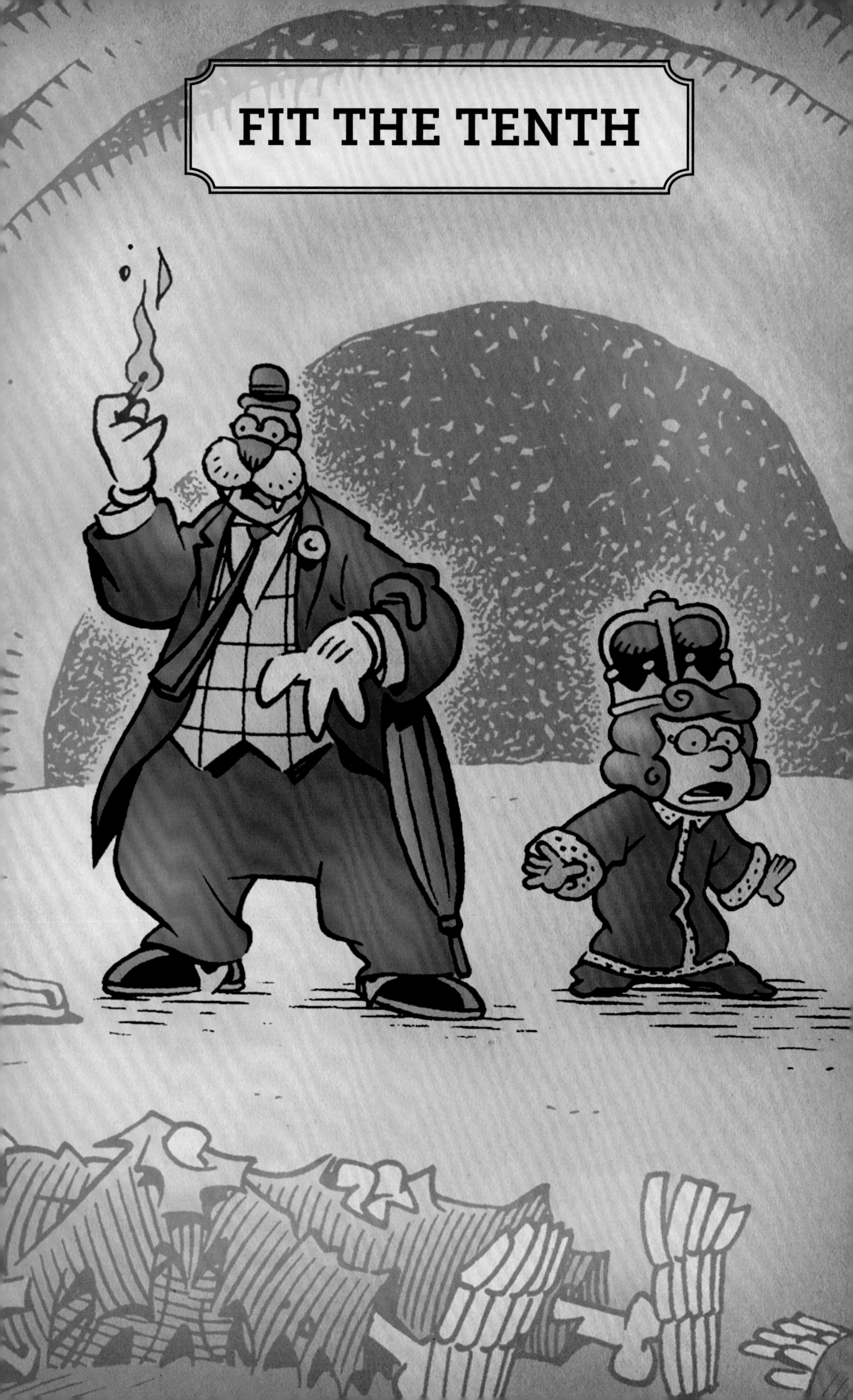
FIT THE TENTH

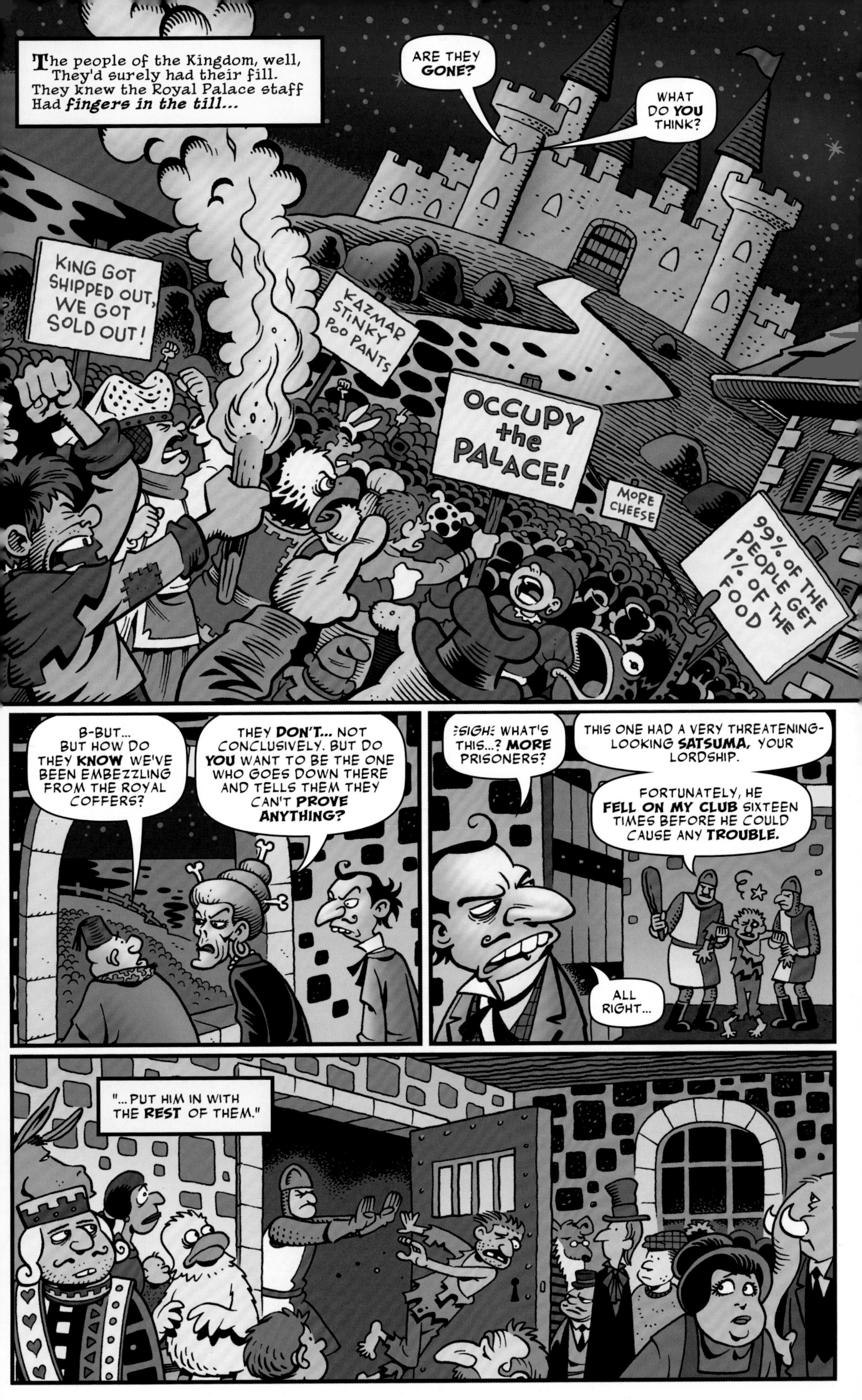
The people of the Kingdom, well,
They'd surely had their fill.
They knew the Royal Palace staff
Had ***fingers in the till...***
ARE THEY **GONE?**
WHAT DO **YOU** THINK?
KING GOT SHIPPED OUT, WE GOT SOLD OUT!
KAZMAR STINKY POO PANTS
OCCUPY the PALACE!
MORE CHEESE
99% OF THE PEOPLE GET 1% OF THE FOOD
B-BUT... BUT HOW DO THEY **KNOW** WE'VE BEEN EMBEZZLING FROM THE ROYAL COFFERS?
THEY **DON'T...** NOT CONCLUSIVELY. BUT DO **YOU** WANT TO BE THE ONE WHO GOES DOWN THERE AND TELLS THEM THEY CAN'T **PROVE ANYTHING?**
:SIGH: WHAT'S THIS...? **MORE** PRISONERS?
THIS ONE HAD A VERY THREATENING-LOOKING **SATSUMA,** YOUR LORDSHIP.
FORTUNATELY, HE **FELL ON MY CLUB** SIXTEEN TIMES BEFORE HE COULD CAUSE ANY **TROUBLE.**
ALL RIGHT...
"...PUT HIM IN WITH THE **REST** OF THEM."

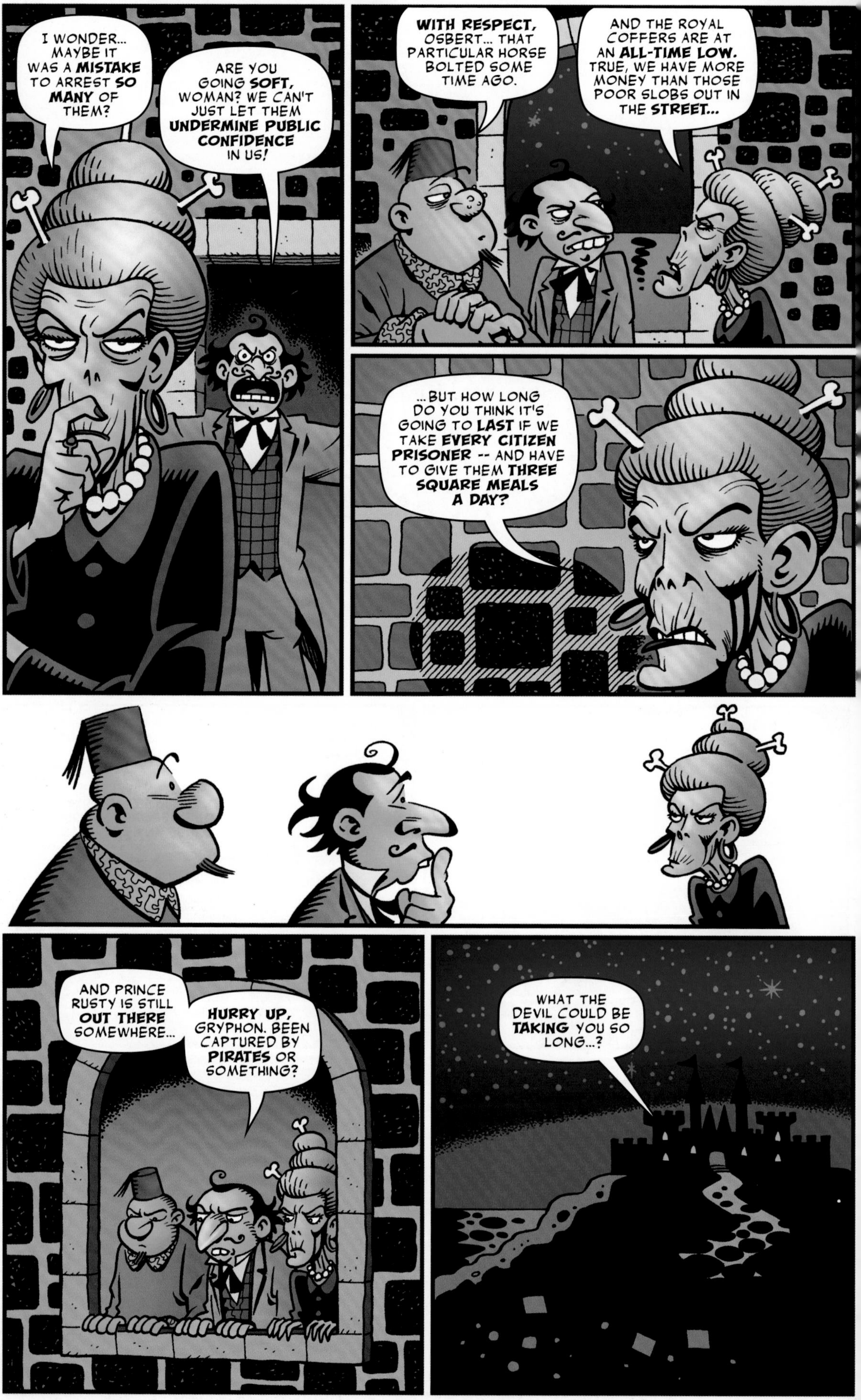
I WONDER... MAYBE IT WAS A **MISTAKE** TO ARREST **SO MANY** OF THEM?
ARE YOU GOING **SOFT,** WOMAN? WE CAN'T JUST LET THEM **UNDERMINE PUBLIC CONFIDENCE** IN US!
WITH RESPECT, OSBERT... THAT PARTICULAR HORSE BOLTED SOME TIME AGO.
AND THE ROYAL COFFERS ARE AT AN **ALL-TIME LOW.** TRUE, WE HAVE MORE MONEY THAN THOSE POOR SLOBS OUT IN THE **STREET...**
...BUT HOW LONG DO YOU THINK IT'S GOING TO **LAST** IF WE TAKE **EVERY CITIZEN PRISONER** -- AND HAVE TO GIVE THEM **THREE SQUARE MEALS A DAY?**
AND PRINCE RUSTY IS STILL **OUT THERE** SOMEWHERE...
HURRY UP, GRYPHON. BEEN CAPTURED BY **PIRATES** OR SOMETHING?
WHAT THE DEVIL COULD BE **TAKING** YOU SO LONG...?

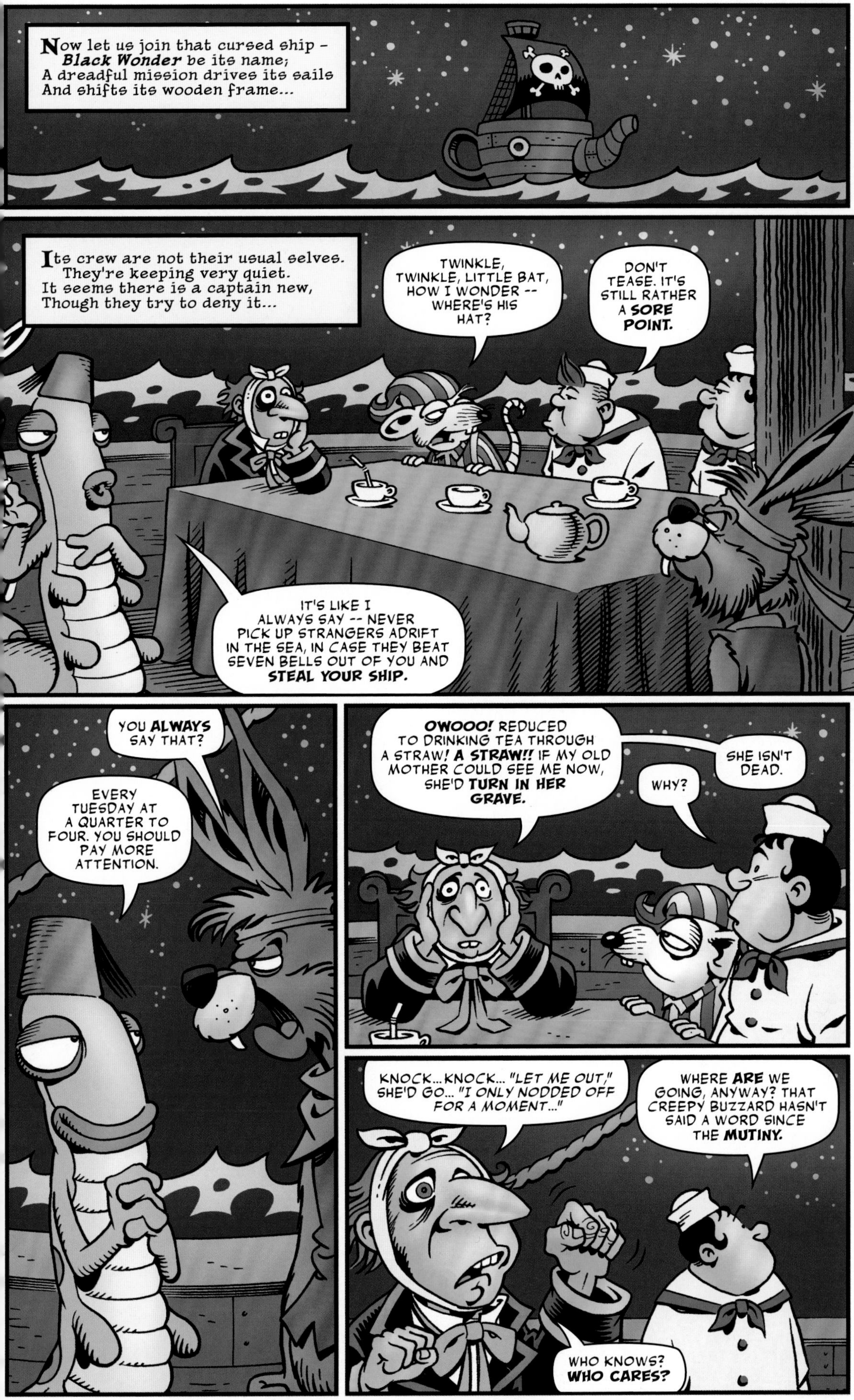
Now let us join that cursed ship – *Black Wonder* be its name; A dreadful mission drives its sails And shifts its wooden frame...
Its crew are not their usual selves. They're keeping very quiet. It seems there is a captain new, Though they try to deny it...
TWINKLE, TWINKLE, LITTLE BAT, HOW I WONDER -- WHERE'S HIS HAT?
DON'T TEASE. IT'S STILL RATHER A **SORE POINT.**
IT'S LIKE I ALWAYS SAY -- NEVER PICK UP STRANGERS ADRIFT IN THE SEA, IN CASE THEY BEAT SEVEN BELLS OUT OF YOU AND **STEAL YOUR SHIP.**
YOU **ALWAYS** SAY THAT?
EVERY TUESDAY AT A QUARTER TO FOUR. YOU SHOULD PAY MORE ATTENTION.
OWOOO! REDUCED TO DRINKING TEA THROUGH A STRAW! **A STRAW!!** IF MY OLD MOTHER COULD SEE ME NOW, SHE'D **TURN IN HER GRAVE.**
WHY?
SHE ISN'T DEAD.
KNOCK... KNOCK... *"LET ME OUT,"* SHE'D GO... *"I ONLY NODDED OFF FOR A MOMENT..."*
WHERE **ARE** WE GOING, ANYWAY? THAT CREEPY BUZZARD HASN'T SAID A WORD SINCE THE **MUTINY.**
WHO KNOWS? **WHO CARES?**

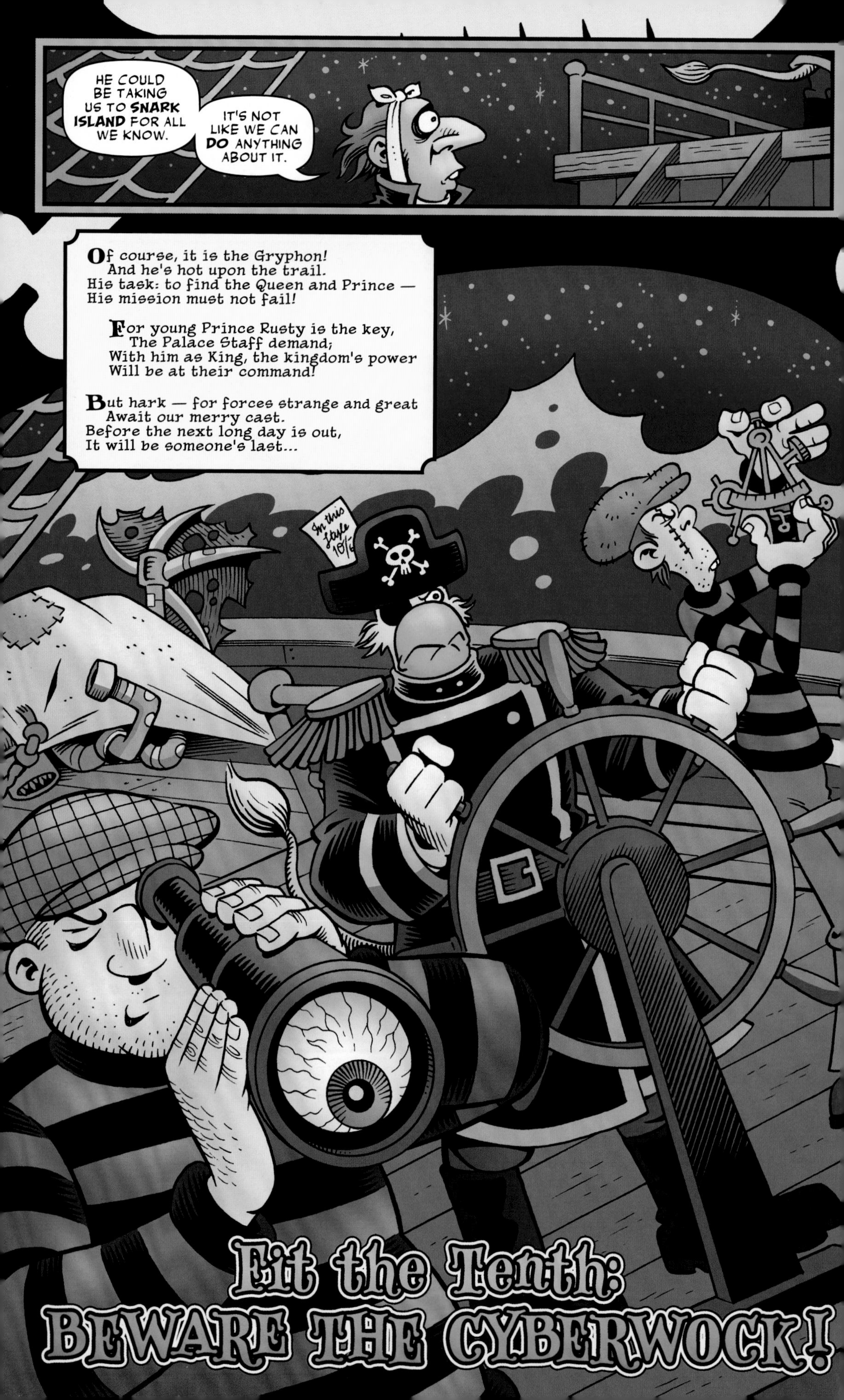
HE COULD BE TAKING US TO SNARK ISLAND FOR ALL WE KNOW.
IT'S NOT LIKE WE CAN DO ANYTHING ABOUT IT.
Of course, it is the Gryphon!
And he's hot upon the trail.
His task: to find the Queen and Prince —
His mission must not fail!
For young Prince Rusty is the key,
The Palace Staff demand;
With him as King, the kingdom's power
Will be at their command!
But hark — for forces strange and great
Await our merry cast.
Before the next long day is out,
It will be someone's last...
Fit the Tenth:
BEWARE THE CYBERWOCK!

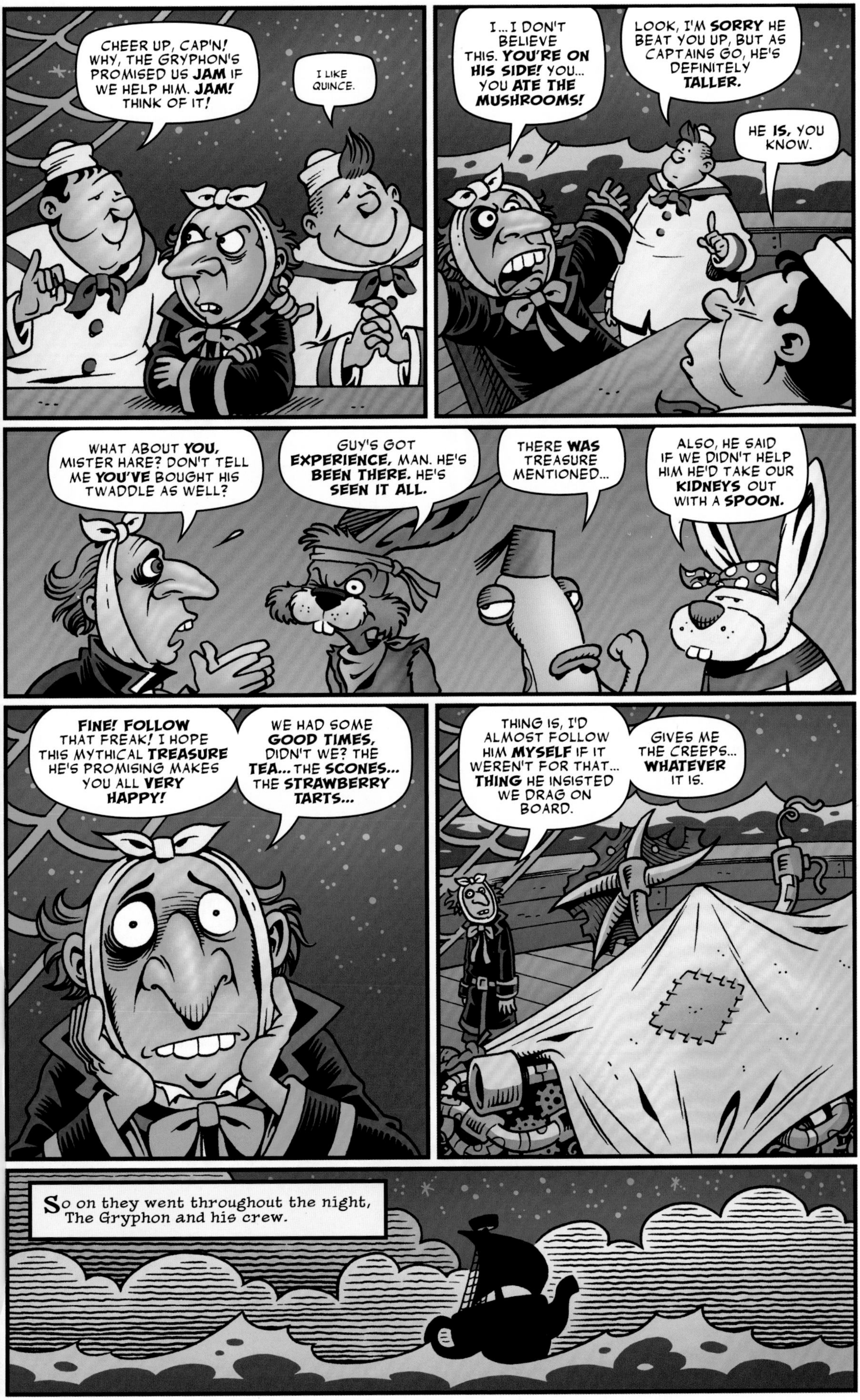

CHEER UP, CAP'N! WHY, THE GRYPHON'S PROMISED US JAM IF WE HELP HIM. JAM! THINK OF IT!
I LIKE QUINCE.
I...I DON'T BELIEVE THIS. YOU'RE ON HIS SIDE! YOU... YOU ATE THE MUSHROOMS!
LOOK, I'M SORRY HE BEAT YOU UP, BUT AS CAPTAINS GO, HE'S DEFINITELY TALLER.
HE IS, YOU KNOW.
WHAT ABOUT YOU, MISTER HARE? DON'T TELL ME YOU'VE BOUGHT HIS TWADDLE AS WELL?
GUY'S GOT EXPERIENCE, MAN. HE'S BEEN THERE. HE'S SEEN IT ALL.
THERE WAS TREASURE MENTIONED...
ALSO, HE SAID IF WE DIDN'T HELP HIM HE'D TAKE OUR KIDNEYS OUT WITH A SPOON.
FINE! FOLLOW THAT FREAK! I HOPE THIS MYTHICAL TREASURE HE'S PROMISING MAKES YOU ALL VERY HAPPY!
WE HAD SOME GOOD TIMES, DIDN'T WE? THE TEA... THE SCONES... THE STRAWBERRY TARTS...
THING IS, I'D ALMOST FOLLOW HIM MYSELF IF IT WEREN'T FOR THAT... THING HE INSISTED WE DRAG ON BOARD.
GIVES ME THE CREEPS... WHATEVER IT IS.
So on they went throughout the night,
The Gryphon and his crew.

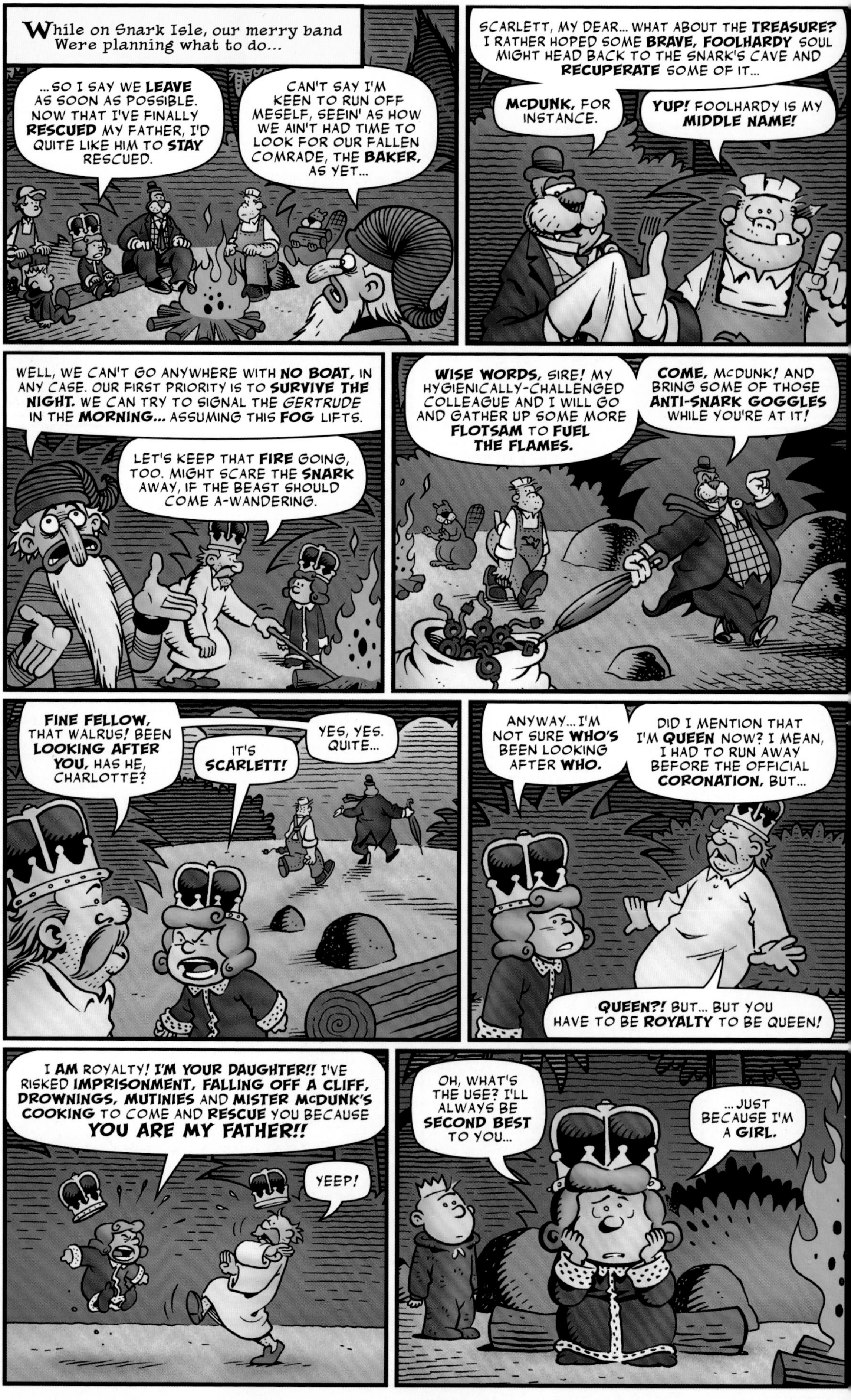
While on Snark Isle, our merry band Were planning what to do...
...SO I SAY WE LEAVE AS SOON AS POSSIBLE. NOW THAT I'VE FINALLY RESCUED MY FATHER, I'D QUITE LIKE HIM TO STAY RESCUED.
CAN'T SAY I'M KEEN TO RUN OFF MESELF, SEEIN' AS HOW WE AIN'T HAD TIME TO LOOK FOR OUR FALLEN COMRADE, THE BAKER, AS YET...
SCARLETT, MY DEAR... WHAT ABOUT THE TREASURE? I RATHER HOPED SOME BRAVE, FOOLHARDY SOUL MIGHT HEAD BACK TO THE SNARK'S CAVE AND RECUPERATE SOME OF IT...
McDUNK, FOR INSTANCE.
YUP! FOOLHARDY IS MY MIDDLE NAME!
WELL, WE CAN'T GO ANYWHERE WITH NO BOAT, IN ANY CASE. OUR FIRST PRIORITY IS TO SURVIVE THE NIGHT. WE CAN TRY TO SIGNAL THE GERTRUDE IN THE MORNING... ASSUMING THIS FOG LIFTS.
LET'S KEEP THAT FIRE GOING, TOO. MIGHT SCARE THE SNARK AWAY, IF THE BEAST SHOULD COME A-WANDERING.
WISE WORDS, SIRE! MY HYGIENICALLY-CHALLENGED COLLEAGUE AND I WILL GO AND GATHER UP SOME MORE FLOTSAM TO FUEL THE FLAMES.
COME, McDUNK! AND BRING SOME OF THOSE ANTI-SNARK GOGGLES WHILE YOU'RE AT IT!
FINE FELLOW, THAT WALRUS! BEEN LOOKING AFTER YOU, HAS HE, CHARLOTTE?
IT'S SCARLETT!
YES, YES. QUITE...
ANYWAY... I'M NOT SURE WHO'S BEEN LOOKING AFTER WHO.
DID I MENTION THAT I'M QUEEN NOW? I MEAN, I HAD TO RUN AWAY BEFORE THE OFFICIAL CORONATION, BUT...
QUEEN?! BUT... BUT YOU HAVE TO BE ROYALTY TO BE QUEEN!
I AM ROYALTY! I'M YOUR DAUGHTER!! I'VE RISKED IMPRISONMENT, FALLING OFF A CLIFF, DROWNINGS, MUTINIES AND MISTER McDUNK'S COOKING TO COME AND RESCUE YOU BECAUSE YOU ARE MY FATHER!!
YEEP!
OH, WHAT'S THE USE? I'LL ALWAYS BE SECOND BEST TO YOU...
...JUST BECAUSE I'M A GIRL.

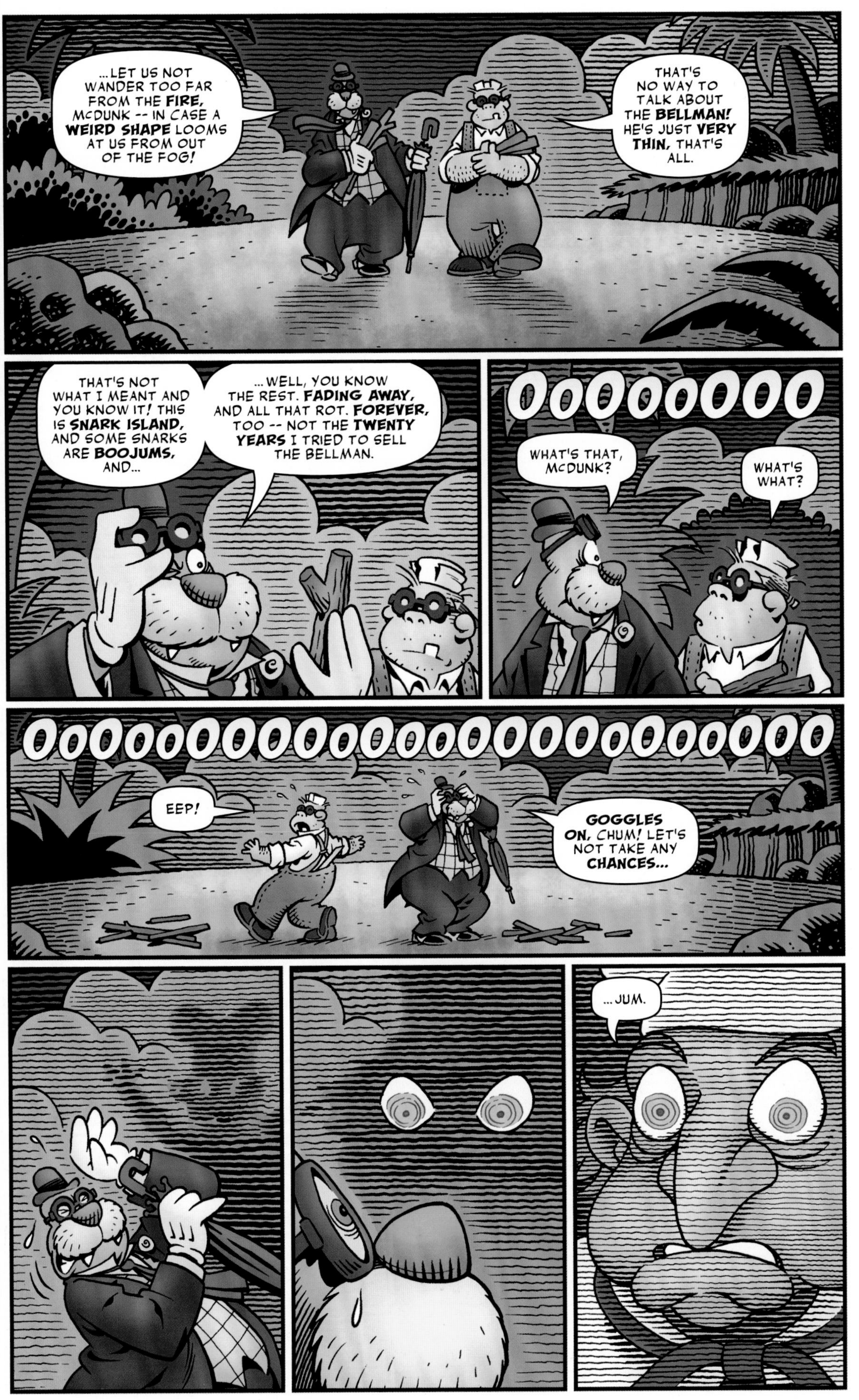
...LET US NOT WANDER TOO FAR FROM THE FIRE, McDUNK -- IN CASE A WEIRD SHAPE LOOMS AT US FROM OUT OF THE FOG!
THAT'S NO WAY TO TALK ABOUT THE BELLMAN! HE'S JUST VERY THIN, THAT'S ALL.
THAT'S NOT WHAT I MEANT AND YOU KNOW IT! THIS IS SNARK ISLAND, AND SOME SNARKS ARE BOOJUMS, AND...
...WELL, YOU KNOW THE REST. FADING AWAY, AND ALL THAT ROT. FOREVER, TOO -- NOT THE TWENTY YEARS I TRIED TO SELL THE BELLMAN.
OOOOOOOO
WHAT'S THAT, McDUNK?
WHAT'S WHAT?
OOOOOOOOOOOOOOOOOOOOOOOOO
EEP!
GOGGLES ON, CHUM! LET'S NOT TAKE ANY CHANCES...
...JUM.

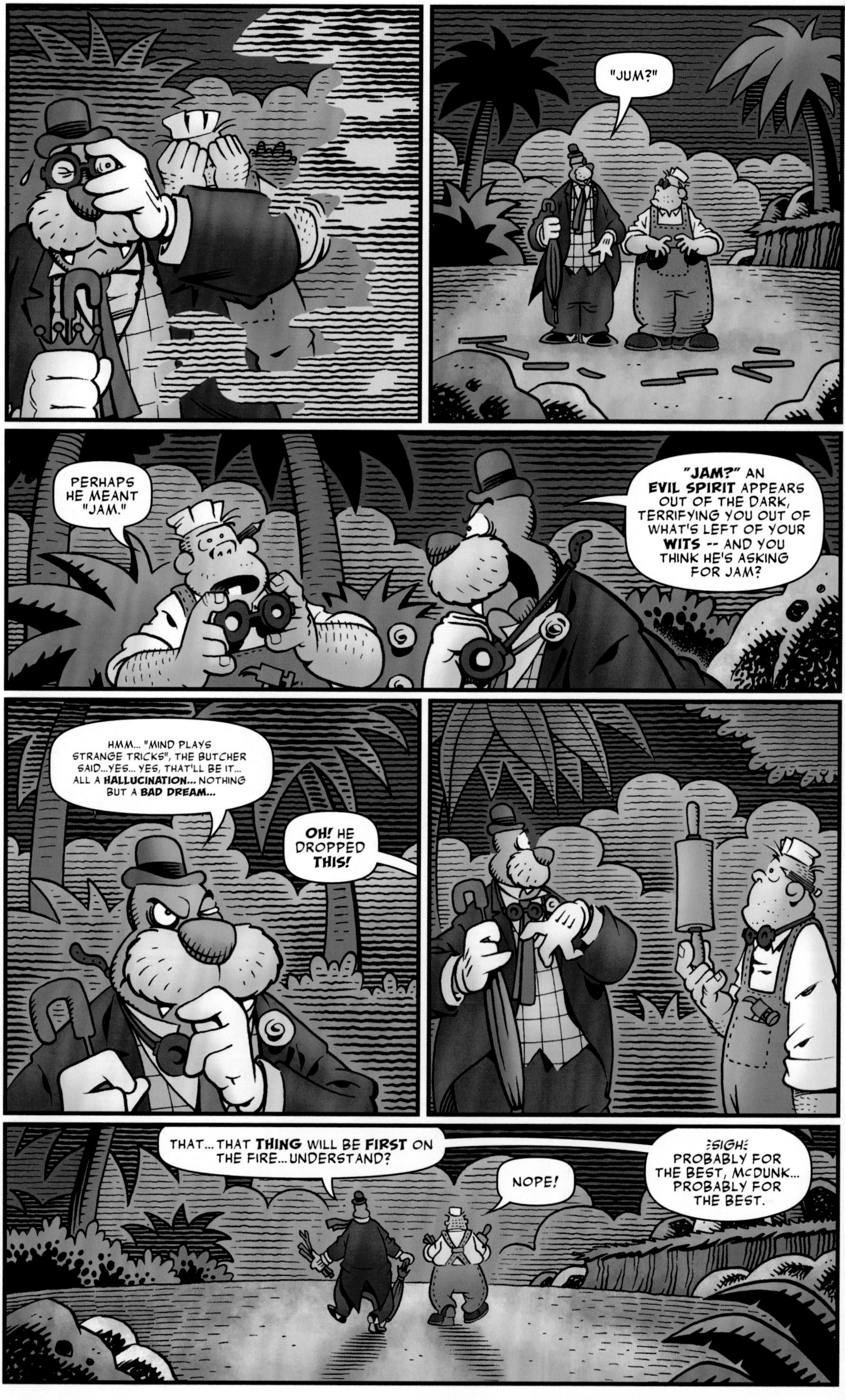
"JUM?"
PERHAPS HE MEANT "JAM."
"JAM?" AN EVIL SPIRIT APPEARS OUT OF THE DARK, TERRIFYING YOU OUT OF WHAT'S LEFT OF YOUR WITS -- AND YOU THINK HE'S ASKING FOR JAM?
HMM... "MIND PLAYS STRANGE TRICKS", THE BUTCHER SAID...YES... YES, THAT'LL BE IT... ALL A HALLUCINATION... NOTHING BUT A BAD DREAM...
OH! HE DROPPED THIS!
THAT... THAT THING WILL BE FIRST ON THE FIRE... UNDERSTAND?
NOPE!
SIGH PROBABLY FOR THE BEST, McDUNK... PROBABLY FOR THE BEST.

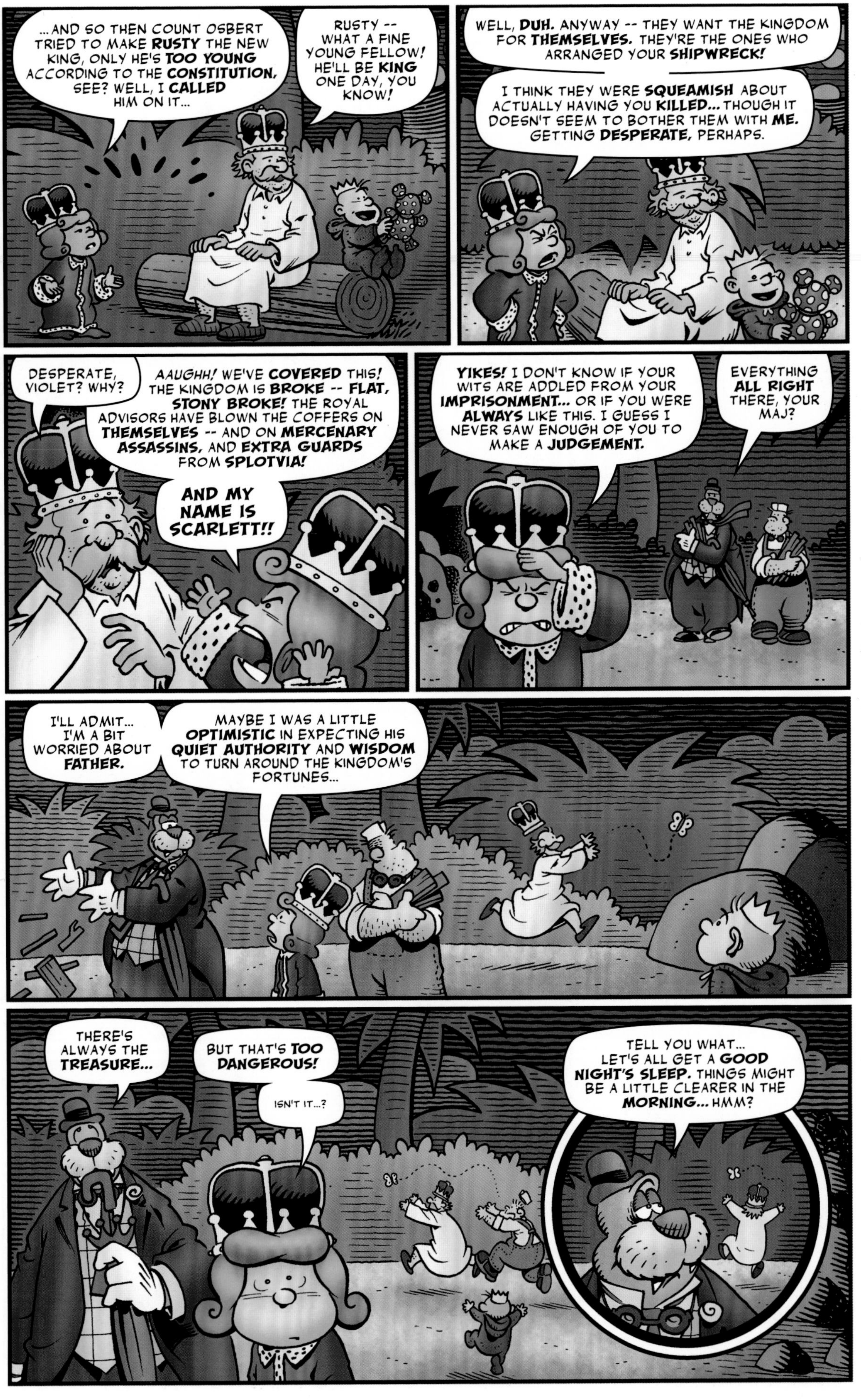
...AND SO THEN COUNT OSBERT TRIED TO MAKE RUSTY THE NEW KING, ONLY HE'S TOO YOUNG ACCORDING TO THE CONSTITUTION, SEE? WELL, I CALLED HIM ON IT...
RUSTY -- WHAT A FINE YOUNG FELLOW! HE'LL BE KING ONE DAY, YOU KNOW!
WELL, DUH. ANYWAY -- THEY WANT THE KINGDOM FOR THEMSELVES. THEY'RE THE ONES WHO ARRANGED YOUR SHIPWRECK!
I THINK THEY WERE SQUEAMISH ABOUT ACTUALLY HAVING YOU KILLED... THOUGH IT DOESN'T SEEM TO BOTHER THEM WITH ME. GETTING DESPERATE, PERHAPS.
DESPERATE, VIOLET? WHY?
AAUGHH! WE'VE COVERED THIS! THE KINGDOM IS BROKE -- FLAT, STONY BROKE! THE ROYAL ADVISORS HAVE BLOWN THE COFFERS ON THEMSELVES -- AND ON MERCENARY ASSASSINS, AND EXTRA GUARDS FROM SPLOTVIA!
AND MY NAME IS SCARLETT!!
YIKES! I DON'T KNOW IF YOUR WITS ARE ADDLED FROM YOUR IMPRISONMENT... OR IF YOU WERE ALWAYS LIKE THIS. I GUESS I NEVER SAW ENOUGH OF YOU TO MAKE A JUDGEMENT.
EVERYTHING ALL RIGHT THERE, YOUR MAJ?
I'LL ADMIT... I'M A BIT WORRIED ABOUT FATHER.
MAYBE I WAS A LITTLE OPTIMISTIC IN EXPECTING HIS QUIET AUTHORITY AND WISDOM TO TURN AROUND THE KINGDOM'S FORTUNES...
THERE'S ALWAYS THE TREASURE...
BUT THAT'S TOO DANGEROUS!
ISN'T IT...?
TELL YOU WHAT... LET'S ALL GET A GOOD NIGHT'S SLEEP. THINGS MIGHT BE A LITTLE CLEARER IN THE MORNING... HMM?

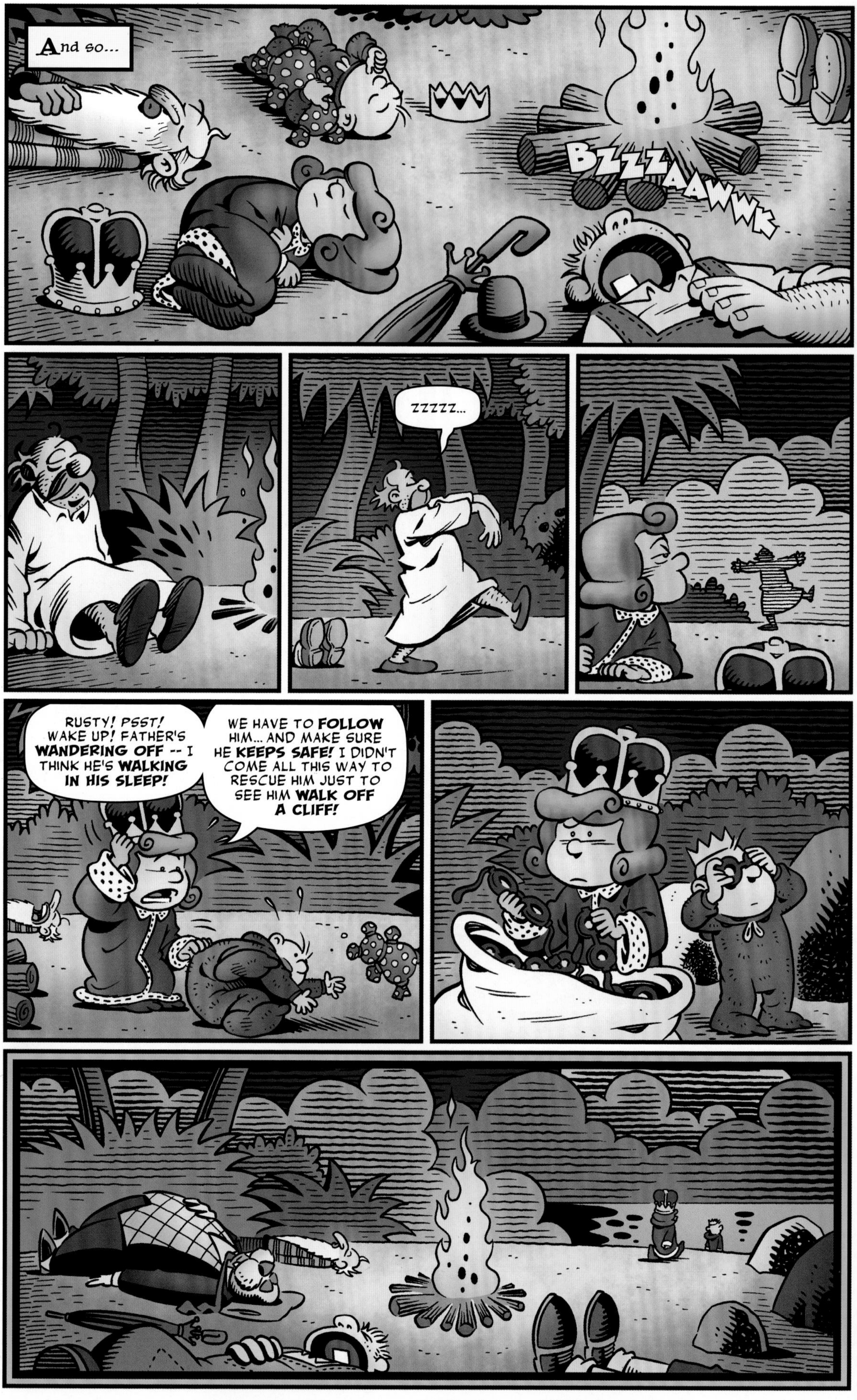
And so...
BZZZAAWWK
ZZZZZ...
RUSTY! PSST! WAKE UP! FATHER'S WANDERING OFF -- I THINK HE'S WALKING IN HIS SLEEP!
WE HAVE TO FOLLOW HIM... AND MAKE SURE HE KEEPS SAFE! I DIDN'T COME ALL THIS WAY TO RESCUE HIM JUST TO SEE HIM WALK OFF A CLIFF!

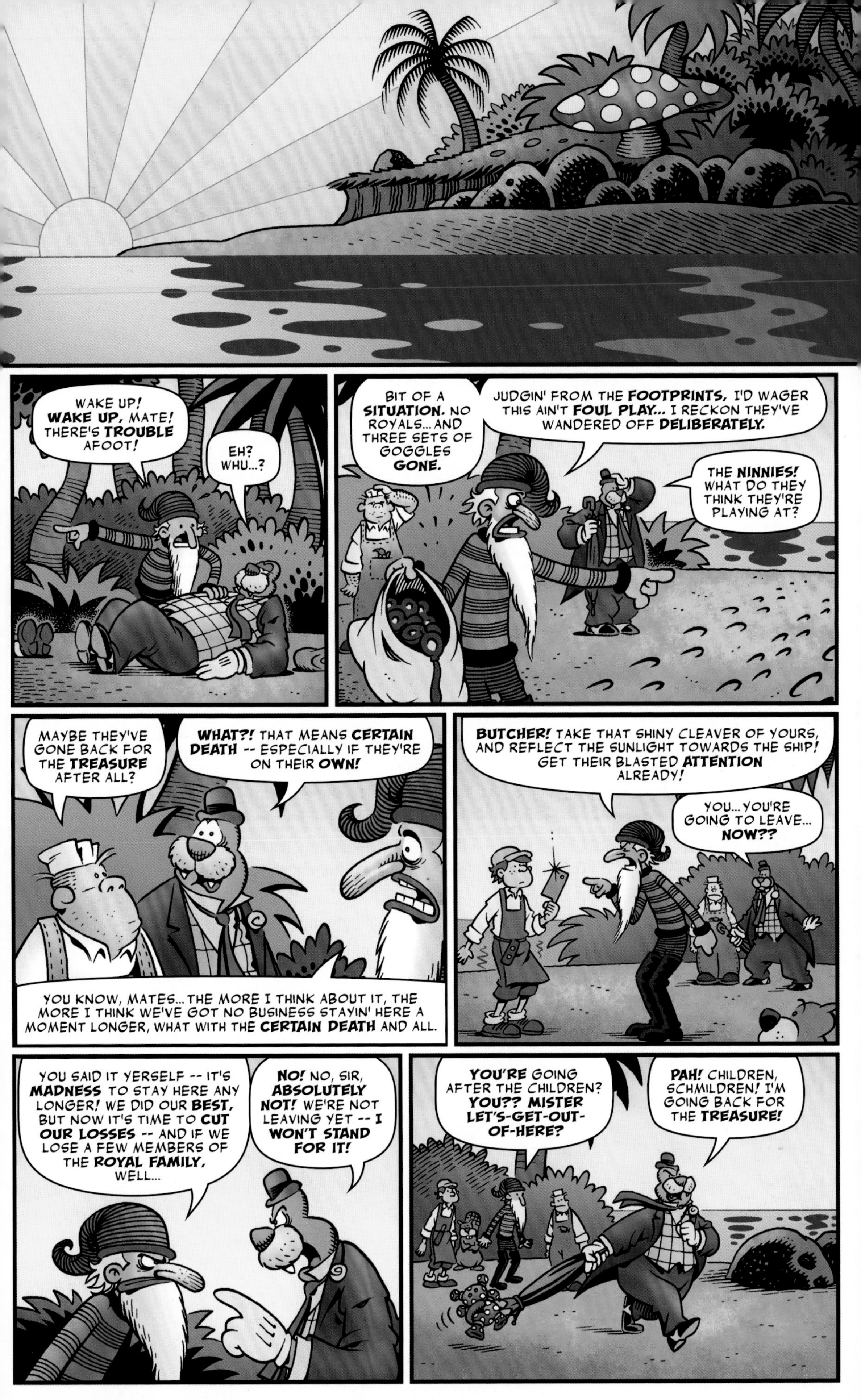
WAKE UP! WAKE UP, MATE! THERE'S TROUBLE AFOOT!
EH? WHU...?
BIT OF A SITUATION. NO ROYALS... AND THREE SETS OF GOGGLES GONE.
JUDGIN' FROM THE FOOTPRINTS, I'D WAGER THIS AIN'T FOUL PLAY... I RECKON THEY'VE WANDERED OFF DELIBERATELY.
THE NINNIES! WHAT DO THEY THINK THEY'RE PLAYING AT?
MAYBE THEY'VE GONE BACK FOR THE TREASURE AFTER ALL?
WHAT?! THAT MEANS CERTAIN DEATH -- ESPECIALLY IF THEY'RE ON THEIR OWN!
YOU KNOW, MATES... THE MORE I THINK ABOUT IT, THE MORE I THINK WE'VE GOT NO BUSINESS STAYIN' HERE A MOMENT LONGER, WHAT WITH THE CERTAIN DEATH AND ALL.
BUTCHER! TAKE THAT SHINY CLEAVER OF YOURS, AND REFLECT THE SUNLIGHT TOWARDS THE SHIP! GET THEIR BLASTED ATTENTION ALREADY!
YOU... YOU'RE GOING TO LEAVE... NOW??
YOU SAID IT YERSELF -- IT'S MADNESS TO STAY HERE ANY LONGER! WE DID OUR BEST, BUT NOW IT'S TIME TO CUT OUR LOSSES -- AND IF WE LOSE A FEW MEMBERS OF THE ROYAL FAMILY, WELL...
NO! NO, SIR, ABSOLUTELY NOT! WE'RE NOT LEAVING YET -- I WON'T STAND FOR IT!
YOU'RE GOING AFTER THE CHILDREN? YOU?? MISTER LET'S-GET-OUT-OF-HERE?
PAH! CHILDREN, SCHMILDREN! I'M GOING BACK FOR THE TREASURE!

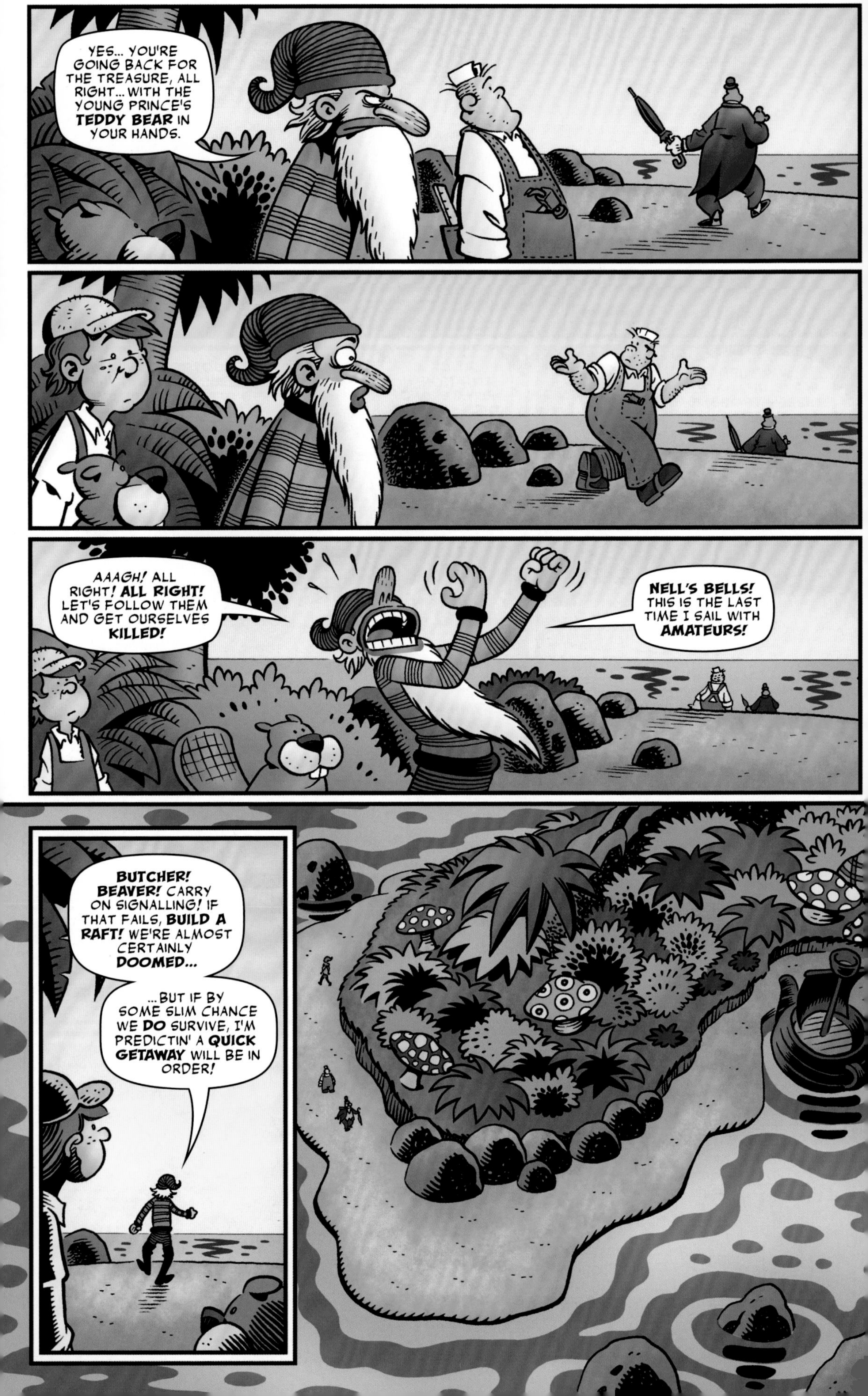
YES... YOU'RE GOING BACK FOR THE TREASURE, ALL RIGHT... WITH THE YOUNG PRINCE'S TEDDY BEAR IN YOUR HANDS.
AAAGH! ALL RIGHT! ALL RIGHT! LET'S FOLLOW THEM AND GET OURSELVES KILLED!
NELL'S BELLS! THIS IS THE LAST TIME I SAIL WITH AMATEURS!
BUTCHER! BEAVER! CARRY ON SIGNALLING! IF THAT FAILS, BUILD A RAFT! WE'RE ALMOST CERTAINLY DOOMED...
...BUT IF BY SOME SLIM CHANCE WE DO SURVIVE, I'M PREDICTIN' A QUICK GETAWAY WILL BE IN ORDER!

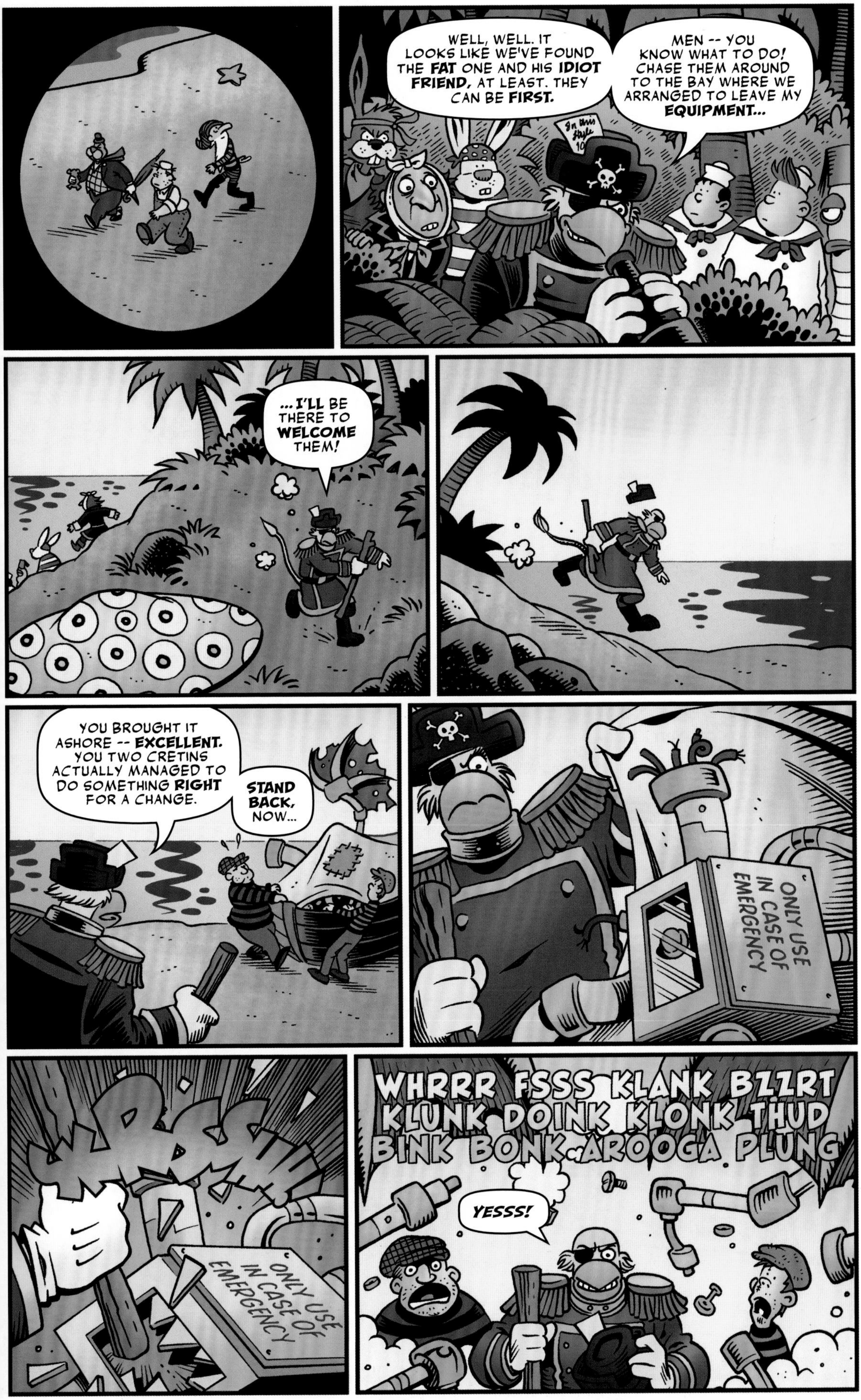

WELL, WELL. IT LOOKS LIKE WE'VE FOUND THE FAT ONE AND HIS IDIOT FRIEND, AT LEAST. THEY CAN BE FIRST.
MEN -- YOU KNOW WHAT TO DO! CHASE THEM AROUND TO THE BAY WHERE WE ARRANGED TO LEAVE MY EQUIPMENT...
...I'LL BE THERE TO WELCOME THEM!
YOU BROUGHT IT ASHORE -- EXCELLENT. YOU TWO CRETINS ACTUALLY MANAGED TO DO SOMETHING RIGHT FOR A CHANGE.
STAND BACK, NOW...
ONLY USE IN CASE OF EMERGENCY
ONLY USE IN CASE OF EMERGENCY
WHRRR FSSS KLANK BZZRT KLUNK DOINK KLONK THUD BINK BONK AROOGA PLUNG
YESSS!

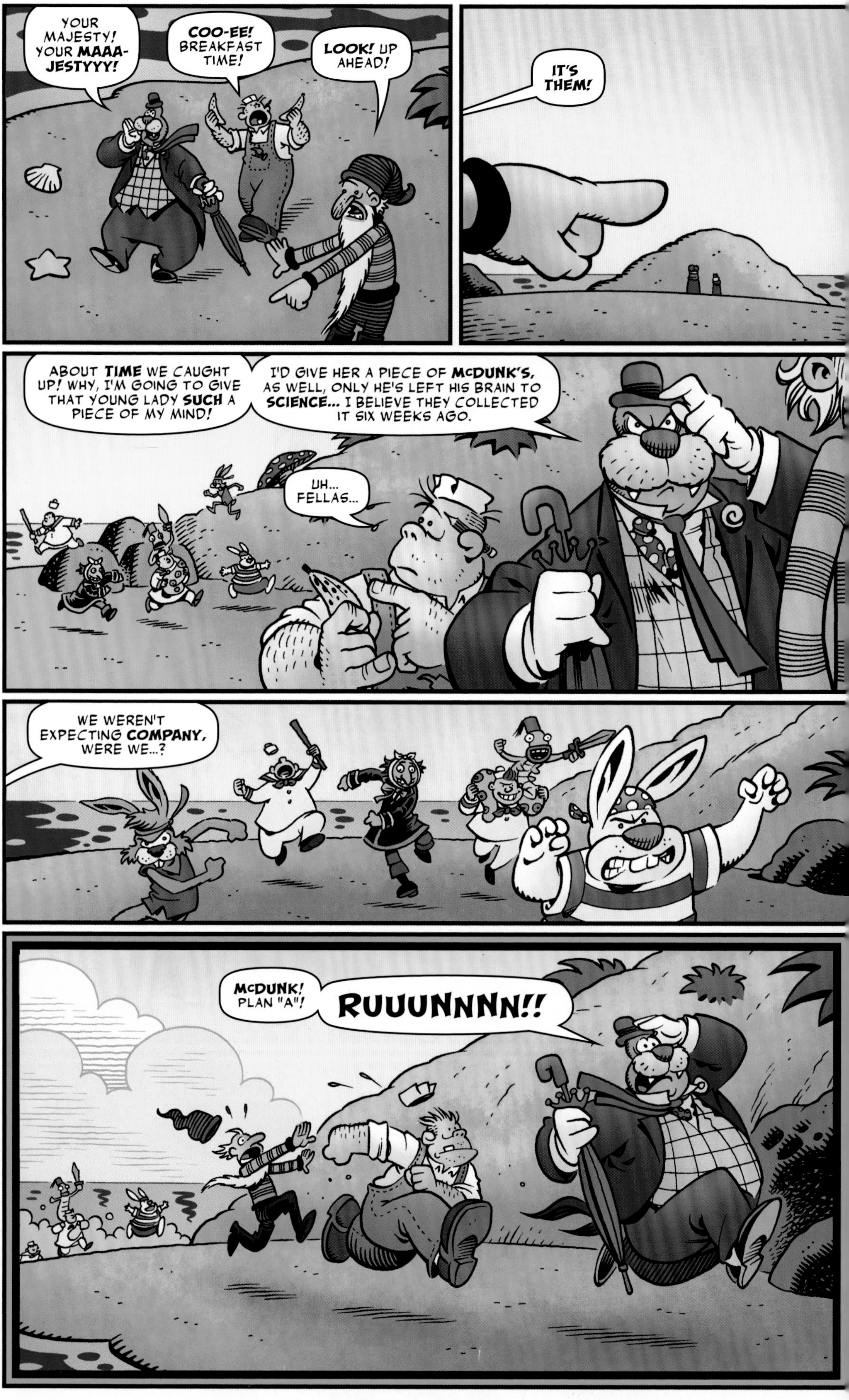
YOUR MAJESTY! YOUR MAAA-JESTYYY!
COO-EE! BREAKFAST TIME!
LOOK! UP AHEAD!
IT'S THEM!
ABOUT TIME WE CAUGHT UP! WHY, I'M GOING TO GIVE THAT YOUNG LADY SUCH A PIECE OF MY MIND!
I'D GIVE HER A PIECE OF McDUNK'S, AS WELL, ONLY HE'S LEFT HIS BRAIN TO SCIENCE... I BELIEVE THEY COLLECTED IT SIX WEEKS AGO.
UH... FELLAS...
WE WEREN'T EXPECTING COMPANY, WERE WE...?
McDUNK! PLAN "A"!
RUUUNNNN!!

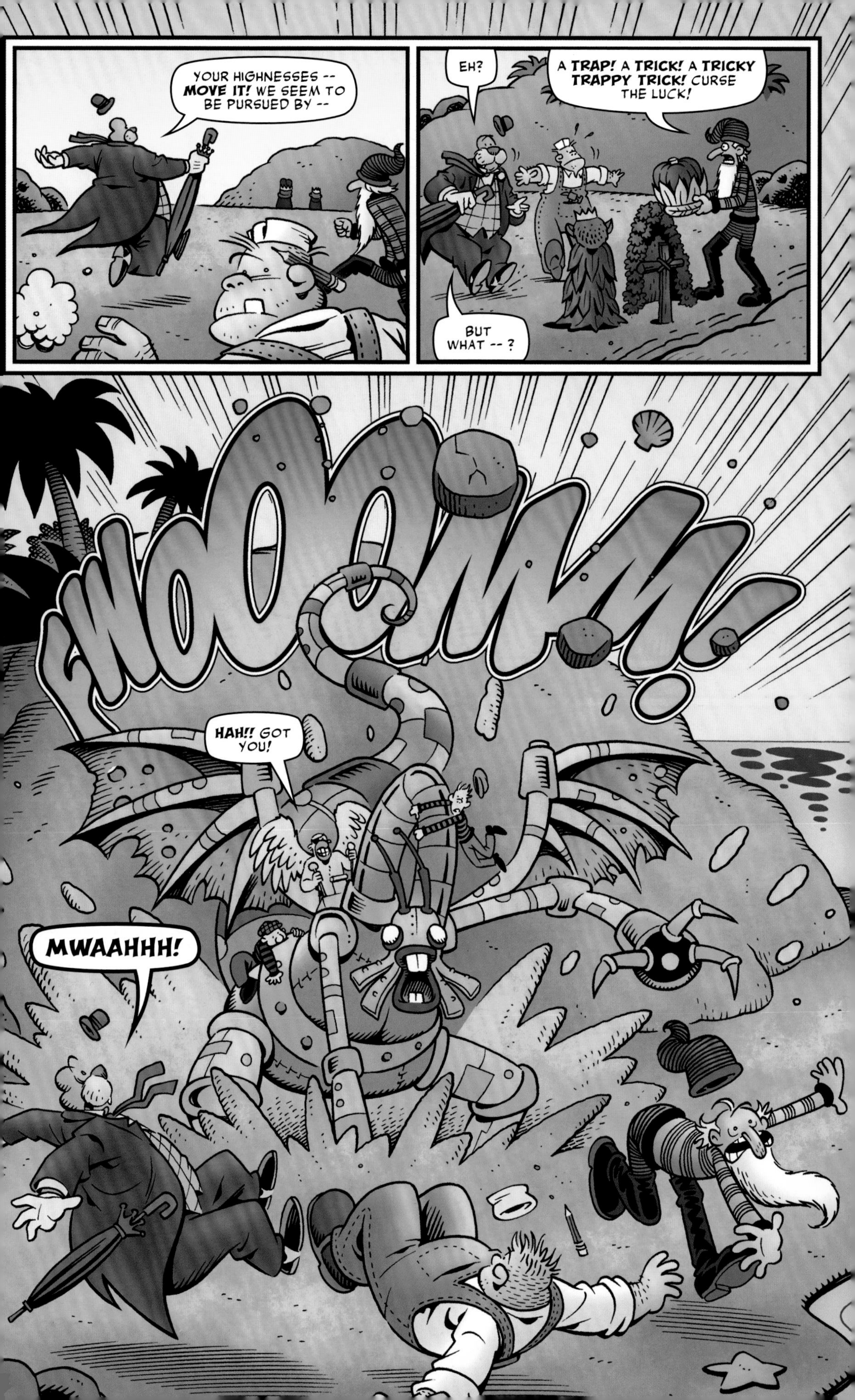
YOUR HIGHNESSES -- **MOVE IT!** WE SEEM TO BE PURSUED BY --
EH?
A **TRAP!** A **TRICK!** A **TRICKY TRAPPY TRICK!** CURSE THE LUCK!
BUT WHAT -- ?
WHOOMM!
HAH!! GOT YOU!
MWAAHHH!

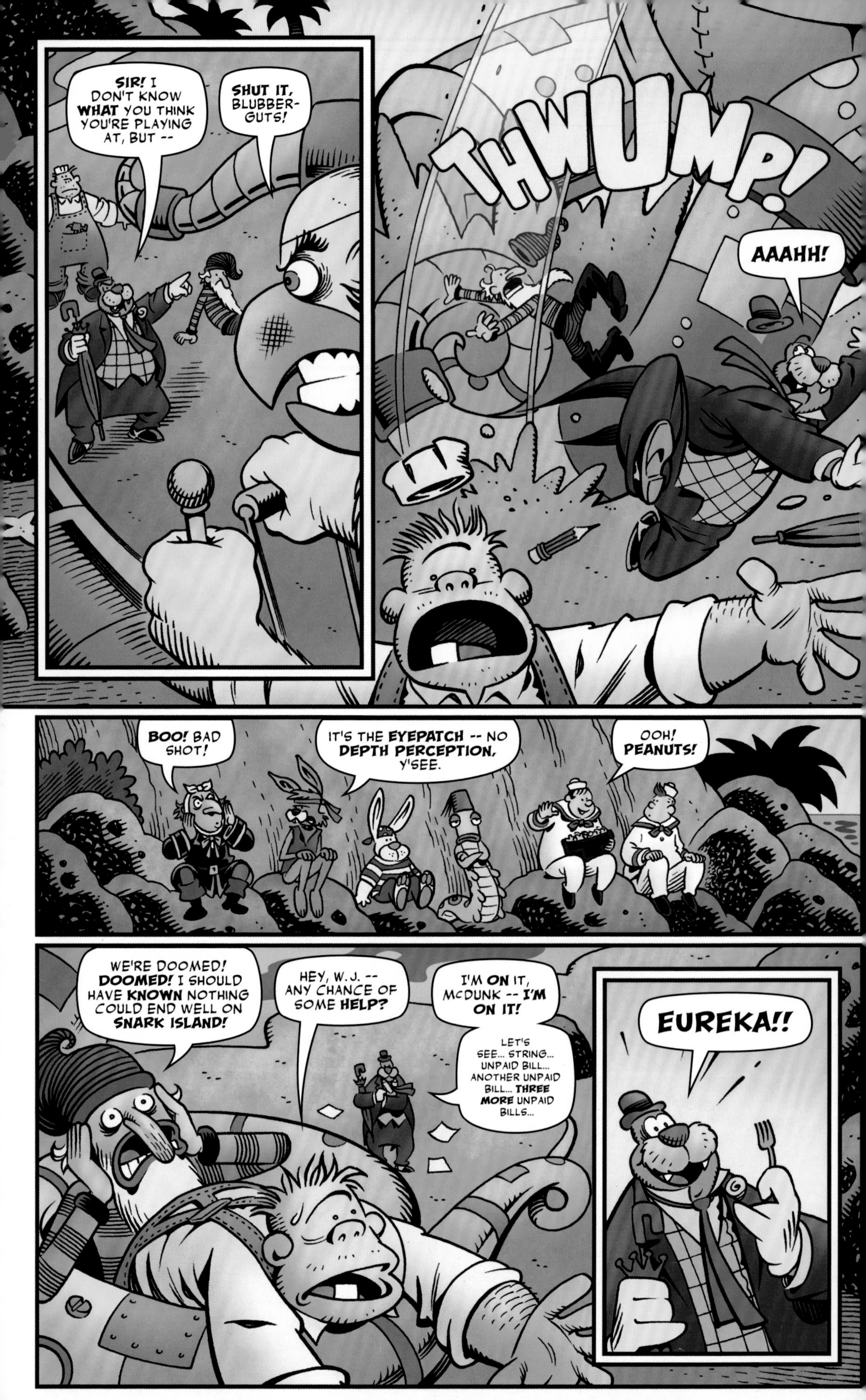

SIR! I DON'T KNOW WHAT YOU THINK YOU'RE PLAYING AT, BUT --
SHUT IT, BLUBBER-GUTS!
THWUMP!
AAAHH!
BOO! BAD SHOT!
IT'S THE EYEPATCH -- NO DEPTH PERCEPTION, Y'SEE.
OOH! PEANUTS!
WE'RE DOOMED! DOOMED! I SHOULD HAVE KNOWN NOTHING COULD END WELL ON SNARK ISLAND!
HEY, W. J. -- ANY CHANCE OF SOME HELP?
I'M ON IT, McDUNK -- I'M ON IT!
LET'S SEE... STRING... UNPAID BILL... ANOTHER UNPAID BILL... THREE MORE UNPAID BILLS...
EUREKA!!

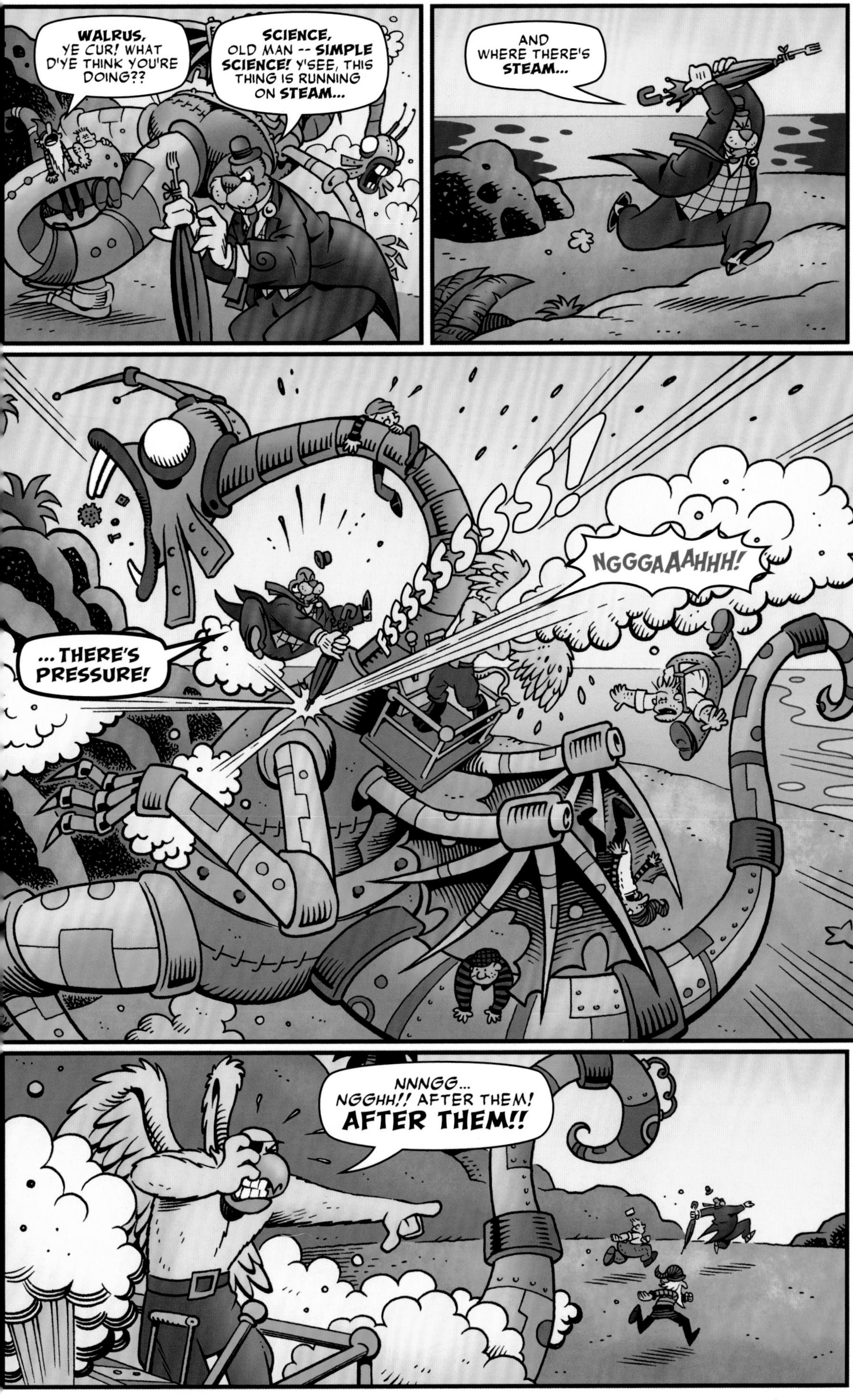
WALRUS, YE CUR! WHAT D'YE THINK YOU'RE DOING??
SCIENCE, OLD MAN -- SIMPLE SCIENCE! Y'SEE, THIS THING IS RUNNING ON STEAM...
AND WHERE THERE'S STEAM...
FSSSSSSSSSS!
NGGGAAAHHH!
...THERE'S PRESSURE!
NNNGG... NGGHH!! AFTER THEM! AFTER THEM!!

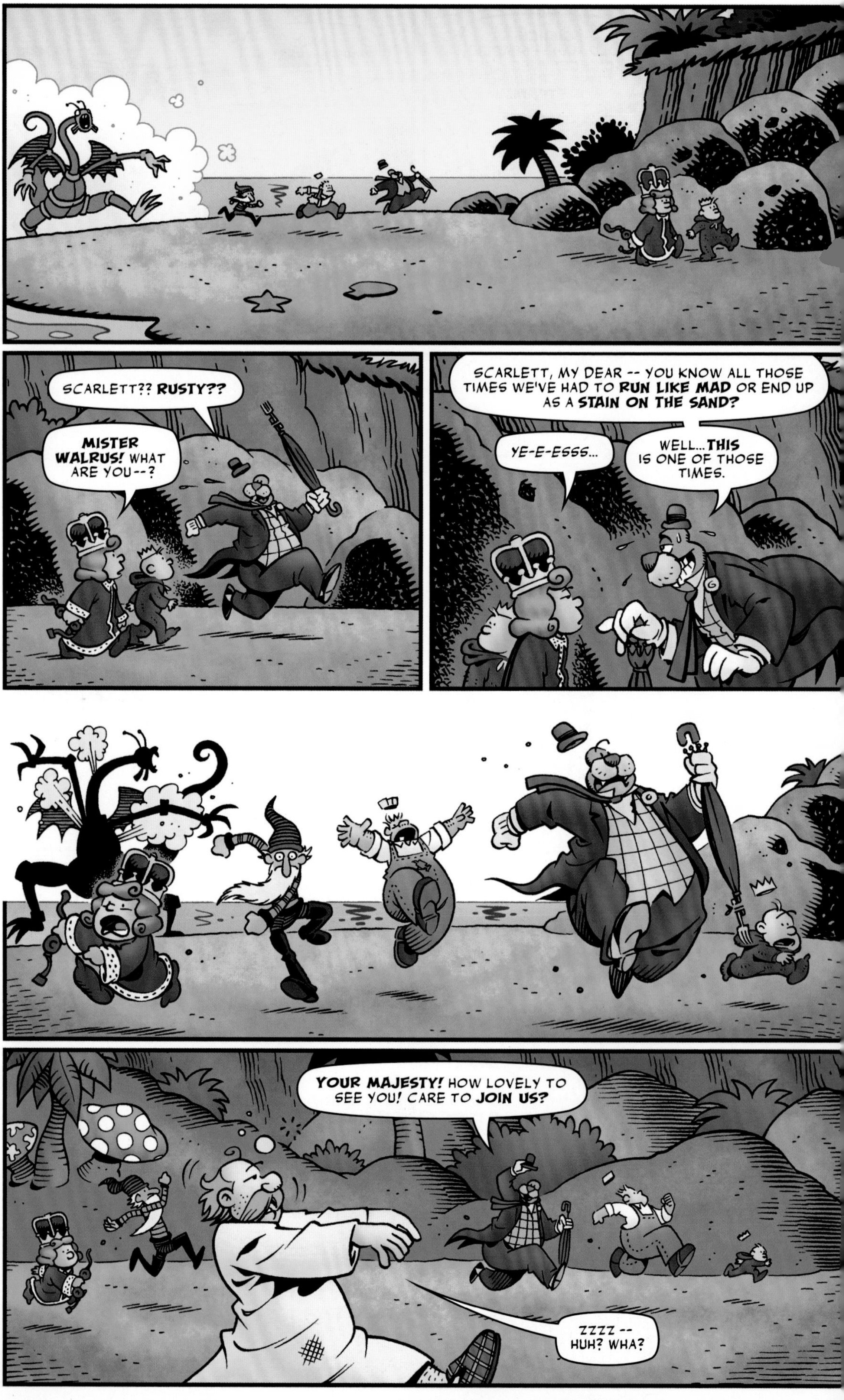

SCARLETT?? **RUSTY??**
MISTER WALRUS! WHAT ARE YOU--?
SCARLETT, MY DEAR -- YOU KNOW ALL THOSE TIMES WE'VE HAD TO **RUN LIKE MAD** OR END UP AS A **STAIN ON THE SAND?**
YE-E-ESSS...
WELL... **THIS** IS ONE OF THOSE TIMES.
YOUR MAJESTY! HOW LOVELY TO SEE YOU! CARE TO **JOIN US?**
ZZZZ -- HUH? WHA?

HEY! WHERE'S IT GONE?

EH?

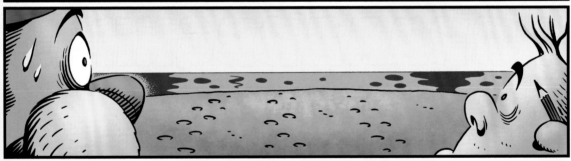

DASHED PECULIAR. **NO SIGN** OF THE BRUTES!

PERHAPS THE **MACHINERY** BROKE DOWN. PERHAPS THEY **TRIPPED AND FELL.**

YES... YES, PERHAPS.

MCDUNK?

GO AND TAKE A LOOK, WILL YOU?

GOOD MAN.

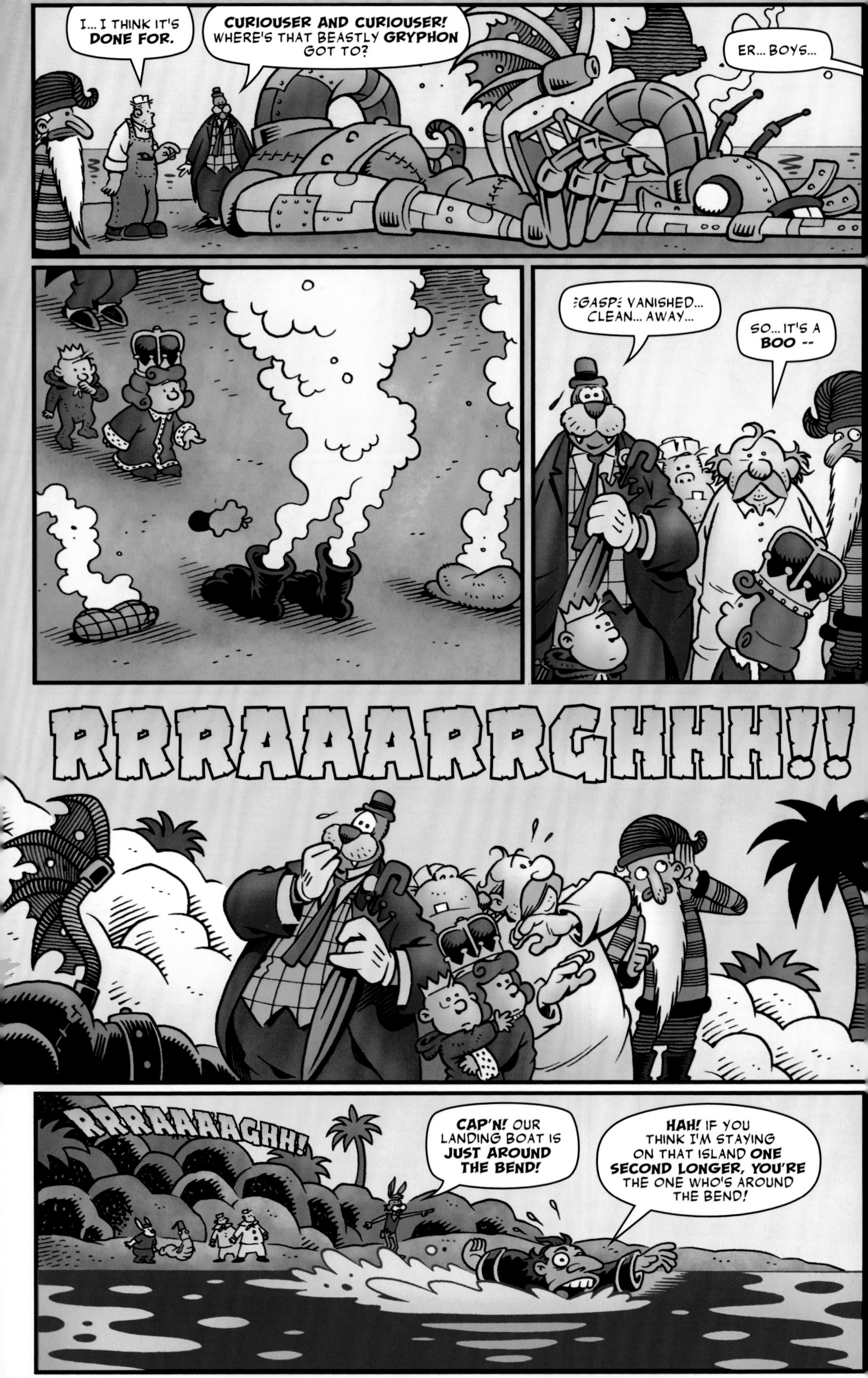

I... I THINK IT'S DONE FOR.
CURIOUSER AND CURIOUSER! WHERE'S THAT BEASTLY GRYPHON GOT TO?
ER... BOYS...
:GASP: VANISHED... CLEAN... AWAY...
SO... IT'S A BOO --
RRRAAAARRGHHH!!
RRRAAAAAGHH!
CAP'N! OUR LANDING BOAT IS JUST AROUND THE BEND!
HAH! IF YOU THINK I'M STAYING ON THAT ISLAND ONE SECOND LONGER, YOU'RE THE ONE WHO'S AROUND THE BEND!

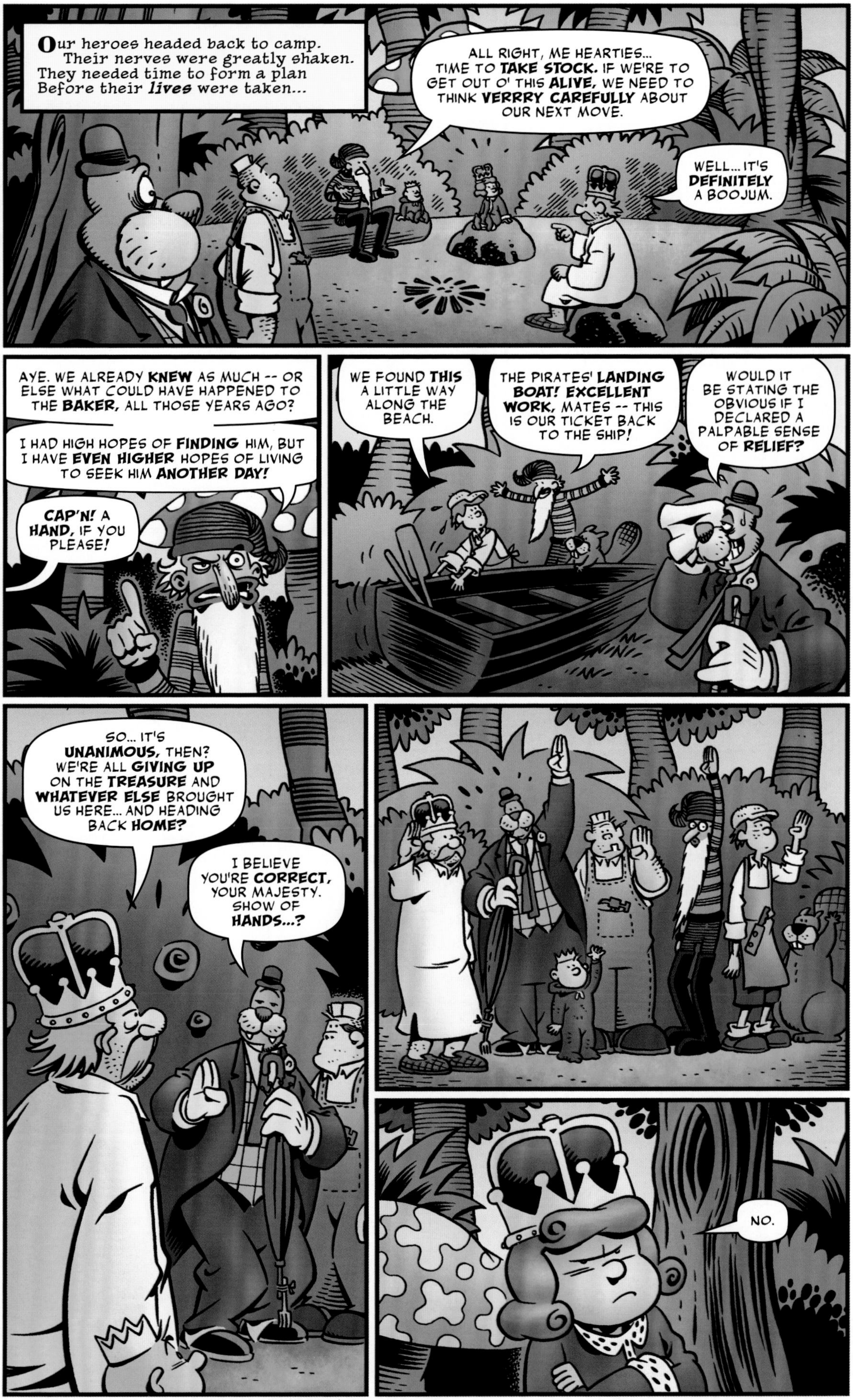
Our heroes headed back to camp. Their nerves were greatly shaken. They needed time to form a plan Before their *lives* were taken...
ALL RIGHT, ME HEARTIES... TIME TO **TAKE STOCK.** IF WE'RE TO GET OUT O' THIS **ALIVE,** WE NEED TO THINK **VERRRY CAREFULLY** ABOUT OUR NEXT MOVE.
WELL... IT'S **DEFINITELY** A BOOJUM.
AYE. WE ALREADY **KNEW** AS MUCH -- OR ELSE WHAT COULD HAVE HAPPENED TO THE **BAKER,** ALL THOSE YEARS AGO?
I HAD HIGH HOPES OF **FINDING** HIM, BUT I HAVE **EVEN HIGHER** HOPES OF LIVING TO SEEK HIM **ANOTHER DAY!**
CAP'N! A **HAND,** IF YOU PLEASE!
WE FOUND **THIS** A LITTLE WAY ALONG THE BEACH.
THE PIRATES' **LANDING BOAT! EXCELLENT WORK,** MATES -- THIS IS OUR TICKET BACK TO THE SHIP!
WOULD IT BE STATING THE OBVIOUS IF I DECLARED A PALPABLE SENSE OF **RELIEF?**
SO... IT'S **UNANIMOUS,** THEN? WE'RE ALL **GIVING UP** ON THE **TREASURE** AND **WHATEVER ELSE** BROUGHT US HERE... AND HEADING BACK **HOME?**
I BELIEVE YOU'RE **CORRECT,** YOUR MAJESTY. SHOW OF **HANDS...?**
NO.

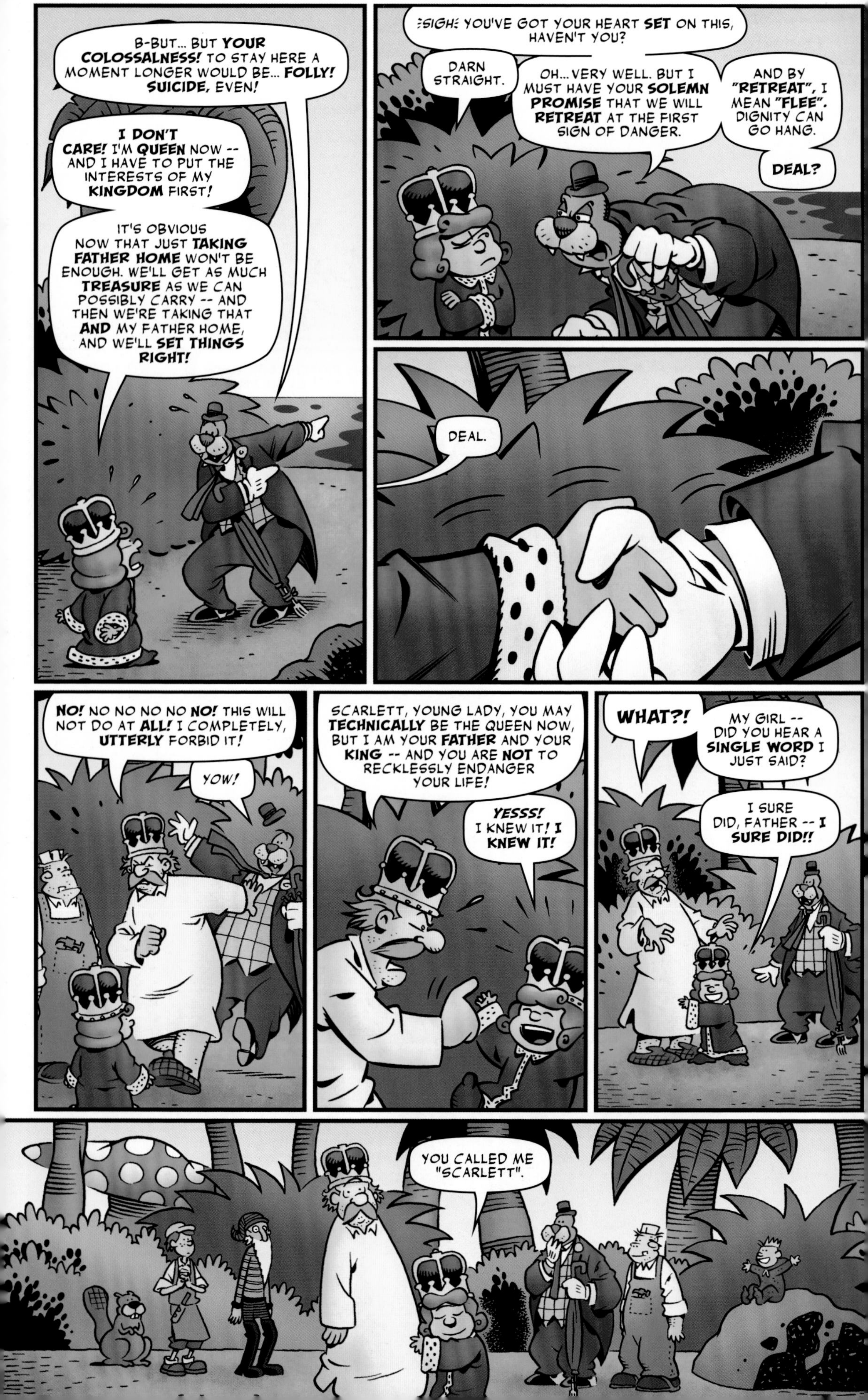
B-BUT... BUT YOUR COLOSSALNESS! TO STAY HERE A MOMENT LONGER WOULD BE... FOLLY! SUICIDE, EVEN!
I DON'T CARE! I'M QUEEN NOW -- AND I HAVE TO PUT THE INTERESTS OF MY KINGDOM FIRST!
IT'S OBVIOUS NOW THAT JUST TAKING FATHER HOME WON'T BE ENOUGH. WE'LL GET AS MUCH TREASURE AS WE CAN POSSIBLY CARRY -- AND THEN WE'RE TAKING THAT AND MY FATHER HOME, AND WE'LL SET THINGS RIGHT!
:SIGH: YOU'VE GOT YOUR HEART SET ON THIS, HAVEN'T YOU?
DARN STRAIGHT.
OH... VERY WELL. BUT I MUST HAVE YOUR SOLEMN PROMISE THAT WE WILL RETREAT AT THE FIRST SIGN OF DANGER.
AND BY "RETREAT", I MEAN "FLEE". DIGNITY CAN GO HANG.
DEAL?
DEAL.
NO! NO NO NO NO NO! THIS WILL NOT DO AT ALL! I COMPLETELY, UTTERLY FORBID IT!
YOW!
SCARLETT, YOUNG LADY, YOU MAY TECHNICALLY BE THE QUEEN NOW, BUT I AM YOUR FATHER AND YOUR KING -- AND YOU ARE NOT TO RECKLESSLY ENDANGER YOUR LIFE!
YESSS! I KNEW IT! I KNEW IT!
WHAT?!
MY GIRL -- DID YOU HEAR A SINGLE WORD I JUST SAID?
I SURE DID, FATHER -- I SURE DID!!
YOU CALLED ME "SCARLETT".

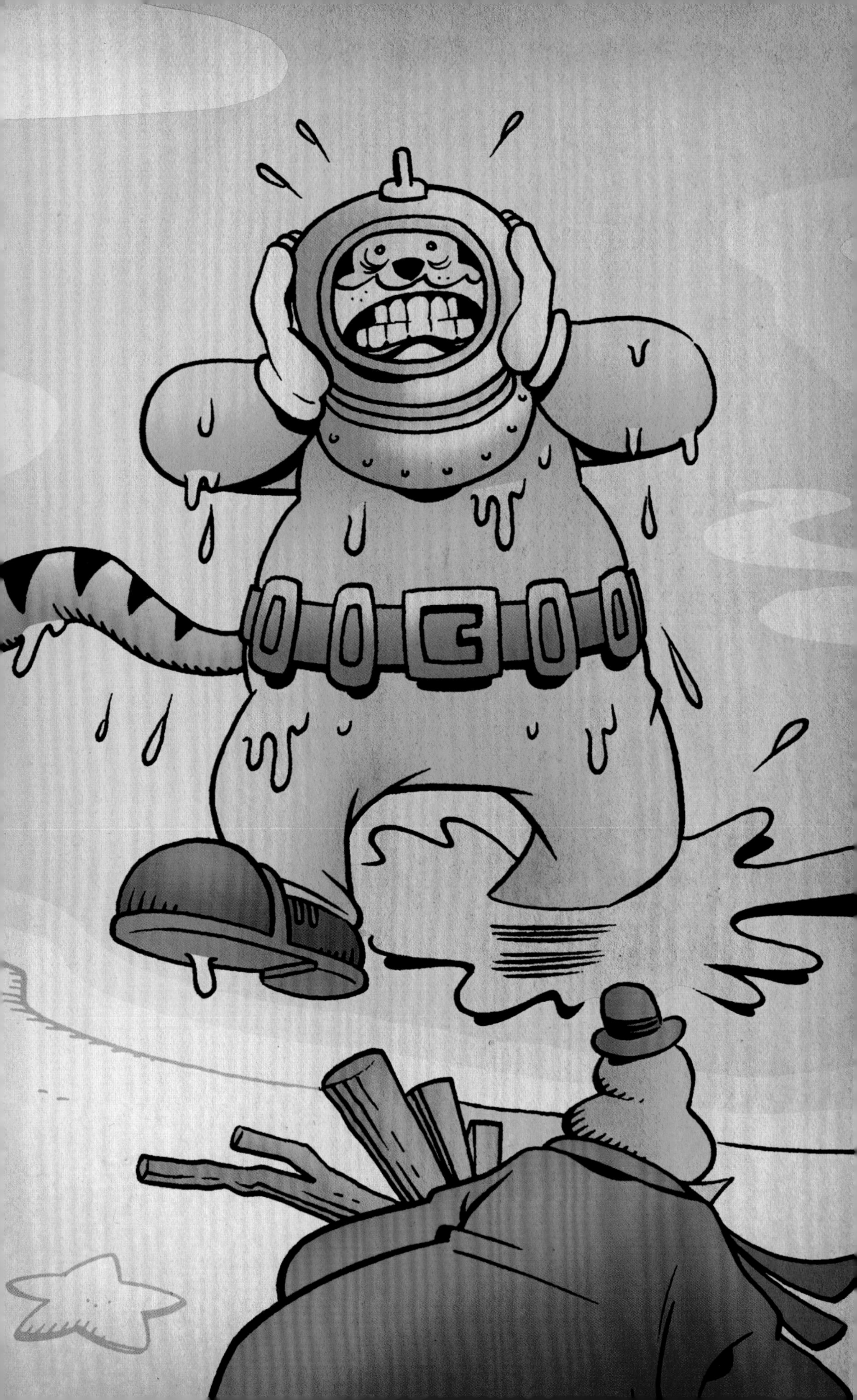

FIT THE ELEVENTH

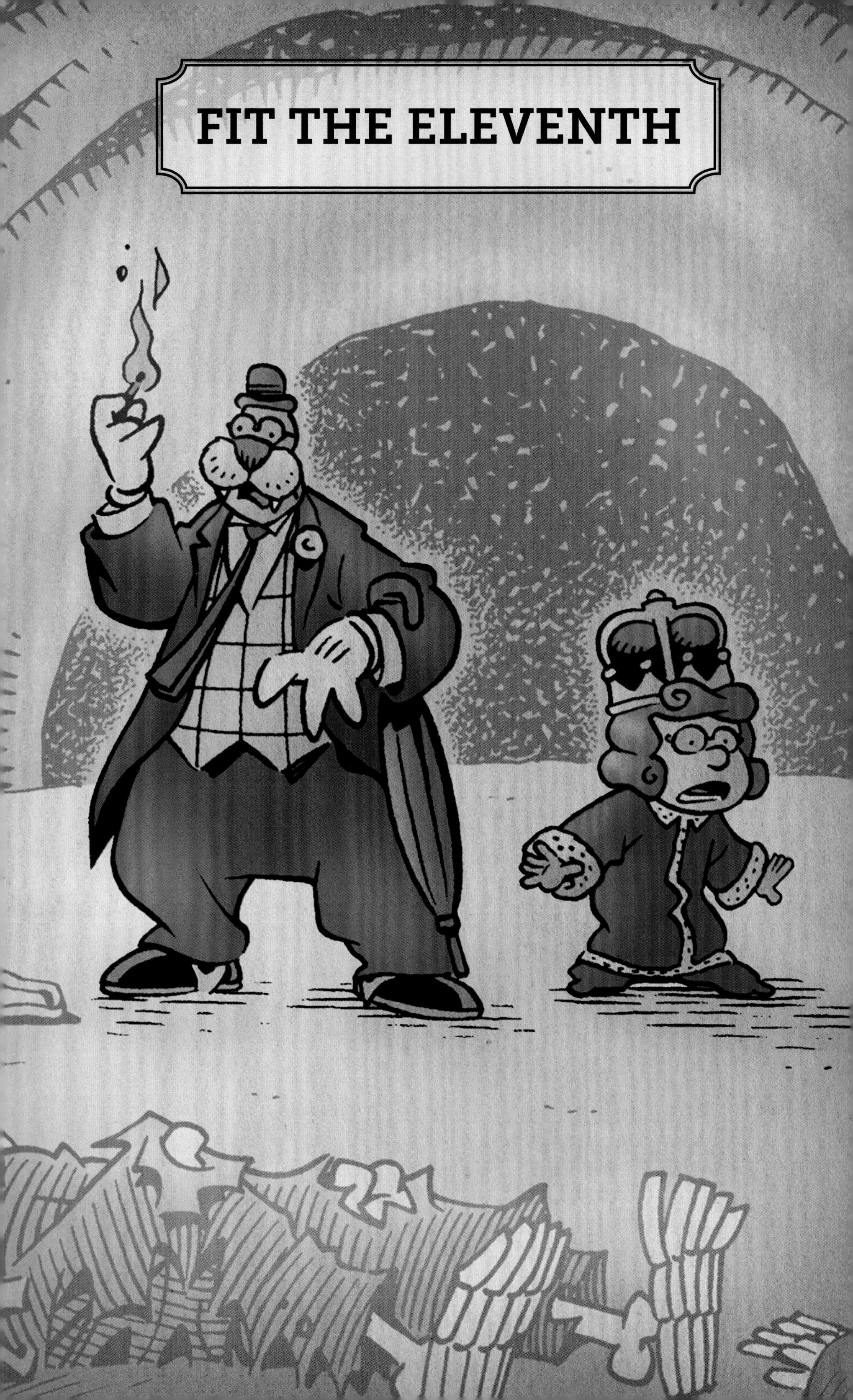

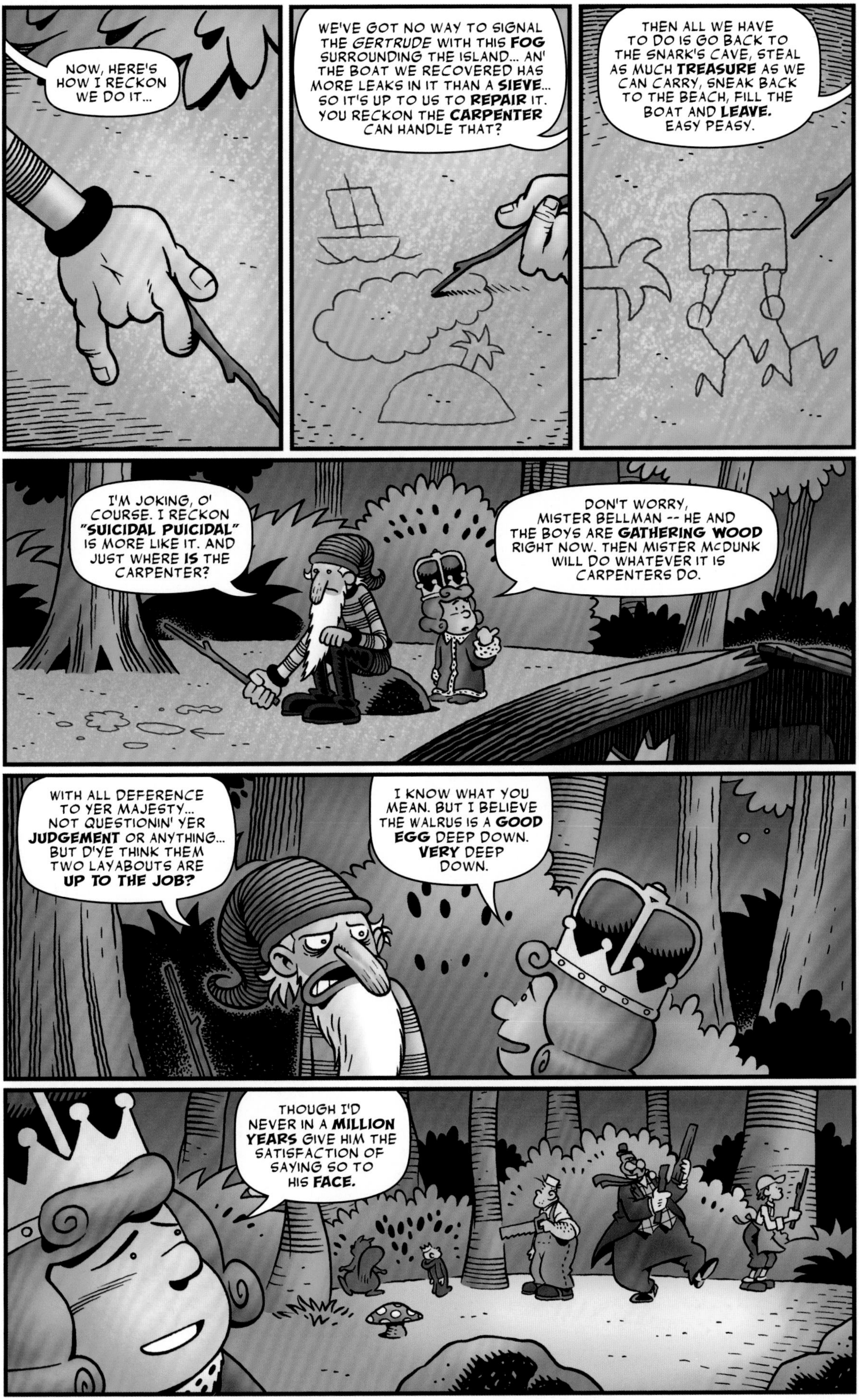
NOW, HERE'S HOW I RECKON WE DO IT...
WE'VE GOT NO WAY TO SIGNAL THE *GERTRUDE* WITH THIS **FOG** SURROUNDING THE ISLAND... AN' THE BOAT WE RECOVERED HAS MORE LEAKS IN IT THAN A **SIEVE**... SO IT'S UP TO US TO **REPAIR** IT. YOU RECKON THE **CARPENTER** CAN HANDLE THAT?
THEN ALL WE HAVE TO DO IS GO BACK TO THE SNARK'S CAVE, STEAL AS MUCH **TREASURE** AS WE CAN CARRY, SNEAK BACK TO THE BEACH, FILL THE BOAT AND **LEAVE.** EASY PEASY.
I'M JOKING, O' COURSE. I RECKON **"SUICIDAL PUICIDAL"** IS MORE LIKE IT. AND JUST WHERE **IS** THE CARPENTER?
DON'T WORRY, MISTER BELLMAN -- HE AND THE BOYS ARE **GATHERING WOOD** RIGHT NOW. THEN MISTER McDUNK WILL DO WHATEVER IT IS CARPENTERS DO.
WITH ALL DEFERENCE TO YER MAJESTY... NOT QUESTIONIN' YER **JUDGEMENT** OR ANYTHING... BUT D'YE THINK THEM TWO LAYABOUTS ARE **UP TO THE JOB?**
I KNOW WHAT YOU MEAN. BUT I BELIEVE THE WALRUS IS A **GOOD EGG** DEEP DOWN. **VERY** DEEP DOWN.
THOUGH I'D NEVER IN A **MILLION YEARS** GIVE HIM THE SATISFACTION OF SAYING SO TO HIS **FACE.**

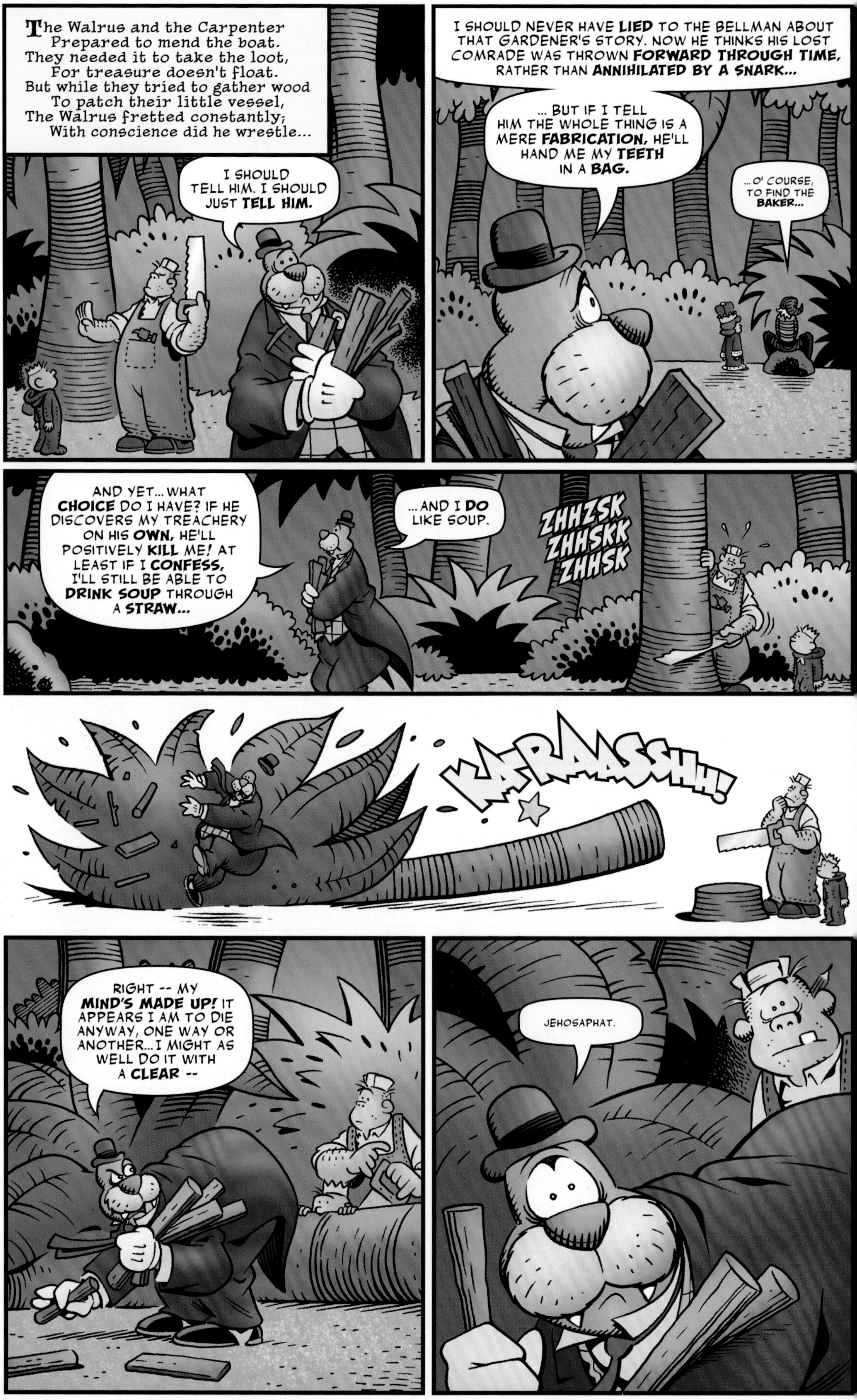
The Walrus and the Carpenter
Prepared to mend the boat.
They needed it to take the loot,
For treasure doesn't float.
But while they tried to gather wood
To patch their little vessel,
The Walrus fretted constantly;
With conscience did he wrestle...
I SHOULD TELL HIM. I SHOULD JUST TELL HIM.
I SHOULD NEVER HAVE LIED TO THE BELLMAN ABOUT THAT GARDENER'S STORY. NOW HE THINKS HIS LOST COMRADE WAS THROWN FORWARD THROUGH TIME, RATHER THAN ANNIHILATED BY A SNARK...
... BUT IF I TELL HIM THE WHOLE THING IS A MERE FABRICATION, HE'LL HAND ME MY TEETH IN A BAG.
...O' COURSE, TO FIND THE BAKER...
AND YET... WHAT CHOICE DO I HAVE? IF HE DISCOVERS MY TREACHERY ON HIS OWN, HE'LL POSITIVELY KILL ME! AT LEAST IF I CONFESS, I'LL STILL BE ABLE TO DRINK SOUP THROUGH A STRAW...
...AND I DO LIKE SOUP.
ZHHZSK ZHHSKK ZHHSK
KA-FRAASSHH!
RIGHT -- MY MIND'S MADE UP! IT APPEARS I AM TO DIE ANYWAY, ONE WAY OR ANOTHER... I MIGHT AS WELL DO IT WITH A CLEAR --
JEHOSAPHAT.

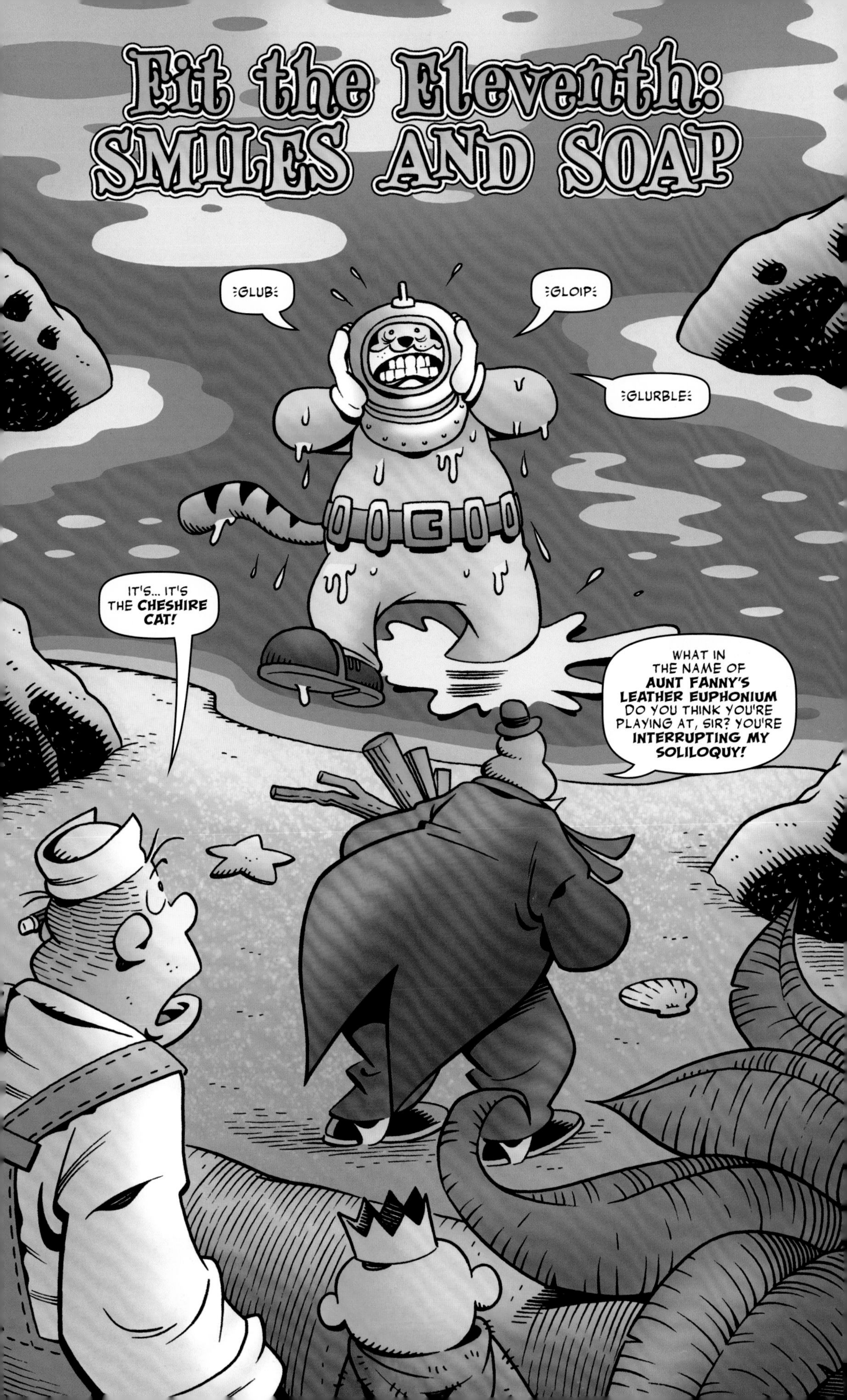
Fit the Eleventh:
SMILES AND SOAP
GLUB
GLOIP
GLURBLE
IT'S... IT'S THE CHESHIRE CAT!
WHAT IN THE NAME OF AUNT FANNY'S LEATHER EUPHONIUM DO YOU THINK YOU'RE PLAYING AT, SIR? YOU'RE INTERRUPTING MY SOLILOQUY!

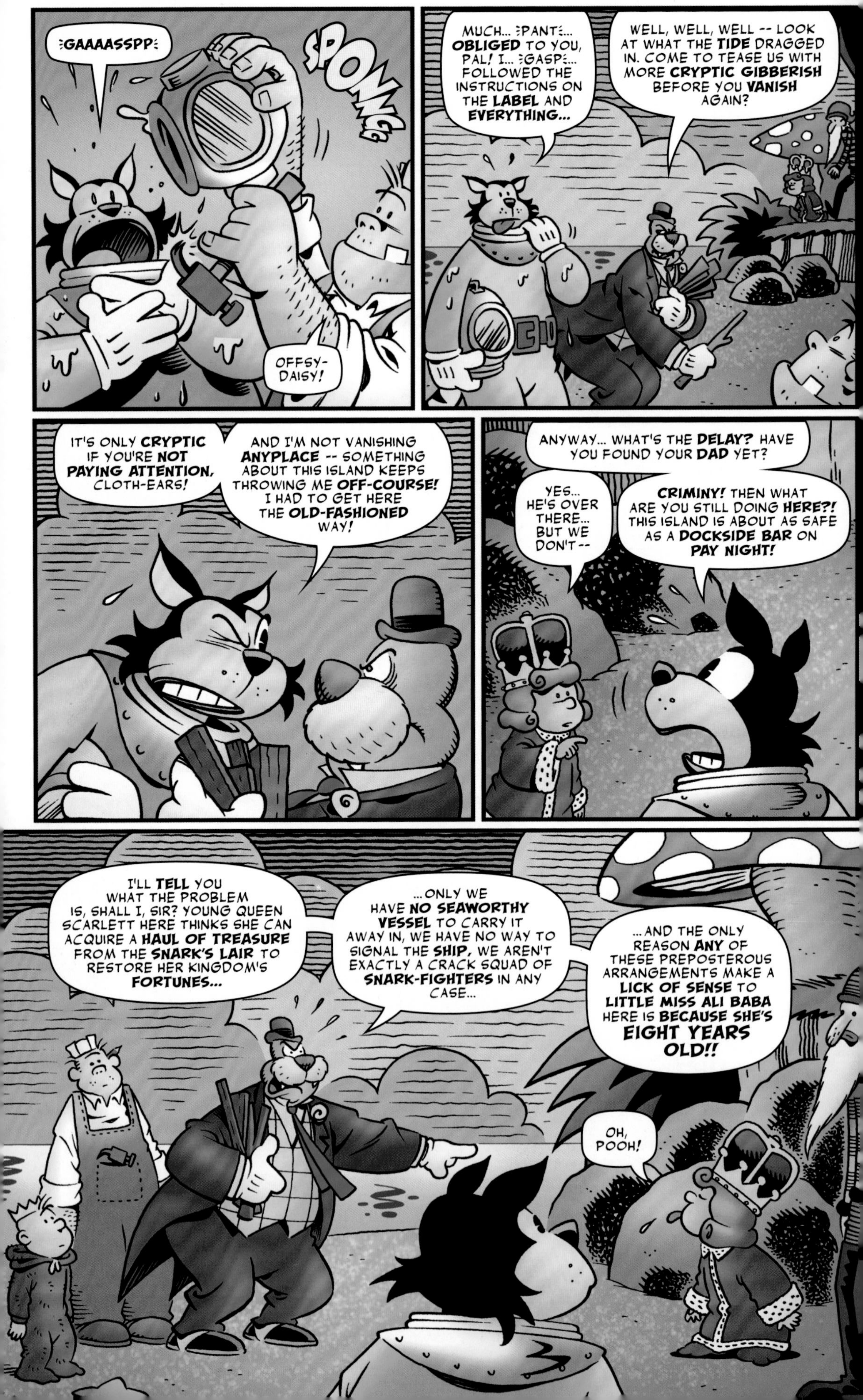

~GAAAASSPP~
SPONNG
OFFSY-DAISY!
MUCH... ~PANT~... OBLIGED TO YOU, PAL! I... ~GASP~... FOLLOWED THE INSTRUCTIONS ON THE LABEL AND EVERYTHING...
WELL, WELL, WELL -- LOOK AT WHAT THE TIDE DRAGGED IN. COME TO TEASE US WITH MORE CRYPTIC GIBBERISH BEFORE YOU VANISH AGAIN?
IT'S ONLY CRYPTIC IF YOU'RE NOT PAYING ATTENTION, CLOTH-EARS!
AND I'M NOT VANISHING ANYPLACE -- SOMETHING ABOUT THIS ISLAND KEEPS THROWING ME OFF-COURSE! I HAD TO GET HERE THE OLD-FASHIONED WAY!
ANYWAY... WHAT'S THE DELAY? HAVE YOU FOUND YOUR DAD YET?
YES... HE'S OVER THERE... BUT WE DON'T --
CRIMINY! THEN WHAT ARE YOU STILL DOING HERE?! THIS ISLAND IS ABOUT AS SAFE AS A DOCKSIDE BAR ON PAY NIGHT!
I'LL TELL YOU WHAT THE PROBLEM IS, SHALL I, SIR? YOUNG QUEEN SCARLETT HERE THINKS SHE CAN ACQUIRE A HAUL OF TREASURE FROM THE SNARK'S LAIR TO RESTORE HER KINGDOM'S FORTUNES...
...ONLY WE HAVE NO SEAWORTHY VESSEL TO CARRY IT AWAY IN, WE HAVE NO WAY TO SIGNAL THE SHIP, WE AREN'T EXACTLY A CRACK SQUAD OF SNARK-FIGHTERS IN ANY CASE...
...AND THE ONLY REASON ANY OF THESE PREPOSTEROUS ARRANGEMENTS MAKE A LICK OF SENSE TO LITTLE MISS ALI BABA HERE IS BECAUSE SHE'S EIGHT YEARS OLD!!
OH, POOH!

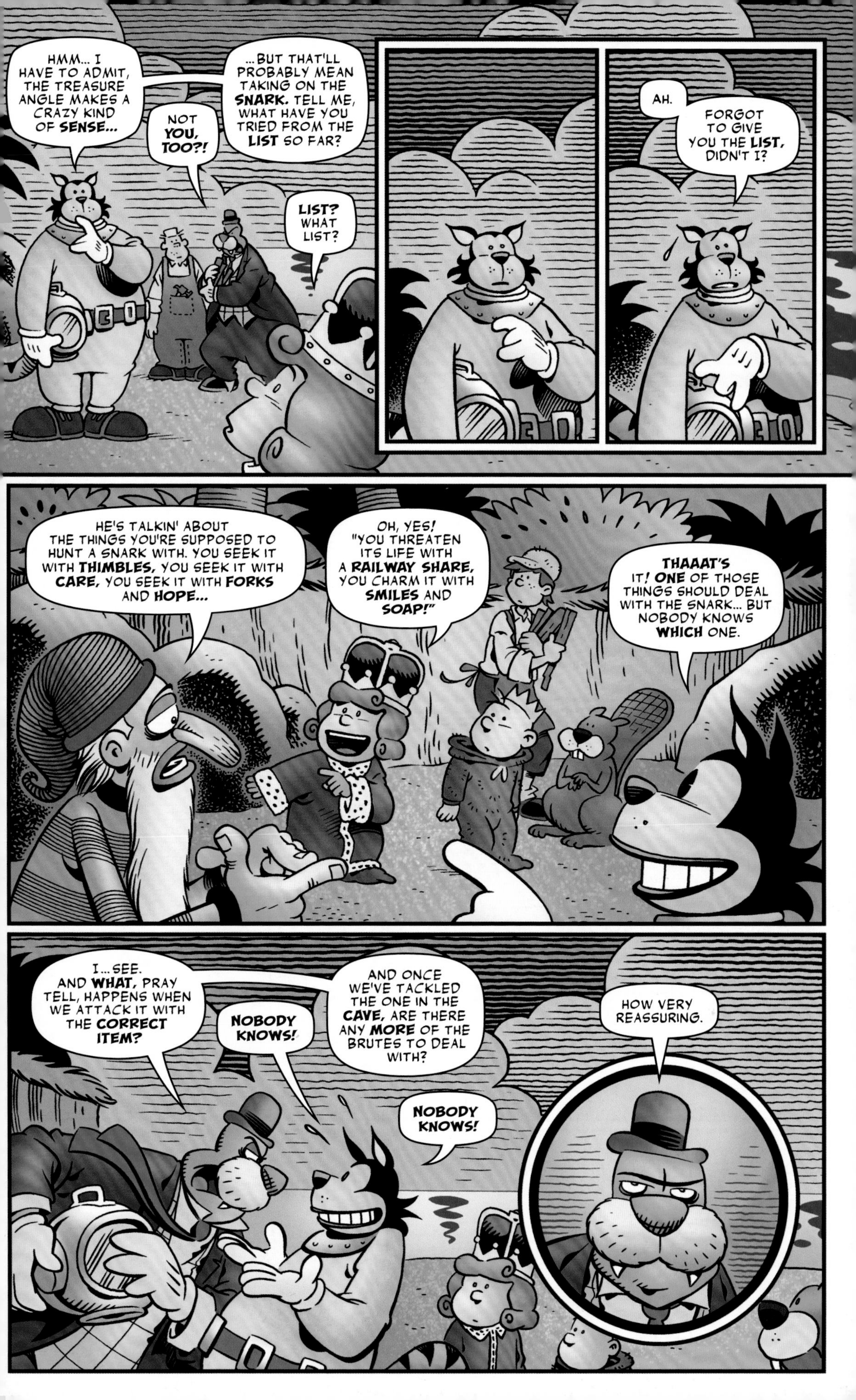
HMM... I HAVE TO ADMIT, THE TREASURE ANGLE MAKES A CRAZY KIND OF SENSE...
...BUT THAT'LL PROBABLY MEAN TAKING ON THE SNARK. TELL ME, WHAT HAVE YOU TRIED FROM THE LIST SO FAR?
NOT YOU, TOO?!
LIST? WHAT LIST?
AH.
FORGOT TO GIVE YOU THE LIST, DIDN'T I?
HE'S TALKIN' ABOUT THE THINGS YOU'RE SUPPOSED TO HUNT A SNARK WITH. YOU SEEK IT WITH THIMBLES, YOU SEEK IT WITH CARE, YOU SEEK IT WITH FORKS AND HOPE...
OH, YES! "YOU THREATEN ITS LIFE WITH A RAILWAY SHARE, YOU CHARM IT WITH SMILES AND SOAP!"
THAAAT'S IT! ONE OF THOSE THINGS SHOULD DEAL WITH THE SNARK... BUT NOBODY KNOWS WHICH ONE.
I... SEE. AND WHAT, PRAY TELL, HAPPENS WHEN WE ATTACK IT WITH THE CORRECT ITEM?
NOBODY KNOWS!
AND ONCE WE'VE TACKLED THE ONE IN THE CAVE, ARE THERE ANY MORE OF THE BRUTES TO DEAL WITH?
NOBODY KNOWS!
HOW VERY REASSURING.

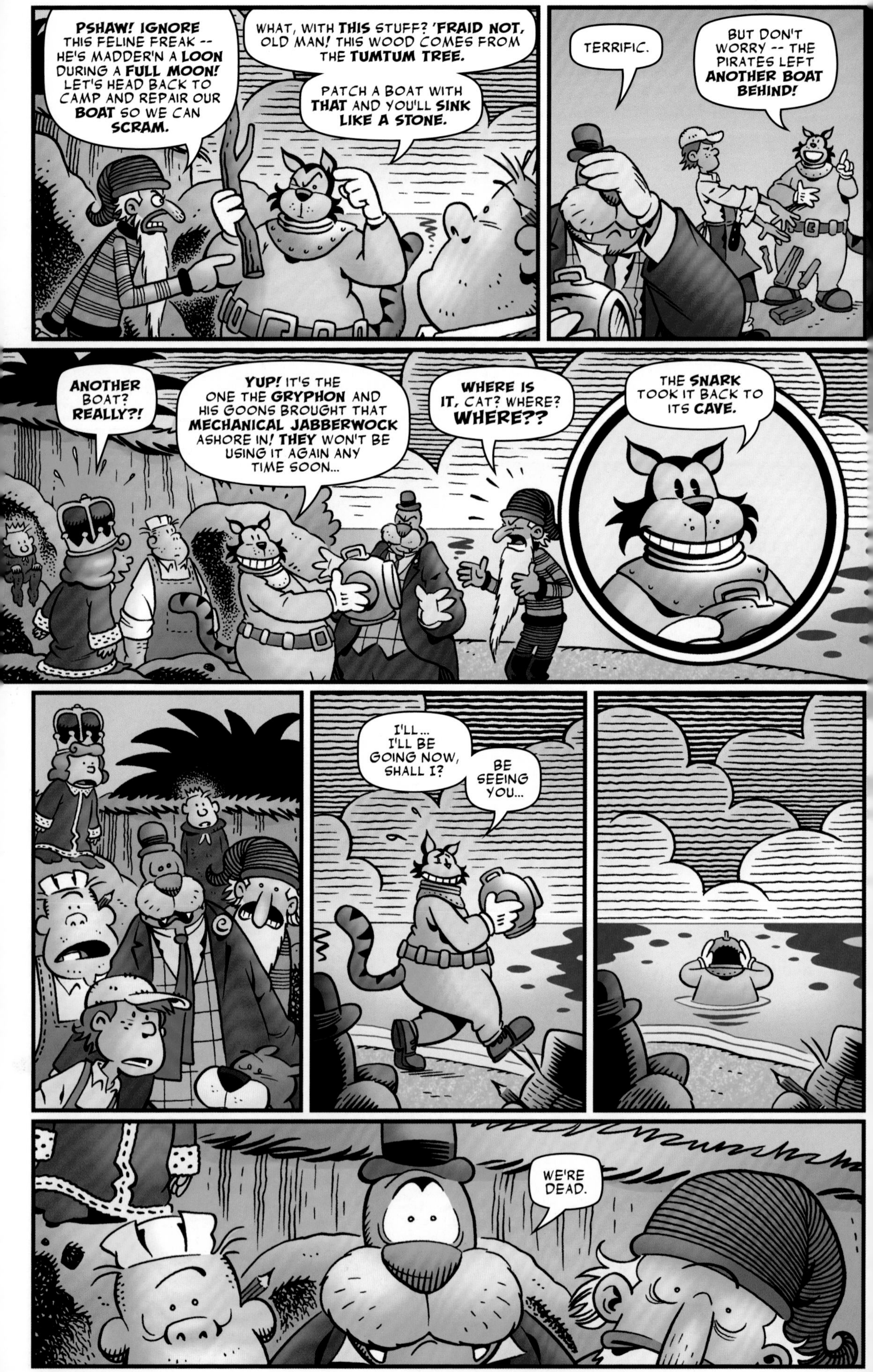
PSHAW! IGNORE THIS FELINE FREAK -- HE'S MADDER'N A LOON DURING A FULL MOON! LET'S HEAD BACK TO CAMP AND REPAIR OUR BOAT SO WE CAN SCRAM.
WHAT, WITH THIS STUFF? 'FRAID NOT, OLD MAN! THIS WOOD COMES FROM THE TUMTUM TREE.
PATCH A BOAT WITH THAT AND YOU'LL SINK LIKE A STONE.
TERRIFIC.
BUT DON'T WORRY -- THE PIRATES LEFT ANOTHER BOAT BEHIND!
ANOTHER BOAT? REALLY?!
YUP! IT'S THE ONE THE GRYPHON AND HIS GOONS BROUGHT THAT MECHANICAL JABBERWOCK ASHORE IN! THEY WON'T BE USING IT AGAIN ANY TIME SOON...
WHERE IS IT, CAT? WHERE? WHERE??
THE SNARK TOOK IT BACK TO ITS CAVE.
I'LL... I'LL BE GOING NOW, SHALL I?
BE SEEING YOU...
WE'RE DEAD.

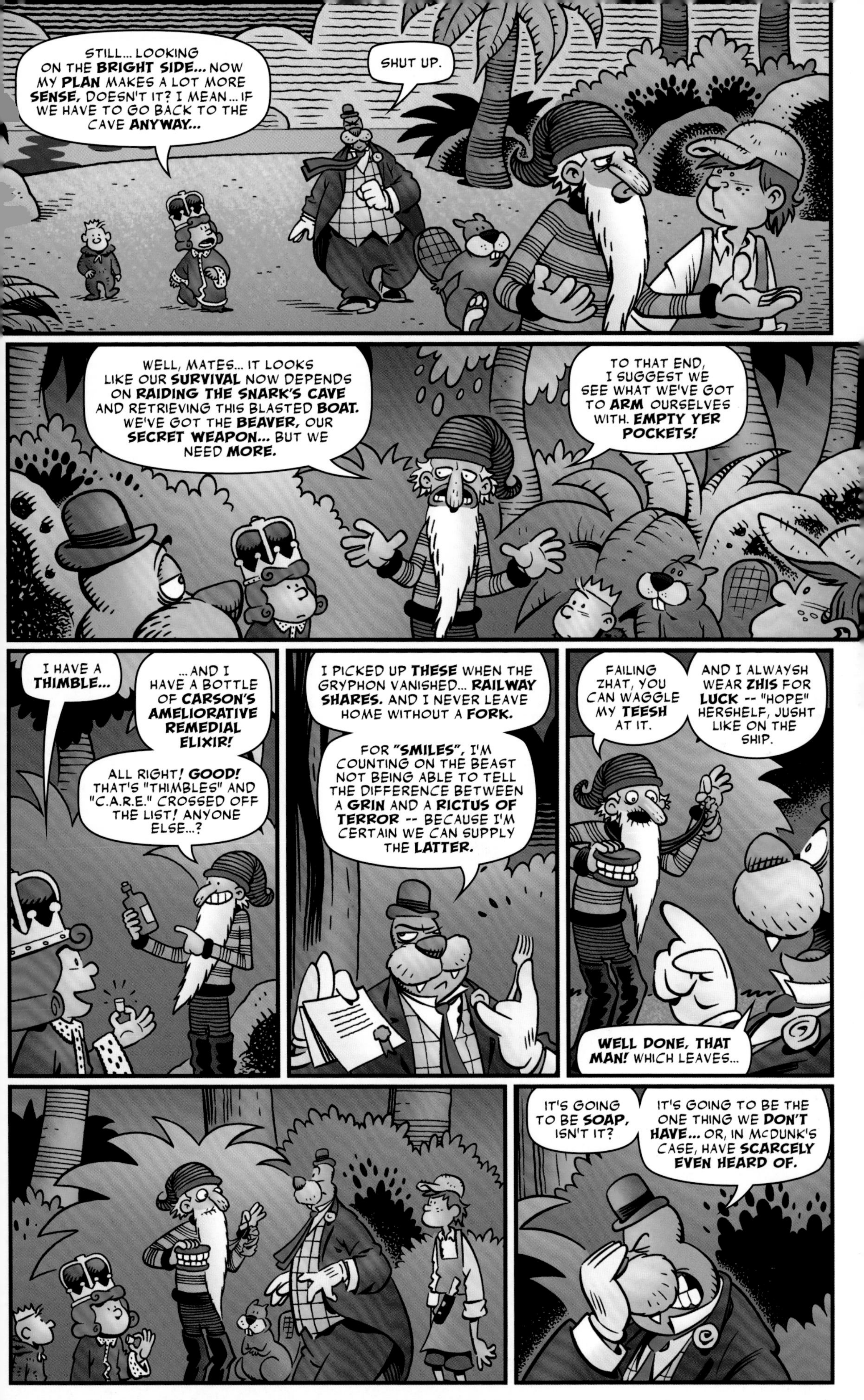
STILL... LOOKING ON THE BRIGHT SIDE... NOW MY PLAN MAKES A LOT MORE SENSE, DOESN'T IT? I MEAN... IF WE HAVE TO GO BACK TO THE CAVE ANYWAY...
SHUT UP.
WELL, MATES... IT LOOKS LIKE OUR SURVIVAL NOW DEPENDS ON RAIDING THE SNARK'S CAVE AND RETRIEVING THIS BLASTED BOAT. WE'VE GOT THE BEAVER, OUR SECRET WEAPON... BUT WE NEED MORE.
TO THAT END, I SUGGEST WE SEE WHAT WE'VE GOT TO ARM OURSELVES WITH. EMPTY YER POCKETS!
I HAVE A THIMBLE...
...AND I HAVE A BOTTLE OF CARSON'S AMELIORATIVE REMEDIAL ELIXIR!
ALL RIGHT! GOOD! THAT'S "THIMBLES" AND "C.A.R.E." CROSSED OFF THE LIST! ANYONE ELSE...?
I PICKED UP THESE WHEN THE GRYPHON VANISHED... RAILWAY SHARES. AND I NEVER LEAVE HOME WITHOUT A FORK.
FOR "SMILES", I'M COUNTING ON THE BEAST NOT BEING ABLE TO TELL THE DIFFERENCE BETWEEN A GRIN AND A RICTUS OF TERROR -- BECAUSE I'M CERTAIN WE CAN SUPPLY THE LATTER.
FAILING ZHAT, YOU CAN WAGGLE MY TEESH AT IT.
AND I ALWAYSH WEAR ZHIS FOR LUCK -- "HOPE" HERSHELF, JUSHT LIKE ON THE SHIP.
WELL DONE, THAT MAN! WHICH LEAVES...
IT'S GOING TO BE SOAP, ISN'T IT?
IT'S GOING TO BE THE ONE THING WE DON'T HAVE... OR, IN McDUNK'S CASE, HAVE SCARCELY EVEN HEARD OF.

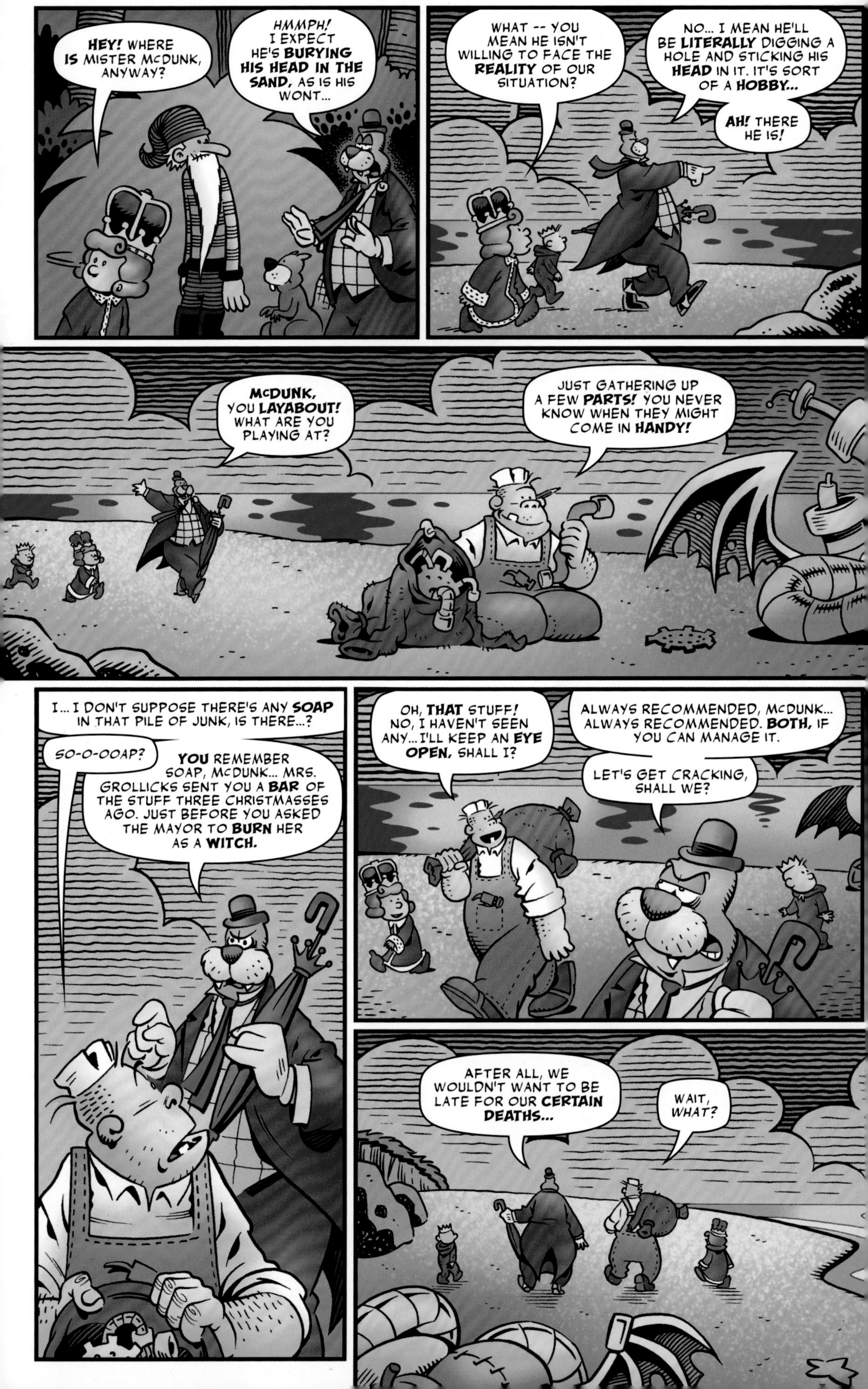
HEY! WHERE IS MISTER McDUNK, ANYWAY?
HMMPH! I EXPECT HE'S BURYING HIS HEAD IN THE SAND, AS IS HIS WONT...
WHAT -- YOU MEAN HE ISN'T WILLING TO FACE THE REALITY OF OUR SITUATION?
NO... I MEAN HE'LL BE LITERALLY DIGGING A HOLE AND STICKING HIS HEAD IN IT. IT'S SORT OF A HOBBY...
AH! THERE HE IS!
McDUNK, YOU LAYABOUT! WHAT ARE YOU PLAYING AT?
JUST GATHERING UP A FEW PARTS! YOU NEVER KNOW WHEN THEY MIGHT COME IN HANDY!
I... I DON'T SUPPOSE THERE'S ANY SOAP IN THAT PILE OF JUNK, IS THERE...?
SO-O-OOAP?
YOU REMEMBER SOAP, McDUNK... MRS. GROLLICKS SENT YOU A BAR OF THE STUFF THREE CHRISTMASSES AGO. JUST BEFORE YOU ASKED THE MAYOR TO BURN HER AS A WITCH.
OH, THAT STUFF! NO, I HAVEN'T SEEN ANY... I'LL KEEP AN EYE OPEN, SHALL I?
ALWAYS RECOMMENDED, McDUNK... ALWAYS RECOMMENDED. BOTH, IF YOU CAN MANAGE IT.
LET'S GET CRACKING, SHALL WE?
AFTER ALL, WE WOULDN'T WANT TO BE LATE FOR OUR CERTAIN DEATHS...
WAIT, WHAT?

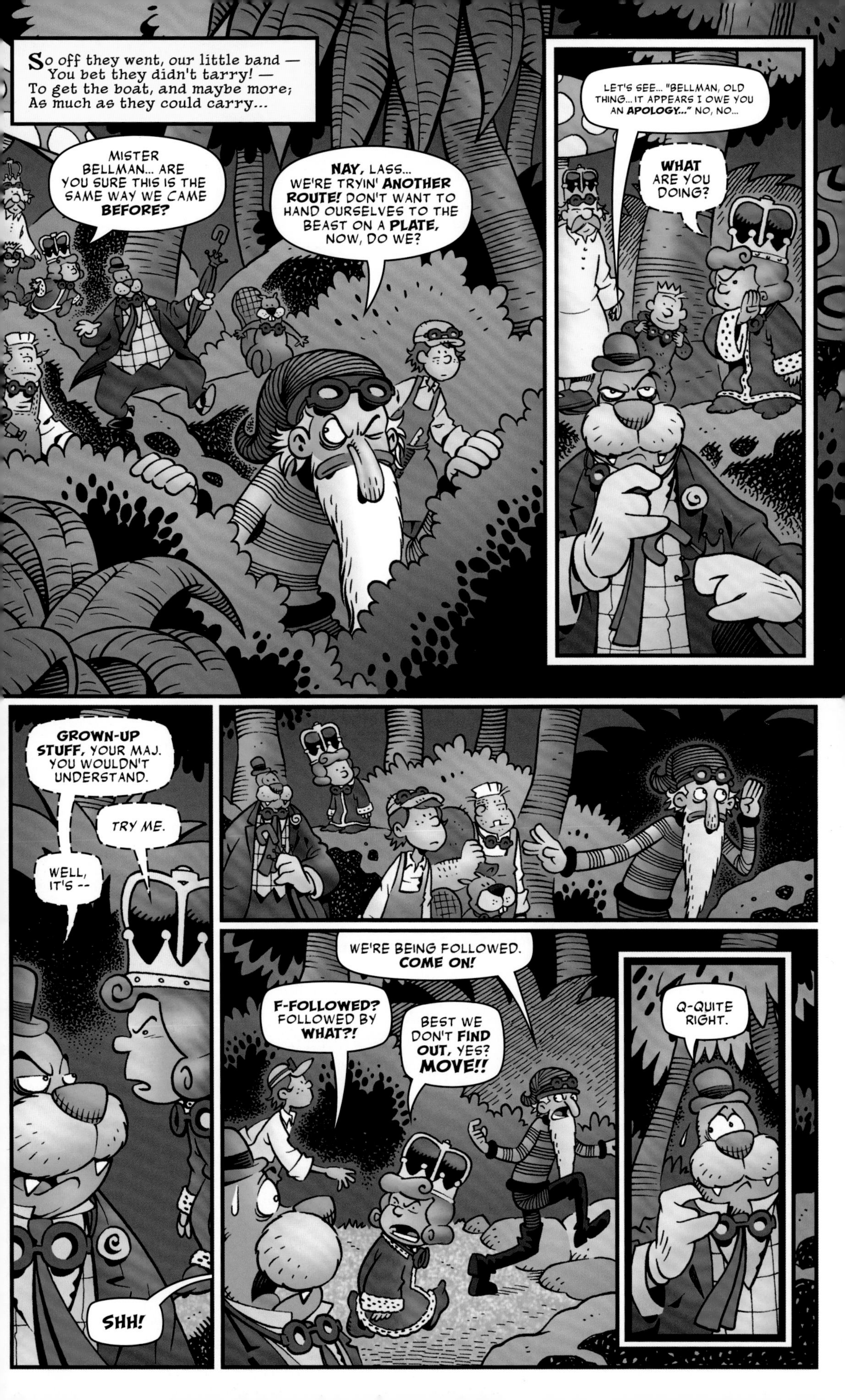

So off they went, our little band —
You bet they didn't tarry! —
To get the boat, and maybe more;
As much as they could carry...
MISTER BELLMAN... ARE YOU SURE THIS IS THE SAME WAY WE CAME BEFORE?
NAY, LASS... WE'RE TRYIN' ANOTHER ROUTE! DON'T WANT TO HAND OURSELVES TO THE BEAST ON A PLATE, NOW, DO WE?
LET'S SEE... "BELLMAN, OLD THING... IT APPEARS I OWE YOU AN APOLOGY..." NO, NO...
WHAT ARE YOU DOING?
GROWN-UP STUFF, YOUR MAJ. YOU WOULDN'T UNDERSTAND.
TRY ME.
WELL, IT'S --
SHH!
WE'RE BEING FOLLOWED. COME ON!
F-FOLLOWED? FOLLOWED BY WHAT?!
BEST WE DON'T FIND OUT, YES? MOVE!!
Q-QUITE RIGHT.

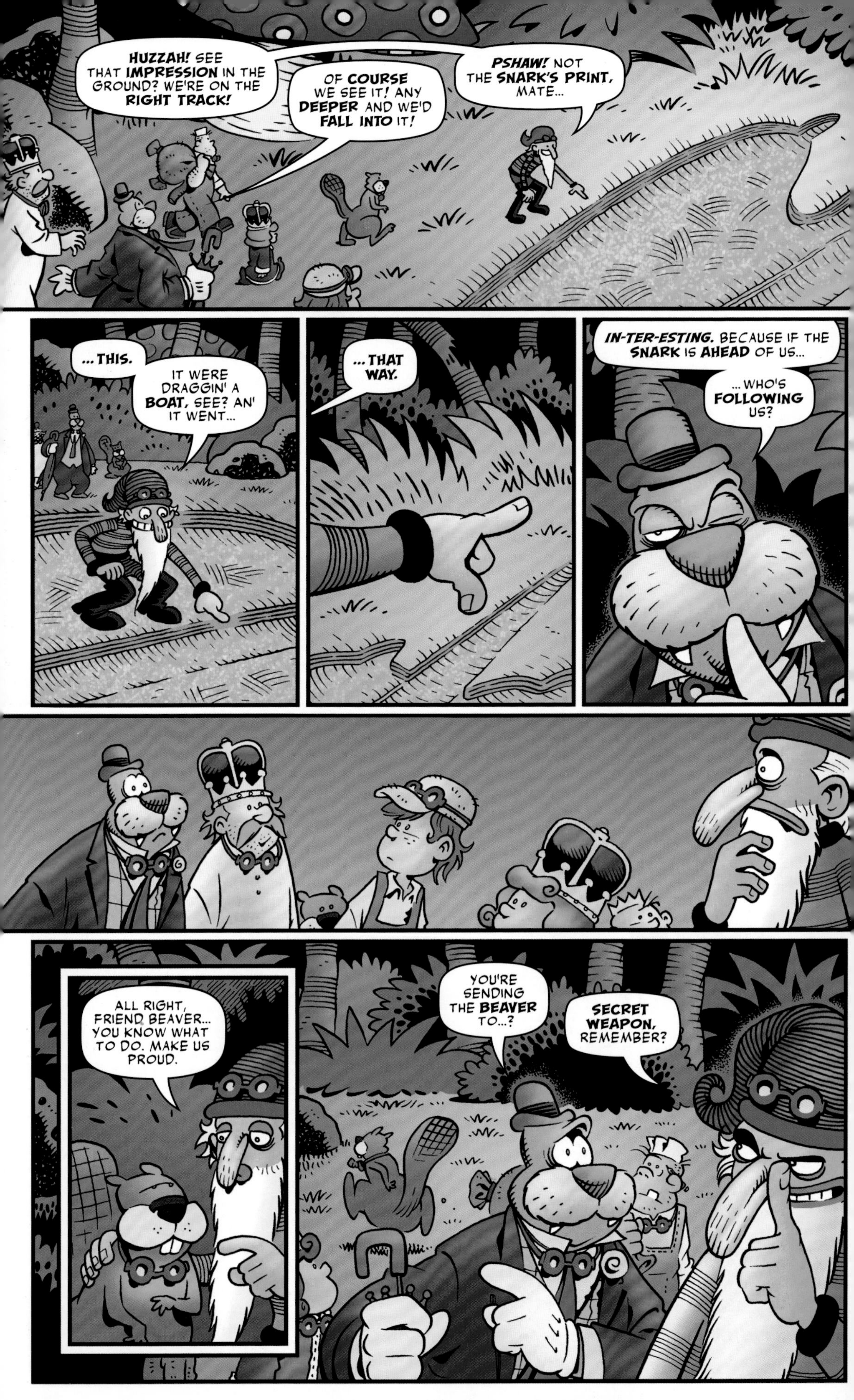
HUZZAH! SEE THAT IMPRESSION IN THE GROUND? WE'RE ON THE RIGHT TRACK!
OF COURSE WE SEE IT! ANY DEEPER AND WE'D FALL INTO IT!
PSHAW! NOT THE SNARK'S PRINT, MATE...
...THIS.
IT WERE DRAGGIN' A BOAT, SEE? AN' IT WENT...
...THAT WAY.
IN-TER-ESTING. BECAUSE IF THE SNARK IS AHEAD OF US...
...WHO'S FOLLOWING US?
ALL RIGHT, FRIEND BEAVER... YOU KNOW WHAT TO DO. MAKE US PROUD.
YOU'RE SENDING THE BEAVER TO...?
SECRET WEAPON, REMEMBER?

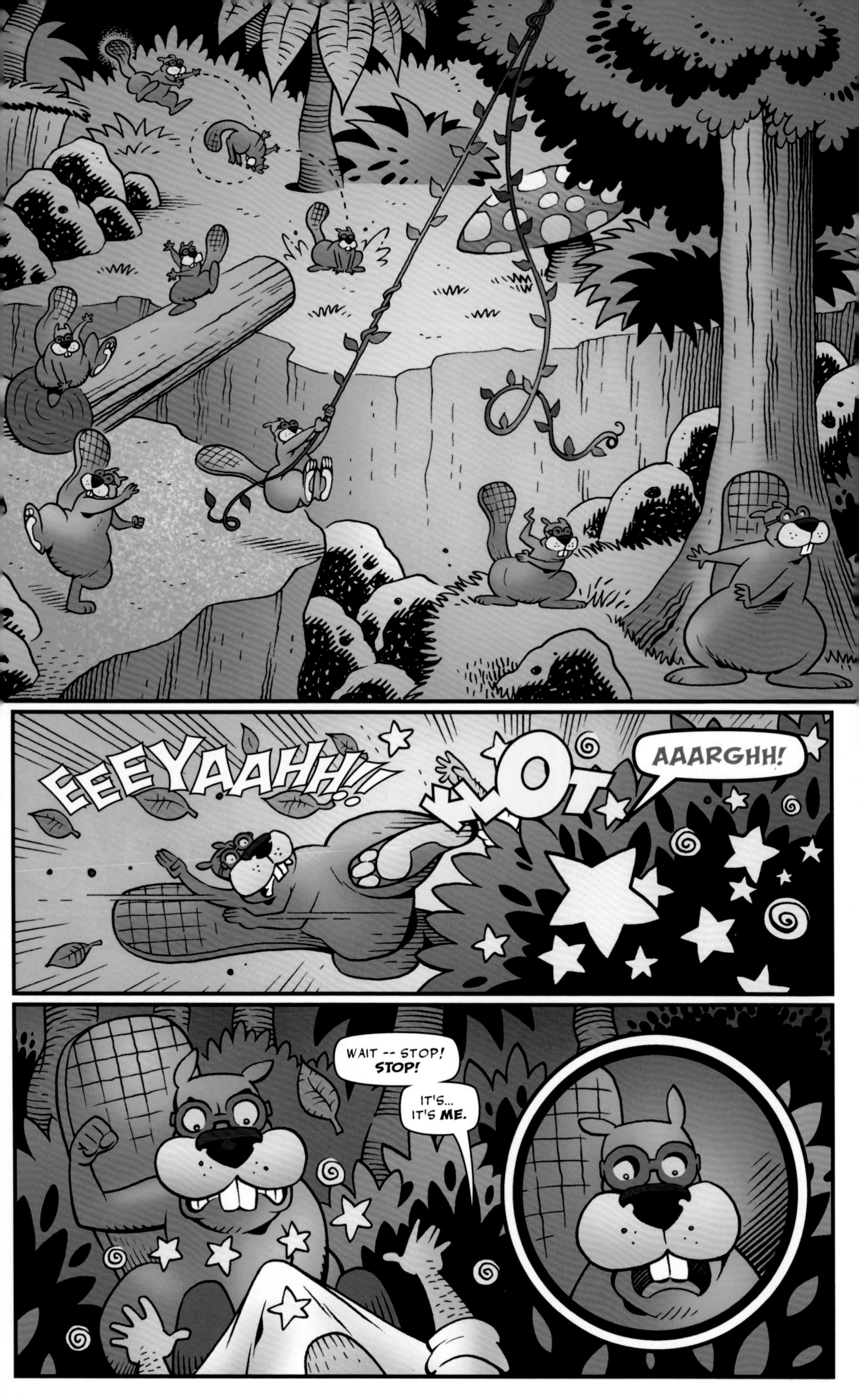
EEEYAAHH!!!
AAARGHH!
WAIT -- STOP! STOP!
IT'S... IT'S ME.

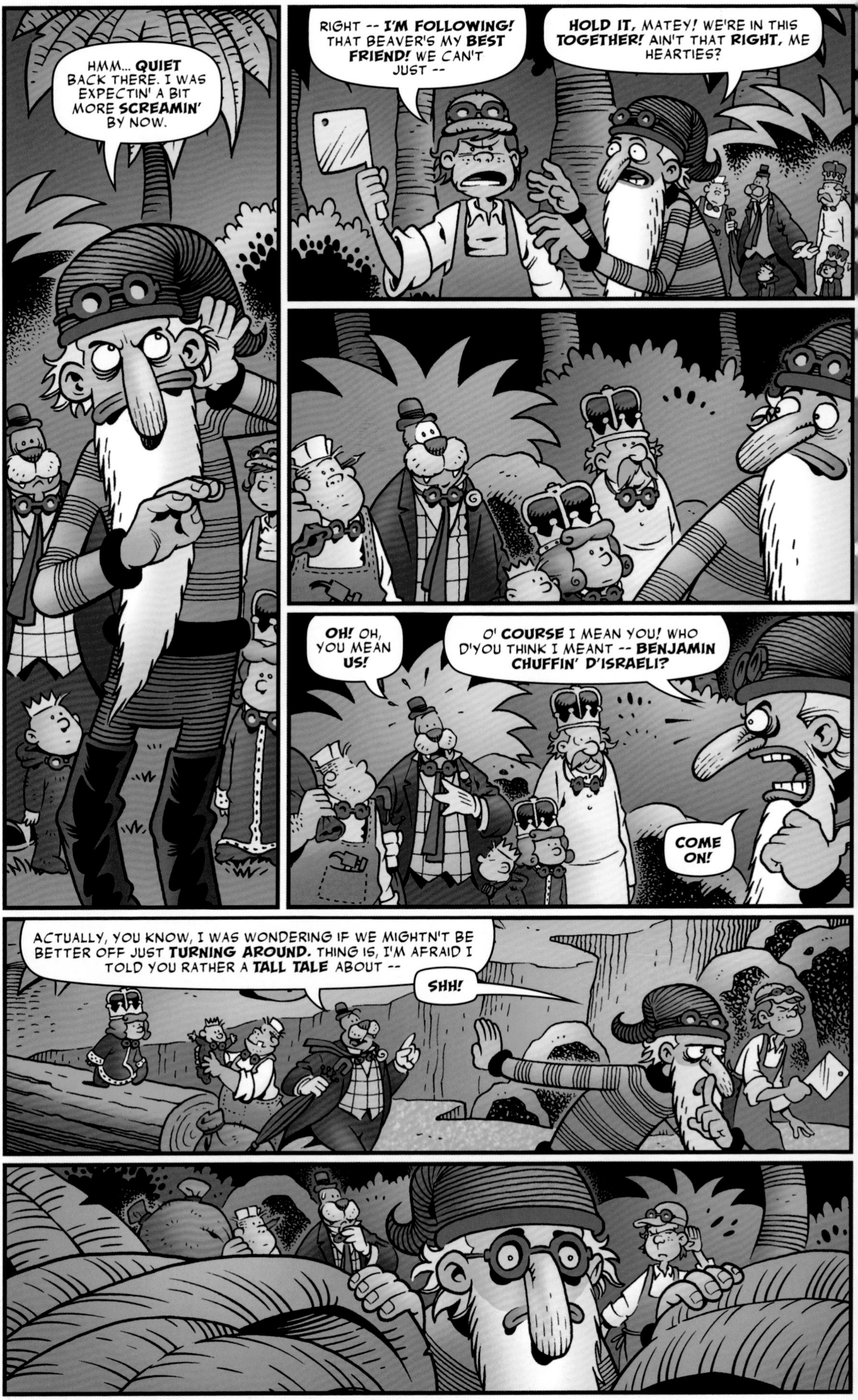
HMM... QUIET BACK THERE. I WAS EXPECTIN' A BIT MORE SCREAMIN' BY NOW.
RIGHT -- I'M FOLLOWING! THAT BEAVER'S MY BEST FRIEND! WE CAN'T JUST --
HOLD IT, MATEY! WE'RE IN THIS TOGETHER! AIN'T THAT RIGHT, ME HEARTIES?
OH! OH, YOU MEAN US!
O' COURSE I MEAN YOU! WHO D'YOU THINK I MEANT -- BENJAMIN CHUFFIN' D'ISRAELI?
COME ON!
ACTUALLY, YOU KNOW, I WAS WONDERING IF WE MIGHTN'T BE BETTER OFF JUST TURNING AROUND. THING IS, I'M AFRAID I TOLD YOU RATHER A TALL TALE ABOUT --
SHH!

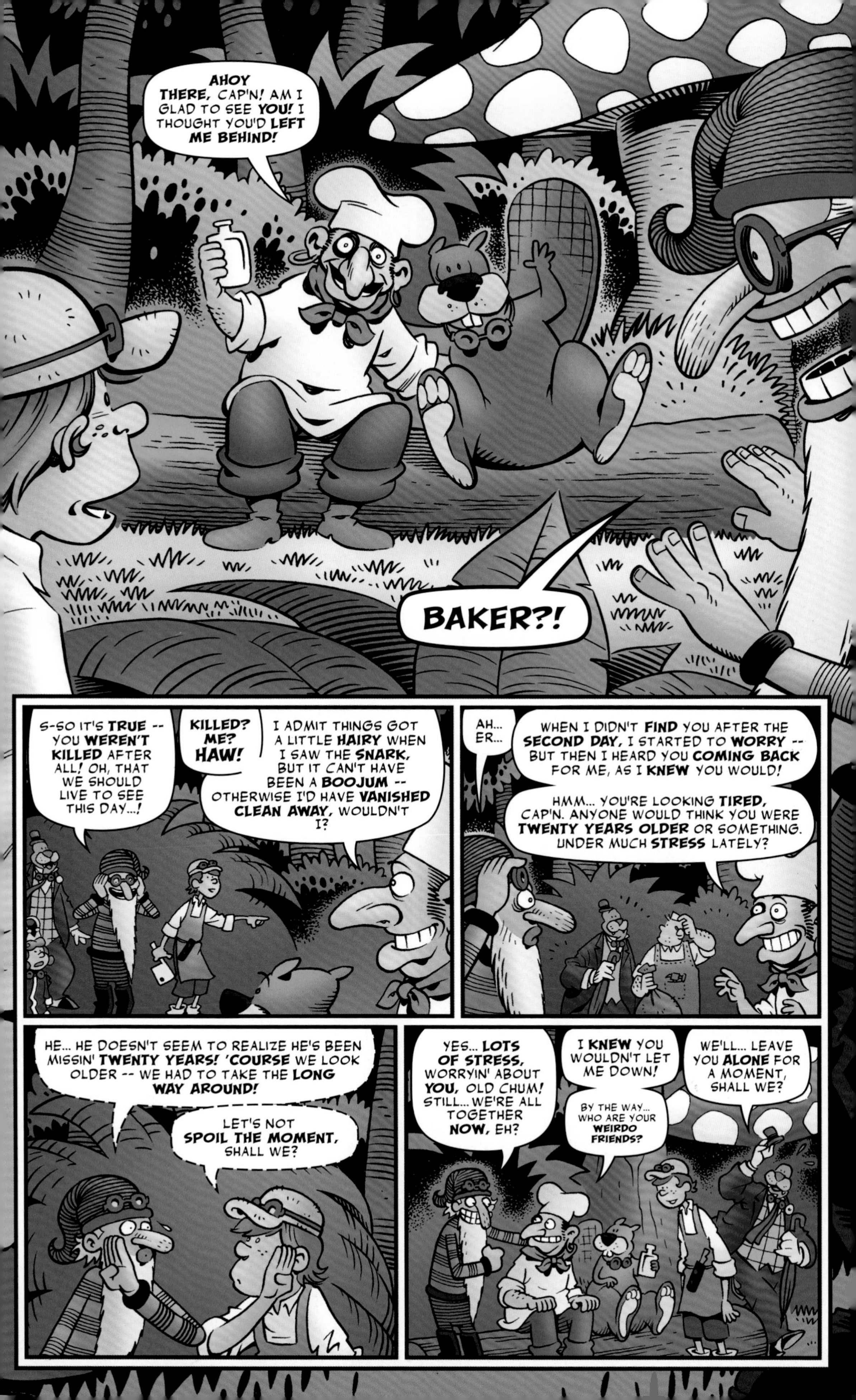
AHOY THERE, CAP'N! AM I GLAD TO SEE YOU! I THOUGHT YOU'D LEFT ME BEHIND!
BAKER?!
S-SO IT'S TRUE -- YOU WEREN'T KILLED AFTER ALL! OH, THAT WE SHOULD LIVE TO SEE THIS DAY...!
KILLED? ME? HAW!
I ADMIT THINGS GOT A LITTLE HAIRY WHEN I SAW THE SNARK, BUT IT CAN'T HAVE BEEN A BOOJUM -- OTHERWISE I'D HAVE VANISHED CLEAN AWAY, WOULDN'T I?
AH... ER...
WHEN I DIDN'T FIND YOU AFTER THE SECOND DAY, I STARTED TO WORRY -- BUT THEN I HEARD YOU COMING BACK FOR ME, AS I KNEW YOU WOULD!
HMM... YOU'RE LOOKING TIRED, CAP'N. ANYONE WOULD THINK YOU WERE TWENTY YEARS OLDER OR SOMETHING. UNDER MUCH STRESS LATELY?
HE... HE DOESN'T SEEM TO REALIZE HE'S BEEN MISSIN' TWENTY YEARS! 'COURSE WE LOOK OLDER -- WE HAD TO TAKE THE LONG WAY AROUND!
LET'S NOT SPOIL THE MOMENT, SHALL WE?
YES... LOTS OF STRESS, WORRYIN' ABOUT YOU, OLD CHUM! STILL... WE'RE ALL TOGETHER NOW, EH?
I KNEW YOU WOULDN'T LET ME DOWN!
BY THE WAY... WHO ARE YOUR WEIRDO FRIENDS?
WE'LL... LEAVE YOU ALONE FOR A MOMENT, SHALL WE?

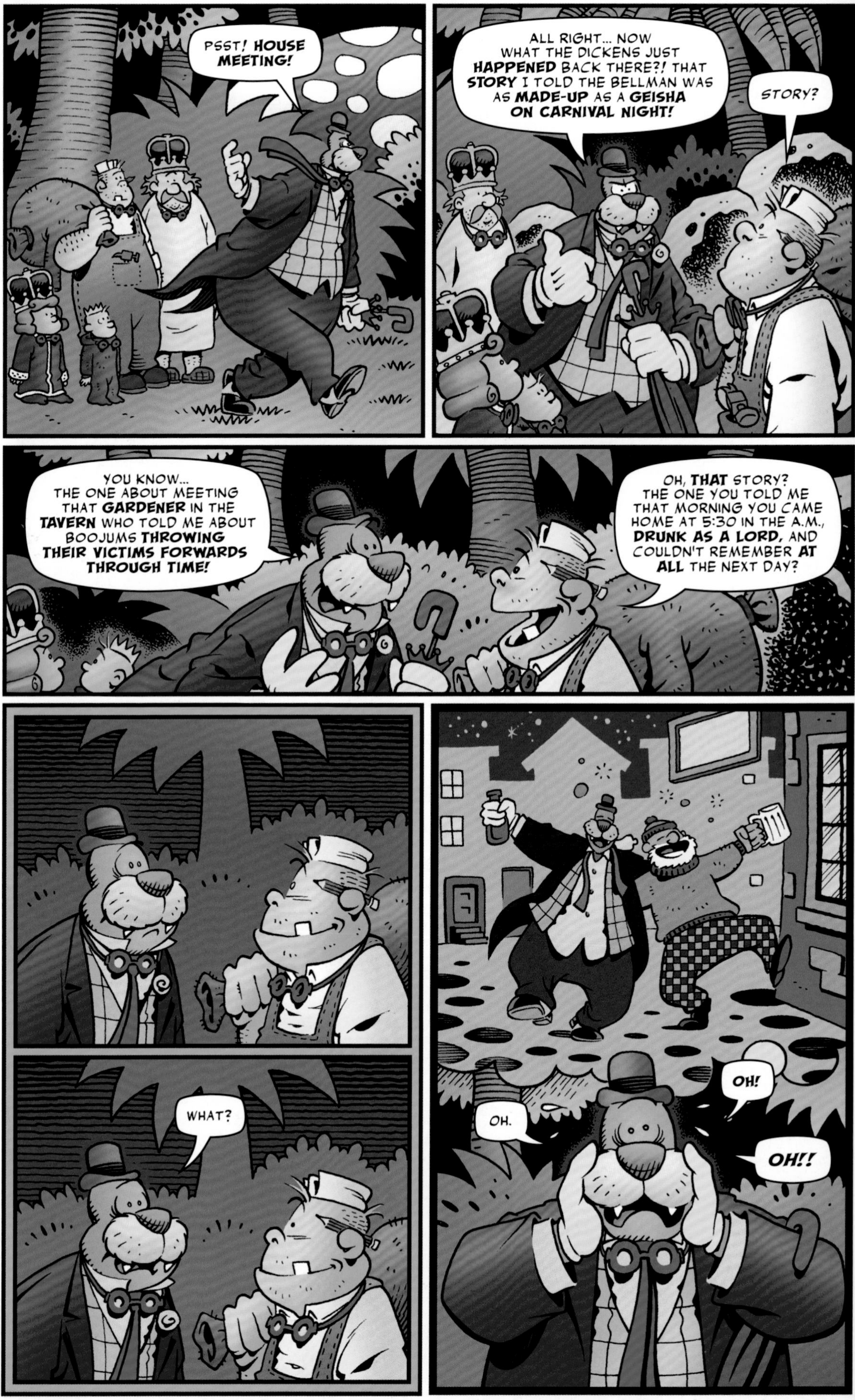

PSST! HOUSE MEETING!
ALL RIGHT... NOW WHAT THE DICKENS JUST HAPPENED BACK THERE?! THAT STORY I TOLD THE BELLMAN WAS AS MADE-UP AS A GEISHA ON CARNIVAL NIGHT!
STORY?
YOU KNOW... THE ONE ABOUT MEETING THAT GARDENER IN THE TAVERN WHO TOLD ME ABOUT BOOJUMS THROWING THEIR VICTIMS FORWARDS THROUGH TIME!
OH, THAT STORY? THE ONE YOU TOLD ME THAT MORNING YOU CAME HOME AT 5:30 IN THE A.M., DRUNK AS A LORD, AND COULDN'T REMEMBER AT ALL THE NEXT DAY?
WHAT?
OH.
OH!
OH!!

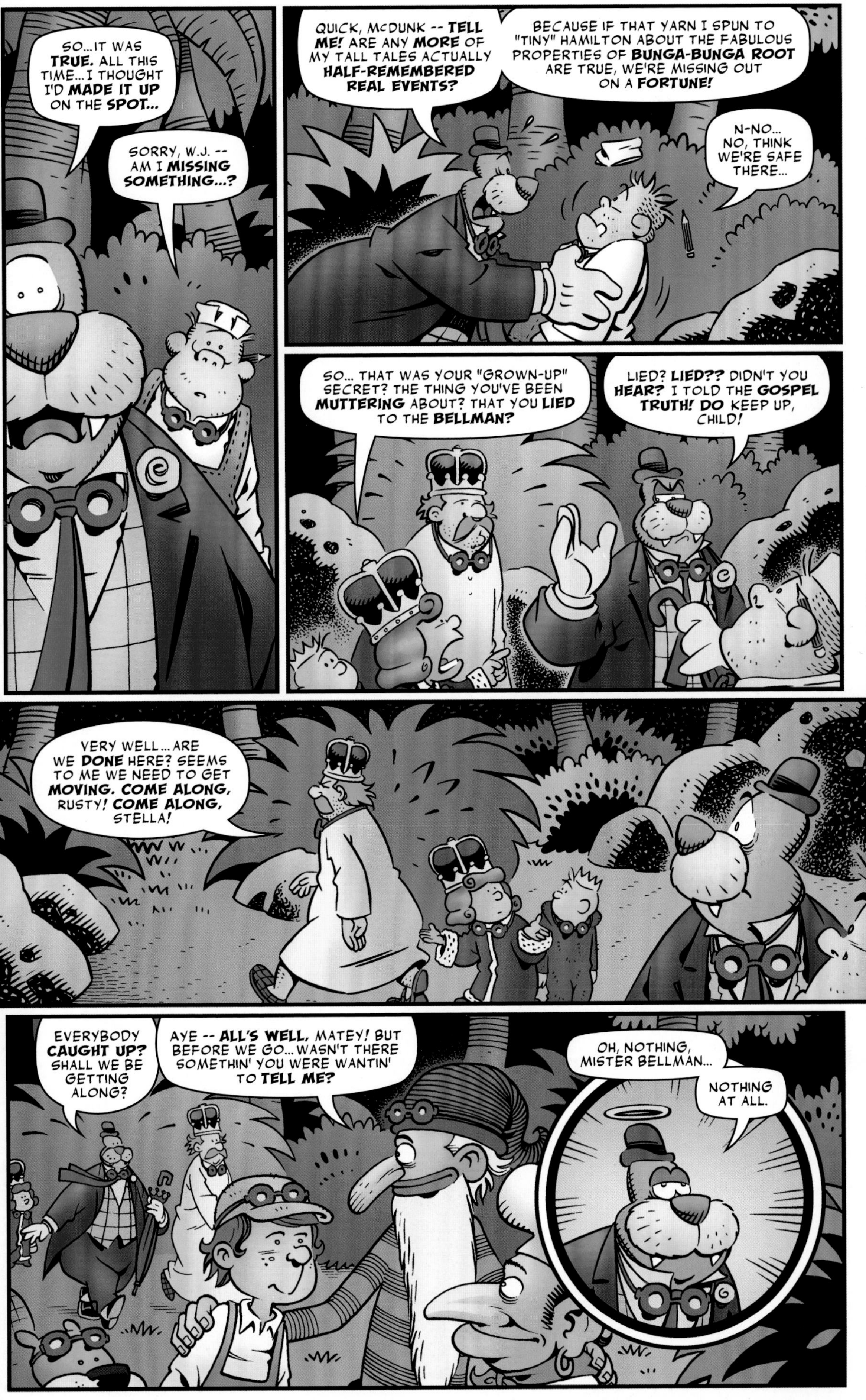
SO...IT WAS TRUE. ALL THIS TIME...I THOUGHT I'D MADE IT UP ON THE SPOT...
SORRY, W.J. -- AM I MISSING SOMETHING...?
QUICK, McDUNK -- TELL ME! ARE ANY MORE OF MY TALL TALES ACTUALLY HALF-REMEMBERED REAL EVENTS?
BECAUSE IF THAT YARN I SPUN TO "TINY" HAMILTON ABOUT THE FABULOUS PROPERTIES OF BUNGA-BUNGA ROOT ARE TRUE, WE'RE MISSING OUT ON A FORTUNE!
N-NO... NO, THINK WE'RE SAFE THERE...
SO... THAT WAS YOUR "GROWN-UP" SECRET? THE THING YOU'VE BEEN MUTTERING ABOUT? THAT YOU LIED TO THE BELLMAN?
LIED? LIED?? DIDN'T YOU HEAR? I TOLD THE GOSPEL TRUTH! DO KEEP UP, CHILD!
VERY WELL... ARE WE DONE HERE? SEEMS TO ME WE NEED TO GET MOVING. COME ALONG, RUSTY! COME ALONG, STELLA!
EVERYBODY CAUGHT UP? SHALL WE BE GETTING ALONG?
AYE -- ALL'S WELL, MATEY! BUT BEFORE WE GO... WASN'T THERE SOMETHIN' YOU WERE WANTIN' TO TELL ME?
OH, NOTHING, MISTER BELLMAN...
NOTHING AT ALL.

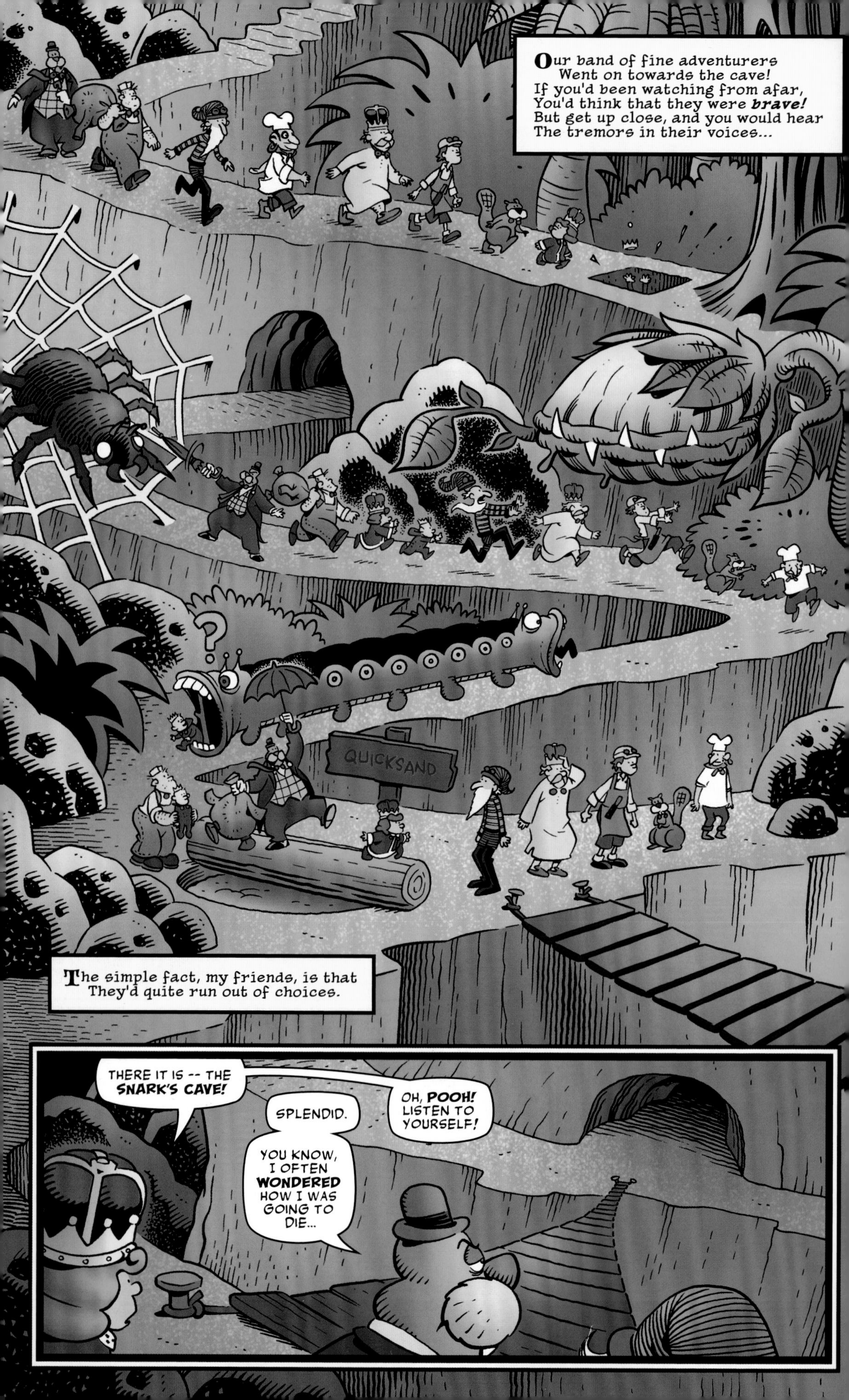
Our band of fine adventurers
Went on towards the cave!
If you'd been watching from afar,
You'd think that they were ***brave!***
But get up close, and you would hear
The tremors in their voices...
?
QUICKSAND
The simple fact, my friends, is that
They'd quite run out of choices.
THERE IT IS -- THE **SNARK'S CAVE!**
SPLENDID.
OH, **POOH!** LISTEN TO YOURSELF!
YOU KNOW, I OFTEN **WONDERED** HOW I WAS GOING TO DIE...

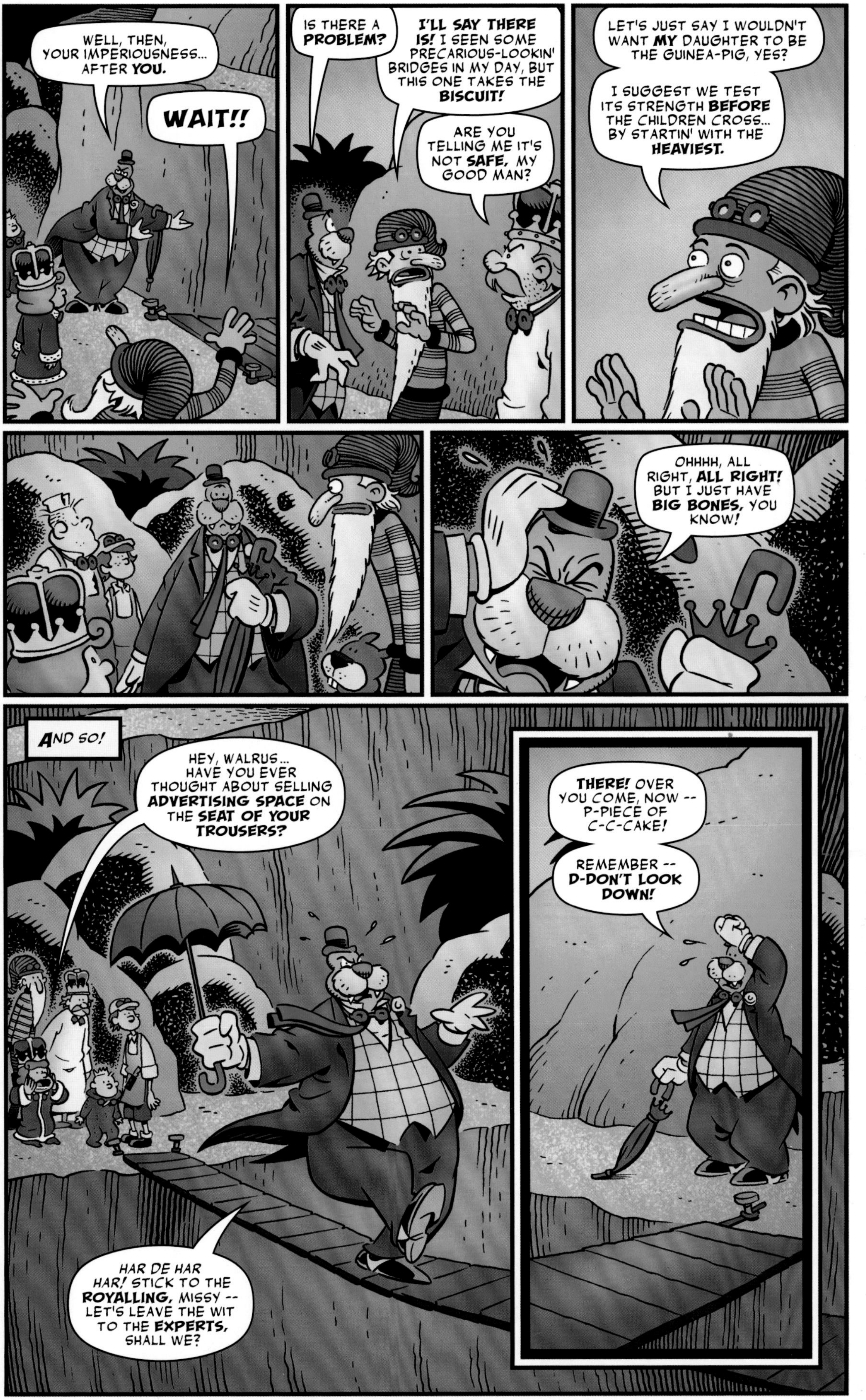
WELL, THEN, YOUR IMPERIOUSNESS... AFTER **YOU.**
WAIT!!
IS THERE A **PROBLEM?**
I'LL SAY THERE IS! I SEEN SOME PRECARIOUS-LOOKIN' BRIDGES IN MY DAY, BUT THIS ONE TAKES THE **BISCUIT!**
ARE YOU TELLING ME IT'S NOT **SAFE,** MY GOOD MAN?
LET'S JUST SAY I WOULDN'T WANT **MY** DAUGHTER TO BE THE GUINEA-PIG, YES?
I SUGGEST WE TEST ITS STRENGTH **BEFORE** THE CHILDREN CROSS... BY STARTIN' WITH THE **HEAVIEST.**
OHHHH, ALL RIGHT, **ALL RIGHT!** BUT I JUST HAVE **BIG BONES,** YOU KNOW!
AND SO!
HEY, WALRUS... HAVE YOU EVER THOUGHT ABOUT SELLING **ADVERTISING SPACE** ON THE **SEAT OF YOUR TROUSERS?**
HAR DE HAR HAR! STICK TO THE **ROYALLING,** MISSY -- LET'S LEAVE THE WIT TO THE **EXPERTS,** SHALL WE?
THERE! OVER YOU COME, NOW -- P-PIECE OF C-C-CAKE!
REMEMBER -- **D-DON'T LOOK DOWN!**

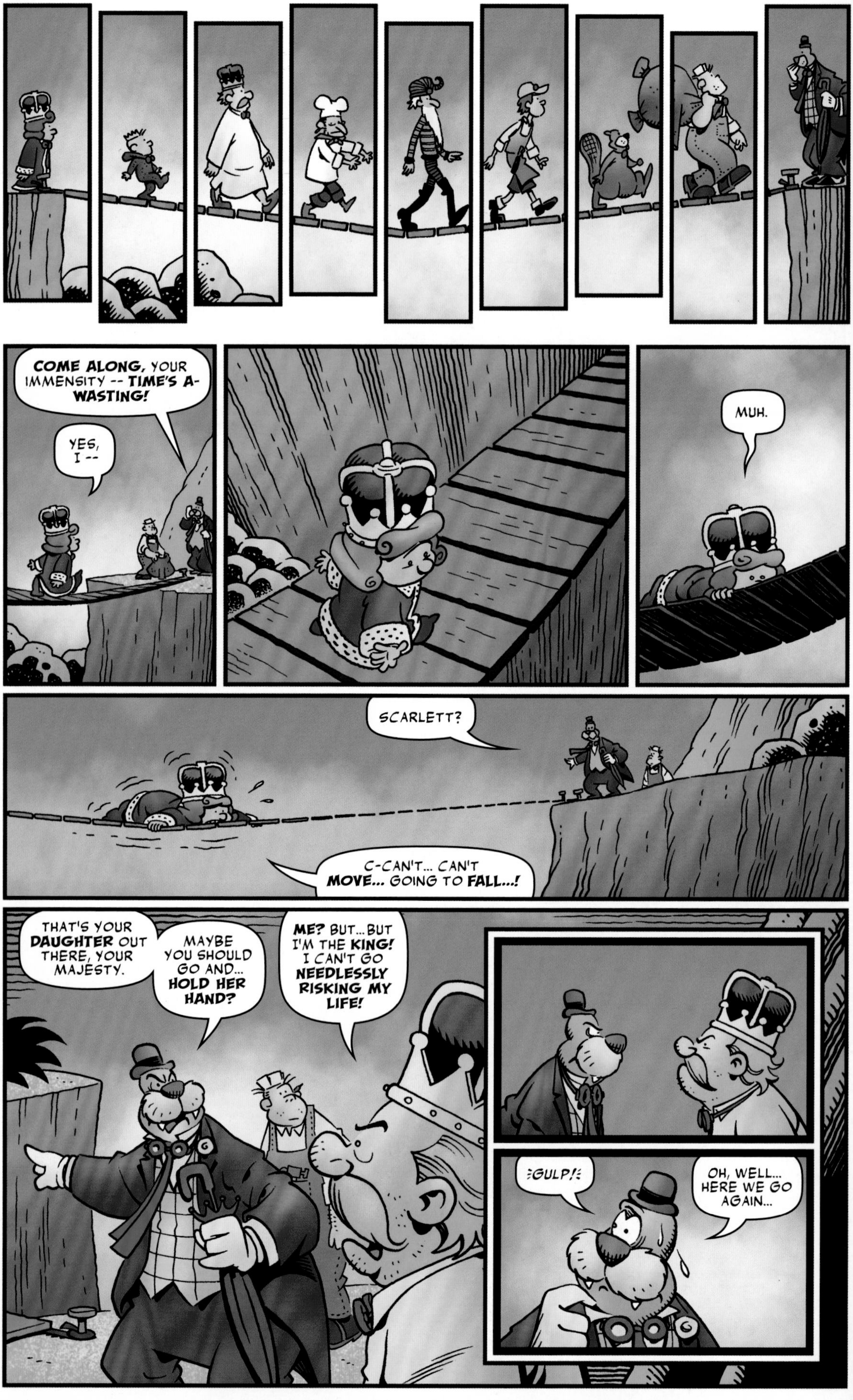
COME ALONG, YOUR IMMENSITY -- TIME'S A-WASTING!
YES, I --
MUH.
SCARLETT?
C-CAN'T... CAN'T MOVE... GOING TO FALL...!
THAT'S YOUR DAUGHTER OUT THERE, YOUR MAJESTY.
MAYBE YOU SHOULD GO AND... HOLD HER HAND?
ME? BUT...BUT I'M THE KING! I CAN'T GO NEEDLESSLY RISKING MY LIFE!
GULP!
OH, WELL... HERE WE GO AGAIN...

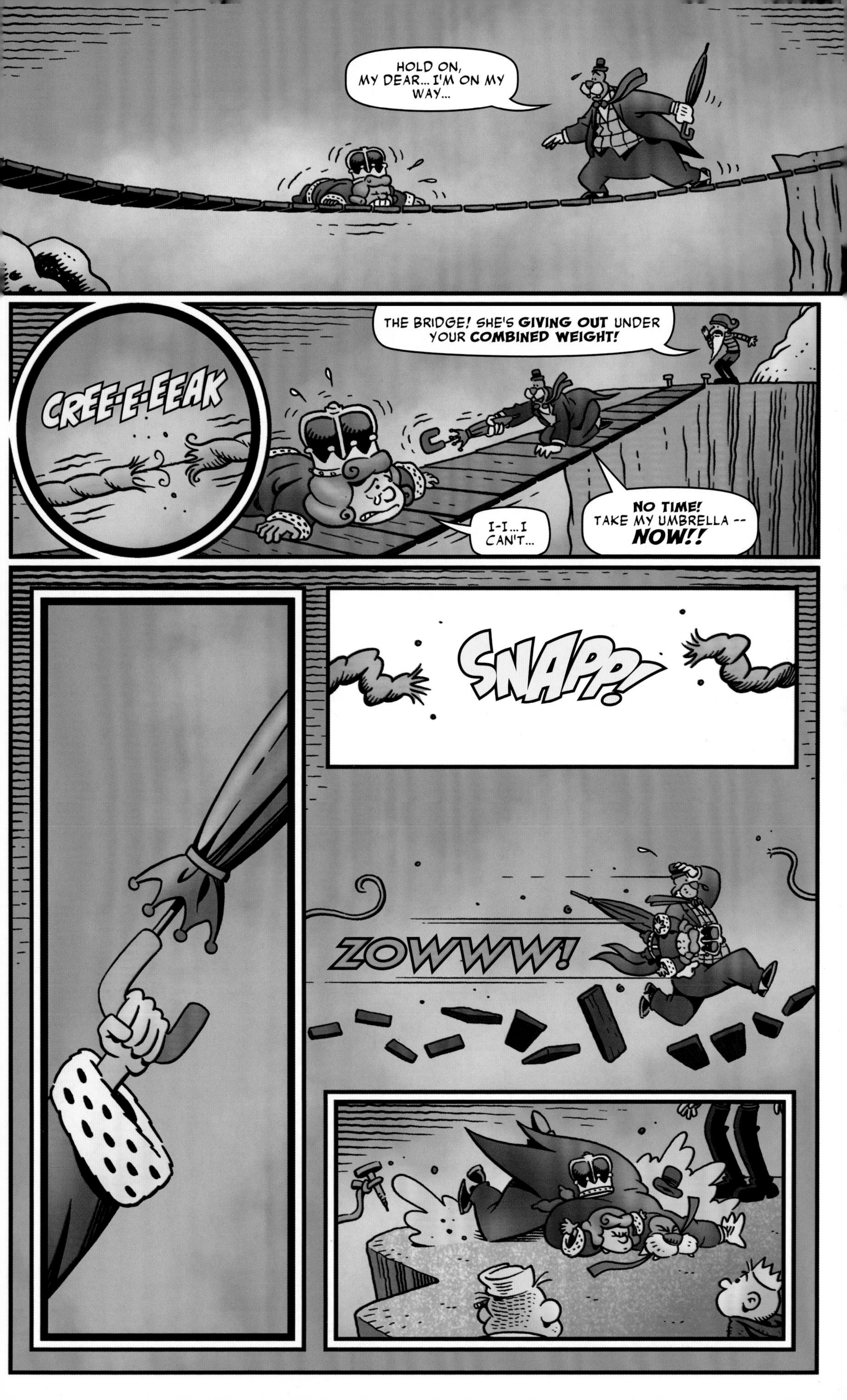
HOLD ON, MY DEAR... I'M ON MY WAY...
CREE-E-EEAK
THE BRIDGE! SHE'S GIVING OUT UNDER YOUR COMBINED WEIGHT!
I-I... I CAN'T...
NO TIME! TAKE MY UMBRELLA -- NOW!!
SNAPP!
ZOWWW!

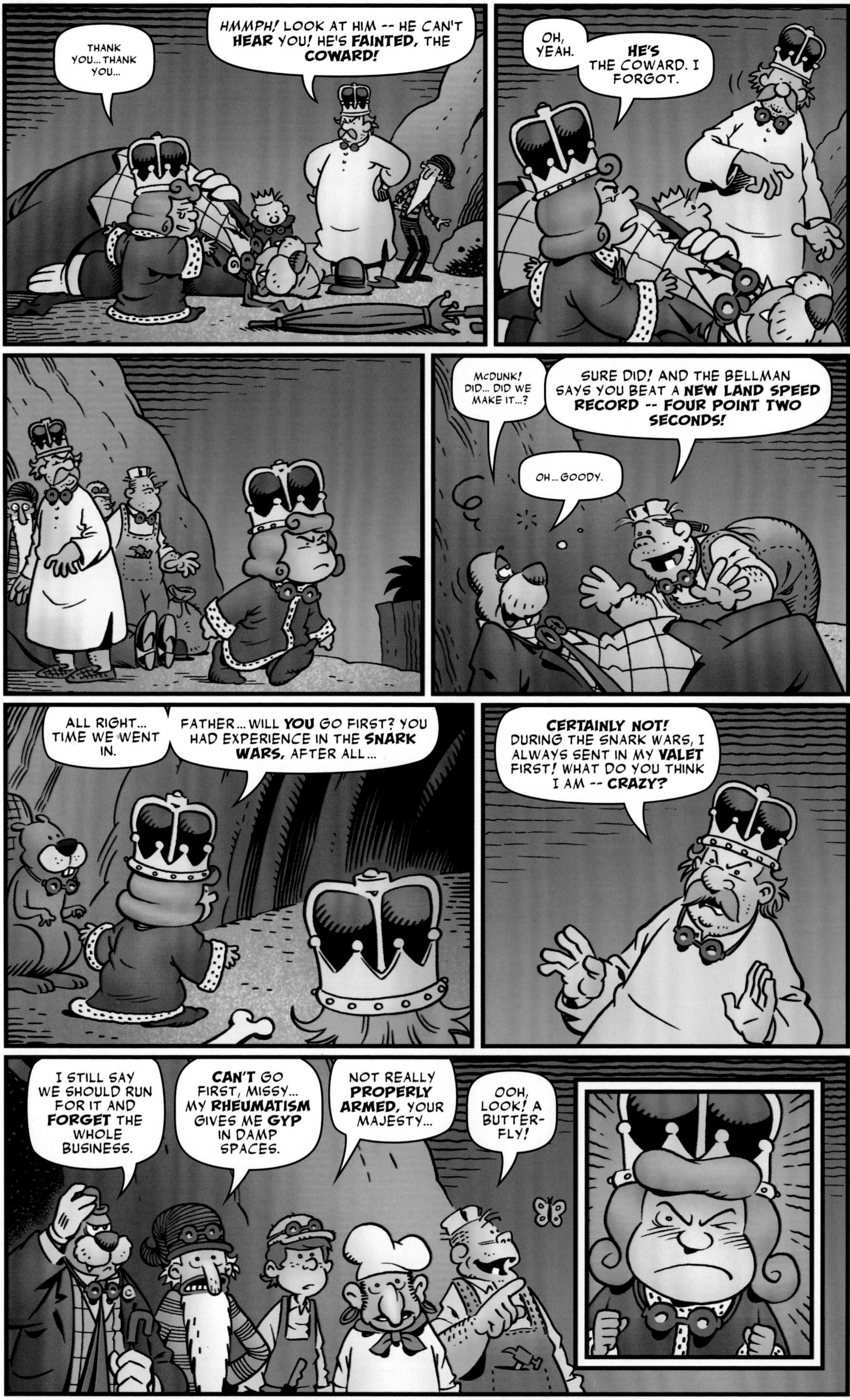
THANK YOU... THANK YOU...
HMMPH! LOOK AT HIM -- HE CAN'T HEAR YOU! HE'S FAINTED, THE COWARD!
OH, YEAH.
HE'S THE COWARD. I FORGOT.
McDUNK! DID... DID WE MAKE IT...?
SURE DID! AND THE BELLMAN SAYS YOU BEAT A NEW LAND SPEED RECORD -- FOUR POINT TWO SECONDS!
OH... GOODY.
ALL RIGHT... TIME WE WENT IN.
FATHER... WILL YOU GO FIRST? YOU HAD EXPERIENCE IN THE SNARK WARS, AFTER ALL...
CERTAINLY NOT! DURING THE SNARK WARS, I ALWAYS SENT IN MY VALET FIRST! WHAT DO YOU THINK I AM -- CRAZY?
I STILL SAY WE SHOULD RUN FOR IT AND FORGET THE WHOLE BUSINESS.
CAN'T GO FIRST, MISSY... MY RHEUMATISM GIVES ME GYP IN DAMP SPACES.
NOT REALLY PROPERLY ARMED, YOUR MAJESTY...
OOH, LOOK! A BUTTER-FLY!

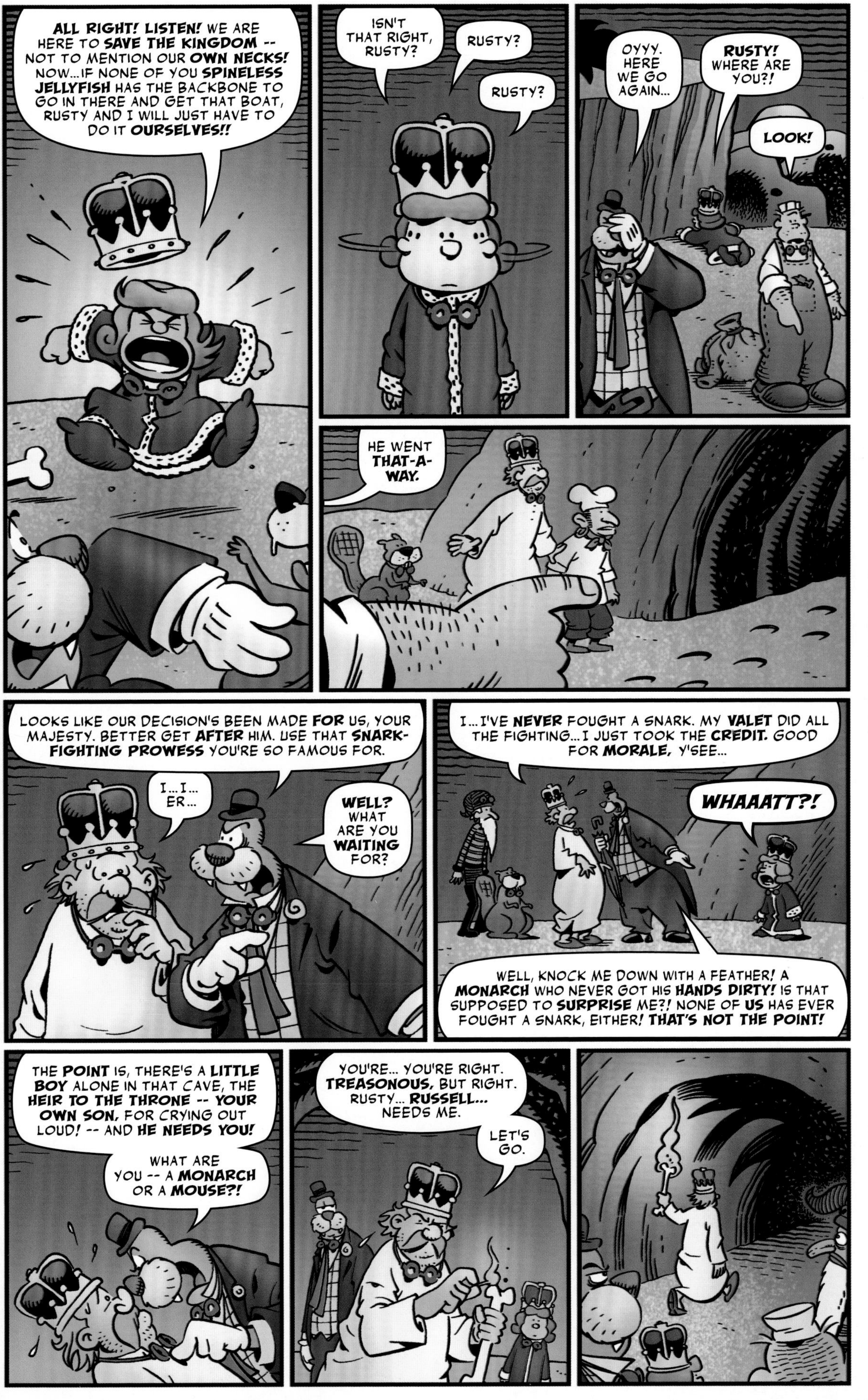
ALL RIGHT! LISTEN! WE ARE HERE TO SAVE THE KINGDOM -- NOT TO MENTION OUR OWN NECKS! NOW...IF NONE OF YOU SPINELESS JELLYFISH HAS THE BACKBONE TO GO IN THERE AND GET THAT BOAT, RUSTY AND I WILL JUST HAVE TO DO IT OURSELVES!!
ISN'T THAT RIGHT, RUSTY?
RUSTY?
RUSTY?
OYYY. HERE WE GO AGAIN...
RUSTY! WHERE ARE YOU?!
LOOK!
HE WENT THAT-A-WAY.
LOOKS LIKE OUR DECISION'S BEEN MADE FOR US, YOUR MAJESTY. BETTER GET AFTER HIM. USE THAT SNARK-FIGHTING PROWESS YOU'RE SO FAMOUS FOR.
I...I... ER...
WELL? WHAT ARE YOU WAITING FOR?
I...I'VE NEVER FOUGHT A SNARK. MY VALET DID ALL THE FIGHTING...I JUST TOOK THE CREDIT. GOOD FOR MORALE, Y'SEE...
WHAAATT?!
WELL, KNOCK ME DOWN WITH A FEATHER! A MONARCH WHO NEVER GOT HIS HANDS DIRTY! IS THAT SUPPOSED TO SURPRISE ME?! NONE OF US HAS EVER FOUGHT A SNARK, EITHER! THAT'S NOT THE POINT!
THE POINT IS, THERE'S A LITTLE BOY ALONE IN THAT CAVE, THE HEIR TO THE THRONE -- YOUR OWN SON, FOR CRYING OUT LOUD! -- AND HE NEEDS YOU!
WHAT ARE YOU -- A MONARCH OR A MOUSE?!
YOU'RE... YOU'RE RIGHT. TREASONOUS, BUT RIGHT. RUSTY... RUSSELL... NEEDS ME.
LET'S GO.

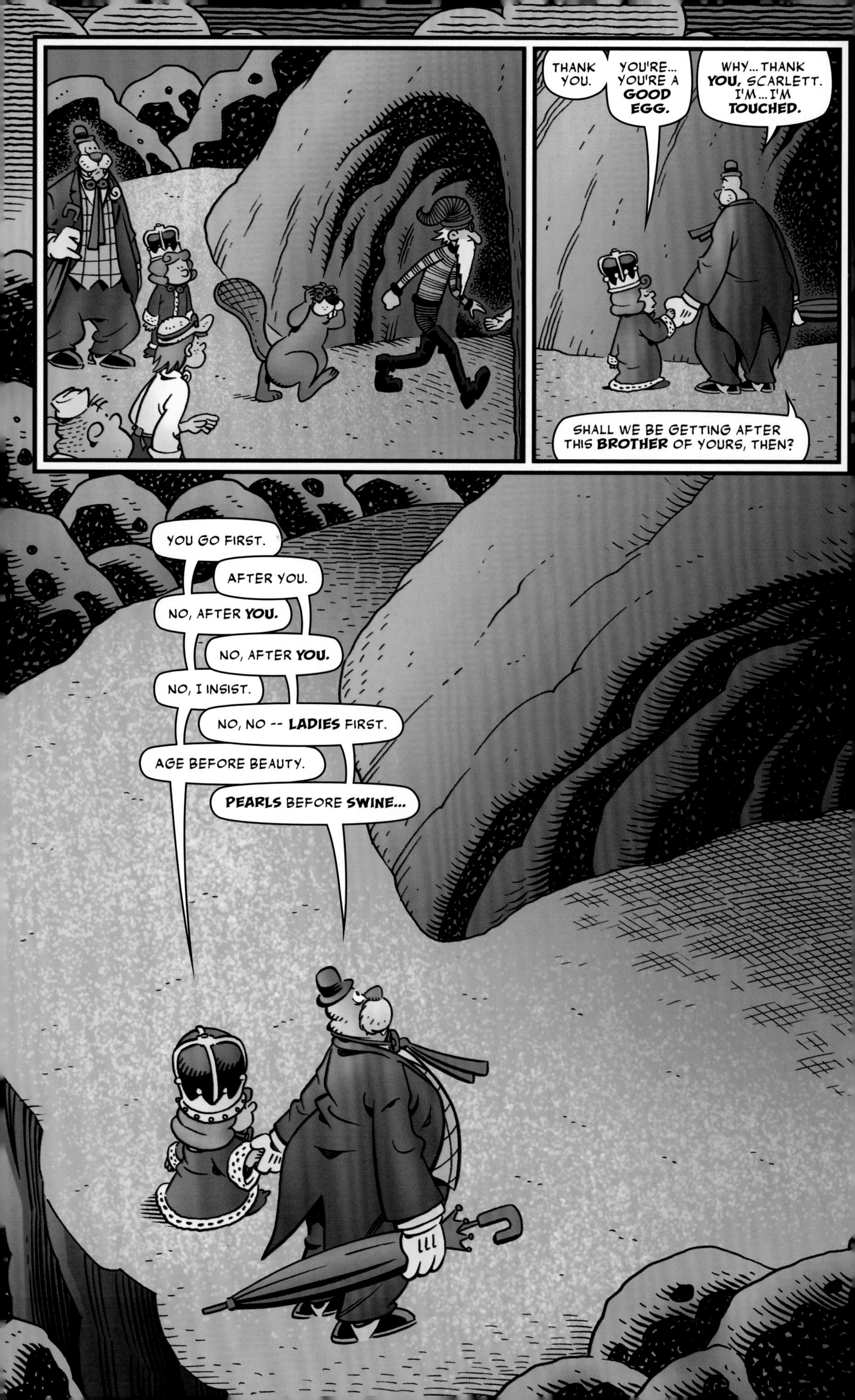
THANK YOU.
YOU'RE... YOU'RE A GOOD EGG.
WHY... THANK YOU, SCARLETT. I'M... I'M TOUCHED.
SHALL WE BE GETTING AFTER THIS BROTHER OF YOURS, THEN?
YOU GO FIRST.
AFTER YOU.
NO, AFTER YOU.
NO, AFTER YOU.
NO, I INSIST.
NO, NO -- LADIES FIRST.
AGE BEFORE BEAUTY.
PEARLS BEFORE SWINE...

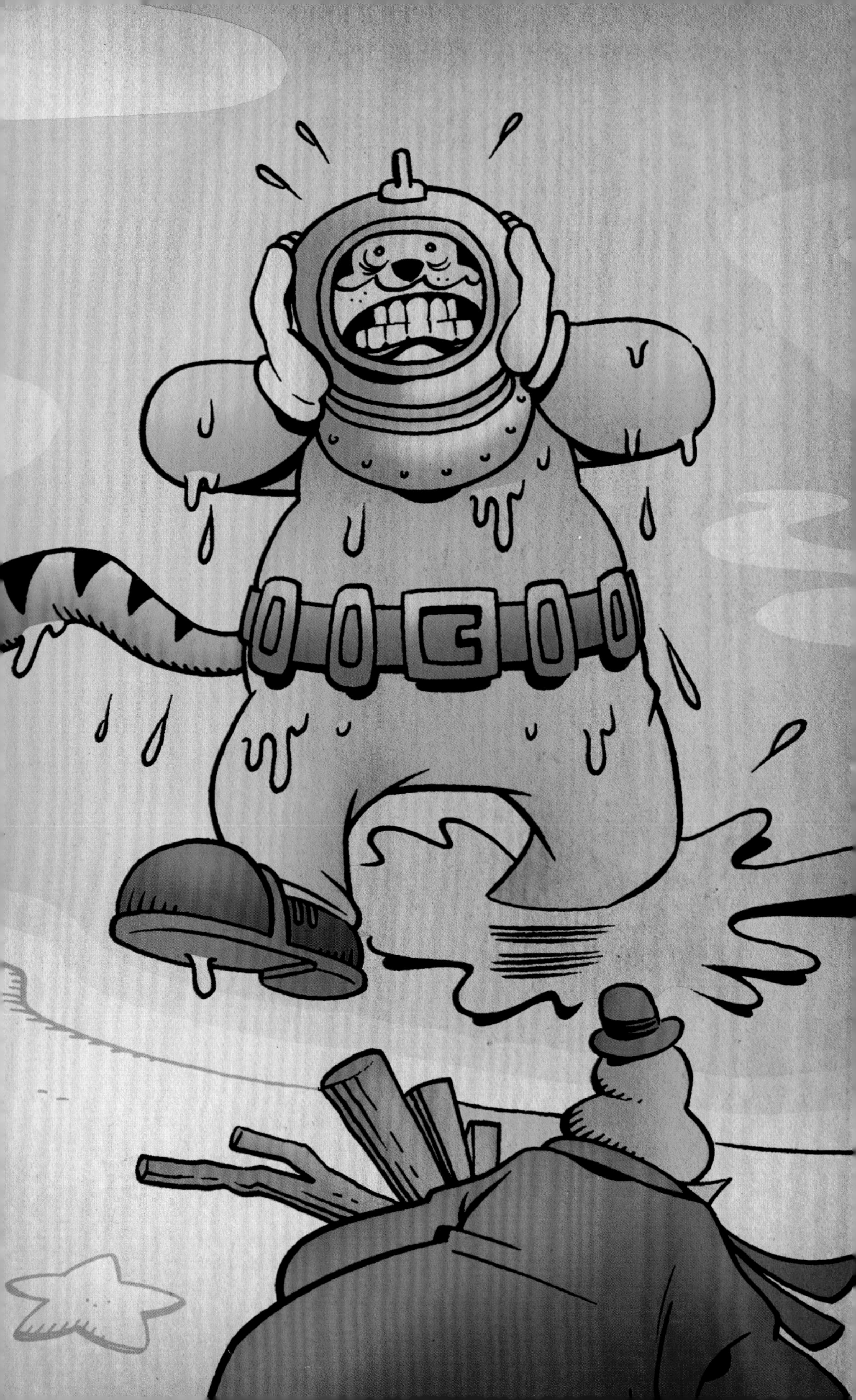

FIT THE TWELFTH

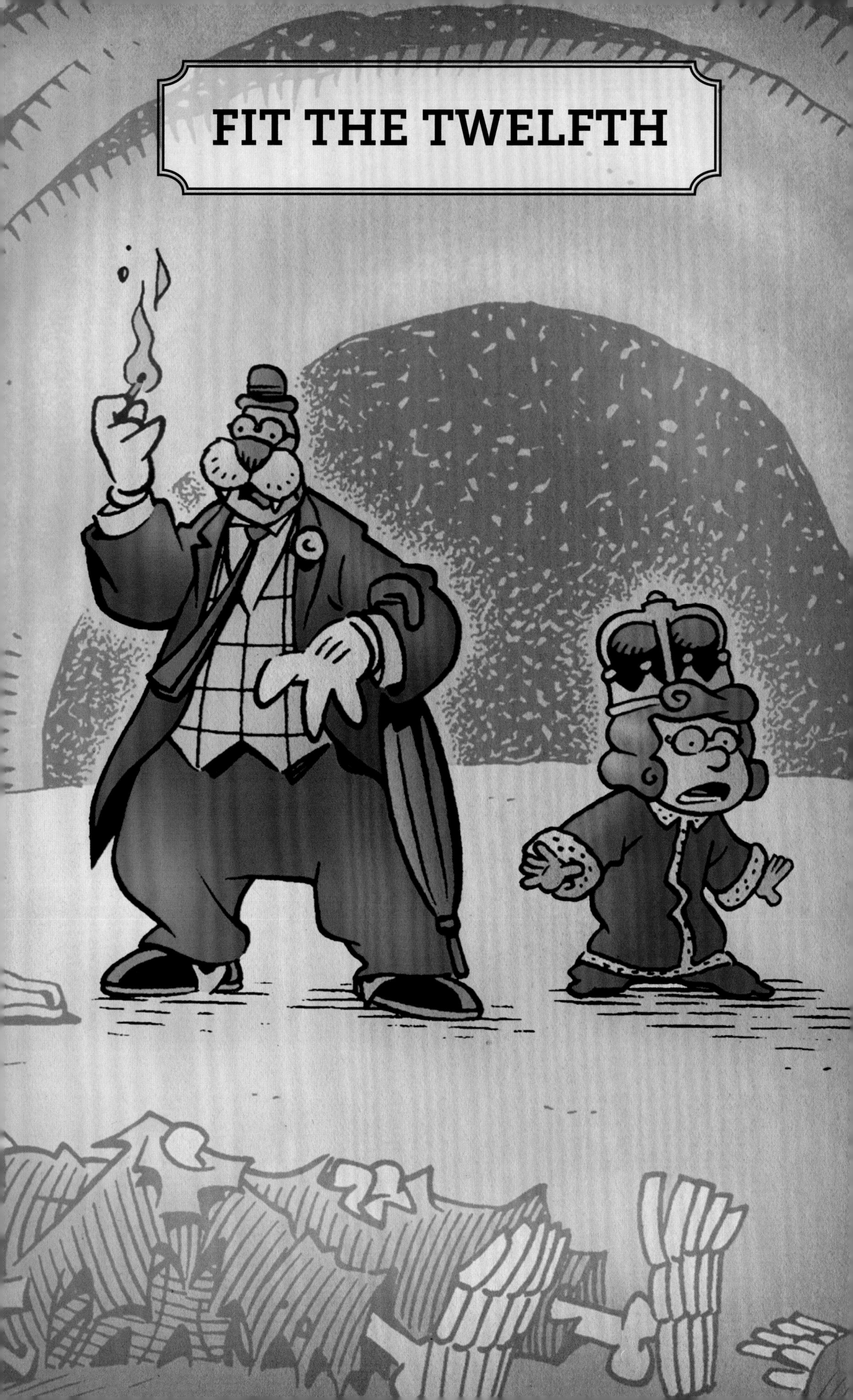

Our band of bold adventurers
Had gone inside the cave.
The hardest part of all of this:
Pretending to be **brave**...

D-DO YOU WANT ME TO **HOLD YOUR HAND**, YOUR M-MAJESTY?

N-NO... I'M O-OKAY...

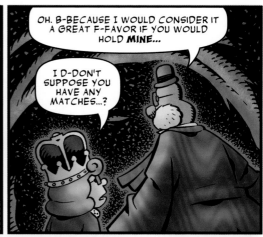

OH. B-BECAUSE I WOULD CONSIDER IT A GREAT F-FAVOR IF YOU WOULD HOLD **MINE**...

I D-DON'T SUPPOSE YOU HAVE ANY MATCHES...?

HMM... I USUALLY KEEP SOME IN MY **HAT**... HOPEFULLY THEY'RE STILL DRY...

THERE! WE HAVE LIGHT!

NOW ALL WE HAVE TO DO IS CATCH UP TO THE...

...OTHERS.

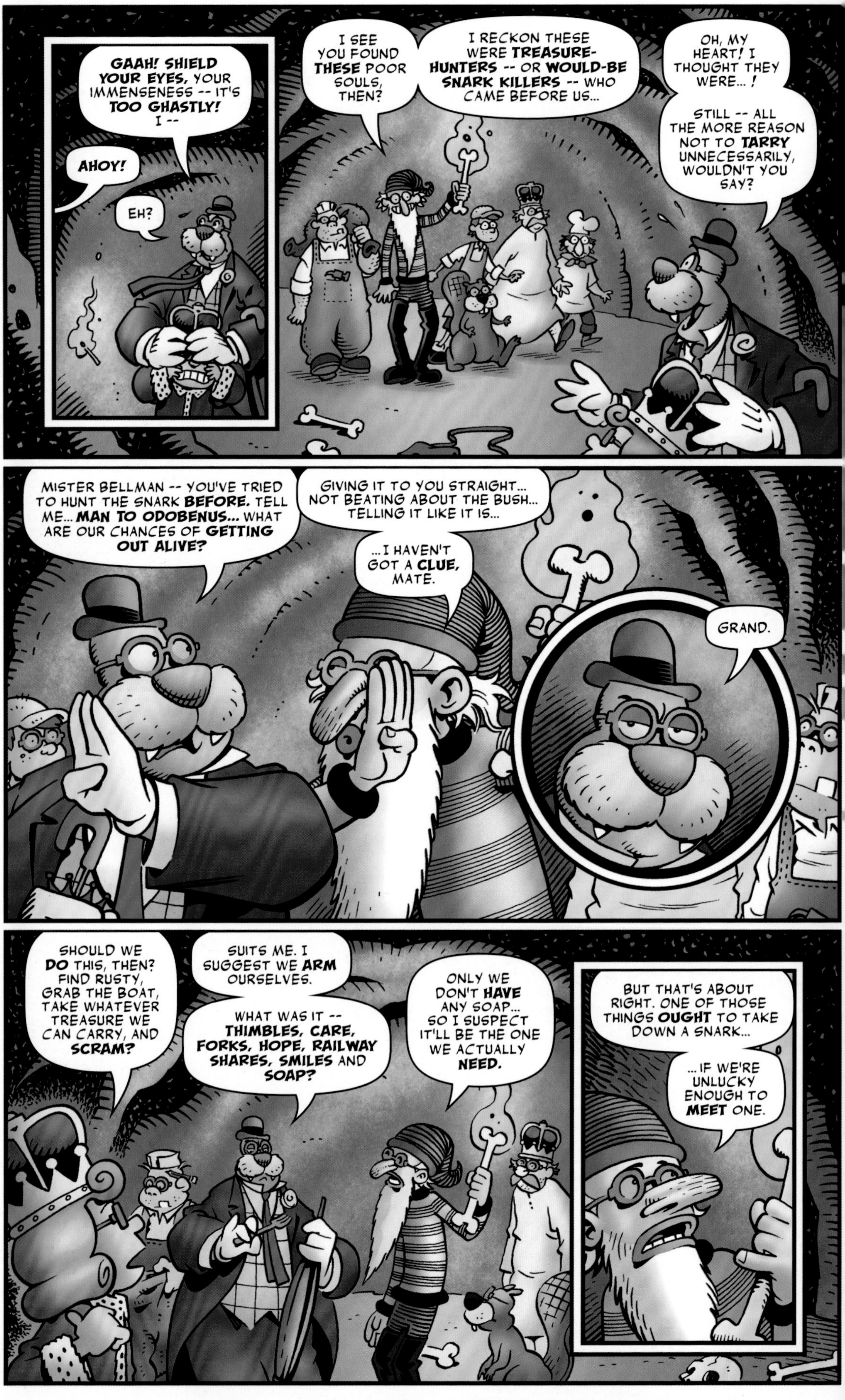
GAAH! SHIELD YOUR EYES, YOUR IMMENSENESS -- IT'S TOO GHASTLY! I --
AHOY!
EH?
I SEE YOU FOUND THESE POOR SOULS, THEN?
I RECKON THESE WERE TREASURE-HUNTERS -- OR WOULD-BE SNARK KILLERS -- WHO CAME BEFORE US...
OH, MY HEART! I THOUGHT THEY WERE... !
STILL -- ALL THE MORE REASON NOT TO TARRY UNNECESSARILY, WOULDN'T YOU SAY?
MISTER BELLMAN -- YOU'VE TRIED TO HUNT THE SNARK BEFORE. TELL ME... MAN TO ODOBENUS... WHAT ARE OUR CHANCES OF GETTING OUT ALIVE?
GIVING IT TO YOU STRAIGHT... NOT BEATING ABOUT THE BUSH... TELLING IT LIKE IT IS...
...I HAVEN'T GOT A CLUE, MATE.
GRAND.
SHOULD WE DO THIS, THEN? FIND RUSTY, GRAB THE BOAT, TAKE WHATEVER TREASURE WE CAN CARRY, AND SCRAM?
SUITS ME. I SUGGEST WE ARM OURSELVES.
WHAT WAS IT -- THIMBLES, CARE, FORKS, HOPE, RAILWAY SHARES, SMILES AND SOAP?
ONLY WE DON'T HAVE ANY SOAP... SO I SUSPECT IT'LL BE THE ONE WE ACTUALLY NEED.
BUT THAT'S ABOUT RIGHT. ONE OF THOSE THINGS OUGHT TO TAKE DOWN A SNARK...
...IF WE'RE UNLUCKY ENOUGH TO MEET ONE.

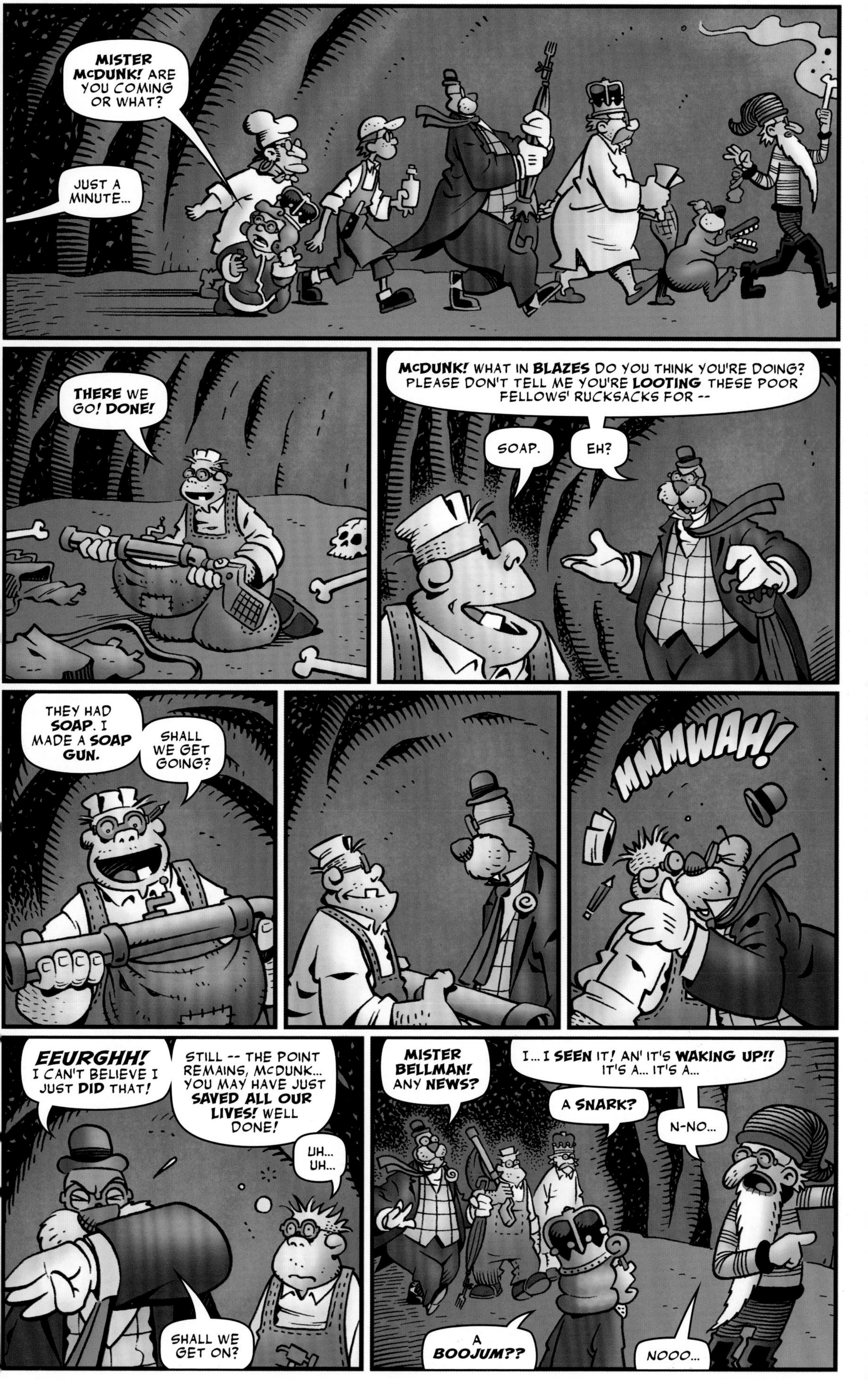
MISTER McDUNK! ARE YOU COMING OR WHAT?
JUST A MINUTE...
THERE WE GO! DONE!
McDUNK! WHAT IN BLAZES DO YOU THINK YOU'RE DOING? PLEASE DON'T TELL ME YOU'RE LOOTING THESE POOR FELLOWS' RUCKSACKS FOR --
SOAP.
EH?
THEY HAD SOAP. I MADE A SOAP GUN.
SHALL WE GET GOING?
MMMWAH!
EEURGHH! I CAN'T BELIEVE I JUST DID THAT!
STILL -- THE POINT REMAINS, McDUNK... YOU MAY HAVE JUST SAVED ALL OUR LIVES! WELL DONE!
UH... UH...
SHALL WE GET ON?
MISTER BELLMAN! ANY NEWS?
I... I SEEN IT! AN' IT'S WAKING UP!! IT'S A... IT'S A...
A SNARK?
N-NO...
A BOOJUM??
NOOO...

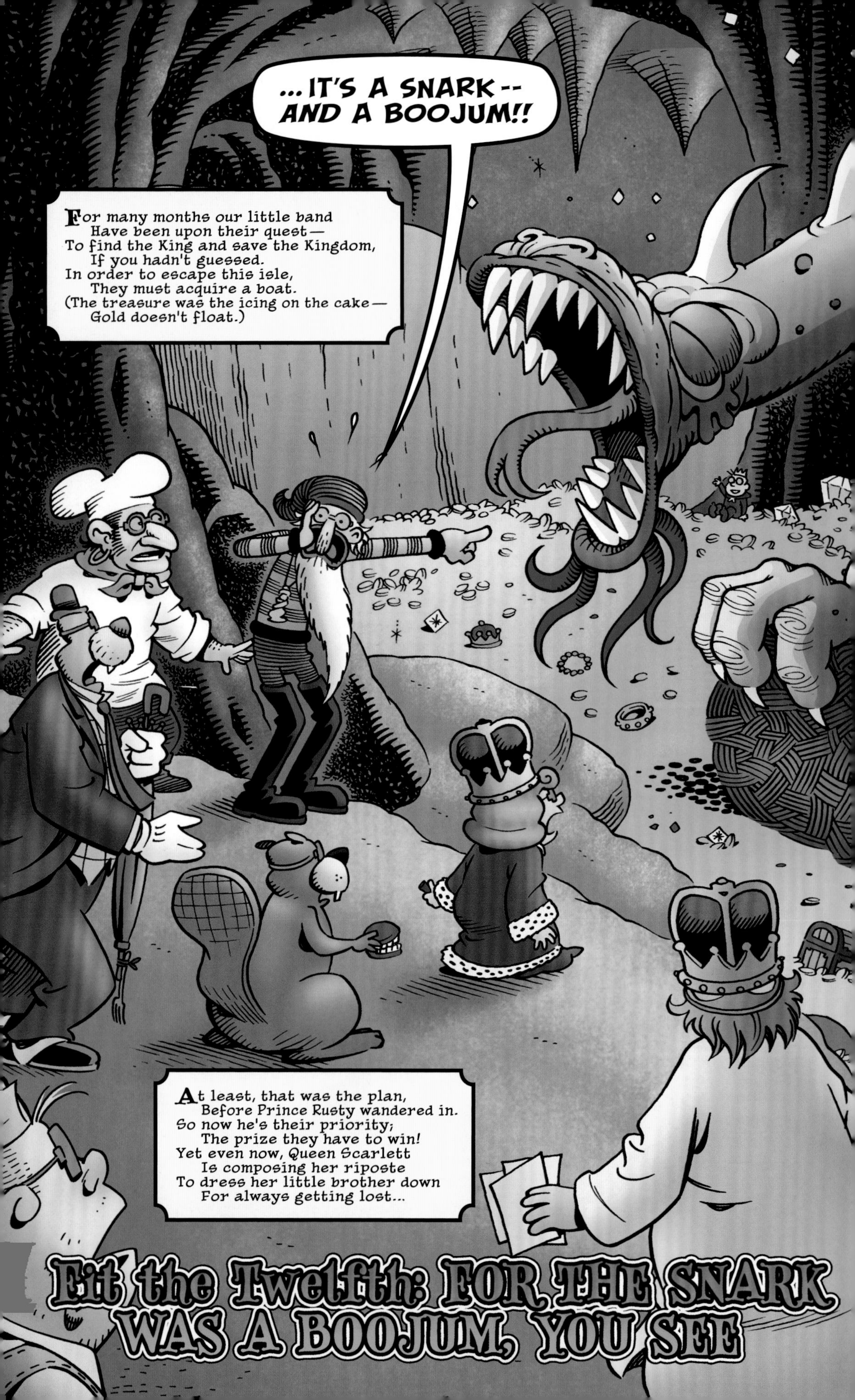
...IT'S A SNARK -- AND A BOOJUM!!
For many months our little band
Have been upon their quest—
To find the King and save the Kingdom,
If you hadn't guessed.
In order to escape this isle,
They must acquire a boat.
(The treasure was the icing on the cake—
Gold doesn't float.)
At least, that was the plan,
Before Prince Rusty wandered in.
So now he's their priority;
The prize they have to win!
Yet even now, Queen Scarlett
Is composing her riposte
To dress her little brother down
For always getting lost...
Fit the Twelfth: FOR THE SNARK WAS A BOOJUM, YOU SEE

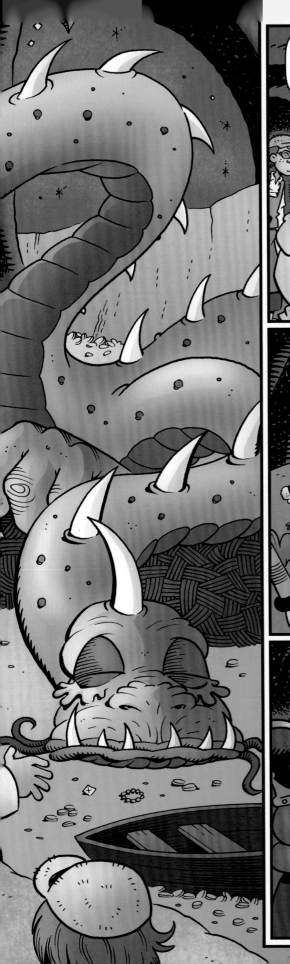

RIGHT -- YOU LOT CREATE A DIVERSION. *I* GRAB THE YOUNG PRINCE. THE CARPENTER **FIRES SOAP** AT THE BEAST WHILE **YOU BOYS** GRAB THE BOAT. THEN -- **BACK TO THE BEACH,** LICKETY SPLIT.

GOTCHA.

AND **ME**?

YOU?

BEST YOU STAY **OUT OF THE WAY,** MISSY. CAN'T BE **TRIPPING OVER** YOU, WHAT?

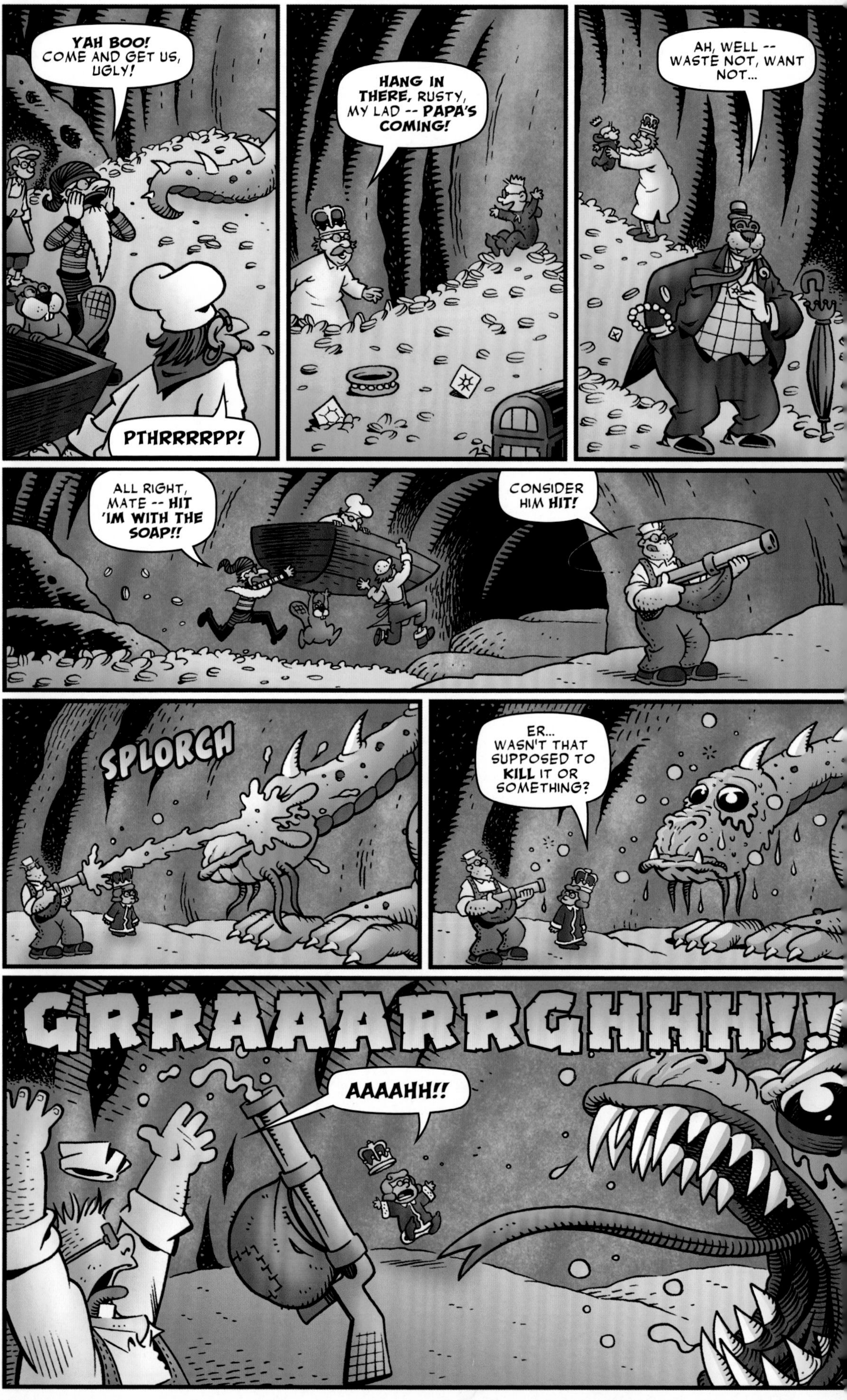
YAH BOO! COME AND GET US, UGLY!
PTHRRRRPP!
HANG IN THERE, RUSTY, MY LAD -- PAPA'S COMING!
AH, WELL -- WASTE NOT, WANT NOT...
ALL RIGHT, MATE -- HIT 'IM WITH THE SOAP!!
CONSIDER HIM HIT!
SPLORCH
ER... WASN'T THAT SUPPOSED TO KILL IT OR SOMETHING?
GRRAAAARRGHHH!!
AAAAHH!!

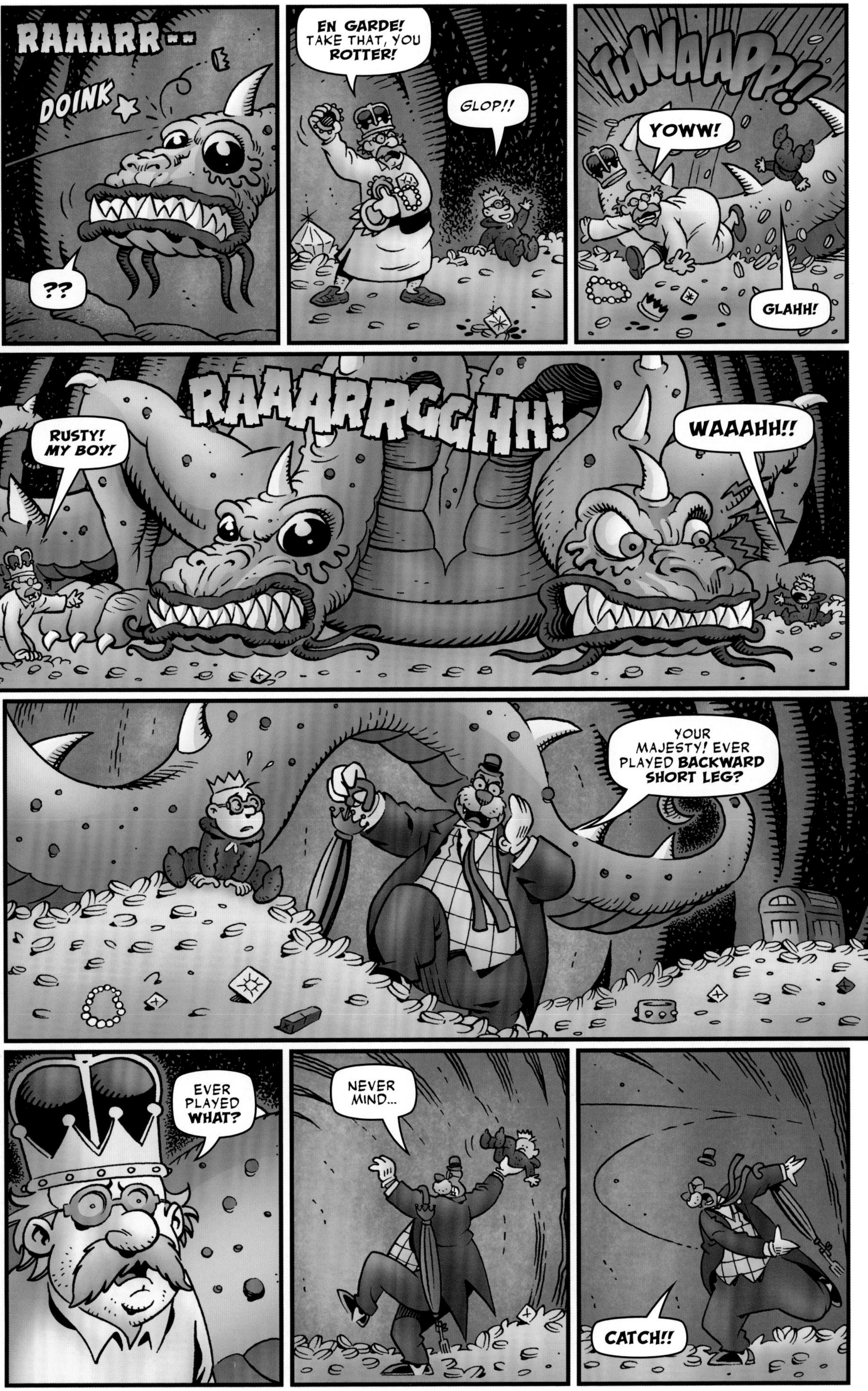
RAAARR..
DOINK
??
EN GARDE! TAKE THAT, YOU ROTTER!
GLOP!!
THWAAPP!!
YOWW!
GLAHH!
RAAARRGGHH!
RUSTY! MY BOY!
WAAAHH!!
YOUR MAJESTY! EVER PLAYED BACKWARD SHORT LEG?
EVER PLAYED WHAT?
NEVER MIND...
CATCH!!

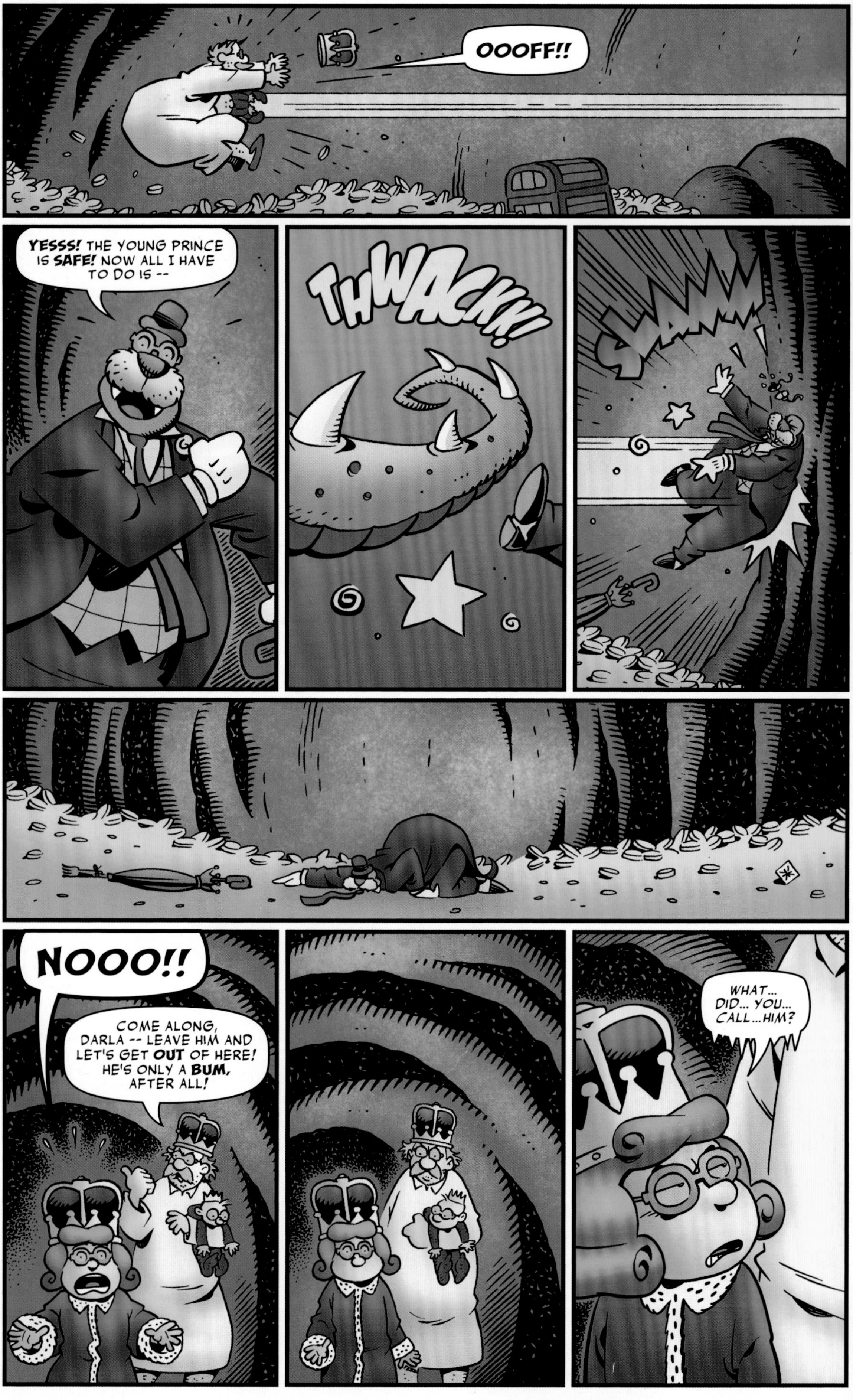
OOOFF!!
YESSS! THE YOUNG PRINCE IS SAFE! NOW ALL I HAVE TO DO IS --
THWACKK!!
NOOO!!
COME ALONG, DARLA -- LEAVE HIM AND LET'S GET OUT OF HERE! HE'S ONLY A BUM, AFTER ALL!
WHAT... DID... YOU... CALL...HIM?

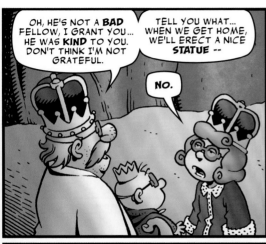

OH, HE'S NOT A **BAD** FELLOW, I GRANT YOU... HE WAS **KIND** TO YOU. DON'T THINK I'M NOT GRATEFUL.

TELL YOU WHAT... WHEN WE GET HOME, WE'LL ERECT A NICE **STATUE** --

NO.

"NO?"

NO. THAT... THAT AVARICIOUS... COWARDLY... RIDICULOUS... **WONDERFUL** WALRUS IS TEN TIMES THE MAN YOU'LL **EVER** BE.

I'M... I'M GOING TO GET HIM. AND YOU CAN'T STOP ME.

NONSENSE! NOW LISTEN HERE, YOUNG LADY -- I AM YOUR **KING,** AND I **ORDER** YOU TO --

HAH! YOU'RE **NOT** THE KING! YOU WON'T BE KING AGAIN UNTIL YOU RETURN TO **RECLAIM YOUR THRONE!** I'M STILL OFFICIALLY THE **QUEEN** UNTIL THAT HAPPENS --

-- AND YOU... ARE... OVERRULED!!

B-BUT YOU SAID IT YOURSELF! HE'S... HE'S **GREEDY! LAZY! WORTHLESS!!**

AND HE WAS **THERE** FOR ME. I KNOW THAT'S HARD FOR YOU TO GET YOUR HEAD AROUND, BUT HE WAS.

HE WAS THERE FOR ME...

...AND I'M GOING TO BE THERE FOR **HIM.**

RAAAARRGHH!!

QUICK, YOUR MAJESTY! IT'S **NOT SAFE** STANDING HERE -- WE'LL WAIT AT THE MOUTH OF THE CAVE! McDUNK'S GOT HER BACK!

BUT IF SHE'S NOT BACK IN **FIVE MINUTES** -- WE'LL **HAVE** TO GO **WITHOUT HER!**

B-BUT... BUT...

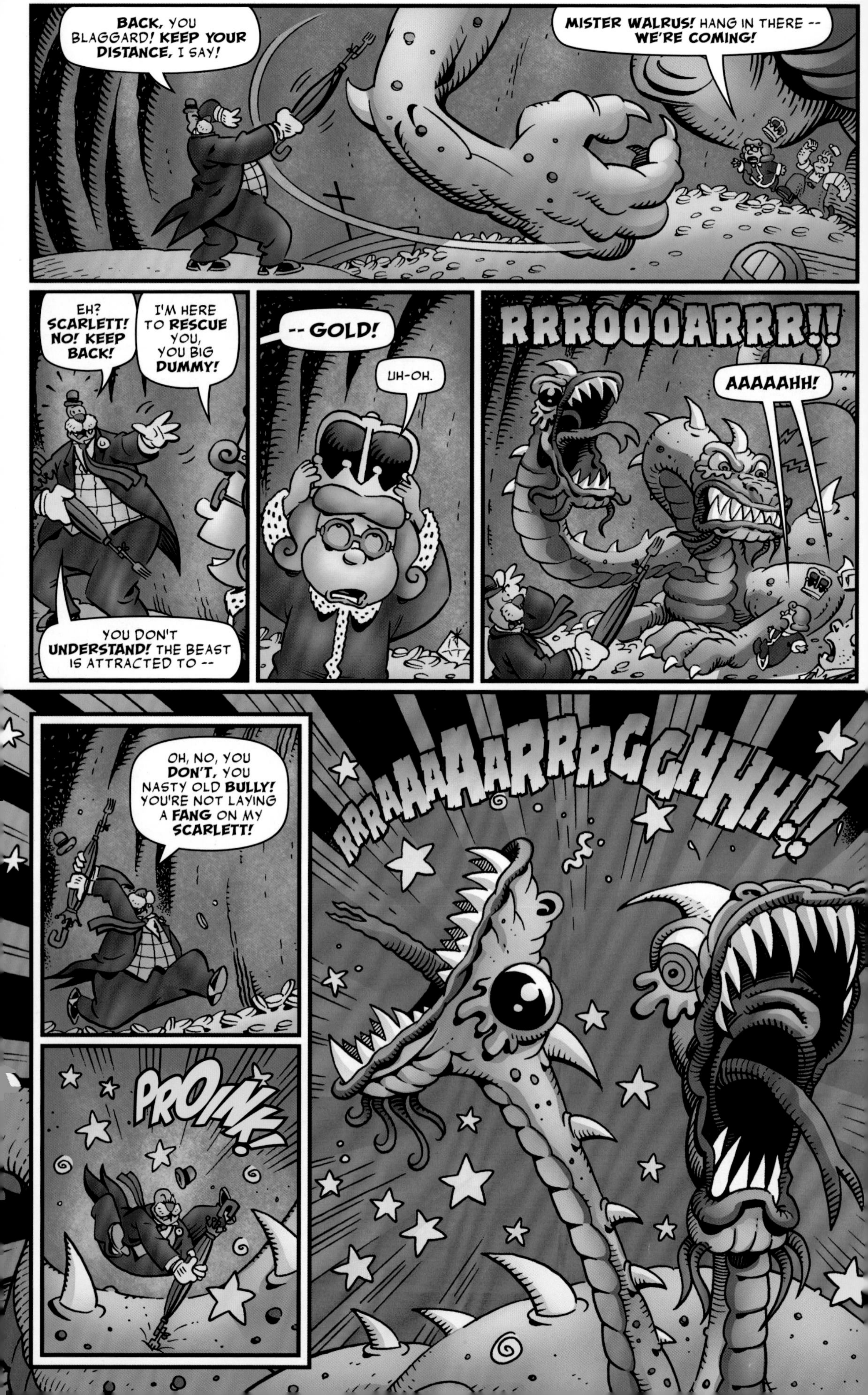
BACK, YOU BLAGGARD! KEEP YOUR DISTANCE, I SAY!
MISTER WALRUS! HANG IN THERE -- WE'RE COMING!
EH? SCARLETT! NO! KEEP BACK!
I'M HERE TO RESCUE YOU, YOU BIG DUMMY!
YOU DON'T UNDERSTAND! THE BEAST IS ATTRACTED TO --
-- GOLD!
UH-OH.
RRROOOARRRR!!
AAAAAHH!
OH, NO, YOU DON'T, YOU NASTY OLD BULLY! YOU'RE NOT LAYING A FANG ON MY SCARLETT!
RRRAAAAAARRRRGGHHHH!!
PROINK!

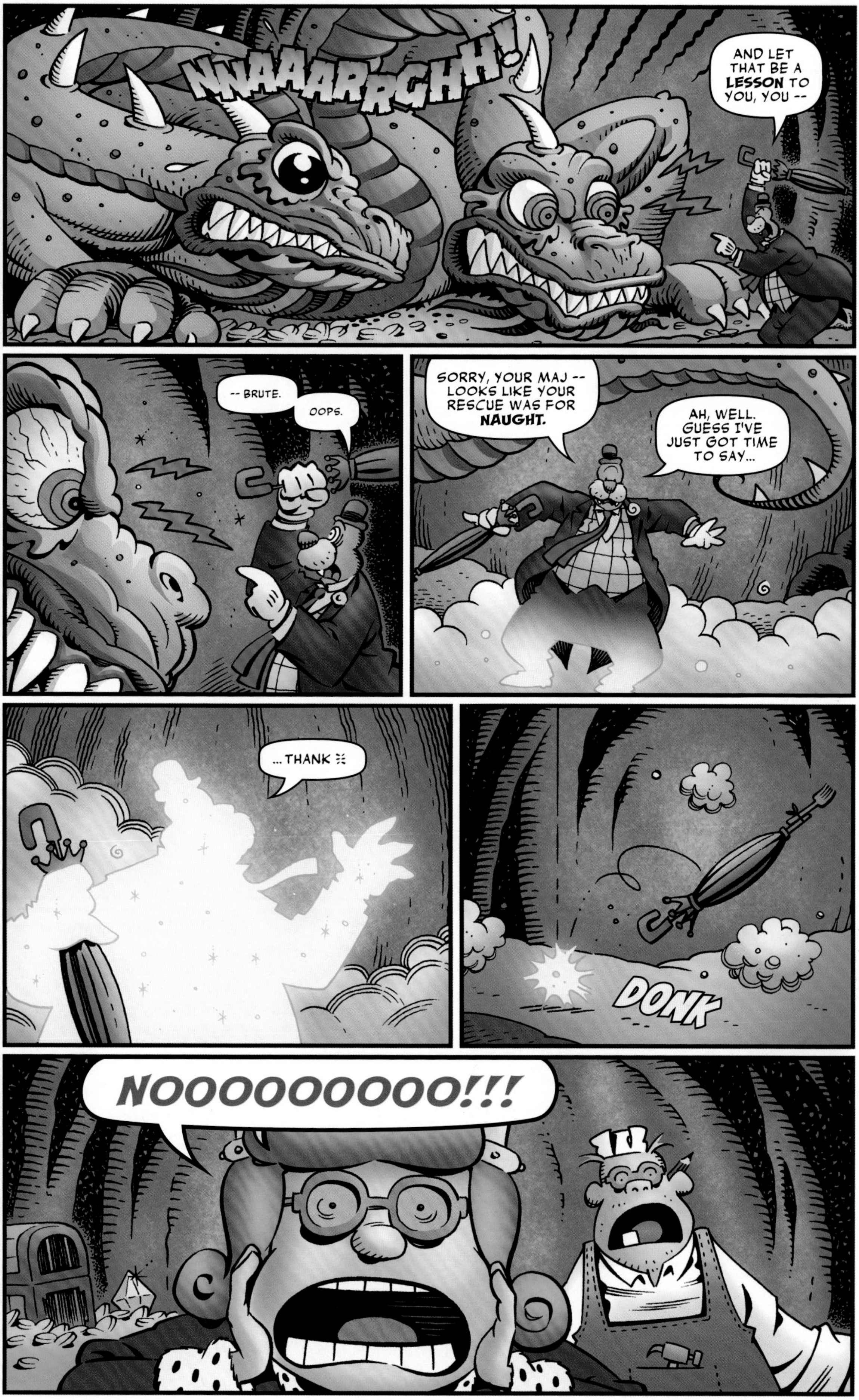
NNAAAARRRGHH!
AND LET THAT BE A **LESSON** TO YOU, YOU --
-- BRUTE.
OOPS.
SORRY, YOUR MAJ -- LOOKS LIKE YOUR RESCUE WAS FOR **NAUGHT.**
AH, WELL. GUESS I'VE JUST GOT TIME TO SAY...
...THANK
DONK
NOOOOOOOOO!!!

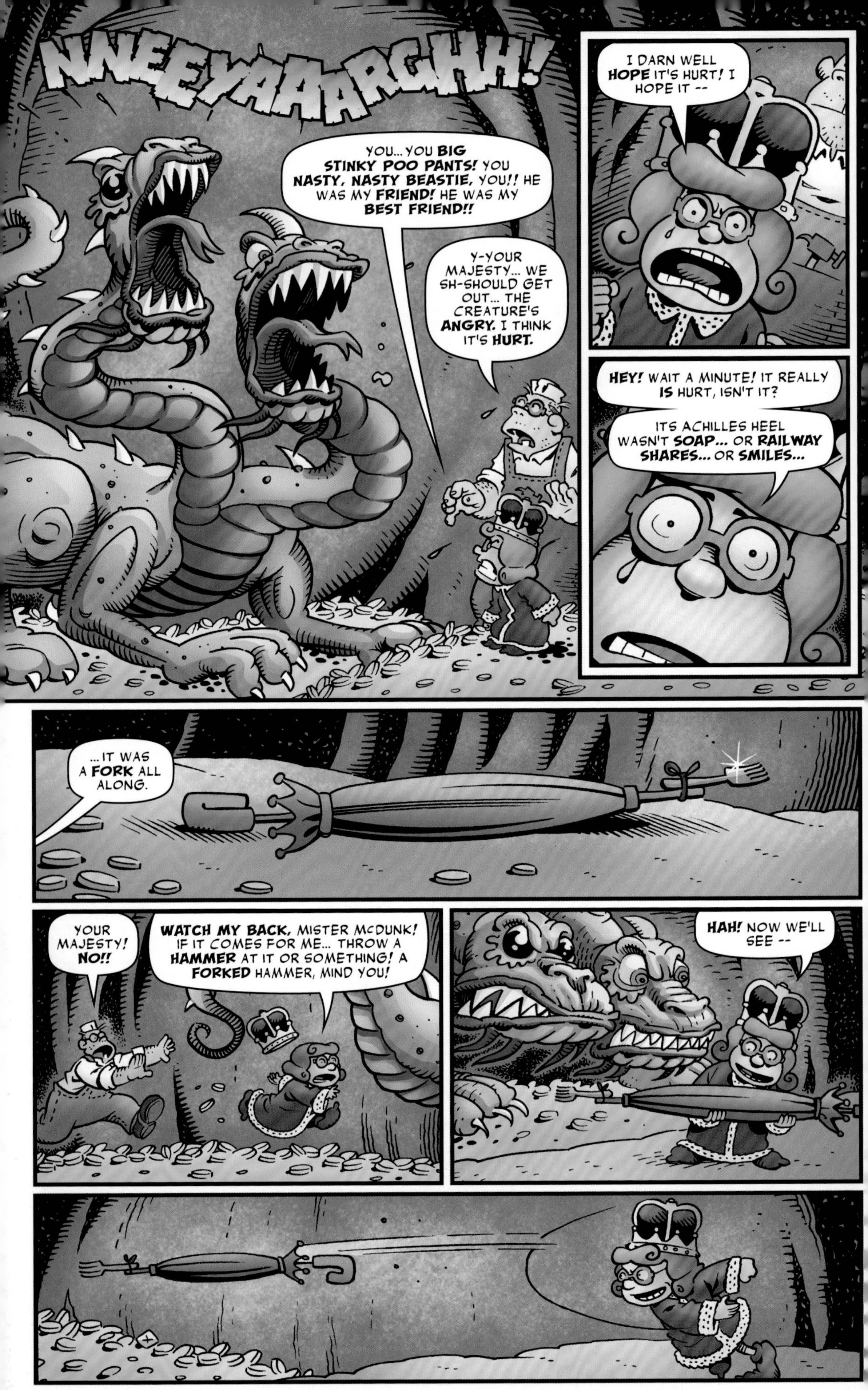
NNEEYAAARGHH!
YOU... YOU BIG STINKY POO PANTS! YOU NASTY, NASTY BEASTIE, YOU!! HE WAS MY FRIEND! HE WAS MY BEST FRIEND!!
Y-YOUR MAJESTY... WE SH-SHOULD GET OUT... THE CREATURE'S ANGRY. I THINK IT'S HURT.
I DARN WELL HOPE IT'S HURT! I HOPE IT --
HEY! WAIT A MINUTE! IT REALLY IS HURT, ISN'T IT?
ITS ACHILLES HEEL WASN'T SOAP... OR RAILWAY SHARES... OR SMILES...
...IT WAS A FORK ALL ALONG.
YOUR MAJESTY! NO!!
WATCH MY BACK, MISTER McDUNK! IF IT COMES FOR ME... THROW A HAMMER AT IT OR SOMETHING! A FORKED HAMMER, MIND YOU!
HAH! NOW WE'LL SEE --

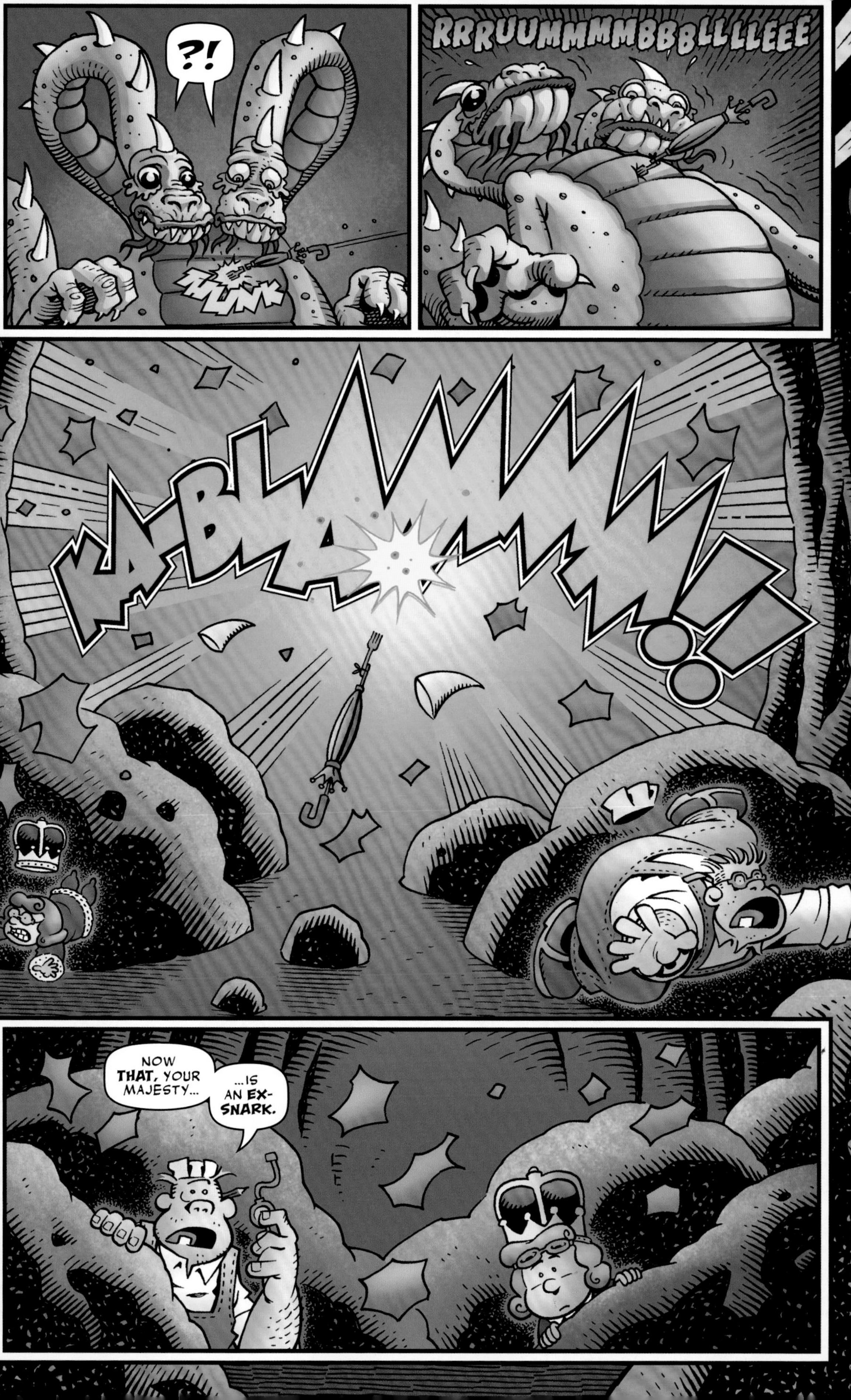
?!
THUNK
RRRUUMMMMBBBLLLLEEE
KABLAM!!
NOW THAT, YOUR MAJESTY...
...IS AN EX-SNARK.

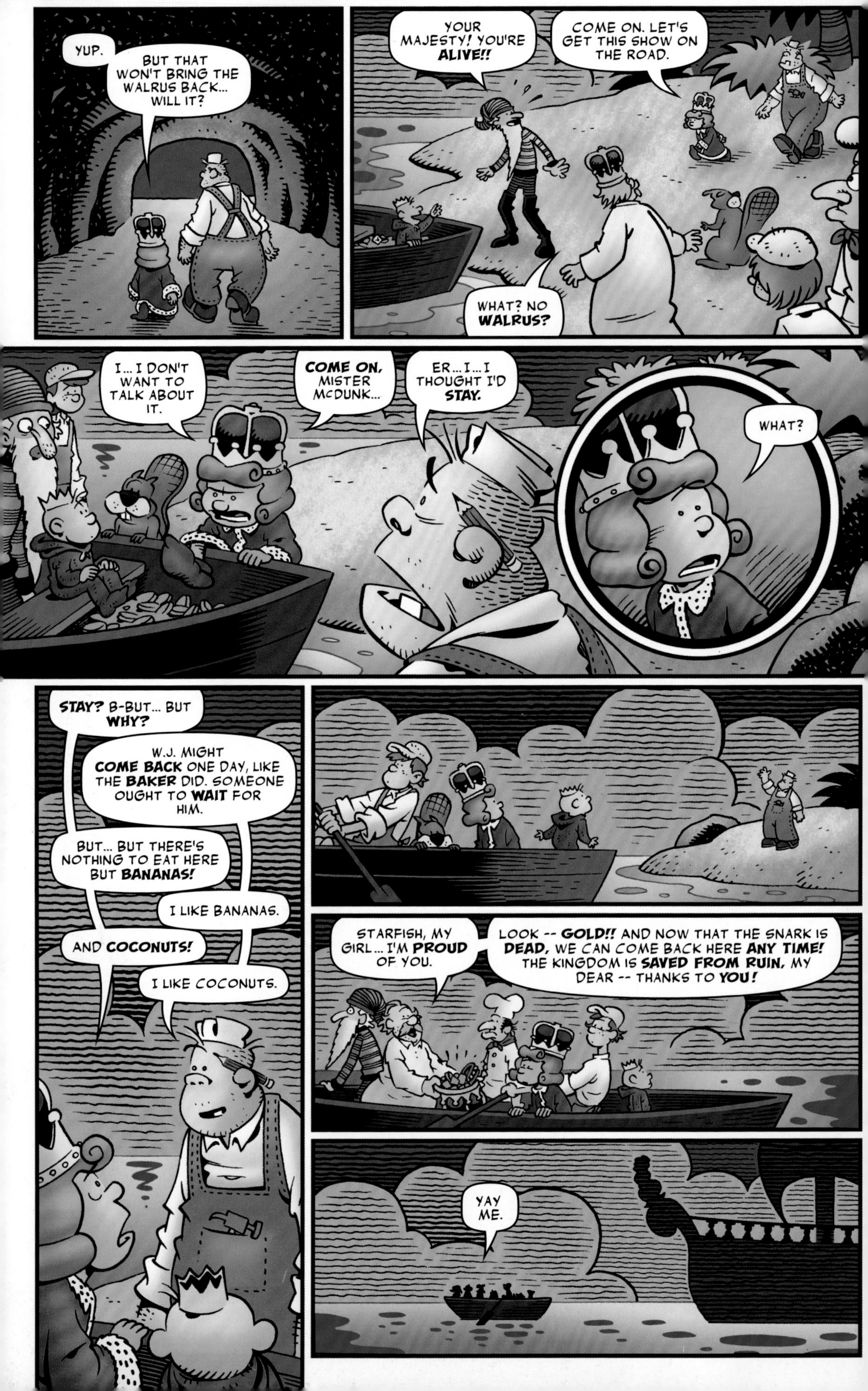
YUP.
BUT THAT WON'T BRING THE WALRUS BACK... WILL IT?
YOUR MAJESTY! YOU'RE ALIVE!!
COME ON. LET'S GET THIS SHOW ON THE ROAD.
WHAT? NO WALRUS?
I... I DON'T WANT TO TALK ABOUT IT.
COME ON, MISTER McDUNK...
ER... I... I THOUGHT I'D STAY.
WHAT?
STAY? B-BUT... BUT WHY?
W.J. MIGHT COME BACK ONE DAY, LIKE THE BAKER DID. SOMEONE OUGHT TO WAIT FOR HIM.
BUT... BUT THERE'S NOTHING TO EAT HERE BUT BANANAS!
I LIKE BANANAS.
AND COCONUTS!
I LIKE COCONUTS.
STARFISH, MY GIRL... I'M PROUD OF YOU.
LOOK -- GOLD!! AND NOW THAT THE SNARK IS DEAD, WE CAN COME BACK HERE ANY TIME! THE KINGDOM IS SAVED FROM RUIN, MY DEAR -- THANKS TO YOU!
YAY ME.

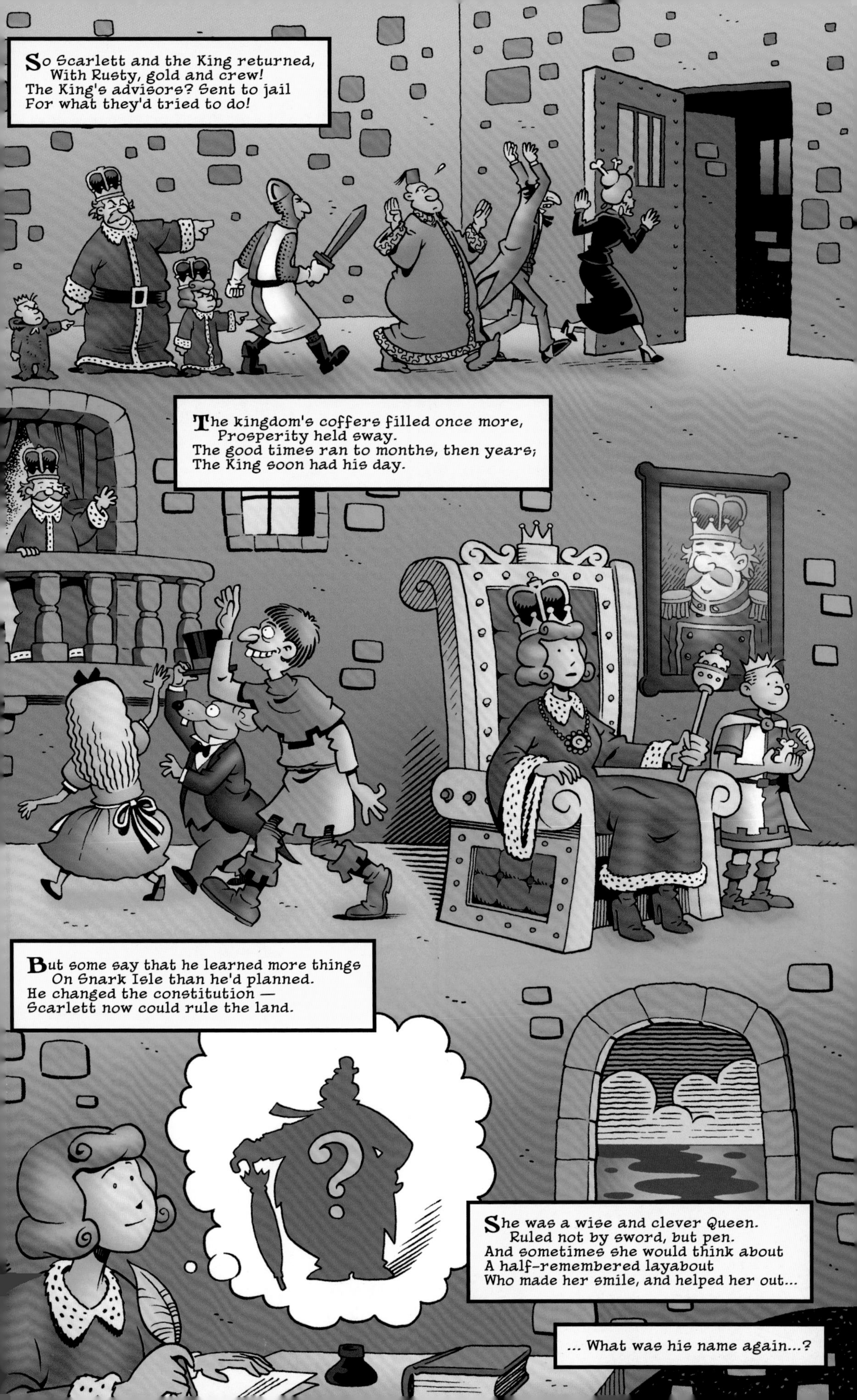
So Scarlett and the King returned,
With Rusty, gold and crew!
The King's advisors? Sent to jail
For what they'd tried to do!
The kingdom's coffers filled once more,
Prosperity held sway.
The good times ran to months, then years;
The King soon had his day.
But some say that he learned more things
On Snark Isle than he'd planned.
He changed the constitution —
Scarlett now could rule the land.
She was a wise and clever Queen.
Ruled not by sword, but pen.
And sometimes she would think about
A half-remembered layabout
Who made her smile, and helped her out...
... What was his name again...?

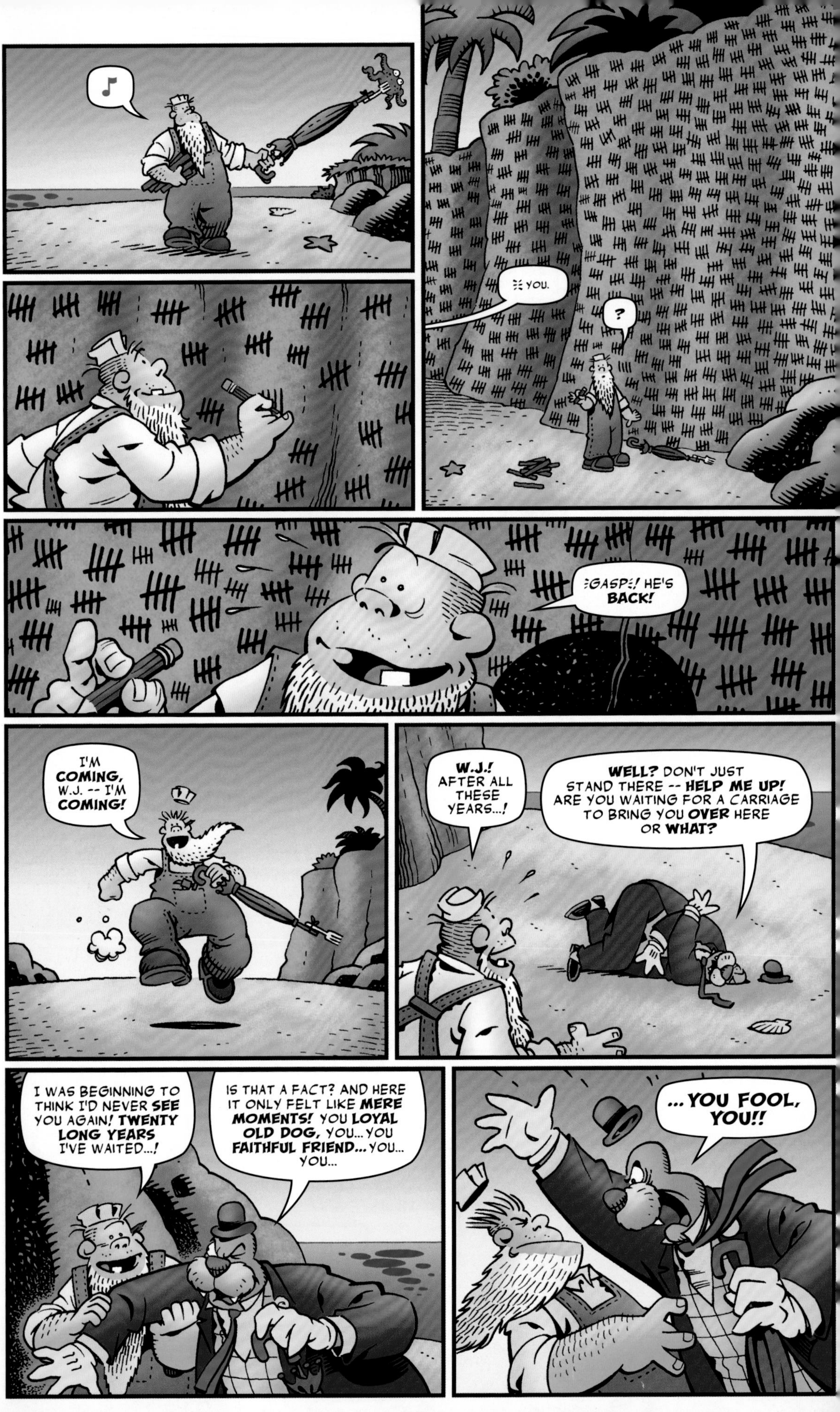
♪
:: YOU.
?
:GASP:! HE'S BACK!
I'M COMING, W.J. -- I'M COMING!
W.J.! AFTER ALL THESE YEARS...!
WELL? DON'T JUST STAND THERE -- HELP ME UP! ARE YOU WAITING FOR A CARRIAGE TO BRING YOU OVER HERE OR WHAT?
I WAS BEGINNING TO THINK I'D NEVER SEE YOU AGAIN! TWENTY LONG YEARS I'VE WAITED...!
IS THAT A FACT? AND HERE IT ONLY FELT LIKE MERE MOMENTS! YOU LOYAL OLD DOG, YOU... YOU FAITHFUL FRIEND... YOU... YOU...
...YOU FOOL, YOU!!

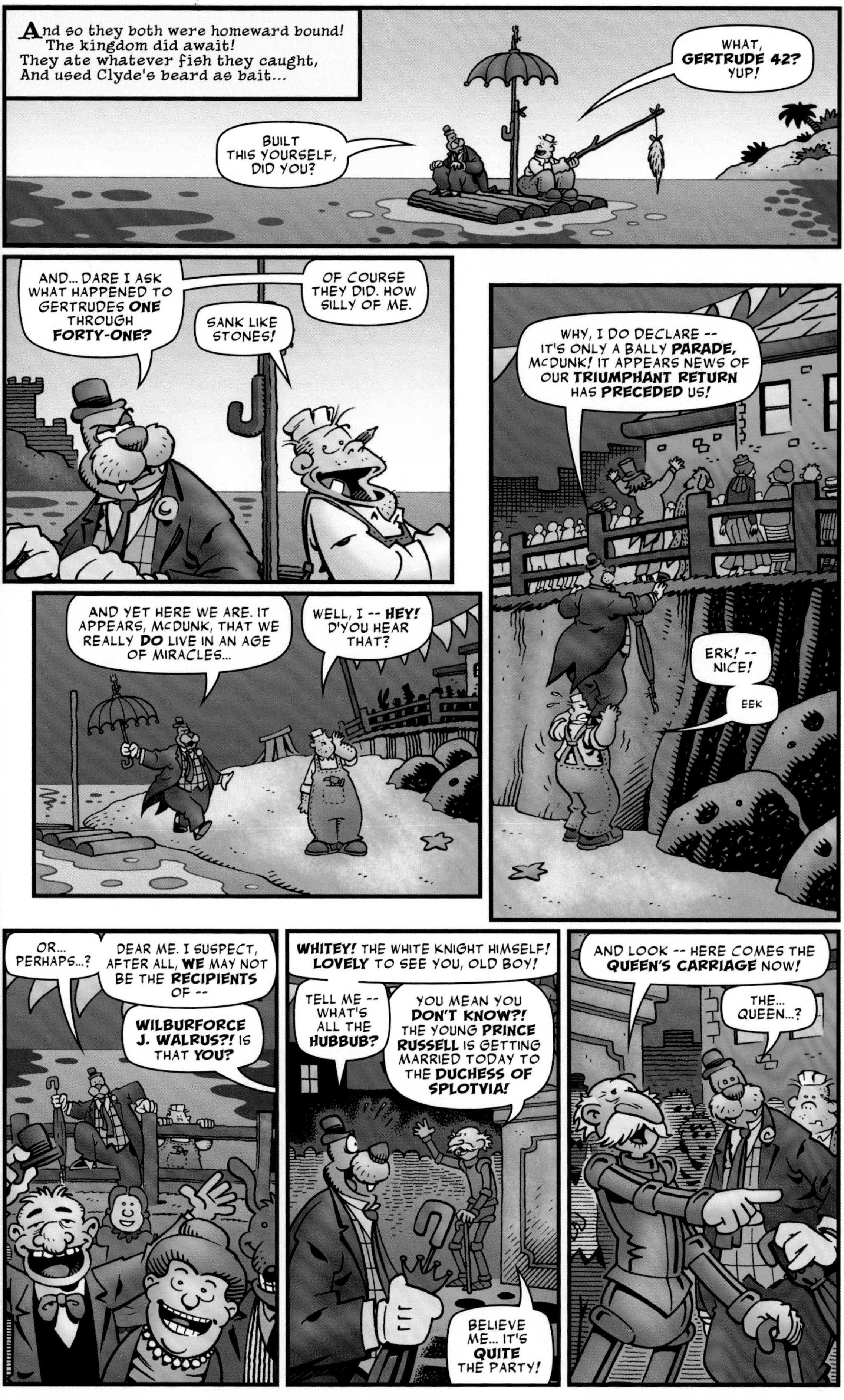

And so they both were homeward bound!
The kingdom did await!
They ate whatever fish they caught,
And used Clyde's beard as bait...
WHAT, GERTRUDE 42? YUP!
BUILT THIS YOURSELF, DID YOU?
AND... DARE I ASK WHAT HAPPENED TO GERTRUDES ONE THROUGH FORTY-ONE?
SANK LIKE STONES!
OF COURSE THEY DID. HOW SILLY OF ME.
AND YET HERE WE ARE. IT APPEARS, McDUNK, THAT WE REALLY DO LIVE IN AN AGE OF MIRACLES...
WELL, I -- HEY! D'YOU HEAR THAT?
WHY, I DO DECLARE -- IT'S ONLY A BALLY PARADE, McDUNK! IT APPEARS NEWS OF OUR TRIUMPHANT RETURN HAS PRECEDED US!
ERK! -- NICE!
EEK
OR... PERHAPS...?
DEAR ME. I SUSPECT, AFTER ALL, WE MAY NOT BE THE RECIPIENTS OF --
WILBURFORCE J. WALRUS?! IS THAT YOU?
WHITEY! THE WHITE KNIGHT HIMSELF! LOVELY TO SEE YOU, OLD BOY!
TELL ME -- WHAT'S ALL THE HUBBUB?
YOU MEAN YOU DON'T KNOW?! THE YOUNG PRINCE RUSSELL IS GETTING MARRIED TODAY TO THE DUCHESS OF SPLOTVIA!
BELIEVE ME... IT'S QUITE THE PARTY!
AND LOOK -- HERE COMES THE QUEEN'S CARRIAGE NOW!
THE... QUEEN...?

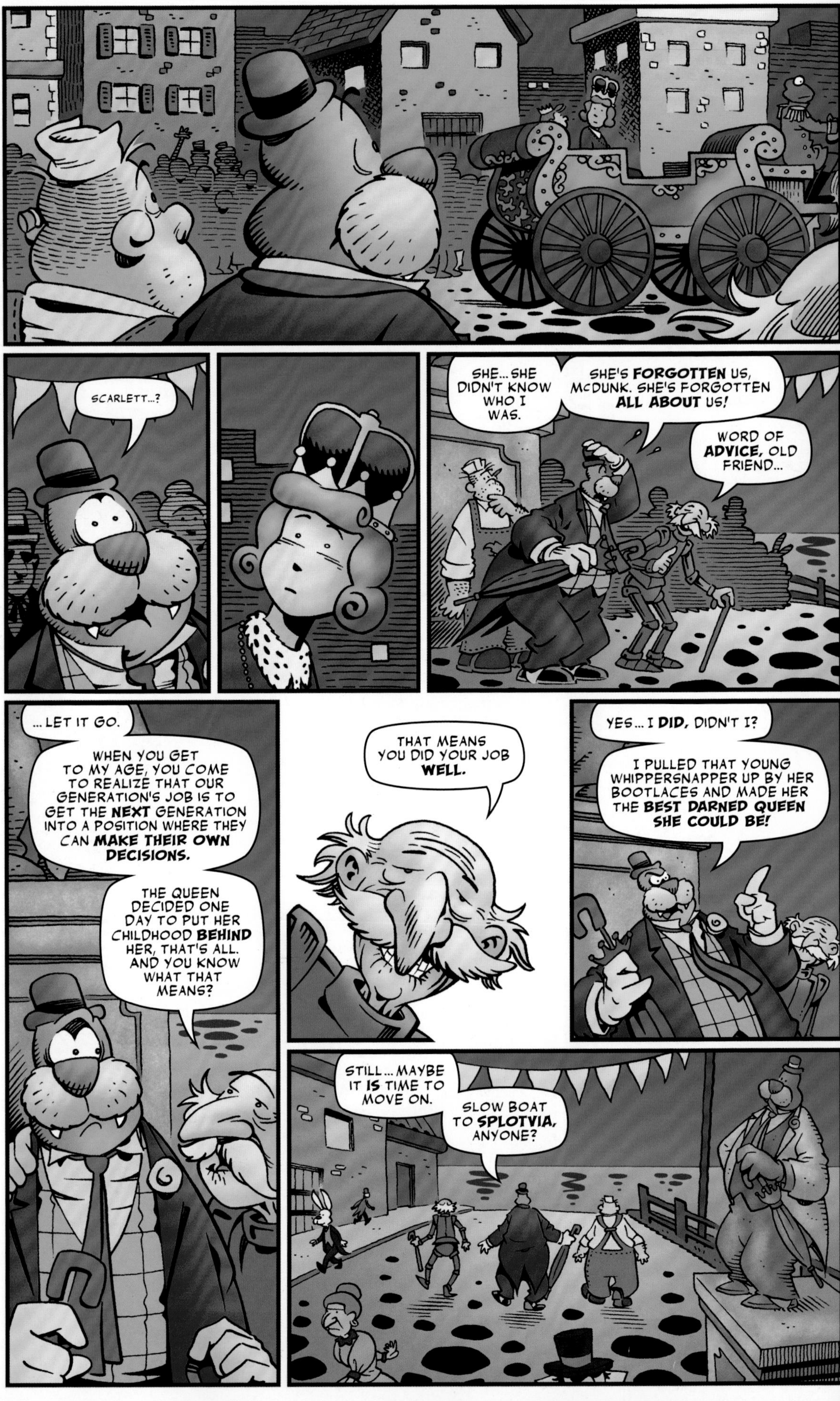
SCARLETT...?
SHE... SHE DIDN'T KNOW WHO I WAS.
SHE'S FORGOTTEN US, McDUNK. SHE'S FORGOTTEN ALL ABOUT US!
WORD OF ADVICE, OLD FRIEND...
... LET IT GO.
WHEN YOU GET TO MY AGE, YOU COME TO REALIZE THAT OUR GENERATION'S JOB IS TO GET THE NEXT GENERATION INTO A POSITION WHERE THEY CAN MAKE THEIR OWN DECISIONS.
THE QUEEN DECIDED ONE DAY TO PUT HER CHILDHOOD BEHIND HER, THAT'S ALL. AND YOU KNOW WHAT THAT MEANS?
THAT MEANS YOU DID YOUR JOB WELL.
YES... I DID, DIDN'T I?
I PULLED THAT YOUNG WHIPPERSNAPPER UP BY HER BOOTLACES AND MADE HER THE BEST DARNED QUEEN SHE COULD BE!
STILL... MAYBE IT IS TIME TO MOVE ON.
SLOW BOAT TO SPLOTVIA, ANYONE?

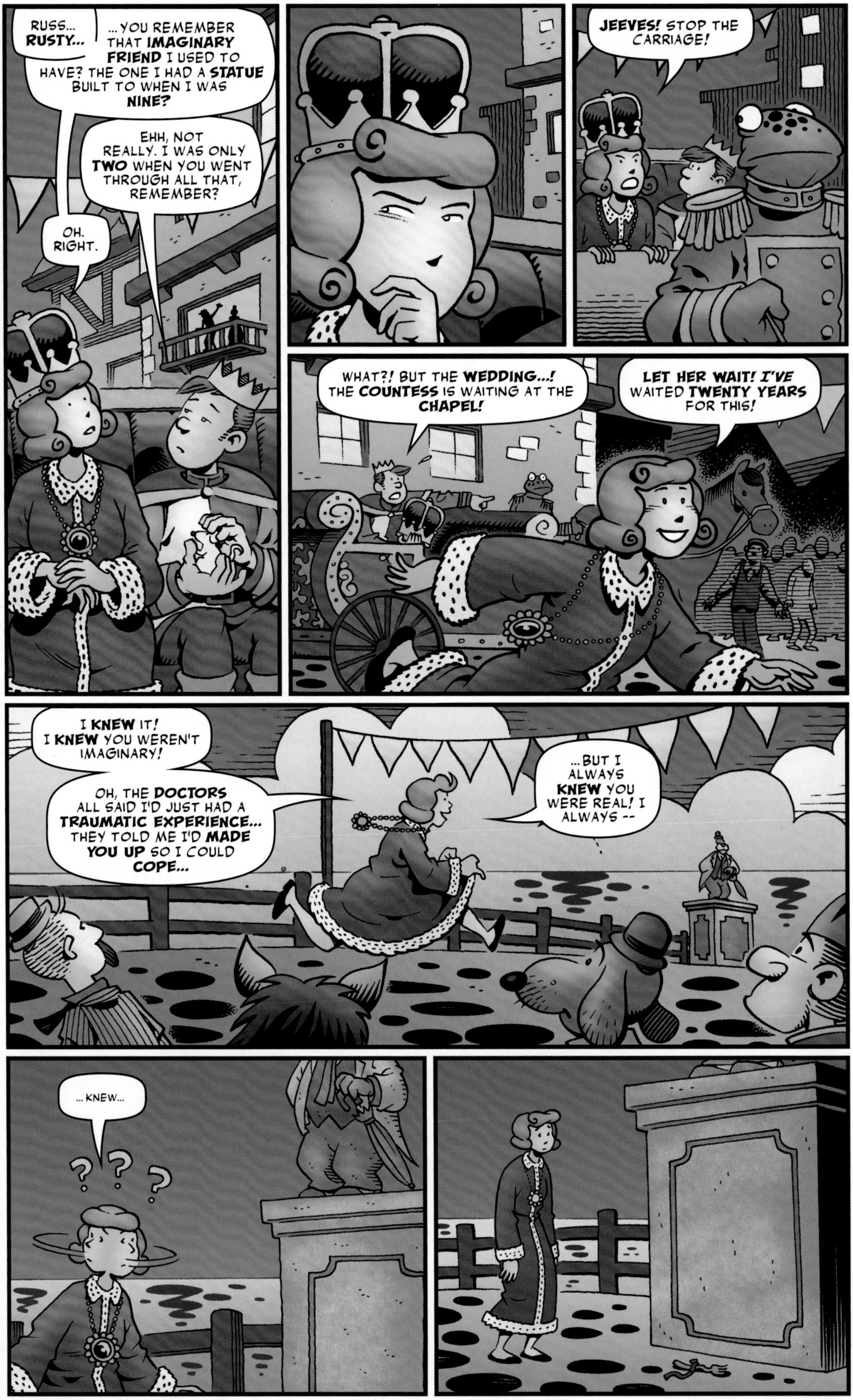
RUSS... RUSTY...
...YOU REMEMBER THAT IMAGINARY FRIEND I USED TO HAVE? THE ONE I HAD A STATUE BUILT TO WHEN I WAS NINE?
EHH, NOT REALLY. I WAS ONLY TWO WHEN YOU WENT THROUGH ALL THAT, REMEMBER?
OH. RIGHT.
JEEVES! STOP THE CARRIAGE!
WHAT?! BUT THE WEDDING...! THE COUNTESS IS WAITING AT THE CHAPEL!
LET HER WAIT! I'VE WAITED TWENTY YEARS FOR THIS!
I KNEW IT! I KNEW YOU WEREN'T IMAGINARY!
OH, THE DOCTORS ALL SAID I'D JUST HAD A TRAUMATIC EXPERIENCE... THEY TOLD ME I'D MADE YOU UP SO I COULD COPE...
...BUT I ALWAYS KNEW YOU WERE REAL! I ALWAYS --
... KNEW...

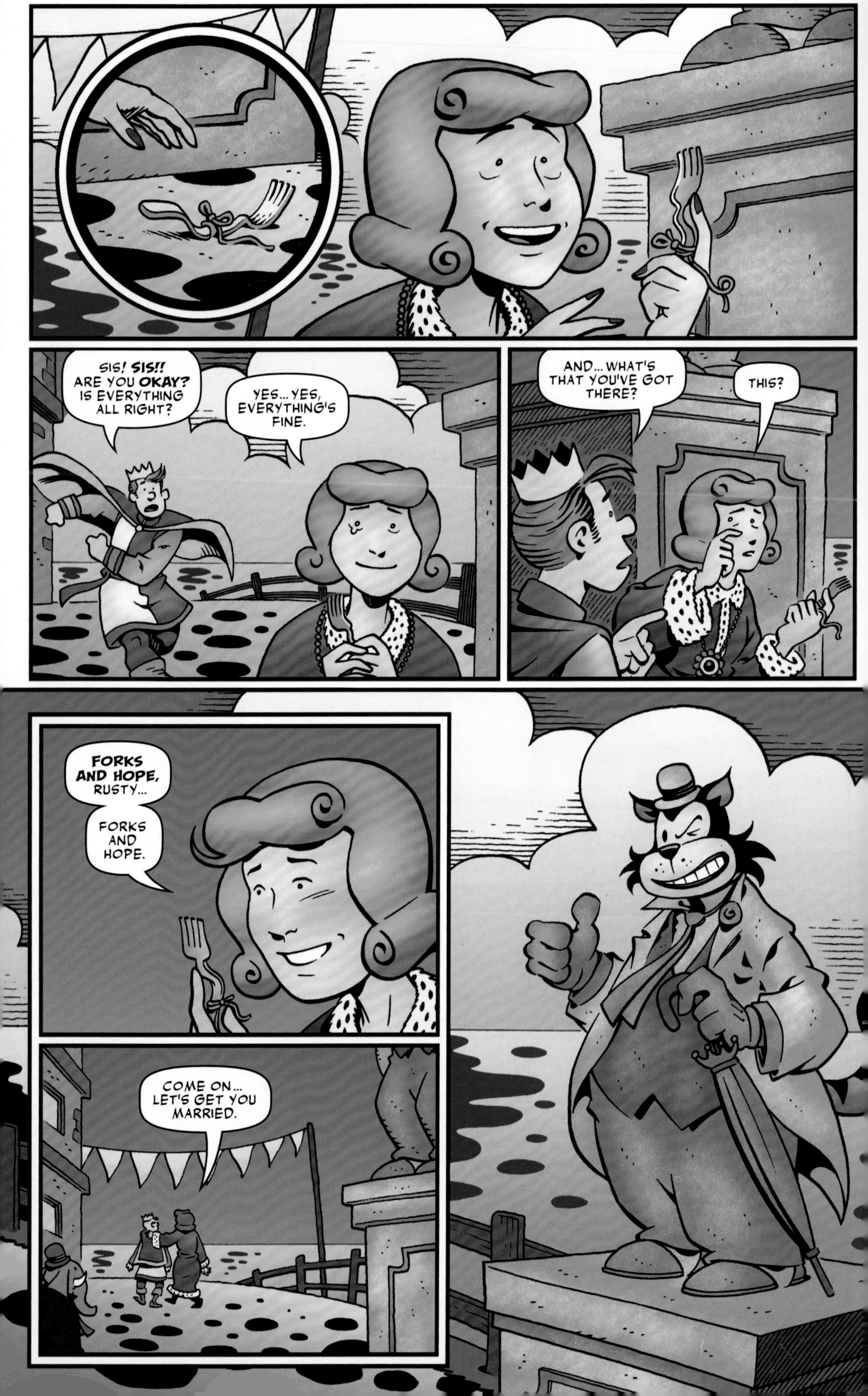
SIS! SIS!! ARE YOU OKAY? IS EVERYTHING ALL RIGHT?
YES... YES, EVERYTHING'S FINE.
AND... WHAT'S THAT YOU'VE GOT THERE?
THIS?
FORKS AND HOPE, RUSTY...
FORKS AND HOPE.
COME ON... LET'S GET YOU MARRIED.

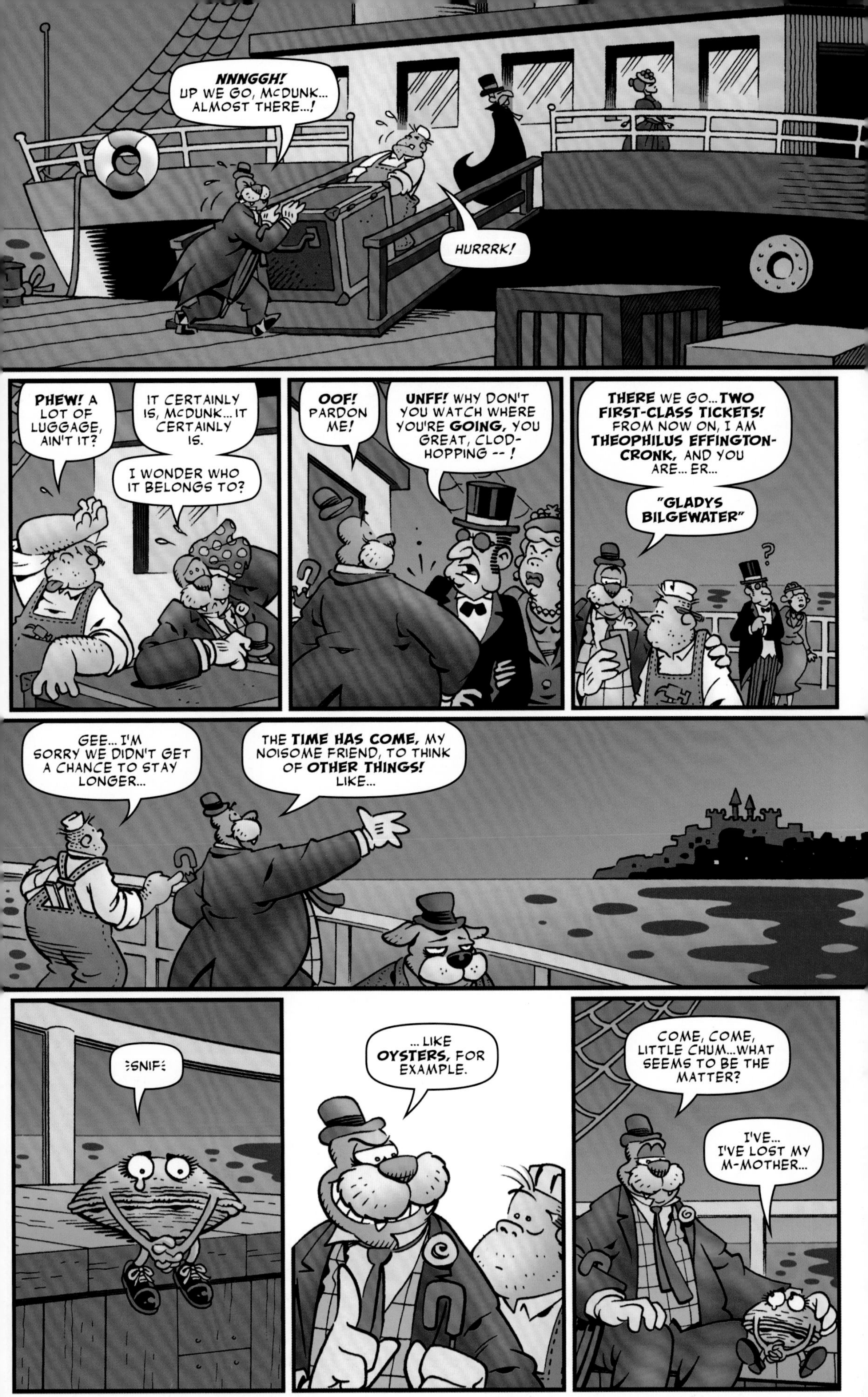

NNNGGH! UP WE GO, McDUNK... ALMOST THERE...!
HURRRK!
PHEW! A LOT OF LUGGAGE, AIN'T IT?
IT CERTAINLY IS, McDUNK... IT CERTAINLY IS.
I WONDER WHO IT BELONGS TO?
OOF! PARDON ME!
UNFF! WHY DON'T YOU WATCH WHERE YOU'RE GOING, YOU GREAT, CLOD-HOPPING -- !
THERE WE GO... TWO FIRST-CLASS TICKETS! FROM NOW ON, I AM THEOPHILUS EFFINGTON-CRONK, AND YOU ARE... ER...
"GLADYS BILGEWATER"
?
GEE... I'M SORRY WE DIDN'T GET A CHANCE TO STAY LONGER...
THE TIME HAS COME, MY NOISOME FRIEND, TO THINK OF OTHER THINGS! LIKE...
SNIF
... LIKE OYSTERS, FOR EXAMPLE.
COME, COME, LITTLE CHUM... WHAT SEEMS TO BE THE MATTER?
I'VE... I'VE LOST MY M-MOTHER...

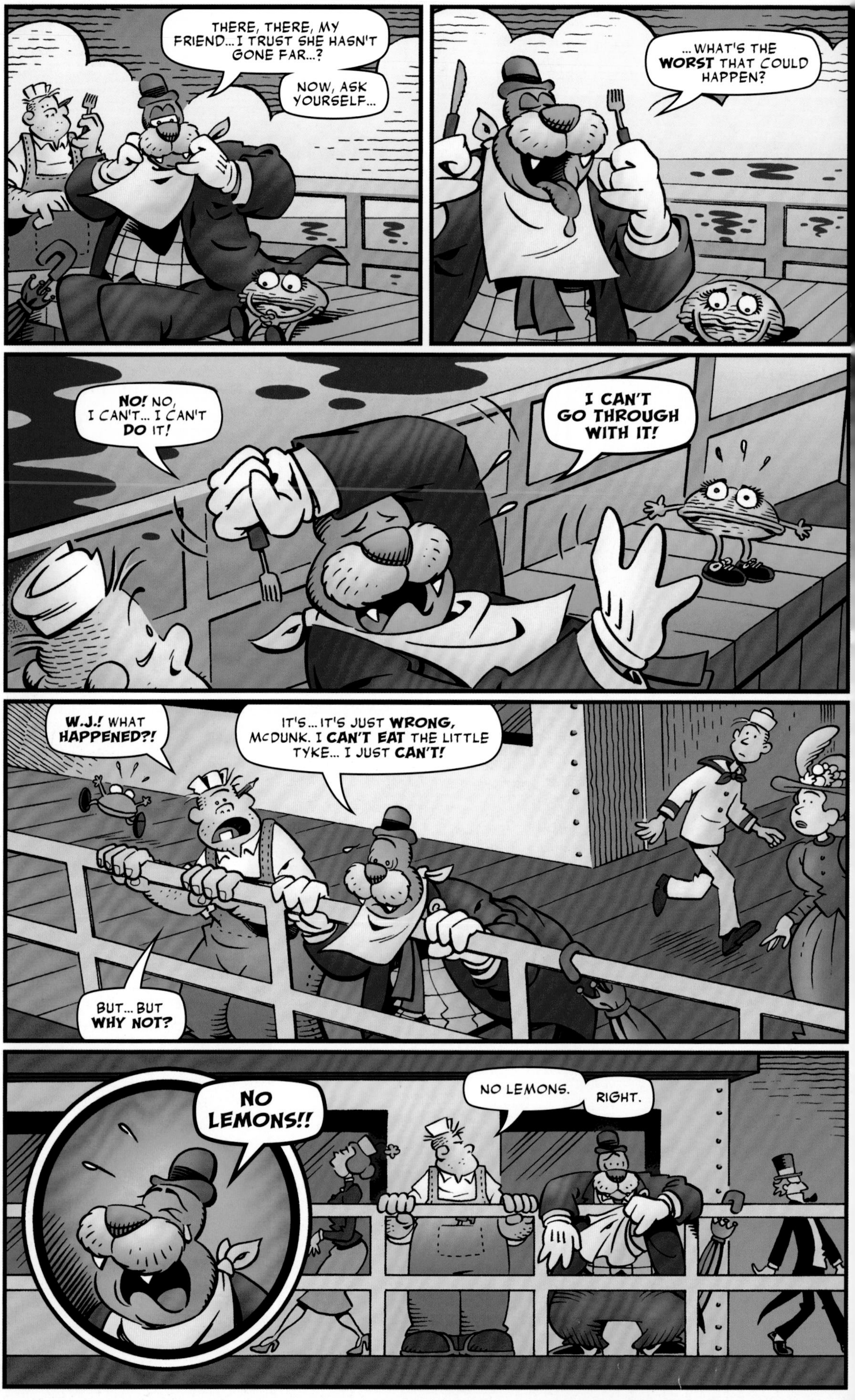
THERE, THERE, MY FRIEND... I TRUST SHE HASN'T GONE FAR...?
NOW, ASK YOURSELF...
...WHAT'S THE WORST THAT COULD HAPPEN?
NO! NO, I CAN'T... I CAN'T DO IT!
I CAN'T GO THROUGH WITH IT!
W.J.! WHAT HAPPENED?!
IT'S... IT'S JUST WRONG, McDUNK. I CAN'T EAT THE LITTLE TYKE... I JUST CAN'T!
BUT... BUT WHY NOT?
NO LEMONS!!
NO LEMONS.
RIGHT.

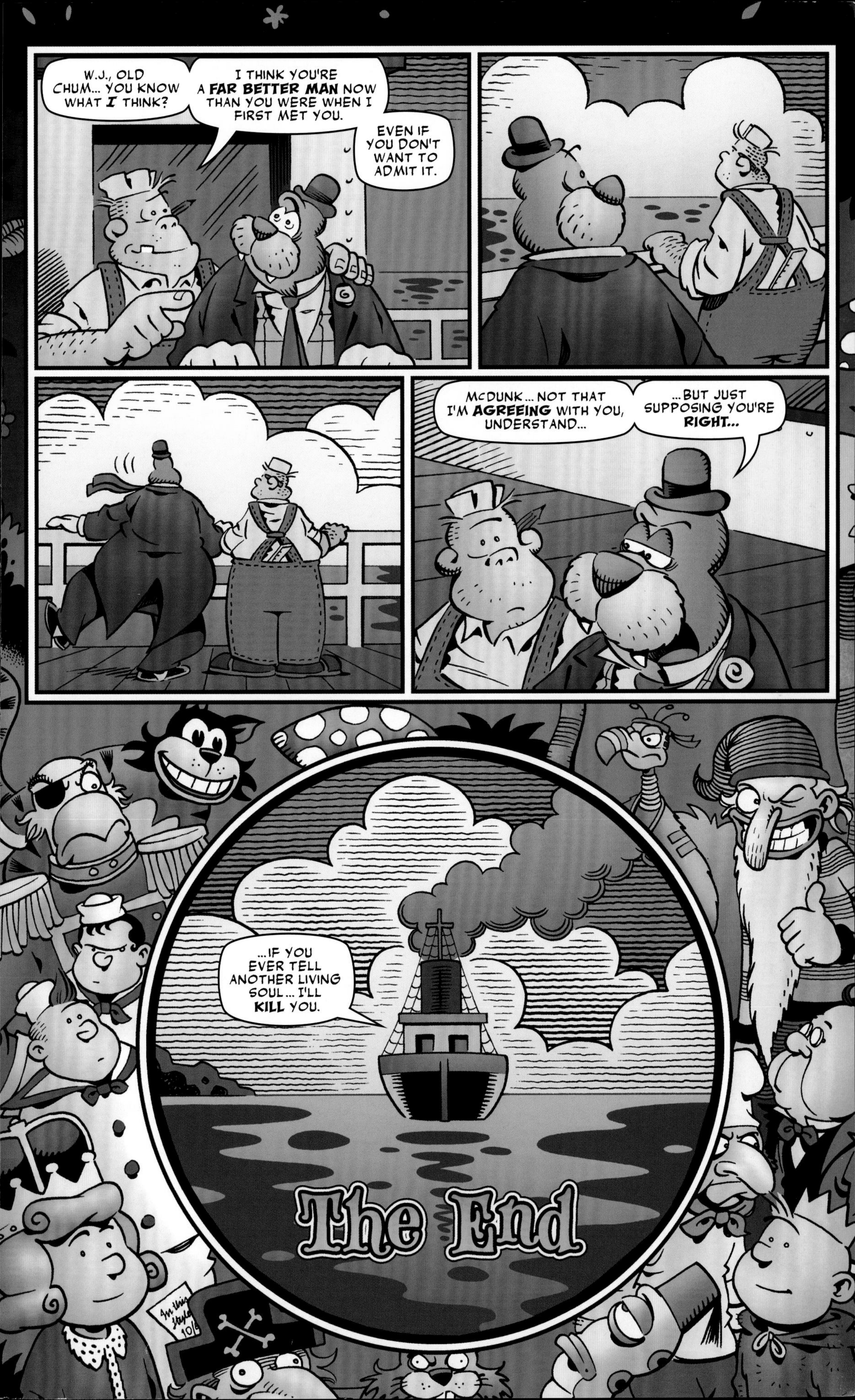
W.J., OLD CHUM... YOU KNOW WHAT I THINK?
I THINK YOU'RE A FAR BETTER MAN NOW THAN YOU WERE WHEN I FIRST MET YOU.
EVEN IF YOU DON'T WANT TO ADMIT IT.
McDUNK... NOT THAT I'M AGREEING WITH YOU, UNDERSTAND...
...BUT JUST SUPPOSING YOU'RE RIGHT...
...IF YOU EVER TELL ANOTHER LIVING SOUL... I'LL KILL YOU.
The End

COVER GALLERY

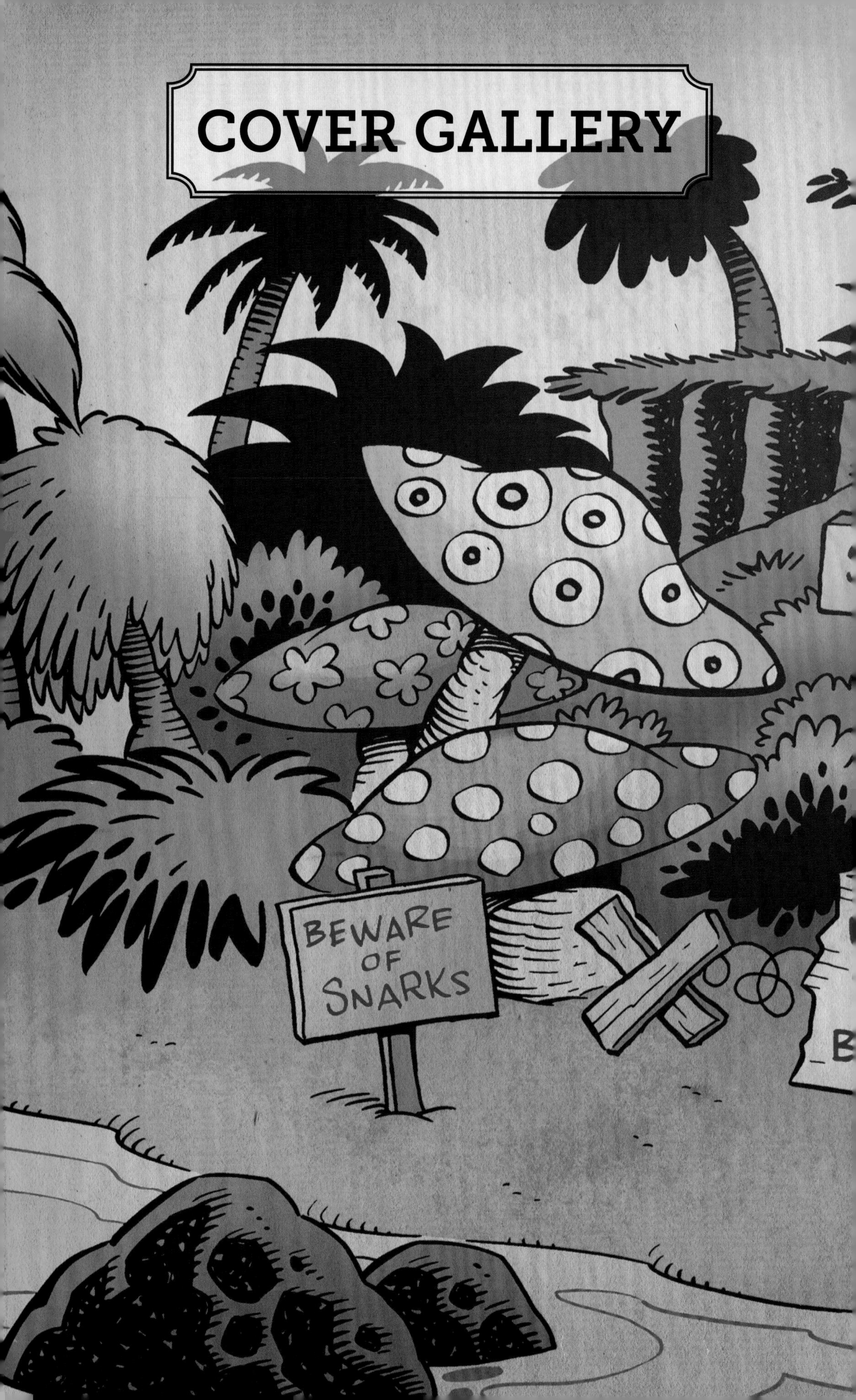
BEWARE OF SNARKS

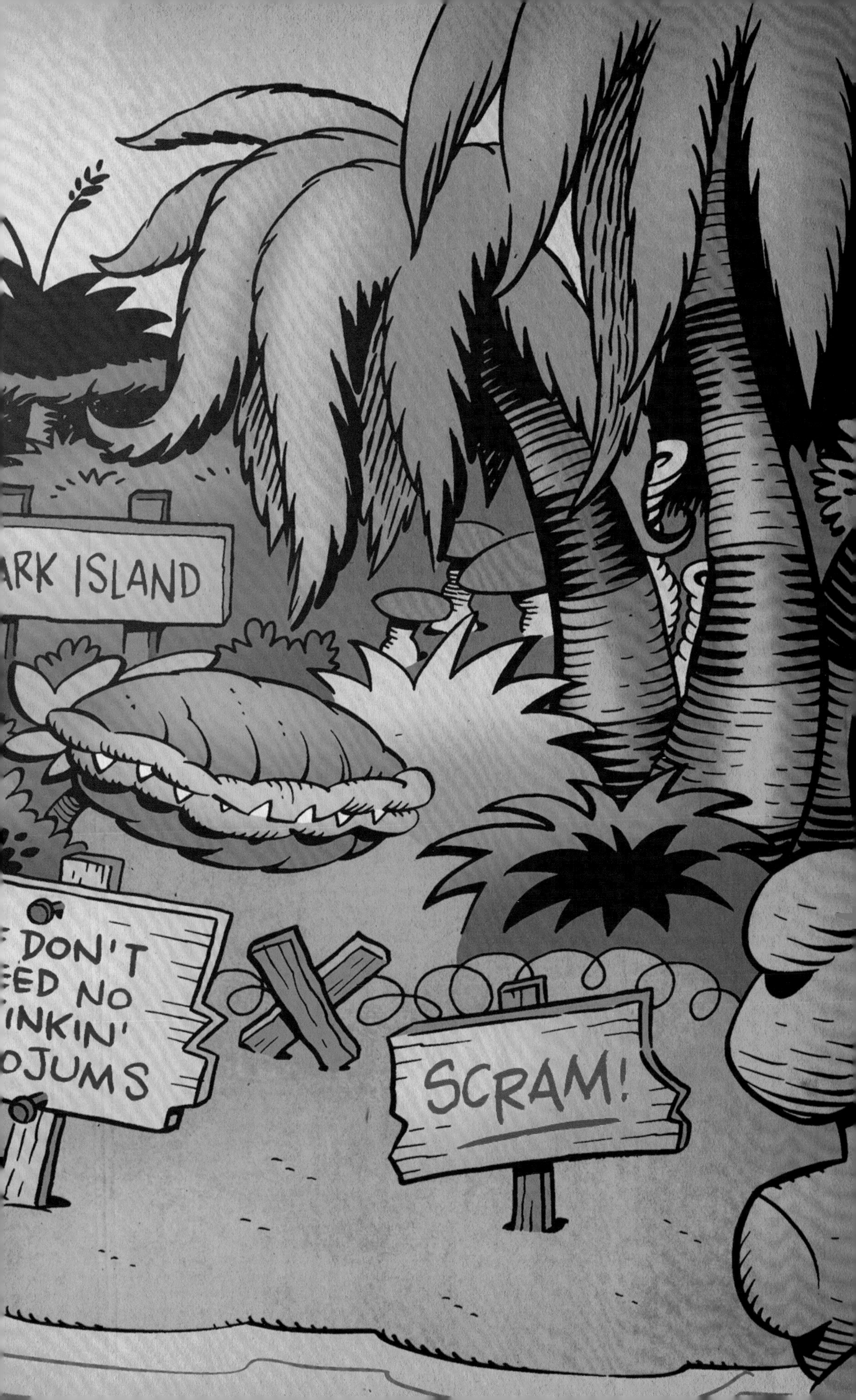
ARK ISLAND
DON'T
ED NO
INKIN'
OJUMS
SCRAM!

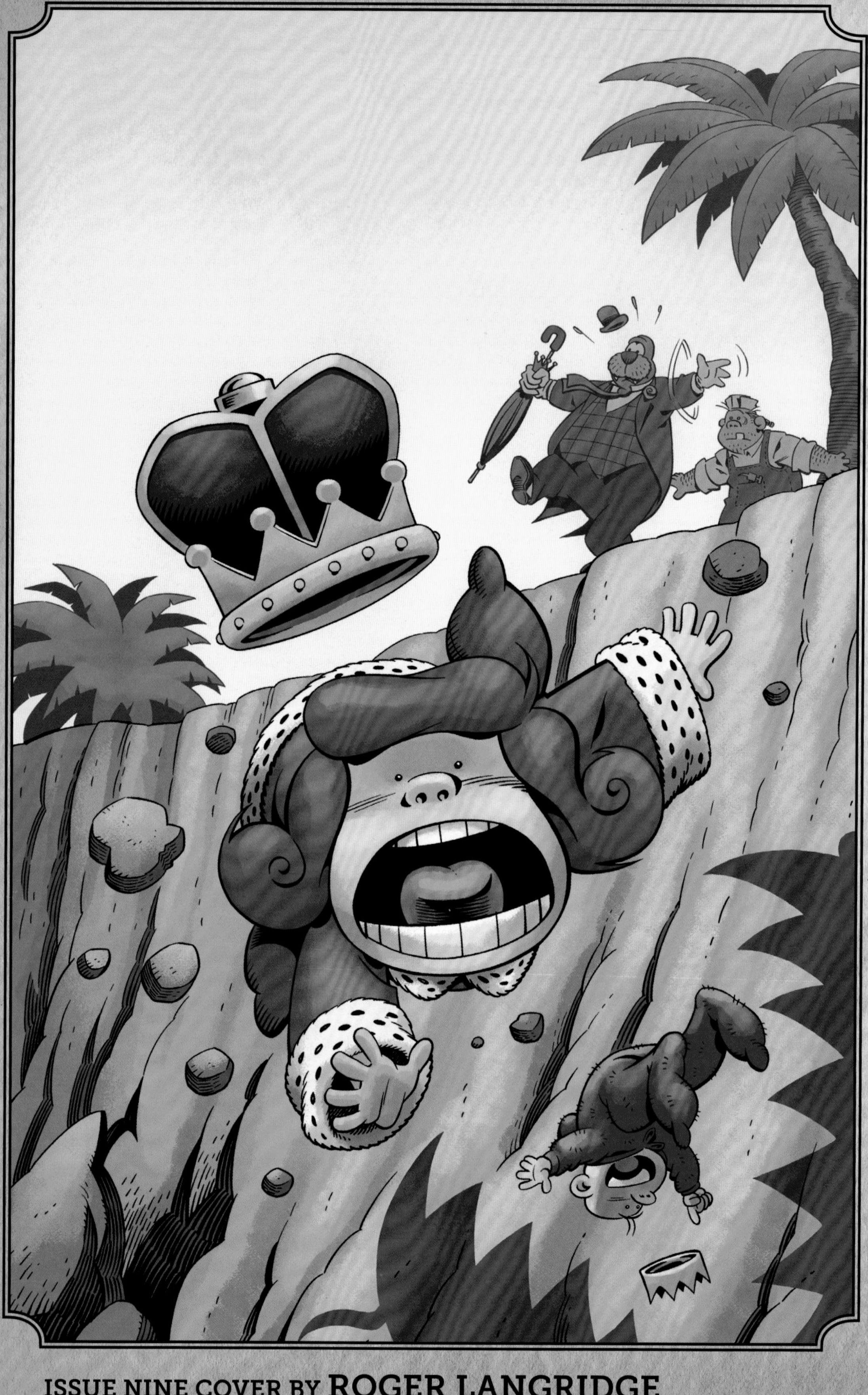

ISSUE NINE COVER BY **ROGER LANGRIDGE**
WITH COLORS BY **MATTHEW WILSON**

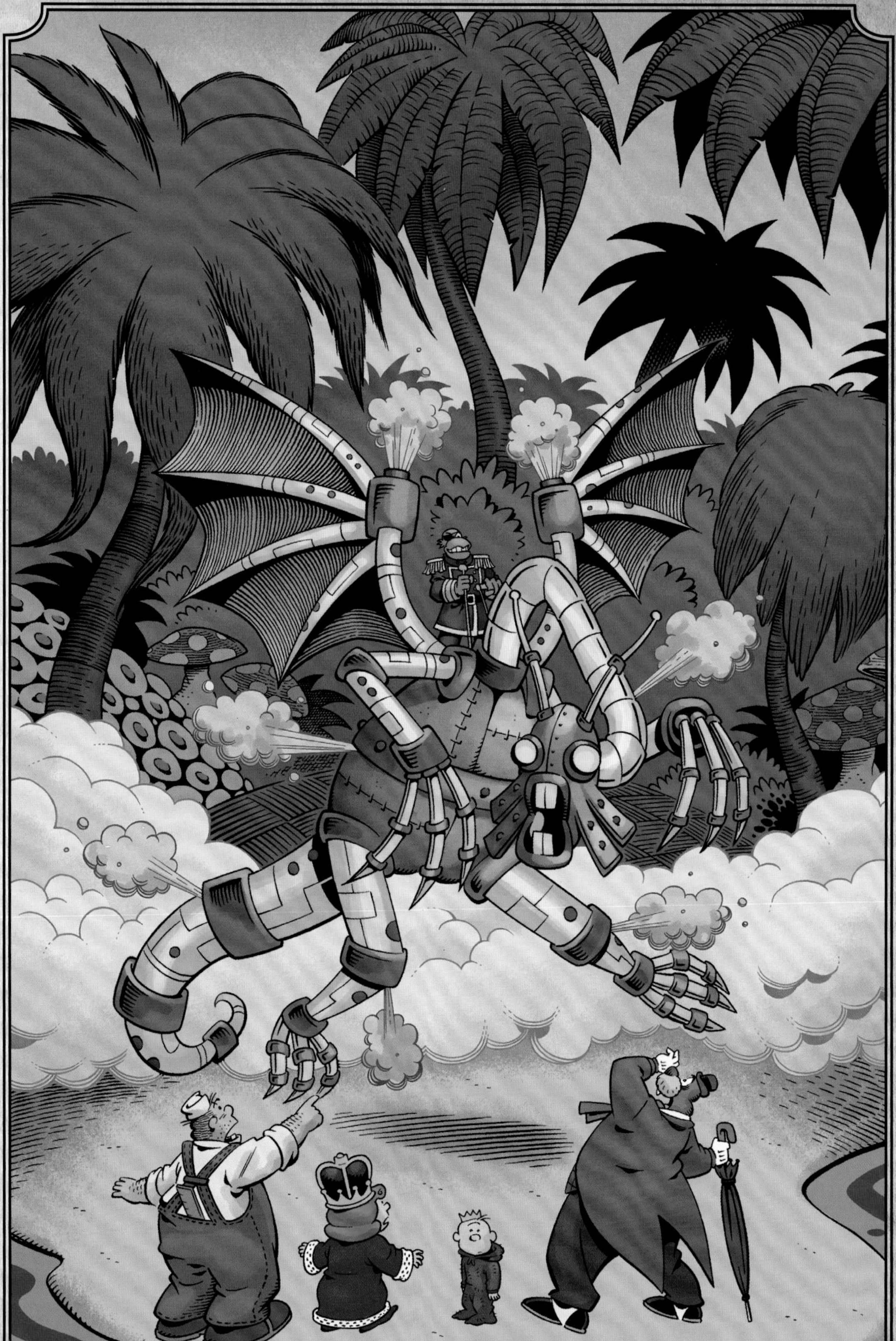

ISSUE TEN COVER BY **ROGER LANGRIDGE**
WITH COLORS BY **MATTHEW WILSON**

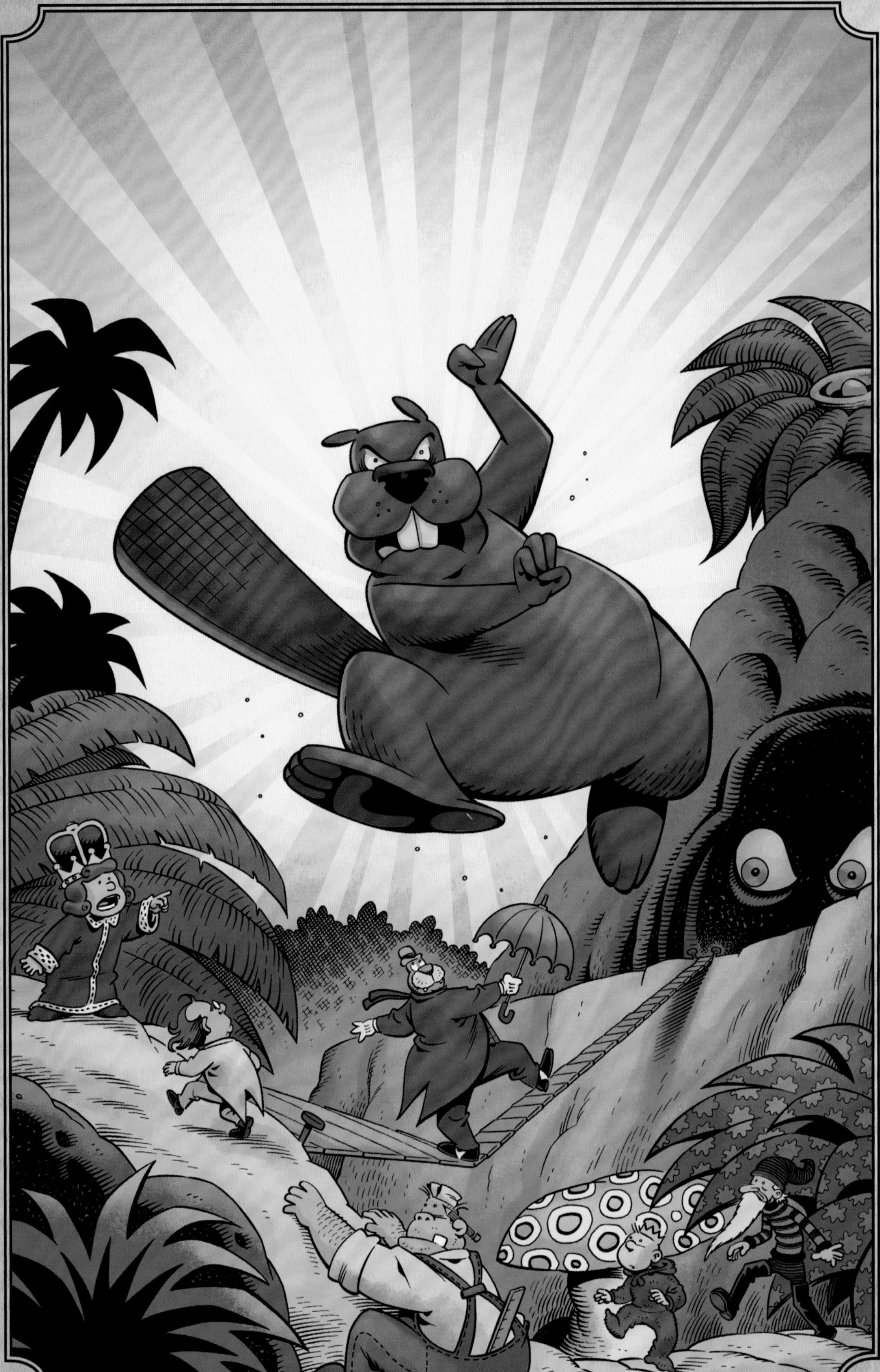

ISSUE ELEVEN COVER BY **ROGER LANGRIDGE**
WITH COLORS BY **MATTHEW WILSON**

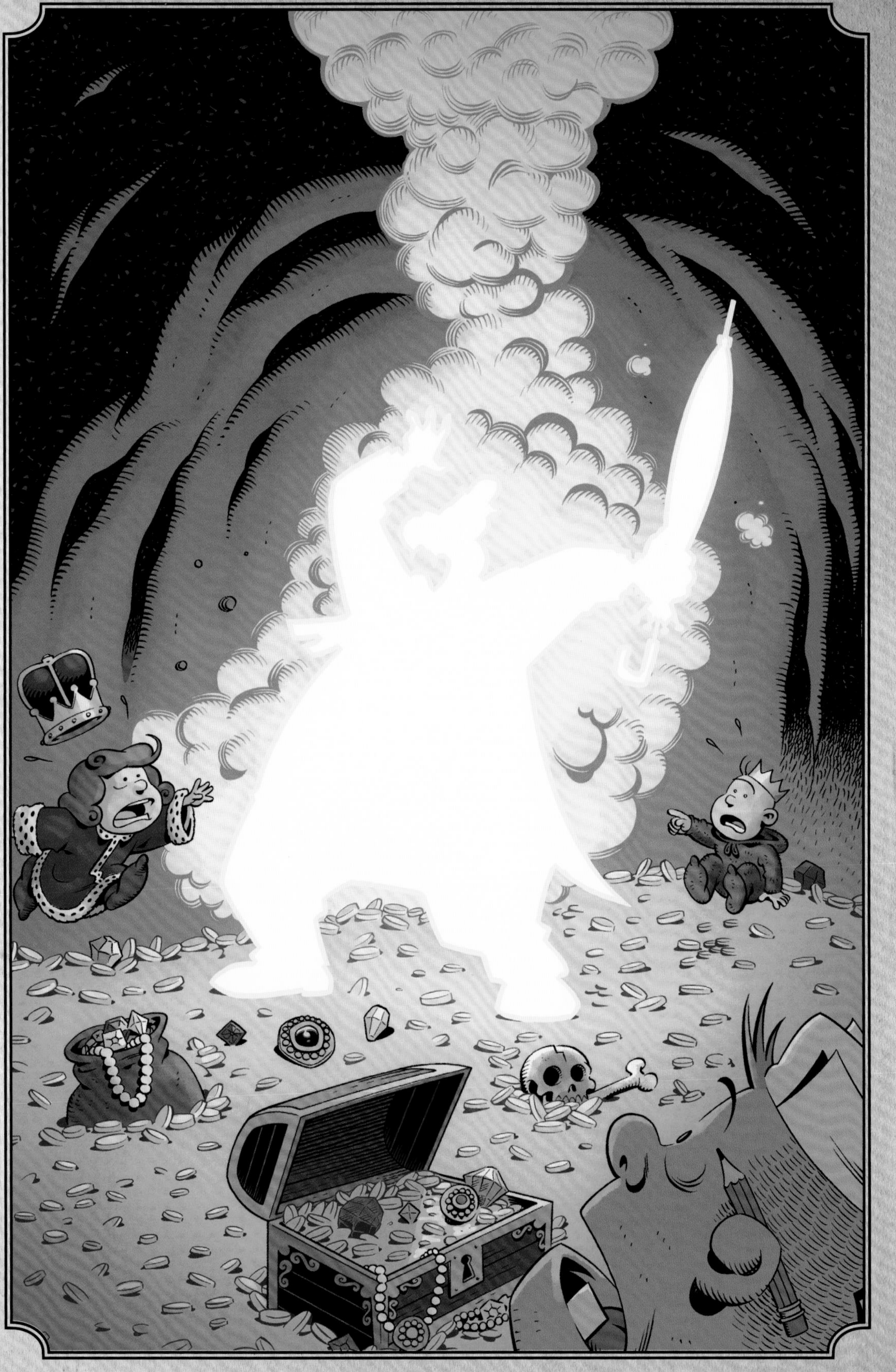

ISSUE TWELVE COVER BY **ROGER LANGRIDGE**
WITH COLORS BY **MATTHEW WILSON**

ROGER LANGRIDGE'S

SNARKED!

SKETCH GALLERY

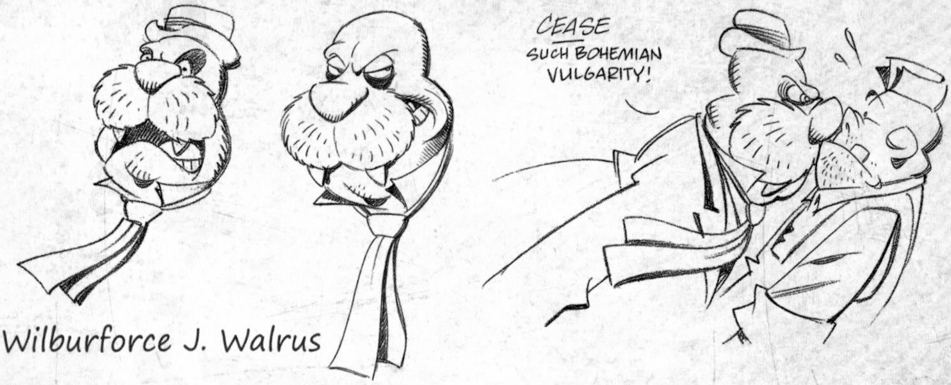
CEASE
SUCH BOHEMIAN
VULGARITY!

Wilburforce J. Walrus

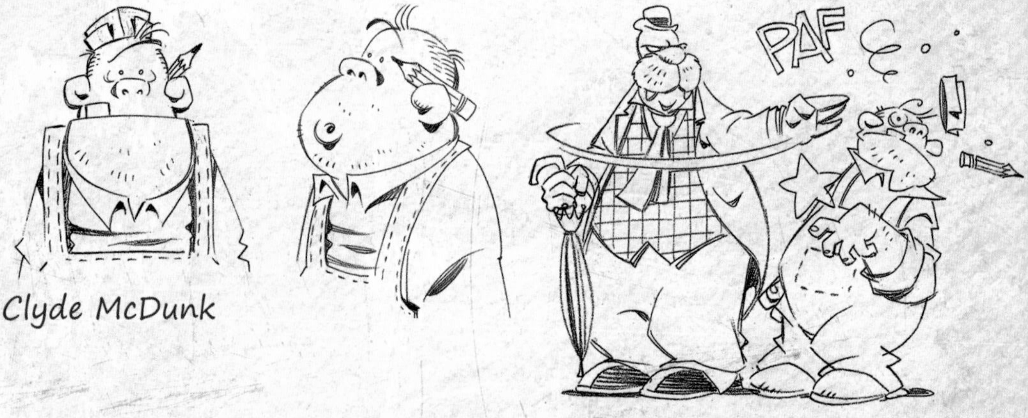
PAF

Clyde McDunk

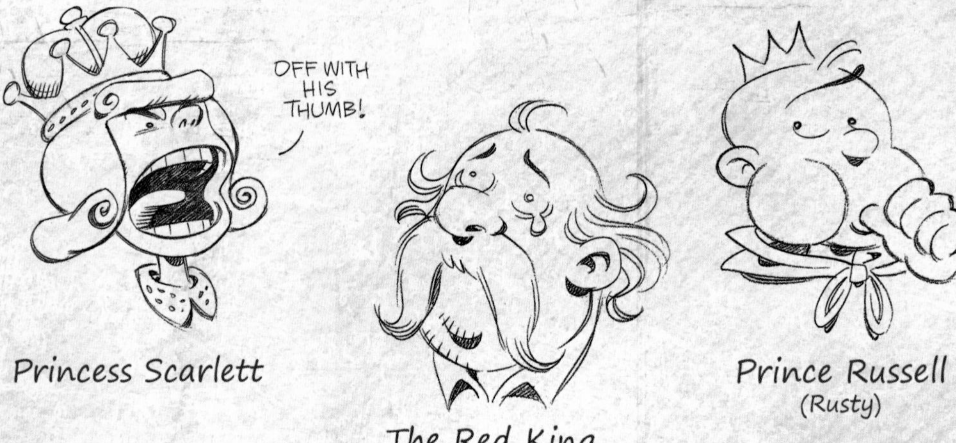
OFF WITH
HIS
THUMB!

Princess Scarlett

The Red King

Prince Russell
(Rusty)

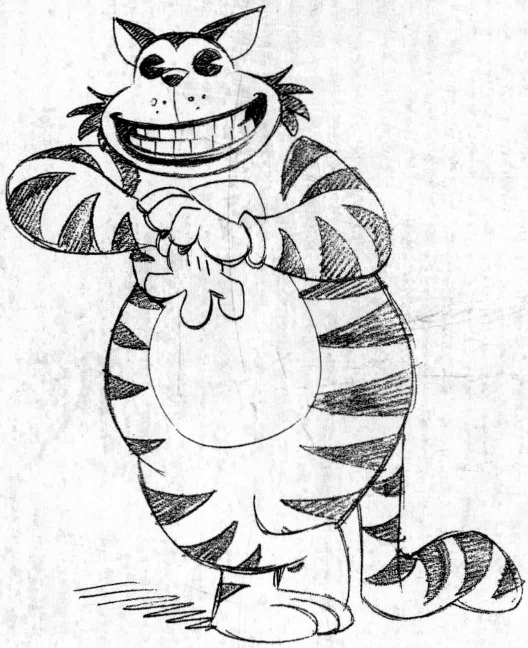

Cheshire Cat

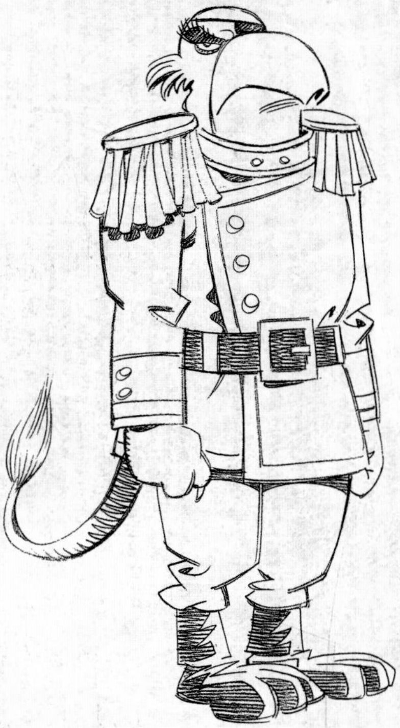

Gryphon

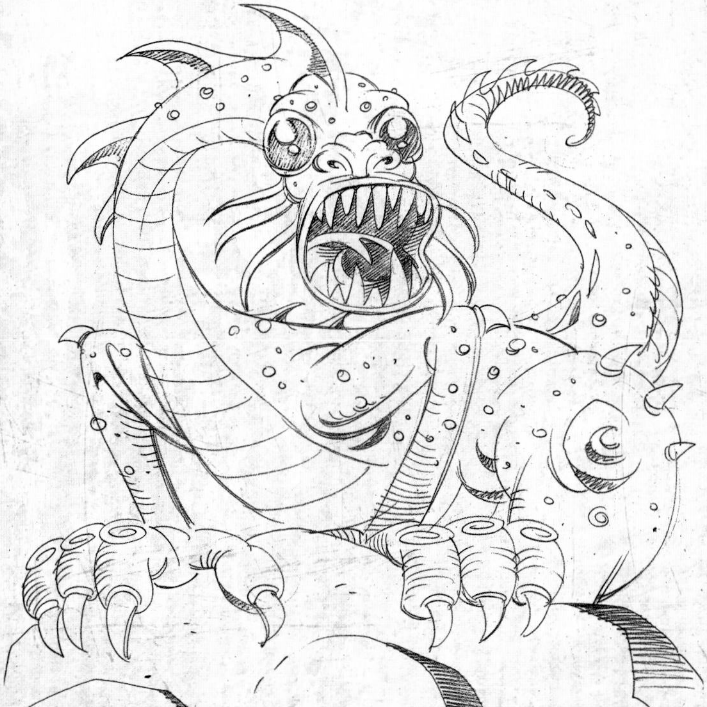

The Snark

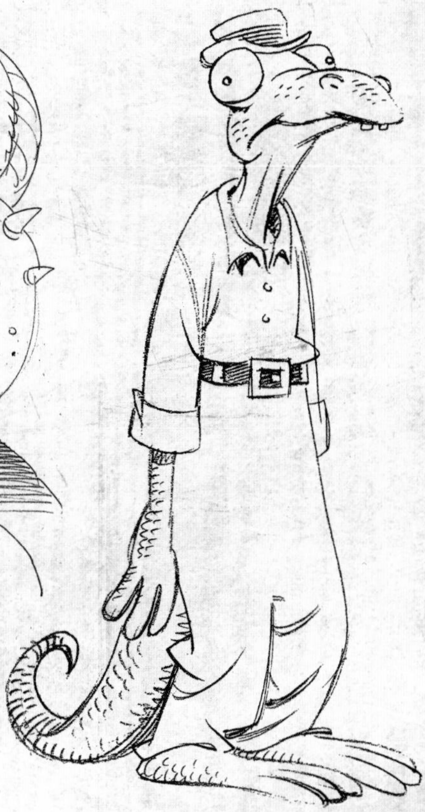

Bill the Lizard

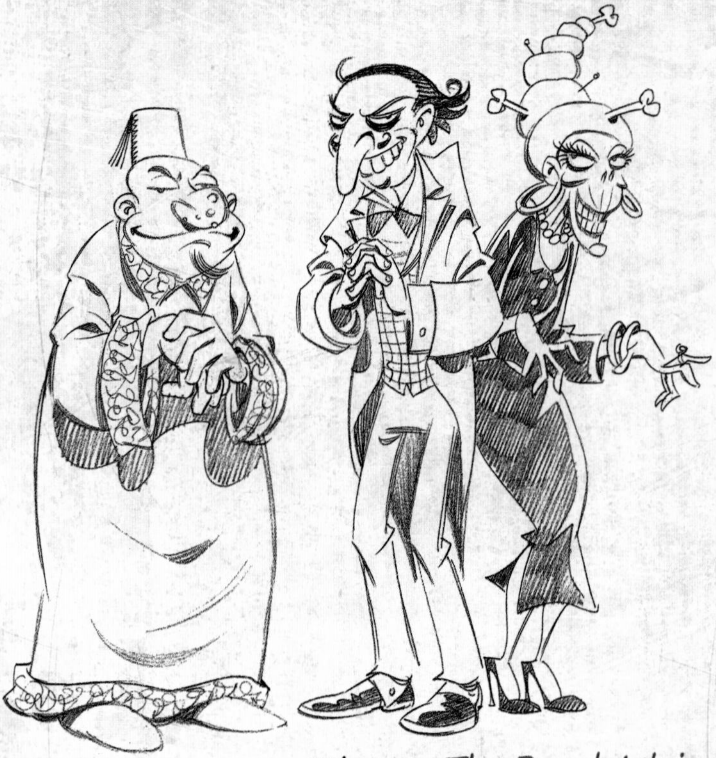

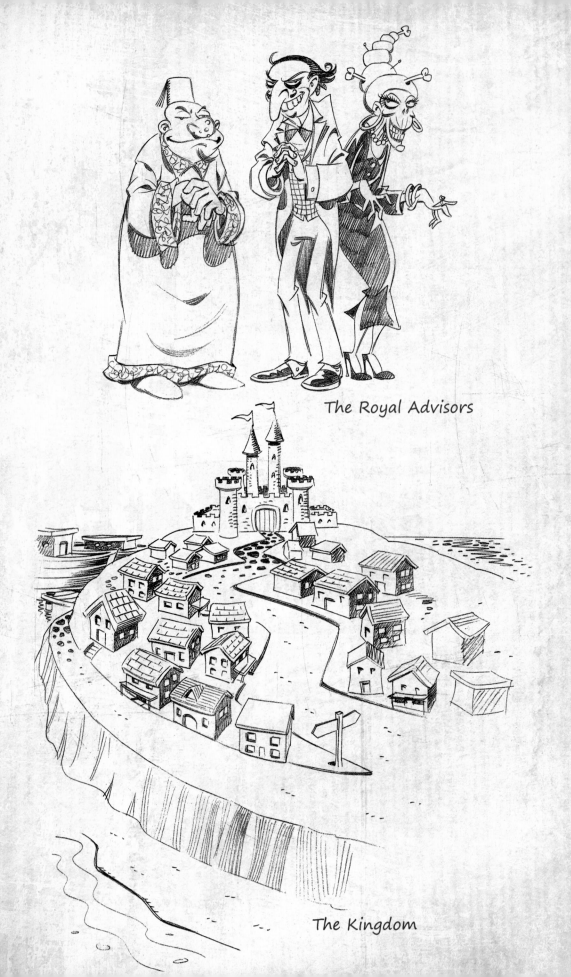

The Royal Advisors

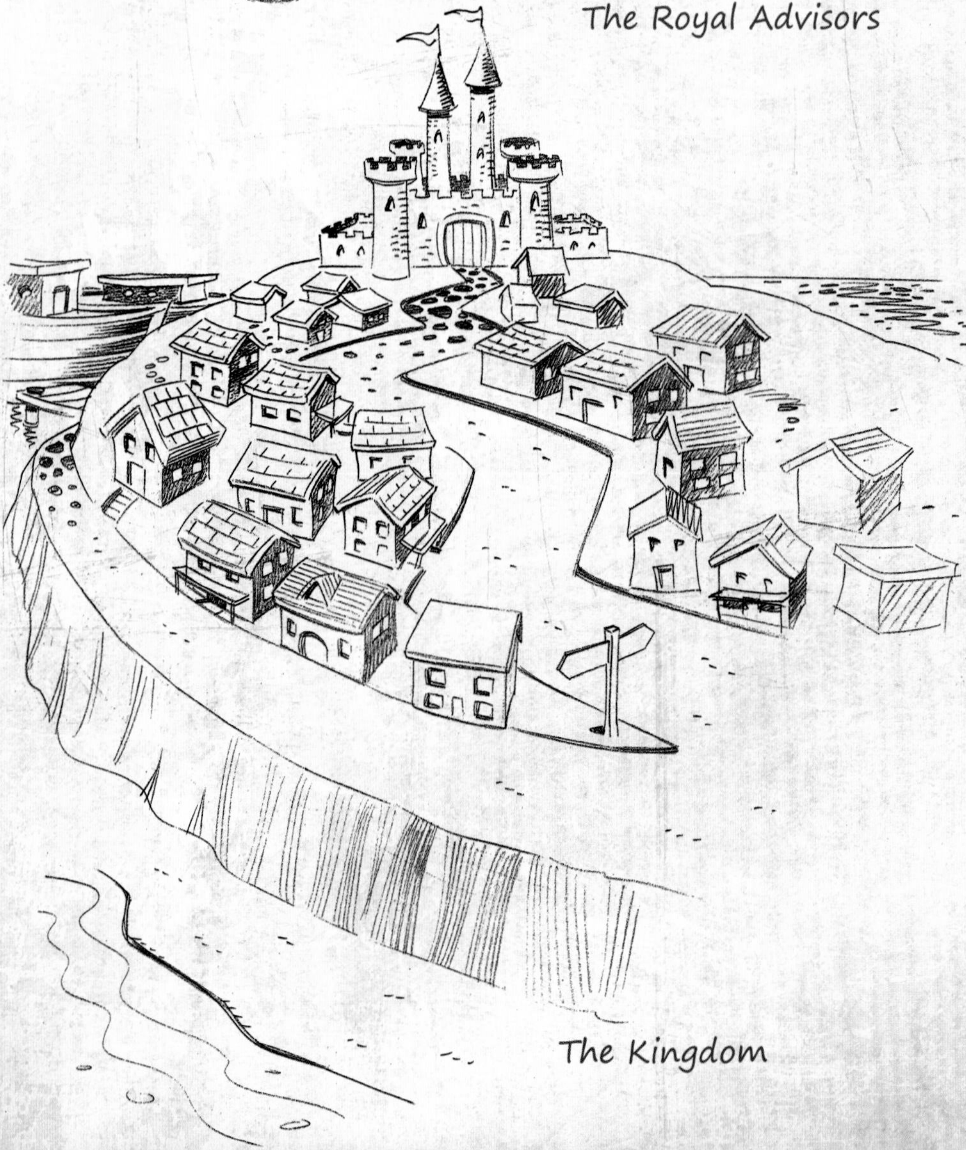

The Kingdom